FORBIDDEN LOVE

"Tallia." The word was a shuddering whisper. Tynan lifted her jaw with a gentle finger to look into her pale smokey eyes. The unbridled adoration he saw there elicited a faint groan from his lips. Gently he pulled her toward him.

Oblivious to all but the anticipation of feeling those strong arms cradling her body, and those firm full lips caressing hers, Tallia leaned into him. His lips closed over hers; his tongue probed deeply into her mouth. Her senses swirled. A kaleidoscope of color burst behind her eyelids as tremendous heat rushed to her limbs. She was melting. Goddess above!

Tynan felt her willing body pressing against his. His blood boiled with desire for the beautiful young woman in his arms. Then reason intruded. Tallia belonged to a noble house. She was a Zarmist. Her destiny didn't lie with a man who roamed the wasteland and who rarely returned to civilization. Slowly, he withdrew from the embrace.

"Tallia," he whispered, his voice so choked he barely recognized it as his own. "We have to stop now. In another moment, it will be too late."

Cover posed by professional models.

To Share A Sunset

SHARICE KENDYL

LEISURE BOOKS   NEW YORK CITY

—DEDICATION—

To Sharry and to Bernice, each to the other, for support and inspiration, and to our mothers, Edith and Margaret, who bequeathed to us their love for the written word.

A LEISURE BOOK ®

October 1990

Published by

Dorchester Publishing Co., Inc.
276 Fifth Avenue
New York, NY 10001

CHAPTER ONE

AGAINST THE ENORMOUS SPHERE OF STARKLY OUT-
lined molten gold suspended on the evening
horizon, the silhouette of a man seated on a
giant horselike beast appeared out of the wasteland.
As the dry prairie grasses blazed with the gilded fire
of the sun's final grasping rays, Tynan dismounted.
His steed, the faralk, waited patiently, its single
horn glittering indigo in the evening light, its eyes
taking on the red glow of nocturnal vision.

The grass rustled softly as Tynan moved to squat
at the edge of the bluff. Autumn, the changeable
season, was upon them. Insects, long since inured
to this cursed land of solitude, hummed in eerie
cadence, warning of the storms to come. In the
valley far below lay his destination, the town of
Promise. But he refused to consider it yet. The
solitude of the distant mountain range beckoned

him, and he turned to view the snow-crowned summits. Only the gods knew what lay beyond those impenetrable jagged peaks.

Imprisoned and isolated by nature's elements, this expanse of land, Karaundo, stretched from unconquerable mountains fringing the northern and eastern boundaries to an inhospitable ocean on the southern and western boundaries. Only Karaundo's periphery of foothills and fertile coast-line were more than sparsely settled, for the center of the territory was an immense and unfertile expanse of rock and barren soil.

Tynan's breath issued in small clouds of steam as he watched the sunset's reflected fire blaze from the mountains' pinnacles. Finally, he turned back to the source of the flaming glow. How many sunsets had he seen? Too many, and yet never enough to attain the answers his spirit craved. Always, the sight prompted him to search his soul, to analyze his emotions.

Even now, he appreciated the beauty of the harsh wilderness around him but he had no desire to share it. His appetite for companionship had perished with his family. The craving for vengeance, no longer the burning compulsion it had been two years ago, remained a cold, uncompromising knot deep in his gut. Four men had yet to meet death at his hand, four of the twelve who had tortured and murdered every member of the House of Keane, except himself. And he had yet to discover the leader's identity. So be it. As a member of King Quillan's Guild of Royal Executioners, the new wasteland patrol, he could continue his solitary life and fulfill the king's orders to bring those men to justice and thereby satisfy Tynan's need for revenge.

He turned his eyes away from the final prismatic burst of color on the horizon to the land below. The town's lights pinpointed Promise's position in the darkened canyon. With a flick of his lean, tanned hand, he discarded the blade of grass he'd been chewing and rose to approach his steed. Leaning his hard, unshaven cheek against the stallion's, he grasped the gnarled ebony horn protruding from its forehead while stroking its neck with his other hand.

"Chaz, I have to go below," he muttered. "Will you come?" Many times in the past, the animal had willingly borne Tynan to destinations it normally shunned, predominately the towns of men. He hoped this time would be no different.

Chaz nudged Tynan, disengaging himself from the embrace. Ruby eyes studied the man. Slowly, he swung his huge raven head to investigate the valley below. Tynan waited, allowing the faralk to evaluate the scene. Chaz snorted in disgust before finally, deliberately, nodding his enormous head.

"Thank you, old friend," Tynan said softly as he moved to mount.

Impenetrable darkness blanketed the valley as Tynan rode toward the distant lights and, not for the first time, he blessed his companion's night vision. Clouds obscured the stars, and neither of the two moons had yet risen. While Chaz's soft cloven hooves moved silently and surely ahead, Tynan relaxed. Lulled by the rocking gait of the faralk, secure in the warmth of his cape of cohabear fur, he endured the crackling crispness of the night air with little discomfort. Eventually a slight aberration in gait and rigidity of muscles in the beast beneath him signaled the outskirts of the town.

Promise barely deserved the appellation as the tiny farming community boasted few inhabitants. Yet, as with many of these small border towns, it served a purpose of having a man or two in the king's employ. Through them, orders were relayed to the Royal Executioners, which was the reason for Tynan's visit to the town. Tonight was the designated contact night between Tynan and a bartender in Promise and Tynan hoped to receive further information concerning the men he'd been ordered to apprehend and judge, the men he'd be happy to see die.

He appraised the town's layout, and his experienced eye proclaimed it totally indefensible. There was no pattern to the side streets which ran off in indiscriminate directions from the central one. Boardwalks flanked the excessively wide main avenue while dilapidated wooden buildings lined either side, nary a hand's breadth separating many of them. It was almost an open invitation to the marauding bands of criminals who sought refuge in the wasteland. Shaking his head in disgust, he headed in the direction of the tavern.

The solitude of the village began to unnerve him as he plodded slowly down the street, the only sound the almost silent plop, plop of the huge faralk's soft hooves. He looked up at the oil lamps, glowing brightly, suspended from their hooks above the deserted street, emphasizing the unnatural stillness. Where were the people? As he neared the opposite end of the town, the illumination from the street lamps became muted, the shadows deepened. His nerves taut, Tynan finally sighted the tavern. Light radiated glaringly from its windows and the racket he'd come to associate with such premises spilled through its doors. He stopped.

The village's desolation solved one problem for him. There were no garies at the hitching posts. The huge feline beasts were Chaz's natural enemy and since faralks were not the usual mode of transportation, there were no facilities for stabling Chaz. With a sigh of gratitude to Galacia, goddess of peace and life, he stroked the neck of his faithful companion before dismounting.

Stealthily crossing the weathered boardwalk, Tynan paused to one side of the entrance, listening to the muffled conversation within. Perhaps he could discover why the town was so empty.

"We got to find a way to bring law enforcers to outpost towns like ours, Jenk, or we won't survive," a deep solemn voice was saying. "Five good men we lost today, and one marriageable young woman, before those murderers rode off."

"I agree with you," replied another voice to which Tynan attached the name Jenk. "Wastelanders like that murdering, thieving Bodan, if that's his name, deserve to die by slow execution."

Tynan released his breath slowly and moved to peer over the door. There were eight subdued men seated within his range of sight, and one slightly aging, though still buxom, barmaid. So, they'd had a run–in with Bodan and Bodan was gone. Once again Tynan was one step too late. Thrul! He cursed, invoking the evil goddess Coran's domain.

He looked over his shoulder at Chaz, a slightly blacker shadow in the darkened street. Wide, nervous, scarlet eyes regarded Tynan. "I won't be long," Tynan muttered to the beast before resolutely pushing the doors aside and stepping into the bar, his right hand resting lightly on the dagger in a sheath at his waist.

Conversation stopped. Tynan paused, surveying the room and its occupants. The wooden bar was scarred, unvarnished. Streaked glasses and dusty liquor bottles lined the shelves on the wall behind it. The sharply pungent aroma of perspiration combined with the smell of musty ale pervaded the hazy atmosphere. His eyes met and held the bartender's hazel ones. Casually identifying himself as a Royal Executioner, he tipped back his huge black hat with the index finger of his left hand; his middle fingers folded, the small finger extended. The man's eyelids flickered in barely concealed astonishment as he recognized the signal. The barman rubbed his left earlobe in apparent nervousness. There were no messages or instructions.

Grayed, splintering floorboards creaked beneath his feet as Tynan shifted, his penetrating emerald gaze sweeping the occupants of the room, who appeared frozen. One man held a mug of ale an inch from his lips, another seemed about to burn his cigar to cinders with the candle he'd been employing to light it. The barmaid stood opposite him, her mouth gaping unbecomingly, revealing stained and broken teeth.

Tynan had known from experience that his wastelander apparel would elicit a reaction. Wastelanders, hardened outlaws, most by choice, some victims of circumstance, were a breed of men feared for their ruthlessness and total disregard for the law. Still, Tynan had chosen the label of wastelander. He remembered one of the many sayings his native friend, Letai, fondly expounded: "It is much easier to hunt a bear if one lives and thinks like a bear."

His mind wandered briefly to the Hytola camp where he'd spent so much time as a youth when Letai's clan had roamed within range of his home, Ravencrest. The nomadic Hytola natives were uncivilized by Karaundoian standards, for they worshipped many strange elemental spirits, but the solitary, gentle people had taught Tynan that the land and its animals were gifts to men and had instilled in him a deep respect for all life. Tynan often missed their undemanding companionship and their peaceful ways.

The barmaid shattered the silence, interrupting Tynan's brief reflection, as her eyes moved beyond him to the hitching post then widened with fear. "He rides a demon-beast." Her audible yet muffled tone was filled with terror as her gaze locked on Chaz's glowing crimson eyes.

The man holding the candle dropped it and his cigar as his gaze followed hers. Ale sloshed over the hand and sleeve of the man holding the mug as he jerked around to gape out the window. "What do you want here, wastelander?"

Recognizing Jenk's voice, Tynan fixed his eyes on the man, studying him. Jenk lounged casually on a sturdy wooden chair at a table in the center of the room, but Tynan recognized the whipcord tension in his muscles. Jenk was not a farmer, and Tynan guessed he was in an occupation just this side of the law. A procurer of goods perhaps, or of women. The shrewdness in Jenk's crystal blue eyes spoke of experience in dealing with many types of people. Yet, even he swallowed nervously as Tynan's cold green gaze raked him dispassionately.

"A drink," Tynan replied as he moved with predatory grace to a vacant table at the rear where he could watch the room and the street beyond. Ignoring the barmaid's blatant reluctance to approach him, Tynan gruffly ordered a mug of rastan. The strong burning liquor would help to warm him against the chill night.

A long moment later the mug was roughly placed before him, a quarter of its contents splattering onto the dirt-encrusted table. The barmaid appeared ready to run, fear of his reaction to her clumsiness etched clearly on her face. Tynan's hand snaked out, grasping her arm. The men remained silent, waiting. "Know where Bodan was heading when he left?" he questioned brusquely.

The woman shook her head mutely, a pulse pounding visibly in her throat.

"You sure?" he prompted.

The stained bodice of her tunic rose and fell at an astonishing rate, as her terrified mud-brown eyes dared to meet his gaze. Licking her colorless, chapped lips nervously, she whispered, "Yes, I'm sure."

Tynan released her, and the noise in the room resumed.

"You a friend of Bodan's, Mister?" queried Jenk, still slouched in his deceptively casual position.

"No," Tynan replied shortly, knowing full well that Jenk and every other man present would understand. One wastelander looking for another, not a friend, meant only one thing.

Jenk nodded slowly and jerked his head in the direction of the door. "He went back to the wasteland, where his kind belongs."

Ignoring the insult, Tynan noticed the man who'd been seated in a shadowy corner near the door rise. Tynan observed him as he strode into the light. He was young, exhibiting the swagger of a bully, his expression belligerent. A farm boy who aspired to being feared and held in awe. A potential wastelander.

Tynan shrugged. If the boy thought to warn Bodan that he was being followed, it would only aid Tynan in his quest. Bodan's pride would force him to find Tynan and face him. And then, fulfilling his duty to his king, Tynan would execute him for his crimes. Yet for Tynan, Bodan's death would be personal. Vengeance was personal.

Tallia approached the tavern. Having never been in such a place, she fervently hoped the need to enter one would not be repeated in the future. A tavern was not the type of establishment frequented by young ladies. She chewed nervously on her lower

13

lip. Beyond those walls·lay her best chance of procuring a desperately needed escort. Surely, this was a fitting end for this day. But this humiliation, for certainly that's what it would amount to, seemed insignificant compared with the tribulations she'd already been forced to endure.

She trembled slightly, still anguished by that afternoon's events. Her roommate Dayna's Uncle Tolar had been Tallia's guide since her departure from the Zarmist College in Maurasia. Sparingly armed within the supposed safety of this small town, Tolar had been cut to ribbons by wastelanders. The commotion had drawn her from her room in time to witness the horrific scene before someone covered his fatally wounded, motionless body. Tallia could not even put a face to his murderers, for by then they had been no more than dusty silhouettes riding away from Promise.

She did not understand such wickedness. The men had to have been in league with the evil goddess Coran and her sorcerers. Only they would sanction such villainous behavior.

Despite her sorrow for Tolar and her compassion for Dayna, Tallia refused to be deterred from her purpose. She had to return home to the Fiefdom of the Twin Suns. Her mind strayed to Eyrsa, who had been her mother's governess, and was now Tallia's governess and the fiefdom's Zarmist, a healer of renowned ability. Tallia was puzzled by Eyrsa's urgent summons that Tallia come home. She would have known the problems Tallia could encounter crossing the wasteland in the autumn. The season for caravans had passed and lone travelers were at the mercy of not only the harsh elements, but the renegade bands of marauders who made their home in the uninhabited terrain. Why had Eyrsa called her home? The question resounded continuously in her mind. Eyrsa's terse request would not have been made without justification.

The innkeeper had informed her that if anybody could be found to provide escort across the wasteland at this time of year, she would locate him in the tavern. She stopped in the shadows, indecisively peering through the dust-caked windows. Brightly illuminated by gaslights throughout, the tavern boasted a long bar and several rough wooden tables. The all-male clientele seemed involved in a boisterous discussion or argument as one tired-looking barmaid moved among them.

Summoning her courage, Tallia took a deep breath to quell her pounding heart and moved to the door. Pausing to take one final calming breath before entering, she started. From the darkness of the street, two red eyes watched her intently. Peering more closely, she noticed the immense size of the beast and the rapier-sharp horn protruding from its forehead. A farak! She'd never seen one in a town before. At the moment, standing motionless, it appeared quite harmless. Tallia checked her curiosity. She had more important things to consider at the moment.

Entering the bar, Tallia's nostrils were immediately assailed by unpleasant odors. With determination, she ignored the stares of the men as she riveted her attention on the large portly figure of the man behind the bar. With small hesitant steps, she

15

approached him. "I require an escort to the Fiefdom of the Twin Suns across the wasteland near the foot of Mount Coran. Can you help me?" she inquired quietly.

"Sorry, lady, you'll have ta speak up," he replied in what Tallia considered an overly loud tone. For an instant, she considered that perhaps he was mocking her.

She lifted her gaze from the man's stained apron to the stubble of his fat jowls, before repeating herself, loudly.

"The only man going in that direction left a few hours ago after killing a number of decent folk. I don't think you would have wanted ta go with him. You aren't going to find any honorable folks crossing the wasteland at this time of year. The last caravan passed a week ago, and they'll be lucky ta make it before the winter storms hit." He paused, continuing more kindly, "You'd best wait for the caravans in the spring."

Tallia raised determined eyes to look the man fully in the face for the first time. His slightly purplish lips curved in a meager smile at her appraisal, deepening the lines around his hazel eyes. "Isn't there anybody who would be willing to escort me? I will pay them well."

"I don't think so, little lady, but I'll ask." He magnified his already loud voice to shout unnecessarily to the occupants in the room who, Tallia was certain, had unashamedly and avidly eavesdropped on the entire conversation. "Anybody here willing ta escort the lady across the wasteland ta the Fiefdom of the Twin Suns? She says she'll pay."

Tallia turned to survey the room as the bartender spoke. Her resolve flickered briefly as she noted the shaking of several heads. Only two men did not immediately indicate a negative reply—a commanding figure, dressed entirely in black, seated at the rear of the room, and a slightly smaller man who sat with apparent ease near the center of the room. Tallia studied them, her apprehension overcome in her desperation to return home.

The dark solitary individual appeared to be a wastelander, the other perhaps a merchant. The quiet appraisal in the second man's glance made her uneasy, and some magnetic force drew her gaze back to the wastelander. Fearsome though he appeared, instinct told her that, of the two, the lone black figure was the man to approach. She studied him. His hair, as black as his attire, fell in a cascade of midnight curls just below his squarish, whisker-shadowed jaw. Cold moss-green eyes returned her gaze with a boldness that flustered her. Tallia lifted her head proudly.

Refusing to be deterred, she moved toward him, ignoring the abruptly silenced men as they realized her destination. With each step, her boldness dwindled, until, when she finally reached his table, she found herself staring intently at the tips of her soft leather boots. Her hands twisted nervously in the folds of her cloak as she attempted to frame her question. "Are you . . . Would you . . ." she stopped, appalled at her stuttering.

Taking a deep breath, she remembered she was no peasant to lower her eyes before an untitled wastelander. Confronting his enigmatic gaze, she began again, more purposefully. "I am Tallia of the House of Darnaz in the Fiefdom of the Twin Suns. It is imperative that I return home as soon as possible. I require escort across the wasteland," she said, stumbling to a halt. Unsure how to continue, she shifted her gaze, fixing it on the gilded hilt of the broadsword visible over his left shoulder. "I can pay well," she concluded lamely, "two hundred gold pentars." She had worn the Twin Sun circlet on her head, as evidence of her status as the daughter of the ruling house of a fiefdom in the hope that no one would demand to see the substance of her money. It wasn't actually a lie. She could pay two hundred gold pentars. She just didn't have the money with her. The funds would only be obtained by her escort when their journey was completed. She held her breath, awaiting the wastelander's reply.

Tynan studied the young woman before him with dispassionate interest. She was very small, little over five feet, and exceedingly beautiful. Rich, dark sable hair tumbled beyond her waist in a thick tangle of silky tresses, framing the creamy loveliness of her complexion. Pale, translucent blue eyes contemplated him hopefully, while a tiny, slightly uptilted, nose lent her a certain haughtiness despite her obvious shyness. He eyed her headdress, the golden metal circlet that dropped to a vee on her forehead. The family emblem of twin suns, a gold one overlapping a black one, was engraved just above the point.

The lady definitely lacked intelligence, or perhaps it was her innocence that accounted for her ignorance of the wasteland ways. Didn't she realize that should she find an escort she'd be risking not only her virtue, but her life? The loss of innocence would be the price of her beauty; the loss of her life would be the price of her affluence. But it was not his concern. His destiny lay along other paths.

Tallia waited for him to conclude his insultingly arrogant appraisal.

"Not interested," he responded coldly.

The girl seemed thunderstruck and appeared to be blinking tears from her eyes. To his amazement, their color shifted from blue to silver. A shock of recognition jolted his soul. He remembered those eyes from somewhere. They were distinctive eyes. Changeable! Where had he seen them before? And why couldn't he remember? The answer eluded him.

She'd obviously not considered the possibility of a refusal, and when he remained silent, she moved away. He watched her approach the man, Jenk. The interest in Jenk's eyes was unmistakable. It was the expression of a man studying a prime piece of stock. A procurer of women then, Tynan concluded. Despite himself, he felt a surge of protectiveness for the girl which disturbed him. He had felt nothing for another human being in two years and had refused to allow himself to care. The pain from the loss of his family was unbearable, and he never wanted to experience it again. So why, now, should he feel the beginnings of compassion for this girl?

Trying to trace the emotion, he examined her more closely. Her appearance, her gestures, her trusting innocence were familiar in a way. Abrupt-

19

ly, a poignant picture of his twin sister invaded his memory. Tynara, sweet beautiful Tynara. She'd looked much as Tallia did now.

Suddenly, the room felt close, the walls confining. Finishing his drink in one gulp, Tynan rose. Throwing a coin at the bartender in a careless gesture, he exited the tavern with smooth purposeful strides. Attempting to suppress the painful memories, he forced himself to think of his quarry. He knew in which direction Bodan was headed now. Perhaps he'd be able to intercept him somewhere in the wasteland.

From her seat, courteously offered by Jenk so they might discuss her plight, Tallia watched the wastelander. Massively muscled, towering, he dwarfed his surroundings. As the cold, mysterious man in black left the tavern, her hope that he might change his mind disappeared. Though she judged him to be rough, tactless, and a man of few words, she'd felt drawn to him. Somehow, she sensed that she'd be safer with him than with any other man. His mannerisms proclaimed him a man of confidence and, since he was a wastelander, that meant he had the self-assurance to survive in that hostile land. He was the man she needed. She shifted slightly in her seat and returned her attention to Jenk.

Outside, Tynan took a deep breath of the crisp night air in another attempt to exorcise the persistent, torturous images from the past. Then with a bound he was astride the faralk's broad back. He urged Chaz to greater and greater speed, fleeing the town, fleeing the past, fleeing the girl who'd invoked the unpleasant memories. Impervious to the stinging flakes of snow which burned his cheeks, he raced into the biting wind that forced tears to his eyes before driving them relentlessly into his hair.

Finally, Chaz's labored breathing penetrated his grief. He signalled his mount to a halt. "Sorry, boy," he apologized, although he knew that the stallion would not have allowed himself to be run had he not desired it. Chaz had been eager to escape his own excruciating memories of man and civilization.

Dismounting, Tynan offered Chaz water from his flask, cupped in the palms of his large hands, before moving off to crouch down in thought. The sound of cold dry snow settling onto drier grasses created a soothing whisper as Tynan leaned against a boulder. The images would not go away. He would have to confront them then, as he had so many times in the past.

A new set of features superimposed themselves over the battered visage of his dying sister as he'd held her in his arms. He forced them away. Tallia of the House of Darnaz meant nothing to him. Tynara, his twin in body and spirit, had meant the world.

The past swirled through his mind. He and his family had taken a caravan trip in search of a Zarmist for his ailing father. Ever the loner, Tynan, one afternoon, left the others to explore the surrounding territory. Ironically, it was on that day, he'd met Chaz. The beast was floundering in quicksand. Tynan rescued him, expecting nothing in return. Everyone knew that the creatures were untamable. But, Tynan had learned from Letai that faralks were not evil as so many people believed, and so Tynan did not fear the animal. Chaz had demonstrated his intelligence with his simple act of gratitude. He'd allowed Tynan to ride him.

Tynan still ached with the numbing shock of what he had found when he returned to the caravan. He would never forget the gray-black column of smoke rising high, slashing dusk's antique gold sky with its sooty imprint or the choking sense of foreboding that communicated itself to his new-found friend and sent man and beast racing like the wind toward the beacon. The caravan had been decimated, burned to the ground in a wanton act of destruction. Beasts of burden slaughtered. His mother, Lady Kyra, defiled before death. His father, Torden, advisor to King Quillan, brutally murdered.

Stumbling blindly through the ravaged caravan, he'd tripped over the headless body of his older brother, Arden, heir to the Fiefdom of Ravencrest. But it was the memory of his sister which tortured him most deeply. She'd not died quickly. Bleeding profusely, battered almost beyond recognition, she'd clung to life, waiting for Tynan's return. Her shining green eyes, clouded with the newly discovered knowledge of life's injustice, gazed at him lovingly as he'd cradled her broken body in his arms. "I knew you'd come," she'd said simply.

Guilt still choked him. "I should have been here," he had whispered.

"They would have killed you too," Tynara had

murmured, her reasoning clear even as she drew her last breaths. And then, as he attempted to clean the crusting blood from her ashen brow, she'd described two of her assailants clearly. "I haven't time to tell you more, Tynan," she'd whispered, her breathing becoming more and more shallow. He pleaded with her to hold on. She hadn't heard. Her pupils dilated; her eyes no longer focused.

"Tynan, are you here?" she'd cried suddenly, hysterically.

"I'm here," he'd assured her, the choking pain in his throat preventing him from saying more as he held her petite form tenderly in the circle of his arms.

"I'm frightened, Tynan. Don't leave me. Hold me," she'd whispered hoarsely, her beautiful eyes staring sightlessly at the brilliant blue of the sky above.

"I am holding you, sister." He'd swallowed against the lump in his throat, allowing the tears to course silently down his face. "I won't leave you. I promise."

Then, momentarily her vision had cleared. With tears shining in her luminous emerald eyes, she'd raised one fragile ashen hand to stroke his cheek as she spoke her final words, "I love you, brother. Live . . . for us both."

Blindly watching the setting sun, Tynan had continued to hold her until the tears of grief and guilt had ceased to flow and he'd looked down upon the lifeless body of his twin to realize that she was truly gone from him.

The scene was branded into his brain with a

searing intensity he could never escape. The stench of burning flesh, the sickly sweet smell of congealing blood. Destruction. Death. His mind recoiled with horror even now, but he refused to allow himself escape. The least he could do was remember the atrocity his family had suffered. He had escaped death, and now destiny drove him to avenge the offense. It was his only solace and even that appeasement was too brief.

The memory faded, but the anguish did not. Tynan, clenching his teeth against a misery almost as fresh as it had been that day, yielded to tears. And, as the moisture tracked freely down the hardened planes of his face, he raised embittered eyes to stare at the hazily visible twin spheres of the now risen moons. Why had his family been so brutally killed? A primal cry of grief and rage rose inexorably in his throat, requiring release. "Why?" he demanded of the gods. His cry echoed back to him from the cliffs above. There was no answer. There never would be. Only the grief remained, sustaining him, driving him. He would not be free of it until the last of the men who'd murdered his family had died by his hand.

He'd found the two men Tynara had described, two of the original twelve. They'd revealed much concerning their companions before he, vengeful and grieving, had allowed them the peace of death.

The memory of Tynara caused Tynan's thoughts to return to the image of the young woman in the bar. She meant nothing to him. Why did her visage continue to torment him? She was too trusting, too like his twin sister. Tynara's words echoed in his mind. "Live for us both." Tynara, only twenty-two at the time of her death, had revered life. She would not want the young woman to suffer.

Angry at the direction his thoughts were taking, he whistled shrilly for Chaz. The beast plodded slowly up to him, a ghostly shadow in the misty moonlight attempting to pierce the cloud cover overhead. With swift sure movements, Tynan relieved the stallion of his gear, permitting Chaz to roam freely. The faralk often joined his own kind at night, but so far he'd always returned to Tynan by dawn. A day would come when he would not return, and Tynan knew it and accepted it. He just hoped it wouldn't be too soon. He'd come to rely on Chaz a great deal.

Wrapping himself in the invaluable cloak of fur, he lay down in the lee of the boulder. Tomorrow if his thoughts still bothered him, he would reconsider the matter of the girl.

Tallia rested her arms on the windowsill and stared through the smudged window of her tiny room at the inn. Last night, she had dreamed of Eyrsa, though not the vigorous eighty-year-old woman she knew. Her governess had appeared stooped and frail, her slender frame laboring beneath the weight of illness. Could the dream be a portent?

With worry creasing her brow, Tallia retrieved her indigo prayer crystal from her pack. Seating herself on the edge of the bed, she fixed her gaze on its darkened surface and concentrated, seeking the meditative state. As she sought the words for her

25

prayer, she remembered the tale Eyrsa had told her of how the crystals had come to be used to speak to the gods and goddesses. Toleme, the first king of Karaundo, child of the gods, had used them a long time ago to seek guidance from the father-god, Yaewel. Now she too echoed the actions of this long-ago king. To Yaewel, who had sent his children, Toleme, Galacia, and Coran, to teach mortal man the value of life, she directed her prayer. *Oh, reverer of life, I beseech you to guard the life of your faithful servant Eyrsa. Preserve her health. As always, I bow to your will.*

Replacing her prayer crystal within the safety of her belongings, Tallia turned once again to the view from the window. The sun rose slowly out of the horizon, lighting the faded and dreary town of Promise. She watched for Jenk's arrival, as he'd told her they'd leave shortly after dawn.

Anxiety and uncertainty about her upcoming journey, Twin Suns, Eyrsa, and her choice of escort, plagued her. Half-formed, disquieting thoughts tumbled through her mind in disarray: Eyrsa's message, Tolar's death, Jenk's almost too confident swagger, and, always, the mesmerizing emerald eyes of the wastelander. She shook her head. The constant worry helped not at all. She turned her attention to the street below and saw Jenk.

In the tavern, he had seemed respectable, had treated her with courtesy. Yet, there was something about him that seemed not to fit. Something artificial. Yes, that was it. His look had held nothing but admiration for her, but when she'd met his gaze unexpectedly, she'd found herself almost scorched by the heat of his azure stare. There was something in the expression in his eyes that made her uncomfortable. She found it difficult to trust him, but she had no choice.

A slight frown marred the smoothness of her forehead as she caressed the comforting bulge of the Zarma stone, suspended on a thong beneath her tunic. The stone, retrieved from a place high in the mountains, was an important augmentation of the Zarmistic healers' ability to diagnose illness with instinctive accuracy. Now its calming influence offered her comfort.

With a sigh, she turned her eyes from the town below, now bathed in the too revealing golden light of the risen sun. It was time to ready herself to leave. She checked her appearance in the mirror and critically appraised her image. She saw a seventeen-year-old woman, petite but well-formed. A wealth of sable waves tumbled past her shoulders to caress her tiny waist. She studied the contrast of her dark hair against the alabaster fairness of her complexion as she secured her tresses in a knot at her nape. The action drew her attention to her now accentuated eyes. They were her most unusual feature, and she had never quite liked them. Large and pale silvery-blue, framed by thick black lashes, they were so translucent as to appear almost colorless except when they reflected the shade of clothing she wore.

Squaring her shoulders, she retrieved her pack and left the room to confront whatever lay ahead. She was frightened but the need to get home granted her strength.

Tallia stepped out onto the sloping boardwalk before the inn, her soft leather boots soundless. The town was silent, deserted. Jenk smiled at her reassuringly. "I've brought the garies around. The stableman told me which was yours. She's a beautiful animal," he concluded, eyeing the cream-colored cat with professional discernment.

"Yes, she is," agreed Tallia proudly. "I call her Luma." She reached to scratch the animal behind the ears, surreptitiously contemplating Jenk from beneath her lashes. His chestnut hair fell straight almost to his shoulders, much longer than the styles worn by men in the cities or fiefdoms. But then, she'd seen no bulletins in Promise offering grooming services. Yet, even without that convenience, Jenk was clean, polished. His hair shone with highlights in the morning sunlight, his tanned countenance clean-shaven. Unexpectedly Tallia realized that he returned her scrutiny, and warmth colored her face.

Tynan observed Tallia from a nearby dense shadow between two buildings. Perhaps, in protecting Tallia, who was so much like Tynara, he could, in some measure, atone for his inability to save his twin.

The jerky movement of Tallia's hands betrayed her nervousness, and he almost smiled as he watched her furtively studying Jenk. If he knew what she was doing from this distance, certainly Jenk was aware of her inspection. His gaze shifted to Jenk who also stared at Tallia. Even from this distance, the expression in his eyes was obvious.

The heat of his gaze bordered on the obsessive. Tynan frowned. Was the man perhaps considering Tallia for himself? Whatever Jenk's plan, it would not reach fruition. Tynan's conscience refused to allow him to leave the young woman on her own.

He stepped from the shadows. "Morning."

Tallia whirled. Against the glare of the sun, she saw only the large black form of a man, faceless in the brilliant light streaming into her eyes. Raising her hand as a shield against the glare, she recognized the wastelander. For some unknown reason, her heart fluttered like a captured wild bird as she studied the powerful masculine figure cloaked in sinister black.

At the sound of his greeting, Jenk pivoted to face him, his gaze immediately locating Tynan. "What do you want here, wastelander?" he asked gruffly.

Tynan stared at Jenk, his impenetrable emerald gaze pinning the man, judging him, finding him wanting. Jenk flushed angrily beneath the scrutiny. Without responding to the merchant, Tynan turned his attention to Tallia. "My destination is near the Fiefdom of the Twin Suns. I will escort you."

Tallia stared at him. The man was presumptuous! He'd refused to escort her, forcing her to finalize plans with Jenk. Now he appeared out of nowhere to announce grandly that he had amended his pronouncement, expecting her to alter her decision immediately. It galled her, more so because that was precisely what she wanted to do. Her instincts told her he was the superior protector, and her instincts were seldom wrong. Swallowing her annoyance, she smiled. "How kind of you."

Tynan frowned. Was there an inflection of sarcasm in her tone?

Tallia turned to Jenk. "Jenk of the House of Krampter," she began formally, "I would like to thank you for your courtesy. As . . ." she halted uncertainly, looking at the wastelander.

"Tynan," he stated.

Just Tynan. Of course, a wastelander would lay claim to no house, large or small. She longed to press him for more information but sensed that her questions wouldn't be well accepted. "As Tynan is going in the direction in which I require escort," she continued, "it would be senseless of me to ask you to go hundreds of miles out of your way." She noted the expression in Jenk's eyes, still fixed on Tynan. "I would like to offer you twenty-five silver pentars for your trouble," she concluded, holding out the small triangular-shaped coins to him, hoping it would appease the man's obviously injured pride. She hated to part with the funds, but it was the appropriate gesture for one of her station.

Jenk's gaze shifted from Tynan to Tallia and she instinctively retreated from the rage reflected in his blue eyes. An instant later they had softened, and she was certain she'd imagined the fleeting expression. "Are you sure that is what you want, Lady?" he asked solicitously. "The man is a wastelander." He spoke the last word with obvious distaste.

"I'm sure, Jenk," Tallia replied firmly. "I am most grateful for your concern, but I'll be fine."

His eyes cooled a degree at her obstinacy. "Very well. I have wasted a good deal of time preparing for this journey, so I will take the money you offer."

He reached to take the proffered coins, then turned, mounted his gari and rode silently away.

Tynan knew Tallia had been unaware of the look that had passed between him and Jenk as Jenk left. But Tynan had seen the emotion in Jenk's cold blue eyes which had been akin to hatred, and suspected that he would be meeting Jenk again, in another place, at another time, when the odds were more favorable to Jenk. Thrusting the thought aside, he turned to Tallia. "These are the supplies you'll be needing," he stated, holding out a scrap of paper. "Do you have them?"

Tallia read the list, surprised to discover there were items she didn't have. It had been Jenk's ability to protect her that had concerned her, not his knowledge of the essentials for the trip. Obviously he had not known as much as he'd led her to believe.

"No," she replied to Tynan, frowning in consternation. "There are some things I'm missing. But the merchant will not be open for another two hours."

"Wake him," Tynan replied shortly, then studied Tallia's garb. The knee-length mauve tunic with its thigh-high slit, and the almost sheer hosiery of the same color, habitually worn together, were not suitable attire for the wasteland.

"Do you have any other clothing to wear?" he queried abruptly, refusing to acknowledge the sensations that began coursing through him at his perusal of her shapely limbs.

"What's wrong with these?" Tallia asked in confusion, looking down at her tunic.

"Nothing, if you don't mind freezing. The waste-

31

land winds are constant and cold despite the sun. You'll need clothing like mine. Two sets if you're to travel comfortably out there."

Tallia studied him. His thick-soled black boots reached to mid-calf, lacing in front. Black pants of a soft leather encased his muscular legs like a second skin. Disconcertingly, her heart began fluttering strangely once more. Her gaze travelled higher. She flushed, quickly passing over the molded leather groin guard fastened to a belt at his lean waist. She noticed the soft suede of his shirt, and the fur cape now thrown casually over one shoulder in the warmth of the morning. Nodding her comprehension, her gaze travelled quickly over his arresting features to stop at his huge hat. The totally circular brim was large enough to shade his broad shoulders.

"All right," she concluded thoughtfully. "I'll try to find something at the merchant's."

"Good," replied Tynan. "Only what's on the list. We'll be traveling swiftly, three weeks to Twin Suns."

Tallia gaped at him. Three weeks! That was less than half the time it took to cross the wasteland by caravan.

"Go wake up the merchant," Tynan continued, jerking Tallia out of her stunned state. "Be back in half an hour," he stated before turning and walking off.

Tallia stared after him, feeling like an abandoned child. She didn't want to rudely rouse the merchant. What would she do if he became angry? Why couldn't Tynan have offered to accompany her?

With hesitant steps, she moved in the direction of the mercantile. After glancing over her shoulder to ensure that she wasn't being observed, she opened her purse to study its contents. If she bargained carefully, she would just have enough to purchase the necessary supplies.

Tallia stared at the building apprehensively. Two equal-sized windows bordered the double door and the last remnants of paint hung in loose flakes on the store's planked facade. Grimacing slightly at her latest unpleasant predicament, she knocked timidly, peering through the dirty window into the dim interior. There was no sign of movement. Suspecting that she might well find herself once more without an escort should she fail to meet Tynan at the appointed time, Tallia knocked again loudly. Endless moments passed with still no response. With a disgusted sigh, she resorted to kicking the door, letting her anger at Tynan dissolve itself in her actions. Finally a grumbling reply came from within the shadowed confines.

When Tallia emerged from the mercantile, Tynan was already waiting next to her tethered gari. Juggling the bundle of clothing and supplies she'd bought after mollifying the disgruntled shopkeeper, Tallia hurried as much as possible without breaking into an undignified run. Tynan sat on his faralk, watching her, making no move to dismount to aid her with the packages. Biting back her annoyance, Tallia swiftly stowed the supplies on Luma, then mounted.

"I assume you can control that beast?" He had an expression of such long-suffering male arrogance on his face that Tallia had to lower her head to conceal her exasperation.

"Yes," she replied calmly. "I can control her."

Tynan nodded. "Let's go." He turned the faralk and headed north, not even looking back to see if she followed.

CHAPTER TWO

BEYOND PROMISE, THE LANDSCAPE CHANGED. THE trail climbed steadily to the top of a bluff before dropping unexpectedly over the edge of the mesa, descending into a craterlike bowl carved out of the terrain millions of years ago. It was like descending into another world, one of arid desolation. Beyond the sharp cliff boundaries, dry tufts of grass struggled for a foothold in the hard, cracked earth. Trees, scattered sparingly in their fight for existence, were stunted by the shortage of moisture and twisted into abstract shapes by the constant buffeting of the chilling wind.

Tallia gazed across the wasteland to where the distant mountains rose, no more than purple shadows jutting from the horizon. In that same mountain range, spanning hundreds of miles along the eastern and northern border of the wasteland, lay the Twin Suns Fiefdom and home. Three weeks! Such a short time and yet forever.

Thus far, she'd trailed contentedly behind the faralk. Now, tired of the sameness of the landscape, she urged Luma forward. It seemed like an appropriate time to make the acquaintance of her escort, and conversation would help pass the time.

Tynan's pace increased to match her own, maintaining the distance between them. Irritated, she tightened her legs on Luma's sides. The cat bounded forward, finally coming abreast of Tynan and his mount.

The stallion snorted, side-stepping nervously as he swung his massive head around, narrowly missing Luma's throat with his sharp ebony horn. Luma tensed, startling Tallia with her shrill feline growl of rage. Instinctively, Tallia jerked the reins, dropping back as she struggled to control the enormous cat.

Having calmed her mount, Tallia lifted her eyes to encounter the scorching heat of Tynan's accusing glare. She bit her lip in vexation. Why hadn't she thought more carefully? She should have expected such behavior from the animals; they were, after all, natural enemies.

Could she, utilizing the commitment the beasts felt to their riders, initiate a truce between the faralk and the gari for the duration of the journey? She was certain it was possible, but she'd never communicated with a faralk. He might resist the idea. Nevertheless, the attempt would have to be made as soon as they made camp.

Her decision arrived at, she stared at Tynan's broad back. *He* was another matter but he *was* a wastelander. She'd just have to make allowances for his impolite behavior.

She shifted in the saddle, attempting to settle herself more comfortably within the stiff curve of the leather. The feat seemed impossible, and her lower region already ached.

Tallia sighed and braced herself for a long, uncomfortable day of solitude. With little else to occupy her time, she began, once again, to examine her surroundings. The barrenness brought to mind one of Eyrsa's comments. "There is beauty in all things. You have but to look to see it."

Tallia scrutinized her environment with renewed interest. She did see it. The brilliant rays of the late-morning sun transformed the arid brown soil to gold. Shaded cracks became patterns of black, crisscrossing and interlacing. Hues of ginger and russet lingered along the ocher cliff walls and bits of quartz reflected the sunlight like diamonds set in the bands of the rock. She smiled. Eyrsa would have been pleased with the thoroughness of her observations.

As the morning passed, she saw in the distance a cloud of dust indicating the presence of a herd of the large, shaggy lemac that foraged in the wasteland. And she noted other things, too, that she would have been blind to had she not been trained to look for them. Of particular interest were thick clumps of coppery-leaved vegetation squatted amid the dry grass along the path. She pulled Luma to a halt and dismounted. Bending, she rubbed the thick leathery leaves of the plant between her fingers. The contact produced no aroma and left no residue. Interesting! She detached one small, elongated leaf from the unfamiliar species and tucked it into the small pouch on her belt. She must remember to ask Eyrsa about it.

"Move it!"

She jumped as the arrogant command resounded in the wasteland silence. Tynan scowled impatiently at her atop the broad back of the faralk he had been forced to halt on her account. A situation he obviously did not appreciate. Guiltily, she scrambled back onto the gari as he set off again, arrogantly assuming that she would obey his command.

Why, if he considered her such an inconvenience, had he agreed to escort her? Who was he? What forces drove him? She didn't feel unsafe with him and yet an inexplicable nervousness prevailed. What was he thinking behind those masked emerald eyes and that perpetual frown? Tallia lifted her brows slightly and stared at him contemplatively. She sighed, resigning herself to her position at the rear of their small procession, watching the miles pass and the sun rise higher in the sky.

They'd been traveling for hours and it was now long past midday. Her every pore felt clogged with minuscule particles of soil swept along by the frigid wind. Her stomach growled angrily, reminding her that, in her anticipation of leaving Promise, she'd eaten sparingly of her breakfast. Did the man never stop? True, once he'd turned, wordlessly indicating as he held up his own canteen that she should alleviate her thirst. But even then he had not halted the faralk. She'd been sipping from her own canteen for almost an hour by then, and had continued to when she'd felt it necessary. It had helped alleviate her hunger, marginally. She shook the canteen. It was almost half empty. Her throat, parched and congested with dust, once again ached for water. She unscrewed the cap and let the cool liquid trickle down her throat before resecuring the canteen to her saddle.

The excitement that had bolstered her spirits when they first left Promise had long since faded. Even her curiosity concerning their surroundings seemed unimportant now. Her shoulders ached from gripping the reins, her legs were cramped in their kneeling position on the stiff saddle. Tynan remained in front of her, his posture rigid and uninviting, the incessant movement of his head as he scanned the horizon communicating his constant vigilance. After the near-disaster of her first attempt to establish a casual conversation, she hadn't tried again nor was she about to.

Would he never stop? Tallia directed another glare at his stiffly erect, broad-shouldered torso. She refused to utter a word of complaint. He would expect that, and she wouldn't give him the satisfaction. Despondently, she watched the dust rising from the crisply dried prairie grasses at each implacable step the faralk took. Step, poof, step, poof. It was like walking through a field of puffballs. The soil was beyond dry; it was positively desiccated, cracked, and splintering in its need for moisture. How did the grasses manage to come back each year? The land as far as the eye could see in every direction was entirely dry! Even the snow, what little there was, appeared dehydrated.

What if the last of the small streambeds had dried up? She'd only brought enough drinking water for herself and her mount, and even that she had hoped to replenish at least once or twice. How would she wash? The thought of traveling three weeks through this dust without washing was inconceivable. She already itched from the coat of dust clinging tenaciously to her flesh. And the icy wind aggravated her too. How could the wind be so freezing cold, carrying minuscule ice particles as it hurled the dust relentlessly before it, while the sun blazed so brilliantly that she could feel her face burning? She supposed she could don the hat she'd purchased. But she'd secured it with her other belongings and she couldn't reach it without dismounting. Besides, she'd never worn a hat. When she'd tried it on in the mercantile, it had felt inordinately cumbersome. She'd bought it only because Tynan had said she'd need one.

Tallia, stop it! a familiar voice chastised. It sounded so much like Eyrsa that she actually lifted her self-pitying gaze to look around. The country was barren for miles; there was no one there. She had known there wouldn't be. Eyrsa was in her mind, in all the training she'd received over the years, in the acerbic comments and words of wisdom. And suddenly she knew what her governess would say to her right now. "Lift that chin, girl. You are a member of the House of Darnaz. You are young and alive, and have yet to experience true discomfort. Self-pity is for the weak. You are of my line. You are not weak!" Tallia smiled. It would be so good to hear that raspy voice again. She urged her mount to close a little of the distance between herself and her escort. She was going home!

The sun was low on the horizon when Tynan finally halted. Tallia stopped and, without dismounting, watched him. There were two reasons for staying mounted. First, she wasn't absolutely certain he'd decided to camp. He'd spoken not a word since dismounting, and appeared engrossed in an examination of the terrain. And second, she was reasonably positive that after so many hours in the saddle her legs were going to refuse to operate properly. If she hadn't been able to see them, she would not have believed she still possessed lower extremities.

She waited, inspecting her surroundings. There was a line of stunted bush near by. A huge rock outcropping rose imposingly out of the ground directly in front of her. Other than those two features, the land appeared no different than what they'd seen all day.

"You going to sit there all night?" a brusque resonant voice jerked her from her reverie. As she began to unfold her body from her kneeling position in the gari saddle, Tallia wondered if his voice sounded that way from inadequate use or from a bad temperament. Unable to reach a conclusion, she let the thought slide. Clinging to the pommel for support, she dismounted. Her legs quaked, tingling painfully as the blood began to flow in new directions, but amazingly, they supported her.

Tynan had already relieved the faralk of its burden of supplies, leaving the animal free to roam. What would she do with Luma? They couldn't leave both animals free for the night. Not unless she somehow managed to make Luma and the faralk understand that for this journey they were companions, not adversaries.

"Unsaddle the gari and stow your tack over there," Tynan ordered, indicating a spot adjacent to the outcropping where his own gear rested.

Despite the nature of his words, the husky male timbre of his voice sent strange little shivers along Tallia's spine. He had a wonderful voice, a pity he didn't use it more often. Mentally shaking herself from her extremely inappropriate musing, Tallia was reminded of Dayna. Dayna had been her roommate and only friend during the three interminable months at the conservatory for Zarmistic healers. It had been she who had made the time bearable, and occasionally even fun. What would she have thought of this silent wastelander? Tallia knew the answer. Dayna was cynical, irreverent, outrageous, and totally obsessed with the anatomy of the opposite sex. She'd explained this obsession as 'an addiction to the sensual pleasures of life.' Tallia looked at Tynan again. Perhaps, he had . . . *Stop it, Tallia*. Firmly she squelched her inappropriate thought.

"Build a fire," he ordered, oblivious to her scrutiny, then strolled off leaving Tallia staring after him incredulously. Almost as an afterthought he pivoted and explained curtly, "I'm going hunting." Then he was gone.

Tynan topped a rise a short distance away and looked back to see Tallia lead Luma over to the outcropping with slow painful steps. A twinge of conscience caused him to tighten his lips in irritation. He was not accustomed to worrying about other people.

Annoyingly enough, Tallia had been in his thoughts much of the day, but the ruminating that had plagued him had had little to do with her immediate comfort. Rather, he'd been preoccupied with doubts concerning the wisdom of his agreement to escort her. How was he, a man of twenty-four years who appreciated women, to maintain his distance and deliver the very presentable Tallia to Twin Suns with her honor intact?

He shook his head in self-disgust. He should have let Jenk escort her. With a resigned shrug, he realized his conscience would not have allowed him to do that either. Thrul! He'd just have to continue to maintain his distance while treating her with as much courtesy as he could muster. He'd start by making an effort to remember that she was not accustomed to living in the saddle.

After the first painful steps, relieving Luma of her saddle and the small bundle of supplies did not prove too difficult. Pragmatically, Tallia decided that the first item on her agenda was to introduce the gari to the faralk. Once confident that they could coexist peacefully without constant supervision, she could direct her thoughts to the other things which required attention. High on the list was a quick visit to a nearby copse of brush.

Entwining her fingers gently in the thick ruff of hair that surrounded the feline's neck, Tallia lead the great cat slowly toward the spot where the faralk grazed. The beast lifted his massive head, regarding her approach warily. Wincing at the silent screams of protesting muscles with each step, Tallia kept her eyes on the animal, willing him to allow her near. Luma began to make small coughing sounds of warning deep in her throat. The cream-colored hair along the cat's spine rose revealing the darker tan of her underfur. Tallia halted. Wrapping her arms around the huge creature, she closed her eyes mentally communicating the tranquility she required. Immediately, Luma quieted and allowed Tallia to lead her forward.

Finally, they were within reach of the faralk. Tallia did not fear the beast, but she would have been foolish had she not been wary. Slowly, she extended her hand, palm up, allowing the faralk to make the initial move. He shook his head in warning, tossing his long mane, bringing the deadly ebony horn alarmingly close to Tallia's throat. Sensing that the animal was testing her, intending no real harm, she simply froze. Luma, trusting completely in her mistress, also remained motionless.

Closing her eyes, Tallia attempted to establish a rapport. She felt the soft muzzle of the faralk against her palm. Gently, she moved her hand up, caressing the enormous head. The mind link happened with a rapidity that astounded her. She felt the sensation of running with the wind, enormous muscles flexing, carrying the man who was good. There was a tremendous love in the animal for the man who rode him, a faithfulness that had begun as an obligation. There was also hate for other men, faceless men who'd tried to destroy the majestic creature because they feared its strength and intelligence. Carefully, Tallia sought to channel the impressions she received to Luma.

Luma understood. She had rarely been treated badly by men, but others of her kind had been. She understood the love bond to a human. Now, Tallia reversed the nexus, communicating the gari's feelings to the faralk. Finally, she used what she had gleaned to transmit her thoughts to both animals. Each had a bond to their riders who traveled as companions. Therefore, the gari and the faralk must coexist harmoniously.

Sensing the animals' understanding and acceptance, Tallia turned, directing her thoughts to preparing for the night. The chill wind caressed her and she retrieved one of the leather outfits she'd purchased from her pack. Her muscles protesting her every move, she attended to her own pressing personal needs behind a few stunted shrubs before changing.

Warmer now, she searched for wood to build the fire but there was no wood in the wasteland. A few brittle bushes, which wouldn't burn long enough to scorch a meal, were all that she could find. What did one use for kindling?

Sitting down, she surveyed the area in perplexity. She couldn't let a small challenge like a campfire defeat her. She was an intelligent person. It would just take some thought. Absently, she kneaded the aching muscles in her thighs as she carefully evaluated the barren terrain. Thousands of acres of dry grass and a few stunted copses of brush surrounded her. What was she missing? Well, she couldn't sit here indefinitely. Tynan would return shortly and her own gnawing hunger prodded her to waste little time.

Breaking some twigs off the nearest patches of brush, she carried the armload back to an area she judged the most suitable for a fire. Clearing the region of grasses so the fire wouldn't get away from her, she piled the twigs in the center of the cleared circle, stuffing the grasses in between the branches.

Tynan stopped dead as he approached the edge of the camp. A small rodent, a toiphat, hung suspended from his hand as his gaze riveted on Tallia. He tried to ignore the tightening in his groin, the sudden quickening of his pulse, the rush of blood through his veins. In silent anguish, he raised his eyes skyward in a plea for strength. Before him, Tallia bent over a small mound of twigs, her rounded hips and slender legs snugly encased in form-hugging, black leather breeches. Nudity would have left as much to the imagination, Tynan thought as he struggled unsuccessfully to focus his eyes elsewhere. He crossed the clearing quickly, smothering emotions to which he refused to succumb beneath a shield of temper. "Haven't you got the fire going yet?"

Tynan's voice rumbling out of the deepening shadows startled Tallia so badly that she dropped her tinderbox. The censure in his tone was more than she could tolerate. She was both mentally and physically enervated, her legs ached, her stomach growled hungrily, and she'd racked her brains to determine how to start his blasted fire. "Maybe if you'd told me just what I was supposed to start a fire with in this cursed country, I would have had better luck," she retorted, flushing with both anger and embarrassment.

"You've traveled the wasteland before." The intensity of his expression belied his casual remark.

A test? "Yes, with a caravan," Tallia informed him defensively. "We carried wood with us."

"Dry dung," he informed her before turning his back and dropping the toiphat unceremoniously onto a flat boulder.

"Dung?" Tallia repeated dully. For a fire? She'd never heard of such a thing.

"Yes, dung," he replied absently, as his knife moved in swift slicing movements. Suddenly, he turned to eye her incredulously. "You do know what it is, don't you?"

"Of course I know what it is," Tallia responded, once again feeling defensive. "It's . . . it's . . ."

"Good."

Her stomach roiled as she noticed the quantity of blood greasing Tynan's hands. Quickly, she turned to the slightly less repulsive task of collecting dung.

Peripherally Tynan observed her at her chore. He repressed a grin at the dainty two-fingered manner in which she collected the stuff. A slight wrinkling of her delicate nose and down turning of her lips conveyed her distaste for the project. He shook his head. If the little upper-class lady wanted to travel the wasteland without a caravan, she'd better get used to it. He'd hunt and help with the cooking, but starting the fire would be her responsibility. Finished cleaning the toiphat, he moved to cut a twig and construct a makeshift spit with which to suspend the animal over the fire.

Tallia had just gotten the blaze going nicely when Tynan returned. "We'll have to let the flames die down a bit. It'll give off more heat, and there won't be any danger of scorching the meat." Then he eyed the horizon morosely before moving off to crouch down on a small rise, facing the sunset.

Tallia had been trained to learn from observation. Watching Tynan, she sensed that his action was one of habit, that he was not simply enjoying one of nature's more beautiful displays. Suddenly she recognized a man in mourning, a man with a tortured soul. That she perceived this was not due to the extraordinary power that had begun developing in her mind as a child, for she could not violate the sacred trust that prevented her from invading the mind of another. She simply observed and translated the messages of his body—the tense muscles across his back, the rigid set of his neck and spine, the slightly downcast angle of his head, and the movement of one, lean bronzed hand. Compassion filled her heart as her eyes fixed on that large capable hand as it rhythmically clenched and unclenched.

Turning her gaze away, she granted him his privacy as she proceeded with the repulsive task of suspending the dripping carcass over the fire. Tallia rarely ate meat, and despite her hunger, she was sickened by the thought of eating the animal.

Almost an hour later, Tynan, now just a slightly blacker shadow against the indigo of the night sky, returned to the fire side. He pulled the cohabear fur cape more tightly around his shoulders for protection from the night's chill before seating himself.

Accepting Tynan's uncommunicative mood, Tallia relaxed, letting the crackling of the fire soothe her nerves as she listened to the night sounds. Insects hummed. Night creatures shrieked. A cat screamed its growl of triumph. Perhaps it had been Luma; she'd left the camp to hunt some time ago. But even the tranquil sounds were unable to distract Tallia totally from eating. After several forced mouthfuls, she forgot her hunger and heeded instead her stomach's protests. Unobtrusively, she pushed the remainder of her meal under a loose clump of nearby grass.

Moving to her bedroll, she spread it out near the base of the outcropping, rearranged her own white palatine over her shoulders, and lay down to stare into the flickering flames. She wished she'd been able to wash, but there'd been no stream near. Feeling unclean was high on Tallia's list of the most uncomfortable circumstances in life. "Will there be water to wash with when we camp tomorrow?" she asked abruptly, startling even herself. Her voice seemed entirely out of place in the darkened silence.

Tynan's gaze locked with hers, and for an instant he appeared astounded by her presence. Then, as her words penetrated his thoughts, he shrugged. "Won't know until we get there."

He continued looking at her, his green eyes glittering peculiarly in the flickering firelight, and for the first time Tallia felt uncomfortable in his presence. She trusted him to escort her across the wasteland safely, but he was a man. In truth, she knew little about him. Finally, she could withstand the powerful force of his penetrating scrutiny no longer. "Why are you staring?"

The question betrayed her innocence, and the breathless quality of her utterance communicated her anxiety. Tynan shook his head. One of the most beautiful women he'd ever seen traveled the isolated miles of the wasteland with him, and she didn't understand why he stared. For an instant, in the deceitful illumination of the fire she'd resembled the captivating seductress of his dreams on those solitary nights when he'd been too long without the companionship of a woman. Locking temptation into the recesses of his mind, he racked his brain for a plausible reply to her question. "Just thinking you'll find it cold sleeping that far away from the fire."

"Oh." Tallia studied him. His words made sense, and she could discern no duplicity in his expression. Yet there was a peculiarity, an intimacy, to his statement that suggested it might not be totally truthful. Still, even if it was not, did she really want to know his thoughts? No, she decided, she did not. "Thank you for your concern. I'll move closer to the fire in a while."

Deciding to stop dwelling on the man, she diverted her attention to his mount. "What is the faralk's name?"

"Chaz," he responded absently, his gaze fixed on some distant point.

Tallia nodded. An unusual name for an unusual animal. It had long been suspected that faralks were extremely intelligent. The herds, when seen, always seemed to be in perfect accord. He was a beautiful creature, majestic, powerful, and definitely not evil. Superstition was the reason behind man's hatred of the faralks. In the night, Chaz, grazing not far away, appeared all but invisible except for the gleam of his single onyx horn in the moonlight, and the glowing blood-red eyes, characteristic of faralks in the absence of daylight. Yes, a superstitious person would fear him. Rising, she pulled her bedroll closer to the warmth of the fire. Curling up within the warmth of her fur, she attempted to thrust all thought away as she glanced at Tynan.

He still sat unmoving and she allowed her eyes to roam his stalwart build. He'd removed the large black hat he'd worn most of the day, and his raven hair hung in soft waves almost to his shoulders. One elbow rested on upraised knees and he supported his strong, square, whisker-shadowed chin in the palm of his hand. He seemed very distant. What was he thinking? Why was he such a silent solitary man?

Tallia tensed, struggling against the smothering blanket of his despondency as it abruptly assailed her senses. Her eyes widened with shock at the sensation. She had never perceived a person's emotions so clearly without physical contact. Eventually the impressions subsided and she was able to close her eyes and drift into an uneasy slumber.

The room was enormous, bedecked with elaborate furnishings and thick, luxurious fur rugs. A large gold-framed portrait of an elderly man resided in a place of honor over the huge ivory stone fireplace. A savage wind wailed and shrieked without, yet the draperies which shrouded the room deadened the sound. It should have been a room which inspired admiration and a sense of safety from the raging storm but it did not.

There was a presence in the room—a man, elegantly garbed. Through the haze of the dream, Tallia felt she should recognize the profile of the man who stared with such satisfaction into the flickering flames as he leaned one arm against the high mantel of the hearth. A knock sounded. The man yelled an imperious "Come," as he turned to the portal.

Tallia gasped. It was Lord Krogan, King Quillan's nephew and heir apparent.

51

She observed the entrance of another man. Not as richly attired, he had the manner of a fighter, yet he did not wear the apparel of a royal man-at-arms. His silent stalking steps carried him quickly across the room. "My lord," he intoned nasally as he swept his sword to one side before kneeling to brush Krogan's outstretched fingers with his lips. Rising, he smiled an eerie smile. "You summoned me?"

"Yes." Lord Krogan turned to resume his position before the great hearth. The tilt of his head and the posture of his tall, lean body conveyed the arrogance of one secure in the knowledge of his power.

"How can I serve, my lord?" A malevolent smile curved the fighter's thin lips.

Tallia tossed restlessly. There were undercurrents she did not understand. She wanted to awaken, to rid herself of the foreboding, but she knew she must remain. She needed to know more. She slipped more deeply into the dream.

"There is a small matter which occupies my mind, Flagan." Krogan made an elegant gesture to a paper lying on a nearby table. "I found it necessary to record the details for you as I have another appointment shortly. When you are finished studying it, burn it. I would like you to hand pick the men most suited to the job. Furnish them no more information than necessary."

Flagan moved to retrieve the instructions. He scanned the contents quickly, surprise etching his features. Then, his shrewd onyx eyes lifted to those of his lord. "This girl has some special significance for you, my lord?"

"You have always been very astute, Flagan. It is a test to confirm a suspicion I have. However, you would do well to remember that being a confidant is more than an honored position; it can be a deadly one. If any of my confidences should reach the wrong ears, I will know exactly whose mouth they came from. I sincerely hope you do not talk in your sleep."

Flagan's complexion had taken on a slightly pasty hue as Lord Krogan spoke. Now Krogan laughed, partially dispelling the strained atmosphere. "Come, Flagan, we have been friends for years. I'm sure nothing will occur to change that." He spoke the words with a falsely boisterous confidence as he moved to drop an embracing arm over the shoulders of the slightly shorter man. "You have been one of my most loyal followers, and will be well rewarded on the day that the throne is mine."

Tallia shivered. Evil. It was like a third presence in the room.

Flagan nodded as Krogan walked with him to the door. "I'm afraid we'll have to conclude our visit now, friend." Krogan's voice carried the intonation of command once more. "Return when you have some news for me."

"Yes, my lord." Flagan's response remained slightly subdued as he departed. Krogan grinned a wolfish smile of satisfaction as he returned to the fireside.

The dream shifted. Tallia saw herself clothed in flowing white vestment, barefoot upon moon-washed marble tiling in a castle turret. A shadow moved to greet her, holding a spectral blade of serrated crystal in its upraised hand. The transparent kris plunged. A deep ruby stain spread and darkened, consuming Tallia's image.

"No!" screamed Tallia, eradicating the painful grip of the dream. The raging denial echoed off the nearby outcropping with a force that brought the sleeping Tynan instantly to his feet. He was at her side in a single stride.

Tallia bolted upright; her pale eyes glowed with the force of myriad emotions. Tynan didn't bother trying to identify them. "Tallia," he murmured, placing a gentle hand on her trembling shoulder. "It's all right. Just a nightmare."

Gradually Tallia's mind returned to the small camp, but the horror of her dream wasn't easily dismissed. She knew it was no ordinary dream. Although she'd never had one before, Eyrsa had spoken of a foreseeing. Foretelling visions were entirely inconsistent—sometimes completely symbolic, at other times very detailed. Her life was endangered unless she could alter the course of destiny. Instinctively, she turned to the comforting presence of the man beside her. She felt safe and secure within the circle of his arms, as though they formed a barrier capable of warding off the sense of evil that had escaped the bonds of her dream.

The part of Tynan that was primitive male instinctively responded to the sensation of Tallia's soft feminine form burrowing into his arms. But her very real horror communicated itself to the civilized man who had much practice in exercising his patience and self-control. Stroking her back, he rocked her trembling body until she calmed. "You all right now?"

She nodded, lifting her trembling hands to wipe at her tear-streaked cheeks. "It was no ordinary nightmare."

"Mmhm," he murmured agreeably, still massaging her back, easing the tension from the muscles.

She gazed briefly into his eyes, searchingly. Perhaps she sought some reassurance there. He didn't know. But as he met her gaze, staring into the pale smokey depths, paralysis overcame him. The charismatic radiance reflected there pulled at him, immobilizing him. A compelling force rose from the crystalline abyss of her irises seeking to take more than he was willing to give. He fought it. Shaking his head in self-derision, he banished the nonsensical delusion. He'd allowed himself to be affected by Tallia's fear and the darkness of the night.

Tynan concentrated on her subdued recounting of the dream, listening silently, indulgently, at first. Then he began to speculate. It didn't sound like an ordinary nightmare, and Tallia didn't attempt to interpret it. She spoke as someone who'd overheard a deeply disturbing conversation, and wondered what it meant.

Gut instinct had prevented Tynan's liking the king's nephew. It was unfortunate that King Quillan had never sired any children who survived infancy. Yet even Tynan found it difficult to believe that the evil Tallia had sensed as a third presence in the room related directly to the popular Lord Krogan. Could she have been mistaken? Why would she have been accorded a view into a future involving a man so removed from her own life? The shadow of danger, she had seen, he acknowledged as a forewarning. There was always danger in the wasteland. He shivered, burying a vague feeling of foreboding.

CHAPTER THREE

THE FIRST FAINT FINGERS OF LIGHT STREAKED THE morning sky as Tallia opened her eyes, awakened by the barely discernible sound of Tynan's movements around the camp. Peering from beneath the protective warmth of her fur cape, she observed him with frank curiosity. Last night, while comforting her in the aftermath of the dream, he'd seemed so warm, so understanding. Who was he beneath his somber veneer of aloofness?

Tallia studied him pensively. He seemed unaware of the magnetism that surrounded him like an aura. Despite the early-morning chill, his shirt hung open. Never had she seen a man so perfectly proportioned. The very sight of him caused an unfamiliar tightening in her abdomen and set her heart pounding. She let her eyes wander over his bronzed chest with its rough diamond of crisp raven curls, following a thin line of dark hair over his hard-muscled midriff until it disappeared beneath the snug waistband of his trousers. The clinging leather, devoid of the thick girdle and groin guard, did little to conceal his maleness.

Tallia felt a warm blush beginning to stain her cheeks as she realized where her gaze lingered, and quickly averted her eyes.

Her appreciative gaze returned to his face, profiled against the silvery dawn, admiring the proud slant of his forehead, the straight bridge of his nose, hesitating at the hard line of his mouth. Passing her fingers over the soft fullness of her own lips with a feather-light touch, Tallia wondered what it would be like to feel his lips on hers. Oh, she'd been kissed before, but somehow the quick peck she'd permitted the village boy paled in comparison to the way she envisioned Tynan's kiss. Closing her eyes, she could almost feel it, soft yet firm, gentle yet demanding.

"Get up." The stern voice, laced with irritation, cut sharply into her thoughts.

Tallia's eyes snapped open. How had he known she was awake? Had he been watching her? The evidence of her mortification crept from her neck into her cheeks as she met his gaze. Her breath caught in her throat; embarrassment immobilized her limbs as the heat of his stare held her in its intractable grip. There was something in the depths of his emerald eyes, just for an instant, flickering like a primitive hunger. And then, it was gone.

The spell broken, Tallia scrambled from her bed of dried grass, quickly turning to hide the flaming blush she knew accompanied the heat of her cheeks. Did he know in what directions her thoughts had wandered? Keeping her eyes averted, she hastily packed, disregarding the tingling of her spine which warned her that his intensely observant eyes still lingered on her.

Irritably retrieving his girdle and groin guard, Tynan slipped them on, ignoring the discomfiting constriction with stern determination. Damn her! Didn't she know what that adulatory expression could do to a man alone in the wasteland? He never should have agreed to escort her. Cursing his lack of foresight, he fervently wished he'd visited a woman before making this trek. Tallia's innocent appraisal of his body, as perceptible as any physical caress, had sent a torrent of awareness and desire coursing through his veins. His own susceptibility infuriated him. How was he to protect her from himself?

Last night, holding her in his arms, soothing away the demons of her dreams, he had felt an electrical undercurrent, a surge of energy that leapt from her fragrant skin and reverberated through his soul as he looked into her eyes. Now he fought the reoccurrence of the magnetic sensation with his anger, the one weapon that never failed to sustain him.

He'd made breakfast and eaten while Tallia slept. Now, he watched with impatience, and a touch of amazement, as she took her time consuming a very hearty portion of flat bread-like cakes and dried fruit, while totally ignoring him. In fact, as she closed her eyes savoring the last of the biscuits, he wondered if she even remembered he was there. Finally, noting that she'd finished, he threw his supplies behind Chaz's saddle and jerked the leather straps taut. Mounting, he urged the faralk into a brisk pace that left Tallia scrambling to secure her belongings and ready her mount before he disappeared from view.

When she had finally shortened the distance between them, Tallia noted the rigid set of Tynan's jaw. Certainly, his displeasure was a result of her brazen conduct. She would have to keep a tight rein on her thoughts. No lady would ever appraise a man so boldly or at least not get caught doing so, though she was sure Dayna wouldn't agree. Yet despite her resolve, as the day progressed, Tallia found her eyes lingering repeatedly on the somber figure in black to whom she'd entrusted her safety, observing the set of his wide shoulders, the rippling movements of his steel-sinewed muscles beneath the clinging leather, and the profile of his handsome face.

It was midafternoon when they reached the first creek bed. With the approach of winter, the water level barely covered Chaz's cloven hooves. In the aftermath of the forthcoming winter storms, the stream would swell, engorging the high banks, becoming a raging torrent as it raced for the distant sea. Tallia followed Tynan's lead and dismounted. After appeasing her thirst, she filled her canteen with the fresh clear liquid while the animals drank. With relief she splashed water over her face and neck. It wasn't a bath but it revived her flagging spirits nonetheless.

As Tynan remounted, Tallia sent a prayer of thanks to the goddess Galacia that the storms had not yet struck. Luma, typically feline, had an intense aversion to getting her feet wet. Had the stream been swollen with melting snows, nothing could have induced the beast to cross. Tallia watched as Tynan and his steed forged heedlessly onward, threading their way up the twisted rock-strewn path on the far side of the gully.

Slowly, she mounted then urged Luma on, leaning forward to whisper encouragement to the skittish animal. Luma's first reaction was a disgruntled hiss as she lifted her wet foot, shaking it angrily. She took another step, repeating the procedure. Then, ostensibly deciding to hasten the end of her torment, she emitted an outraged shriek and made one mighty bound for the opposite bank. Tallia struggled to keep her balance as the cat's forward motion propelled the animal halfway up the steep incline. Twisting frantically, Luma clawed for footing. Slipping from the saddle, Tallia groped in panic for the spitting feline's mane. Grasping only air, she fell from Luma's back, tumbling down the hard sandy bank to land unceremoniously in the icy water. Luma, freed of the encumbering weight of her rider, struggled up the bank to stare indignantly down at her.

Beside the gari, Tynan's motionless figure sat in silence upon Chaz—the demon-beast. For an instant, as she squinted at their forms silhouetted on the rise, Tallia fancied the apparition not so far off. The faralk's mighty body with its deadly gleaming horn seemed in perfect harmony with its enigmatic rider. From the shadowed features beneath the broad brim of his hat, Tynan's green eyes glistened with impatience, radiating a mysterious inner fire. Tallia swallowed nervously, lowering her gaze.

Unexpectedly, anger began to displace anxiety. What right had he to stare at her so accusingly? She wanted to voice her indignation, but her dignity forbade it. Instead, she struggled to her feet. The slippery stones of the stream provided poor footing and she slipped, falling to her knees. Couldn't he offer to help? Inquire as to her health? True, she had sustained little injury other than a slight scrape on her elbow and a severe blow to her pride. Still, he could ask! Anxious to vacate the icy water, she tossed the remnants of her pride to the wind and crawled. A degrading display, but one that achieved her objective. Ashore, Tallia pulled herself erect, compressed her lips into a thin line, and stomped up the steep path to Luma's side.

"You said you could handle her." Tynan's deep voice was expressionless, yet its very lack of sentiment conveyed his aggravation.

Tallia no longer cared. She was wet, cold, humiliated, and getting angrier by the minute. Bracing her small feet apart, she placed her hands on her hips and stared up at Tynan with all the hauteur she could muster. Gritting her chattering teeth, she spoke as calmly and emotionlessly as he. "I'm doing the best I can under the circumstances. I am hardly responsible for the inbred dislike Luma has for water."

His eyes darkened dangerously at her tone but Tallia was past caring. With a corner of her shirt, she hastily scrubbed at the mud coating her arms.

There was a moment of complete and utter quiet. "You all right?" his sonorous voice broke the strained silence.

Now he asks? Tallia thought in disgust. "Fine," she muttered with ill-temper.

"We'll camp here." Tynan dismounted and began

to remove the saddle and supplies from Chaz's back.

No apology, Tallia thought, but then she'd not really expected one—not from him. Tallia unloaded Luma and rummaged through the packs for dry clothing before moving back to the stream to wash away the residue of the crusted mud from her skin.

Trembling in reaction to the frigid caress of the wind, she hid herself behind some scraggly bushes near the creek and quickly changed. Then, after eyeing the slightly murky waters of the stream with indecision, she quickly rinsed the mud from her wet clothes before carrying them back to camp to dry near the fire. Tynan was nowhere in sight, a fact that didn't displease Tallia at the moment. Assuming he'd gone hunting, she set about building a fire. As the fire grew, Tallia stood staring dazedly into the flames, warming her hands.

"Tallia," a deep voice suddenly rumbled behind her.

Startled by the unexpected sound, she spun around in alarm, almost stumbling back into the flames of the campfire. Tynan's arm snaked out to catch her, tightening around her waist.

"Oh!" Tallia gasped, unsure whether her shock was induced by the fear conjured by his unannounced presence, or by the fact that the hard muscles of his chest pressed so closely against her breasts.

She stared up at him, captivated by the hard line of his lips, the tension in his square jaw, the muscle that twitched menacingly near the edge of his mouth, the dangerous gleam in the jade pools of his

63

eyes. For an instant, his eyes locked with hers. In the lucid depths she watched a battle without understanding with what he struggled, or if he won. Hypnotized, she remained motionless as his lips parted slightly allowing a sigh to escape before he lowered his head. The first whispery caress of his lips on hers sent exhilarating shocks dancing along her nerve endings. His mouth hardened as he deepened the kiss. Instinctively, Tallia opened her mouth.

As the blood roared in her ears, she permitted her eyes to close, luxuriating in the exotic sensations. A part of her mind, the part that was healer, began to analyze her body's reaction to this dark domineering man. Her body came to life at his warming touch, melting against him with a will of its own. Her insides quivered with a strange heat that stole the strength from her limbs. She had never felt like this before. Dayna was right, it was wonderful!

As he drew away, she ran her tongue lightly over her lips, tasting the lingering saltiness of his mouth. Her eyes flew open as he thrust her away, distancing himself as though burned by her touch.

"I'll be at the stream."

Tallia watched his quickly retreating form in puzzled silence, feeling frustrated without knowing why. She stood for several minutes, allowing the last fleeting sensations of the embrace to scatter in her mind and release her body from their compelling grip. Finally, sighing in confusion, she eyed the moorhen Tynan had dropped by the fire. She'd have to gather more chips before the embers would be hot enough to cook the bird. But first, personal discomfort prompted her to search the terrain for privacy.

Turning away from the stream, a small stand of feathery ortail trees, stunted by the harsh climate of the wasteland, looked as though it might provide the sought-after seclusion. She could collect dung on her way back. Her nose wrinkled in disgust at the reminder of the distasteful task.

Reaching the barrier of stout shrubs, she parted the cascade of wispy dry foliage and uttered an involuntary squeal of delight. A tiny pond, not more than twelve feet in diameter, reposed jewellike within the circular wall of the brush. Her thoughts turned to Tynan and the waiting campfire. *Just a few minutes*, she thought, eyeing the crystalline pool with lustful delight. She tested the water gingerly, expecting icy cold. Surprisingly, the pond was warm. Fed by an underground hot spring, wisps of steam rose and swirled along its surface. Elated at the prospect of clean warm water in which to bathe, she hastily peeled away her clothing and draped it over the nearest branch. Anticipating the pleasure of being clean, she stepped into the tranquil water.

The caress of the water soothed her dry skin as she slipped below the surface. With steady, languid strokes she crossed the pond, rolling onto her back to float lazily on the mirrored surface, assuaging her aching muscles. Then she submerged, letting her long sable hair trail freely through the water. For the first time in her life, she fully appreciated the luxury of a bath. And as she allowed her mind to drift, Tynan's visage intruded on the peacefulness of the moment. She knew she should have told him where she was, but the enticement of the crystal clear pond had precluded all other thoughts.

Tynan stood just beyond the trees, feeling very much the intruder, reluctant to speak, unwilling to break the peacefulness of the moment. The late-afternoon sun shone through the trees, dappling the ivory length of Tallia's body with lacy patterns. She was a creature from another place and time, mythical in the water's mists, enchanting. Unadulterated delight shone from the flushed radiance of her cheeks as, her eyes closed, she floated, sending ripples across the otherwise placid surface of the water.

Suddenly, she twisted and submerged. His breath caught as he was afforded a titillating glimpse of her small tight derriere. She surfaced once more. Her firm young breasts pierced the surface of the pond, their peachy crests taut. Between them, on a leather thong, rested an unfamiliar stone. He wondered about it briefly, until his eyes were drawn to a small diamond-shaped birthmark on her left breast. His lips ached to kiss the slight imperfection that assured him she was not some flawless illusionary creature.

Tynan was gradually drawn out of his dreamy state of mind by the relentlessly increasing pressure of the groin guard as its inflexible shell became painfully constricting. With a rueful shake of his head, he reflected that he might have to give up the protective device for the remainder of their trip. Forcefully tearing his eyes away from the mesmerizing scene, Tynan, uncertain of the strength of his willpower, decided to leave Tallia to her bath. His worry had been appeased. She hadn't reacted to the force of his untimely passion by running away in fear. With a final backward glance at her sylphlike form as she dived once more, he silently returned to camp.

A short time later, Tallia calmly approached the bivouac. The sight of the moorhen, already suspended over a bed of hot coals, caused her to flush guiltily. Tynan, squatted to one side of the fire, stared into the distance. Dropping the unnecessary chips, she approached him. "Tynan, I . . . I'm sorry I didn't build the fire." He looked up, his green-eyed gaze fixing on her inscrutably. Was he angry? "I found a pond, a wonderfully warm pond," she added, emphasizing the attraction. "I just couldn't resist the opportunity for a bath."

Tynan's jaw clenched, combatting the tormenting image her words rekindled. "I know."

Tallia stared at him in puzzlement. "What?"

"I went looking for you."

"Oh." Shocked speechless by his candor, Tallia's face flamed with embarrassment as she wondered exactly when he'd seen her. She didn't know whether to be angry, or happy, or simply outraged at the invasion of her privacy. Strangely enough, happiness won. She wasn't entirely sure what prompted the odd euphoria, but the thought that Tynan had come looking for her was definitely part of the reason. Analyzing her reaction, she realized that if he had come looking for her, it meant that he'd been worried about her. If he worried about her, it meant that he cared about her. A small contented smile curved her lips.

As if by mutual unspoken agreement, neither

Tynan nor Tallia made any reference to their earlier passionate exchange. They ate in silence as the sun descended beyond the distant hills transforming them to deep purple against the blushing firmament. Tallia cleaned the camp area as Tynan moved off to sit quietly on a sandy ridge, his face turned toward the last of the sun's rays.

Tallia, observing the rigid set of his shoulders, pondered his remoteness, the steady clenching and unclenching of his fists. Unsure how to become a part of his nightly routine, or even if she wanted to, she allowed him his solitude. As before, once darkness blanketed the wasteland he returned, silently taking a position near the fire.

Tallia studied his face through the flickering flames. The light cast a reddish hue across his strong cheek bones and onto the wavy crests of his ebony hair. In the shadowy green depths of his eyes lingered the expression of torment she had witnessed before. What haunted his past so strongly? What anguish drove him to wander the wasteland? Whom or what did he seek?

As if sensing her attention, Tynan raised his eyes to hers, the expression gone, cloaked once more in stolidity. Her sympathetic smile evoked no response. As he looked away, she fought the urge to go to him, to assuage the anger and sorrow inseparably entwined within him.

"Would it help to talk about it?" Her softly spoken words implored him to share his pain.

He met her gaze, staring into her pale, translucent eyes. Where did such innocence come from? How could she, who had never suffered, understand the pain of losing loved ones? His throat constricted. Sharing his grief would not eradicate his guilt. He could guess her reaction to the horrific tale. She would gaze at him, her face white with shock and say, "I'm so sorry." Because, after the recounting of his tale, what else would there be for her to say? "Can't change the past." His voice carried a note of regret.

Tallia's observant gaze swept his face. Slowly, she nodded. They had only been traveling two days. There was time yet for her to learn more about him. The set of his chin warned her the subject was closed, at least for now. An acquiescent sigh escaped her. Circumstance decreed she cross this desolate wasteland. Tynan was simply the means. And although she found herself increasingly attracted to him, in all likelihood, once the journey ended, they would never meet again.

"Time to move."

Tallia groaned as the loud male voice intruded on her peaceful slumber. Her eyes opened to a sky still dark with the remnants of night's cloak.

"So early?" she muttered.

"We lost time yesterday. Today we make it up." The matter-of-fact reply did little for her mood. Deciding sleepily that maybe if she ignored him he'd go away, she pulled the cocooning warmth of her cloak over her head. The ploy didn't work, as Tallia realized with chilling clarity seconds later when her fur was torn from her grasp allowing the icy predawn air to caress her flesh. She screamed in shock and outrage.

"Move it." The quietly spoken words did not cool her irritation, but rather tempered it—with wisdom. She rose.

The terrain changed slightly as they forged their way ever further into the depths of the wasteland. Sandy soils and tenacious prairie grasses gave way to enormous rock outcroppings, huge black-veined granite boulders. Wintry wind whistled eerily through odd rock formations balanced precariously on the steep inclines of deep gorges.

On the narrow path ahead of her, Tynan pulled Chaz sharply to a standstill, motioning Tallia to halt behind him. From the wind-swept rise, he eyed an approaching lone rider suspiciously. Few people braved the wasteland this time of year unless they belonged there. Experience prompted wariness in the midst of this desolate land. He waited tensely, his hand poised on the hilt of his black-handled dagger, feeling the comforting pressure of his broadsword against his back. His penetrating gaze scanned the area for any other companions. Ambush was not above most wastelanders. As always, Tynan relied heavily on the primitive instincts that had thus far insured his survival.

The stranger's feline mount side-stepped nervously as the scent of the faralk reached her. Instantly, her rider became alert, his eyes skimming the barren landscape. As his searching gaze found Tynan seated masterfully astride the sleek black demon-beast, he jerked the gari to a halt.

With a deep ravine to his left and a sharp ridge on his right, the stranger's only alternative, other than meeting them, was to return the way he had come. As his eyes stared past Tynan's threatening form, catching sight of Tallia, he finally urged his mount cautiously forward.

Tallia watched Tynan. His first instinctive grip on his weapon eased somewhat, although his hand continued to hover within easy reach. The tension of his body conveyed his alertness. Tallia had the impression that his vigilant gaze recorded the stranger's every movement, the nervous gesture of one hand as it reached to scratch his neck, the almost imperceptible turning of his head as he, too, surveyed the surrounding rocks.

He paused as he reached them. The two men observed each other warily, exchanging stiff nods of greeting. "Lady." The man acknowledged Tallia's presence with a curt nod, though his eyes strayed for only a brief second from the darkly dressed, ominous male at her side. Then, very slowly and purposefully, he raised the index finger of his left hand, middle fingers folded and small finger rigidly extended, to push back his enormous tan-colored hat.

Tynan betrayed not the slightest flicker of recognition of the signal. It wasn't enough. Although he knew King Quillan had commissioned other law bringers to roam the wasteland as Royal Executioners, he'd met few. This man could be one of them, or he could be a wastelander who'd tortured the information from a king's man.

With infinite casualness, he mimicked the gesture. "A silent wind sweeps the wasteland," Tynan said, disliking the flowery identifying words, feeling especially foolish because he knew Tallia listened avidly.

"It blows from Maurasia," the stranger responded.

Ignoring Tallia's quizzical expression, Tynan relaxed somewhat. "There was a storm in Promise, but it moved on," he remarked, indicating the trail ahead with an inclination of his head.

The man nodded, the tense set of his shoulders easing. "The name's Cam," he offered.

"Tynan."

"I'm on my way to Gratifa," Cam remarked, alluding to a small nondescript town bordering the wasteland. "I suspect a squall might strike there."

Tynan nodded his understanding. "Is the way clear ahead?"

"I haven't met anyone other than a couple of old diggers since last week," Cam answered, referring to the men who braved both wasteland and wastelanders to mine for gold.

Tynan nodded and indicated that Tallia should move on. She nodded politely to the stranger before her creamy gari padded forward, past Tynan's mount and down the slight decline beyond the hill's crest. She looked back when Tynan didn't follow immediately and found him watching the stranger's departure. Curiosity ate at her as she waited impatiently for Tynan to rejoin her. Finally, he conveyed some silent instruction to Chaz and rejoined Tallia.

Unable to contain her curiosity, she blurted, "What was that cryptic conversation all about?"

"What cryptic conversation?"

She sighed in exasperation. "You know. The stuff about silent winds and squalls."

"Nothing." A flickering shadow of changing expressions crossed his square tanned features. Tallia, suspicious and puzzled, was denied the opportunity for further questions as Tynan moved past her, increasing Chaz's pace.

The afternoon passed slowly until the sun slid inevitably into the horizon, setting the sky aglow with its fading scarlet rays. Tallia clutched her thick cloak closer, shielding herself from the cold touch of dusk's breath. Still Tynan showed no sign of stopping for the night.

The great black stallion's eyes turned blood-red as darkness descended. Tallia knew the animals had no difficulty seeing at night, but unaccustomed to the eerie darkness of the silent wasteland, she shivered at imaginary shadows. Finally, she called out to Tynan, "Shouldn't we stop soon?"

"What?" He struggled to pull his thoughts back from their wanderings.

"Shouldn't we make camp for the night?" Tallia patiently repeated her request.

"All right." Almost instantly, he chose a spot near an overhanging outcropping. Directing Chaz to it, he halted and slipped effortlessly from the faralk's back, deftly removing his pack in the same economizing motion. Left to roam freely, Chaz immediately moved off to graze.

Wearily, Tallia echoed Tynan's actions. Removing the padded blanket and harness from the feline, she set the gari loose with an appreciative pat. Stretching to ease her tired muscles, she found a comfortable spot near where Tynan knelt to start a fire and dropped to the ground. As the flames caught and the ensuing blaze began to warm the air, she moved closer, welcoming the fire's comforting heat.

Silently, she accepted the cold meat and dried biscuits Tynan offered. He would have to hunt again tomorrow. Hunger appeased, Tallia began to wonder exactly how Tynan had managed to start a fire tonight. There was absolutely no brush in this area of the wasteland, and she'd not seen him collect any dung chips. "How did you start the fire?"

"I saved the chips you collected last night."

"Oh," she responded with some amazement. What a thing to carry in your pack! Seeing that her escort meant to offer no further conversation for the evening, Tallia slipped from the fireside and stood staring across the expansive rocky landscape before slowly, thoughtfully strolling into the blanketing darkness.

She wrapped her fingers around the Zarma stone, hoping to receive some comfort from it. The dream, although she'd thrust it from her conscious thoughts, still nagged incessantly at the recesses of her mind. She wondered if the foretelling dreams would always seem so confusing. The concept of knowing a portion of some future event had intrigued her until she had had the dream.

A soft snort from nearby drew her attention. Chaz regarded her with gentle eyes. Suddenly feeling an overwhelming need for his supporting strength, she approached the beast. He tossed his dark head but didn't move away as she rested her cheek against the velvet hair on his massive neck.

From outside the glow of the firelight, Tynan observed the scene. He sensed the girl's loneliness but made no move to intrude on the strangely poignant embrace between the gentle, diminutive young woman and the immense dreaded demon-beast. The faralk seldom let anyone other than Tynan near. Yet, the animal's instincts were unfailingly accurate. If Chaz befriended Tallia, then she was worthy of that trust.

Tallia felt better when she returned to the fire. She'd always had a close bond with animals. It had been that very bond that had prompted Eyrsa to begin her Zarmistic training in the first place. At five years old, while playing in the fields with several of the village children, Tallia had discovered an injured llamahare in a peasant's trap.

Eyrsa had nodded understandingly, a hint of concern shadowing her eyes, when the young girl carried the animal home and placed her small hands on its twisted leg, instinctively pouring empathetic healing energy into the small body. It was a miracle, Eyrsa had said, making Tallia promise not to reveal her special talent to others. First, they had to practice, Eyrsa had explained, but she allowed Tallia to befriend the animals.

Though not permitted pets, animals seemed drawn to Tallia and she had a way with them that bound them to her despite their wildness. Her contact with the animals had remained a secret. Eyrsa had given her the Zarma stone then, saying that it was a sign of her special talents and that it would enhance her abilities. Tallia treasured the smooth mauve talisman, wearing it suspended on a woven leather thong around her neck. Gradually, over the years, Tallia had become aware that her healing talents were unique. But at the college in Maurasia that truth had struck home forcibly. Few

Zarmists used more than compassion and herbal remedies in their healing. Why was she so different? Why had Eyrsa prompted her to hide her ability as much as possible?

"That's very unusual," Tynan remarked.

She realized he was looking at the Zarma stone, which she had forgotten to tuck back inside her tunic. "A gift from my governess," Tallia replied casually. She'd been careless to let him see it in the first place, especially after all the times Eyrsa had stressed keeping it hidden. But that was before she'd been enrolled in the school. Her training was no longer a secret, she reminded herself. Noting his expression of total incomprehension, she elaborated. "It's a Zarma stone. They are worn by Zarmistic healers, or those in training like myself. They augment the empathetic powers of the mind, making us more efficient healers." He nodded silently, apparently satisfied with her response.

"Is she a Zarmist?"

"Yes," Tallia responded, eager to expound Eyrsa's virtues. "She's the healer in our fiefdom. She never had any children of her own so she sort of adopted my mother and me. Her name is Eyrsa."

Tynan observed the way Tallia's face lit with love at the thought of the healer. He clenched his fist at the memory of the bond he had shared with his own family.

The innocence that graced her tranquil face touched something deep within him. He shrugged off the nebulous emotion. Bidding her good night, he found his own bed and forced himself to close his eyes.

A long-buried boyhood memory surfaced. Moural, the reigning seer and wise man in Letai's village, had been instructing Letai in the course of his destiny. According to the tribe, eighteen was when a boy became a man and his destiny became set and now that Letai was of age, he needed to know what life's path held for him. The old man had told Letai that he would follow the herd spirit, drifting across the open lands in an unknown quest.

At the conclusion of the lesson, the eighteen-year-old Tynan had asked the man if he could see his destiny as clearly as he could see Letai's. The wizened native's reply had been cryptic. "Destiny's path is never easy. Yours will be extremely difficult, with many choices. But you must seek a destiny that is greater than your own, that is the way to truth and freedom. The foundation of your destiny lies within shimmering walls. Choose the path that runs parallel to the Zarma stone. It will not be easy, but I believe it is the one for you."

Zarma stone? The old man's prophecy began to have meaning. Still, how could the healers' Zarma stones have an effect on his life? Sleep was long in coming and even when it did, he tossed and turned restlessly, wary of something he could not explain.

The morning sun shone feebly, its rays barely penetrating the haze of ominous gray clouds. Tynan glanced back along the path. Uneasily, he pulled his cloak closer around his shoulders. The morning showed no sign of warming after the frigid night, a clear indication of the approach of winter. Though the light snow that had fallen during the night didn't hamper their progress, their footprints

77

left a distinct trail.

Tynan recalled Tallia's remark concerning Luma's strange behavior. He had attributed the gari's actions to the change in the weather. Now, his own instincts tingling, he was convinced that they were being followed. Had he been alone he would have circled back to discover the identity of their trackers.

Altering their course from the predetermined path, Tynan directed Chaz northward to the edge of a ridge. There the snow had not covered the rocky ground and following them would be more difficult. Though the maneuver alleviated his uneasiness somewhat, he increased the pace, hoping to put adequate distance between themselves and whoever was behind them.

Tynan remained watchful all afternoon. He could detect no sign of pursuit and finally allowed himself to relax slightly as the sun emerged from behind the clouds and began to melt the last of the snowy mantle despite the constant chill of the mountain winds. The parched earth drank in the melting snows. Tynan had forgotten the way water could rapidly change the wasteland. He watched Tallia bend from Luma's back to pluck a rosy bloom from one of the squat wildflowers that burst through the white mantle as the warmth of the sun touched it. The native plant life took full advantage of the scant water supply provided now by the first hints of winter. Though perilous, this land had a wild dangerous beauty all its own.

Locating a sheltered area beneath a rocky ledge, Tynan stopped to camp just before nightfall. Tonight he wanted a secure camp, one that was not easily besieged. After a hasty meal, Tallia drifted off to sleep but Tynan sat by the remains of the fire, listening intently for any unusual sounds. Chaz wandered off as usual for his nightly adventures. Luma, after making several strange purring sounds, disappeared across the top of the ridge. It was well into the night before Tynan finally nodded off into a light sleep.

He jerked in his sleep, instantly awake. Remaining motionless, he listened intently. Clouds obscured the faces of the twin moons, darkening the landscape, muting the eerie light. Silently, Tynan rose, removed his dagger from its sheath and stuck it into the waistband of his trousers. Then, retrieving his garotte, he slipped into the gray shadows of the nearby rocks, his booted feet soundless on the shale. Though he had heard and seen nothing, he sensed the camp was being watched, felt the chill of that knowledge run up his spine beneath his suede shirt. Keeping his back to the rocks and one eye on the embers of the campfire, he made his way along the edge of the stone outcropping.

On top of the ridge, he dropped onto all fours. The rising sun would soon silhouette him against the sky. He preferred to keep his presence unknown, at least until he could discover who was in the area. He crept soundlessly across the dry ground, listening, watching.

Against the shapeless patterns of rock, a shadow shifted. Tynan fixed his gaze on the area. The man moved again and Tynan worked his way across the top of the ridge and down the other side, scouting the area surrounding the man. He appeared to have no compatriots. Behind his quarry now, he inched forward.

Nearly upon his prey, he rose silently to his feet and pulled the thin wire garrote from his belt. He twisted the ends of the metal strands around each hand and snapped the wire to assure its tightness in his grip.

The other man turned hesitantly at the slight sound. Tynan remained motionless, pressed up against the cold rock wall. After a minute, the man returned to his vigilant watch. Tynan moved. Swiftly, he reached the man's position and with one lithe movement slipped the wire over the man's head, tightening it dangerously around his throat.

His victim reached up, clawing silently at the constricting garrote. Tynan kept the strand taut but loose enough to prevent strangling the man.

"All right," he growled in the man's ear, "who are you?" He loosened the garrote enough to permit the man to reply.

The man shook his head and Tynan angrily tightened the device before continuing his questioning. "Who sent you?"

As the man turned his head, Tynan noted the fear in his eyes. He leaned closer, his own face only inches from the stranger's.

"I'm not going to ask ag—" Tynan's voice faltered as strong arms grasped him roughly from behind. As he struggled to free himself, the wire slipped from his grasp.

Footsteps announced the approach of at least two more men. The moon eased from behind the thick cloud cover, bathing the plateau with pale blue light. Struggling against his captors, Tynan looked up. His eyes widened with shock. Directly before him stood the man he had sought and tracked for the past two years. Bodan!

CHAPTER FOUR

TYNAN FROZE, IGNORING BODAN'S PRETENTIOUS sneer, refusing to allow the man to see his agitation. Silently, Tynan reprimanded himself for his lack of thoroughness. He had known it was unlikely that the man he questioned was alone. Yet, as he'd maneuvered around behind him, he'd detected no accomplices. For more than two years he'd roamed the wasteland, tracking down criminals such as Bodan, and had never been caught off guard before. Yet there he stood as captured prey rather than victorious hunter.

The slight groan of the man he'd attempted to interrogate drew his attention. The fellow rubbed his throat as he struggled to his feet, shooting a venomous glare at Tynan.

The steel of Bodan's dagger pressed against

Tynan's ribs. Bodan jerked his head in the direction of camp, excusing the other men, obviously secure in the belief that he could manage his captive alone. Tynan flexed his arms as he was released and Bodan's compatriots moved past him.

As the illumination from the slivered moon penetrated the darkness, Tynan studied the man he'd sought so diligently over the last months. A hoarse choking noise escaped the criminal's thin lips which were pulled back in a mirthless grin, revealing teeth stained the color of old wood. A gruesome scar encircled the man's throat, indicating that Bodan had survived a hanging. The man's hair hung in thick greasy strings to his shoulders and icy gray eyes set in a swarthy face pocked with blemishes met Tynan's gaze emotionlessly.

Bodan directed a guttural remark to his companion. "Go with the others, Sal. You'll have your revenge, but after we've taken care of the girl." The hissing rasp that passed for mirth wheezed from between Bodan's lips again. "You're gonna sound like me now, pretty boy."

Sal's malicious gaze which had been directed at Tynan turned now to Bodan. There was no love between these men, and wordlessly, Sal moved off.

"Get the girl!"

Tynan's thoughts shifted sharply at Bodan's directive. The girl! What did these men want with Tallia? His brow creased fleetingly in a puzzled frown. Bodan didn't seem to realize that Tynan had been dogging his trail for months. Had his capture been an accident precipitated by fate? Was he merely an obstacle in the pursuit of their true quarry? If that was so, then Tallia was the reason they were there. But why? And how had they known where to find her? Jenk? No, he didn't think so.

Tynan wondered if revealing his identity would distract the man. Probably not. But he would have to act before they reached the camp where he'd be surrounded by who knew how many of Bodan's companions. If he was going to overcome Bodan, now was the time even though the odds were still in the wastelander's favor. Tynan's quick gaze appraised his captor. Bodan was armed with two daggers. One he clenched firmly in his hand; the other, appropriated from Tynan, protruded from the side of his waistband. Tynan decided that waiting would only increase Bodan's odds.

"Let's go." The man's voice rasped near his ear as he nudged Tynan to move in front of him, increasing the pressure on the dagger, drawing blood in the area over Tynan's kidney.

He had to chance it. Tynan lunged forward, diving, rolling. His hand closed on a stone the size of his fist. Still rolling away from Bodan, he twisted, launching the rock with a forceful sidearm cast. The unexpected missile caught Bodan high on the shoulder, throwing him off balance as Tynan scrambled to his feet and hurled himself at the wastelander's legs. Bodan bellowed his rage as he stumbled beneath the onslaught, slashing wildly with the knife even as he fell. Tynan felt a twinge of pain as the blade gashed the flesh of his forearm. He ignored it. Pouncing, he straddled Bodan's sprawling body. Closing one hand in a vise-like grasp around the wrist that held the offending dagger, he drove his clenched fist into his assailant's face. Bodan howled with pain and fury as blood spurted from his nose. Rage seemed to give the man renewed strength. He bucked convulsively. As Tynan struggled to maintain his balance, Bodan rolled, pinning Tynan beneath him. The upraised dagger glittered in the light of the setting moon.

His heart pounding, his breath coming in quick gasping gulps, Tynan strained, his muscles knotted, to keep the hand holding the dagger away from his throat. He tightened his grip on Bodan's wrist, could feel the tendons straining, but still the bones did not snap. Inch by agonizing inch, the dagger descended. Tynan constricted the muscles in his other arm, attempting to dislodge Bodan's shackling grasp as it pinned his wrist to the ground. Bodan had the advantage, using his body weight to augment the strength of his hold. Tynan couldn't budge him. The dagger hovered against his throat, the cold whisper of metal brushed his damp flesh.

Suddenly, a female scream pierced the air. A scream from the past? He would not fail Tynara's memory. This was one of the men who'd tortured and defiled his sister. A red haze of hate penetrated his brain. Bodan *would* pay!

Strength born of grief coursed through his veins. With a surge of adrenaline, he shook off Bodan's grasp on his pinned arm. Clenching his fist into a rock-hard hammer, he slammed it into Bodan's temple. The wastelander's body jerked back.

Dazed, Bodan shook his head to clear it, and Tynan took advantage of his momentary disorientation. Twisting his body, he pivoted, overbalancing his adversary. Quickly, he nailed the wastelander to the ground. Grasping the wrist of the hand still clinging tenaciously to the knife, he wrenched it high above the ground before slamming it into the soil. The knife flew from Bodan's grasp. Coldly, Tynan glared into the face of the man beneath him. He'd been appointed judge, jury, and executioner of the wasteland by the highest power in the land. Tynara's bruised and bleeding spectral image rose hauntingly in his memory. Guilty! He raised his fist to deliver the verdict.

Tynan's breath escaped in a whoosh as a booted foot found its mark against his ribs. Searing fingers of pain clutched his chest, tightening, squeezing his lungs. From behind, rough fingers grasped his hair, wrenching his head back. One of Bodan's men! The pain that racked his body dimmed as self-condemnation clouded his mind. He'd failed to execute the punishment Tynara's memory demanded. Jerked to his feet, his arms yanked painfully behind his back, he was quickly and securely bound. His pitiless gaze remained riveted on the alternately groaning and cursing Bodan. Tynan's chest heaved with the effort to cool the murderous rage threatening to consume him.

Meeting Tynan's gaze, Bodan recognized the intensity mirrored there. Momentarily, he froze. "Who are you?" he rasped.

The time for caution was past. "Tynan," he growled. A single word, yet one that said it all.

A slight widening of Bodan's eyes was the only evidence that Tynan's reputation had preceded him.

"Come on." The order from Sal, slightly hoarse, was accompanied by a powerful tug on the binding on his wrists. "You can talk later. It's the girl we want."

"Shut up, Sal," Bodan ordered. Then he grinned that fiendish grin. "So, you're the fellow who's been following me. Mind telling me why?"

"Not at all." Tynan's cold smile, though more pleasant to look upon, was almost as chilling as Bodan's. "I'm going to kill you."

Bodan looked over Tynan's shoulder at his companions. His grin still fixed firmly in place, he mimicked Tynan's words. "He's going to kill me."

Mocking laughter erupted behind him. Tynan ignored it. The desire for vengeance gripped him like a savage hunger, and blazed in his glittering emerald eyes.

Bodan's eyes returned to meet Tynan's gaze, and his grin faltered. "Why?" Forced mockery still laced his tone, but Tynan also read uncertainty in his voice.

Once again Tynan smiled coldly. Had Bodan even known the names of the people he'd so brutally murdered? "House of Keane, the Fiefdom of Ravencrest." He watched Bodan closely for a sign of recognition. At first the man's forehead puckered slightly in puzzlement. Then, his brow cleared, his gaze hardening.

"You want to kill him now, Bodan?"

Tynan challenged the wastelander with his fearless hate-filled gaze. "No," Bodan replied shortly. "We'll let him watch the sport with the woman first."

Without further comment Tynan was jerked roughly around and shoved down the path to the camp. The sun, almost risen, had begun to bathe the land in its golden glow and, although still cloaked in purple shadow, the rocky path to the prairie below was visible.

Chaz should be back soon, Tynan calculated. But would it be soon enough? Would he be able to help? Absently, Tynan listened to the crunch of stones beneath his feet as he explored his mind for a way to save Tallia from the men who'd captured them. He was still without a plan when they reached the camp.

Caught in the light of a single grasping ray of the morning sun, Tallia looked pale and stricken. She'd been bound, her arms wrenched cruelly behind her back by a man who, judging by his filthy unkempt appearance, was Bodan's twin in character. That these men would dare to touch her enraged him to the point of madness.

"Bodan," Tynan called. Bodan turned. "I will kill you," Tynan asserted calmly. He jerked his tethered arms from Sal's grasp. Instantly, the other men were upon him. He crumpled to his knees as the hilt of a short sword connected with his skull. Fists and boots slammed into his body with painful force. He crouched, rolling into a ball in an attempt to protect himself from the gleefully delivered beating. The sneering jibes of his attackers infiltrated the haze that fogged his thoughts.

"Enough." It was Bodan's rasp. "I want him to

watch the entertainment. Tie his legs so he won't keep trying to act like a hero."

Futilely, Tynan lashed out with his booted feet, and received another kick for his trouble. Fire erupted within his rib cage.

Bodan grasped Tynan's hair in one large fist, yanking him upright to lean against a boulder. "You watch."

Tynan heard Bodan's words as though from a distance as he struggled to maintain consciousness through a pain-induced haze. Blood-flecked spittle escaped the corner of his swollen lips as Tynan glared at Bodan. "Why the girl?" he queried in a hoarser tone than he'd intended.

"Orders." Bodan cocked his head vindictively. "We got orders to extract some information from her and have as much fun as we want doing it. Then we deliver a submissive little girl who won't be any trouble at all to her new master."

"Whose orders?"

"That I can't tell you," replied Bodan astutely. Then as if an idea suddenly occurred to him, his eyes took on a predacious gleam. "She your woman, Tynan?"

"No."

Bodan eyed him with measured assessment, the hint of a mocking smile twisting his mouth. "You want to know what we're gonna do?"

Tynan remained silent.

Bodan continued his tormenting game, testing Tynan. "First, we're gonna ask her a question, nice like. The first wrong answer"—he shrugged and held up the little finger of his left hand to illustrate —"we'll break her finger." Tynan gritted his

89

teeth, remembering his sister's broken limbs. His throat closed as hatred rose like bile, choking him. "The next wrong answer, we'll burn her feet." Bodan gestured to the previous night's fire, now just a bed of crimson coals. "Course then, she won't be able to stand up no more. Now, lying down's a lot more fun. Don't you think?" Tynan continued to glare at him wooden-faced.

Slightly disappointed that he'd been unable to provoke the bound man, Bodan lost interest in the game and turned his attention to the quivering young woman held securely by two of his men while a third stood back.

"It's gonna be some sport." Bodan rasped. "Don't want you to miss nothing." He reached to position Tynan at a better angle against the boulder, and Tynan grit his teeth against the wave of agony radiating outward from his rib cage.

Tynan breathed a pain-filled sigh of relief as Bodan moved off. Now he could work at the bonds. He'd have to move as quickly as possible. He chanced a swift glance in Tallia's direction, and wished he hadn't. Her fearful eyes locked on his, pleading, filling him with a sense of helplessness. He tried to tear his eyes from the scene about to be enacted but couldn't. He watched, letting the sight fuel his rage. Furiously, he rubbed the rough hemp that bound his wrists against the rock at his back, ignoring the pain as the ropes burned into his flesh.

Tallia struggled ineffectually against the rough hands that held her as Bodan walked casually toward her as if he had all the time in the world.

The crooked menacing smile sent shivers of fear rippling across her cold flesh. He stopped directly before her, his eyes lowered, fascinated by the heaving of her breasts. He lifted his dagger to her throat then slowly ran it down the front of her suede shirt, letting it bump suggestively across the leather lacings that held the garment together.

Terror chilled her, raising goose flesh on her arms, and she gasped as the cold steel pressed against her abdomen. With an adept flick of the blade, Bodan sliced the bindings and her shirt fell open. Bound, unable to cover herself, Tallia fixed her gaze on a point below and behind her tormenter. The point of the dirk ran across her breast as he pushed the thick material aside. Tallia lowered her head in an effort to conceal the degradation she felt as Bodan's companions whistled and made lewd remarks. The thick tresses of her hair curtained her face, temporarily obscuring the sight of their lurid sneers.

Her mind reeled with the insanity of the situation. Never had she suspected that such people existed. What demented pleasure did they derive from her debasement? She cringed as filthy hands cruelly fondled her body, pinching her tender breasts. Brutal laughing voices echoed, surrounding her, sending her thoughts spinning in a whirling vortex of frustration. She squeezed her eyes shut as she felt the shirt ripped from her body.

"Who are your parents?" Bodan demanded. She struggled to correlate the question with what was happening to her. "Who?" he demanded again, jerking her face up, forcing her to meet his gaze as he thrust his pock-marked face closer. She gagged at the foul stench of his breath.

Her eyes sought Tynan as one seeking a life line. He appeared to be watching the debacle almost impassively. Except for his eyes. Those beautiful emerald eyes drilled into hers. *Be brave, hold on,* they commanded. Suddenly the nipple of her left breast was twisted brutally, and she cried out at the agony that threaded through her.

"Look at me when I talk to you," the repulsive man rasped in her face. "Who are your parents?"

Uncontrollable tears rolled down Tallia's ashen cheeks. She clenched her teeth against the pain, trying in vain to deaden it with her mind. Another stabbing flash of fire left her gasping for breath. She couldn't hold on. She wasn't strong enough. "Arilan and Rashana Darnaz."

"Wrong answer, bitch."

She heard a snap and her body jerked. Suddenly nauseated, her knees buckled as a wrenching pain in her left hand shot up her arm. She choked on the scream she didn't have the strength to utter as she dropped to the ground. Why were they doing this? She felt the ropes slip from her wrists before she was pulled back to her feet.

"Karr, show the lady your handiwork," Bodan ordered.

Supported by Karr's cruel, groping hands, she swayed unsteadily as her hand was brought before her face. Her little finger stuck out at an odd angle. Dazed, Tallia stared at it almost dispassionately as the initial pain receded, replaced by a dull throbbing sensation that moved slowly up her arm.

Gagging as her stomach contracted with queasiness, she averted her eyes, half believing that if she couldn't see it then it wasn't so.

"You convinced I'm serious now. Your real parents. Who are they?"

Tallia gazed at him blankly. Her real parents?

Abruptly, Bodan's attention was caught by the stone still hanging on its leather thong about her neck. "What's this?" he queried, lifting it curiously.

"M—my Zarma stone," Tallia muttered.

"What's a Zarma stone? Is it worth anything?"

Tallia shook her head. "It h—helps me in my training."

"What training?" he asked impatiently, tugging on the thong, bringing Tallia's face closer to his own and the putrefying stench of his breath.

"Zarmist," Tallia stammered. "I'm training to be a Zarmist."

For an instant the horrible man appeared stunned by her reply. Then a strange sibilant laughter shook his body as he released the stone. "Faid, Rizo," Bodan called, "did you hear that? She's training to be a healer." The sadistic laughter surrounding her increased in volume.

As abruptly as it had started, the evil man's laughter stopped. He raised his dagger and tilted her chin up with it until she looked into his wintry eyes. "Now, I want you to answer my question."

"I—I did," Tallia stuttered, ashamed of the huge tears rolling down her face. Where was the strength Eyrsa had always told her she had? "I know no other parents."

Anger clouded his features. "Lying bitch." He

made a swift movement with the dagger and once again Tallia felt pain. A trickle of warm blood oozed from the gash at the side of her neck and flowed down between her breasts. "Now tell me."

Blindly, Tallia fixed her gaze on the rising sun as her mind desperately sought to hold onto her sanity. She couldn't give him the answer he seemed to seek, for she didn't know what it was.

A sudden vicious blow sent her sprawling. Her head reeled and she fought the threatening black cloak of unconsciousness until, vaguely, she heard a voice over the buzzing in her ears. "Get the coals."

Coals? Were they going to burn her? *No! Oh, please, no!* Through hazed vision she sought Tynan's shape against the boulder. Rigid with fear, she began to squirm toward him, but Karr's heavy-booted foot halted her, shoving her viciously into the dirt.

"Hurry up with the questions, will you," another voice whined. "I want some o' what's between her legs."

No! This couldn't be happening! Why did these men want to hurt her? Lifting her head she looked wildly at Tynan. He sat just as he'd been when she'd last seen him, to all appearances dispassionately viewing the proceedings.

Only Tynan was aware of the insane rage coiling, burning virulently in his gut. He'd loosened the bonds, but not enough to work his large hands from the loops. The lacerated flesh of his wrists burned; the muscles in his hands screamed in protest at the contortions his fingers were making. His arm stung, and his side blazed with the agony of his traumatized ribs. Yet he ignored his own pain, his entire being centered on Tallia, willing her to hold on. Willing her to survive. Her beautiful tender body was already livid with bruises. Her glossy sable hair hung in a tousled mass of tangled curls against the paleness of her tear-streaked face. He caught his breath as she twisted to look at him, and his heart ached at the confusion and panic in her eyes. But it was the sight of the swelling purple contusion distorting the delicacy of her fragile features that drove him to struggle at his bonds with renewed determination. The sun, fully risen now, sat on the horizon. Tynan cursed under his breath. Where was Chaz?

Tallia felt her ankles grasped, and kicked feebly at her tormenters. Their crude laughter grated on her shocked senses.

"The names of your parents," Karr growled in her ear. Weakly, she shook her head. And then anguish contorted her features as searing flames of pain traveled up her leg from the soft sole of her bared foot. Her agonized wail echoed back from the walls of the nearby hill of rock. For a moment consciousness slipped away, but escape was not forthcoming. Stinging slaps to her bruised face renewed her torment. Tears glittered in her eyes.

"All right, girl. You still got one good foot. Up on it and tell me what I want to know." It was Bodan's hideous rasping voice again.

In shock, her senses numbed, Tallia struggled to her knees. Some distant part of her brain wondered if they were going to kill her. She didn't want to die.

They couldn't make her die! For the first time in her life, Tallia felt hate and a strange warmth began penetrating her body from the stone still dangling about her neck, gradually radiating outward, granting renewed strength to her limbs. Tossing her tangled mass of hair, she rose to her feet, no longer the bowed and frightened young girl of seconds earlier. Mindless of the scorching pain in her slender foot, she stood tall, her stance belligerent.

Tynan stared in amazement at the transformation taking place before his eyes. For an instant, he forgot his pain and purpose as his eyes fixed on the strange red glow of the Zarma stone and Tallia's face. The features were hers, yet somehow altered. There was no softness, no innocence in this face. The translucent silvery eyes narrowed with hatred and the planes of her face hardened as her lips thinned in a travesty of a smile. The husky laugh that escaped her lips made his skin crawl. For an instant, superstitious terror clutched his spine in its icy grip. Then, he noticed that all the men's eyes were glued to this strange being. Shoving his own paralyzing astonishment aside, he abandoned caution and used the diversion to work on his bonds.

Her feet planted firmly apart, Tallia glared at Bodan, her colorless eyes illuminated from within by a strange light. Potent power emanated, almost visibly, from her body.

Bodan backed away. She laughed, a deep resonant sound that gurgled from deep within her chest. They feared her now. She could feel it, feel the growing trepidation crawling along their nerve endings. A part of her, alien, unrecognized, revelled in the prepotent sensation.

Slowly, she leveled her gaze on Bodan. "Feel my hate," she hissed, extending one slender arm, her fingers outstretched. She could feel the beat of his heart, hear its quickening. She could sense the small hairs on the back of his neck rising as apprehension spread through his body like a sickness. His dread increased; her strength multiplied. His heart palpitated with the beginning of real terror. Tallia's eyes widened as slowly, oh, so slowly, she turned the fingers of her outstretched hand upward. Almost imperceptibly, her fingers began to close, as mentally she squeezed the organ pounding so rapidly in his chest. Her mind struggled against the act, then was suppressed by a stronger instinct.

Tallia felt the surge of power, rejoiced in the victory to come. Triumphant laughter issued from her lips as Bodan clutched frantically at his chest, staring at her in paralyzed horror.

"Now . . . I know why he wanted . . . you," Bodan gasped. "He should have warned . . . us . . . s . . . s . . ." His dying breath escaped in a hiss as he crumpled to the ground.

Tynan slipped his hands free of the bonds. Refusing to take his eyes from Tallia, he clenched his jaw against a fresh assault of pain as he struggled with the ropes binding his ankles. He stared at Bodan's body in stunned surprise. Tallia couldn't have heard the man's final whispered words for Bodan had backed quite a distance away from her. But Tynan had heard. Who was *he*? Could it possibly be the leader of the party who had killed his family? How would Tynan discover his identity? And what had he wanted with Tallia? The racing questions came to a screeching halt as he looked again in her direction. She'd dropped weakly to her knees. Whatever bolstering powers she'd drawn upon were gone. Having completely forgotten Tynan, Bodan's compatriots approached her, cautiously, their daggers drawn.

"Did you see what she done to Bodan?" Sal asked, apocryphal fear making him unwilling to believe what his eyes had witnessed.

"Yes, I saw," growled Karr.

Faid remained silent, advancing cautiously a few steps behind Sal. Rizo hung back as far as possible, superstitious terror mirrored in his eyes.

Suddenly, an inhuman shriek of fury pierced the air, and the men turned to seek the source of this new threat. A raging black demon with a gleaming onyx horn appeared, lunging down from the rocky hill straight toward Sal, who fell beneath the beast's churning hooves.

Welcoming the diversion caused by Chaz's appearance, Tynan retrieved his weapons from Bodan's body. The raging tempest inside him sought release in assault. Though he grunted in pain as the dagger flew from his fingers, his accuracy was unimpaired. Faid clutched at the hilt protruding from his chest as he slumped to the ground. Peripherally, Tynan saw Rizo deserting the camp. Karr managed only a few panic-stricken leaps before his midsection was pierced by the rapier sharp horn of the avenging faralk. Within moments, the battle was over. In the aftermath, Chaz stood quivering, still consumed by the fury in his blood.

Sal's moan drew Tynan's attention. He needed answers, and perhaps Sal would be able to provide them. The man was regaining consciousness. Lifting Sal's head, his hand came away stained and bloody, and Tynan cursed.

"Sal!" Tynan shouted, slapping the man's cheek. "Hey, Sal, wake up." His eyelids flickered. "Sal," he repeated. "Can you hear me?"

"Yes," came the whispered reply.

"Who was he?" Tynan demanded. His only reply was an expression of confusion in the eyes of the dying man. "The man who hired you to capture the girl," he prompted, "who was he?"

"Don't know."

"Where were you to take her?"

"Why sh—should I tell you?" Sal mumbled obstinately.

Tynan compressed his lips, forcing down his impatience. "Because you're dying. Maybe you can earn a second chance with the goddess Galacia before she abandons you to her sister, Coran, in Thrul."

Sal appeared to consider his words for a moment. "We were supposed to meet a guy . . ." he paused, gasping for breath.

"Where?" Tynan urged, afraid that time was running out.

"The tavern in Lamos."

Lamos. The town was only about a day's ride from the Twin Suns Fiefdom. "Who?"

"Four . . . Finger . . ." His words trailed off into silence.

"Four-Finger Dack?" Tynan queried urgently. It was no use. Sal's eyes stared blindly into a world he no longer saw. Four-Finger Dack! It had to be. He'd ridden with Bodan off and on for years and was another of those Tynan searched for. Dack might know who wanted Tallia, and he was one of the few left from whom Tynan could discover the identity of the man who'd ordered his family killed. So, they'd go to Lamos.

Looking once more at Sal's staring eyes, he reached to close them. "Good luck with the goddess," he muttered.

Every bruise and laceration on his body ached. Wearily, Tynan surveyed the havoc around him. Four bodies lay in various positions, their life fluids slowly staining the parched soil beneath them. Rizo had escaped. Chaz, no longer suffused with fury, stood back snorting and tossing his head, jittery and overwrought by the smell of death. In the center of it all knelt Tallia staring blankly at some distant point. In shock, Tynan concluded. He'd see to her before he took care of the bodies.

"Tallia," he said softly, reaching out to caress her shoulder. His heart ached at the way she cringed from his touch. As she recognized him, tears slowly welled in her soft dusky eyes. "It's all right now," he continued in gentle tones. "They can't hurt you anymore."

She nodded her understanding, but tears continued to flow down her cheeks in a torrent. "Tallia, I need to set your finger before the swelling gets any worse."

She glanced down at the injury in surprise, as if

the physical pain was almost nonexistent compared to the psychological. "Yes," she whispered, "I know."

"It will be painful," he warned.

She merely nodded as she held out her hand to him. Closing her eyes, she took a deep breath, still shaky from suppressed emotion, and sat immobile.

Tynan gently examined the finger, observing her features closely. There was no change in expression. Then as quickly as possible, he jerked on the tiny appendage, setting it back into the socket. An almost inaudible groan made him glance back at her face. Her eyes had opened, and she seemed a shade paler if that were possible.

"It's over now."

Again, she nodded without speaking.

Tynan's eyes fell on her exposed breasts. He winced as he struggled to remove his leather shirt.

"You're badly hurt," Tallia stated as she accepted and donned the garment.

He nodded. "Broken ribs."

"We must bind them until I'm well enough to help you."

Limping slowly to her pack, Tallia retrieved the tunic she'd not worn since leaving Promise. Tearing it into strips, she used it to bind Tynan's rib cage, feeling his pain as her own with each agonized breath he drew. When she finished, she sat back to rest.

Tynan scowled at the sight of her blistered sole. "Come on," he spoke brusquely, "we need to bathe your foot."

Slowly, they made their way to the stream where Tallia dangled her foot in the cooling waters. She needed to exorcise the horror of her encounter with the wastelanders as swiftly as possible. Perhaps putting it into words would help her understand it. "I killed a man, Tynan. How could I have done that?"

Tynan stared at her in surprise. He had been asking himself the same question. Yet, he knew Tallia's question was not the same as his. He wanted to know the method she'd used. She wanted to know how she'd allowed herself to be provoked into an act she viewed as abhorrent. Murder. How could he answer her when he didn't fully understand? Or perhaps he did. For him, violence was a way of life. Physical strength ruled. It was the law of the wasteland. Was what Tallia felt revulsion for the violence she'd discovered in herself, or guilt? He knew about guilt.

Tallia watched him expectantly, her expression despairing. Tynan swallowed. "We all do things we find abhorrent if our lives or the lives of loved ones depend on our actions." He took a deep breath, gazing at the horizon with unseeing eyes as he envisioned the past. "Taking a life is never easy." *Sometimes, though, it is necessary*, he reflected. *Justice is necessary*.

"But, if it comes down to kill or be killed, instinct takes over. Some day you'll forgive yourself." *That's what I keep telling myself*, he thought, unaware that he clenched the fist of his right hand. *He should have been there when his family needed him*. "In the meantime, you'll learn to live with the guilt you impose on yourself. If you don't, your spirit will die, little by little, and the enemy will have won anyway."

CHAPTER FIVE

TALLIA SAT CROSS-LEGGED, HER POSTURE ERECT, HER eyes closed. She concentrated, eliciting all her mental energy. Her hands and feet tingled as vitality flowed through her body. The power surged in waves within her, purifying, healing. Though not consciously aware of Tynan's return to camp, she felt his presence, telepathically recognizing him by the chaotic emotions his nearness produced within her. She emerged from the depths of her mind as one surfacing from deep sleep. His grisly task was concluded then. She opened her eyes. Overhead, the sun had passed its zenith. She'd meditated most of the morning, and already she felt the efficacy of the recuperative trance.

Suppressing speculation concerning the details of Tynan's gruesome task of disposing of the dead wastelanders, she concentrated on her concern for her missing mount. "Has Luma returned yet?"

"No," Tynan replied curtly. Dark shadows beneath his eyes, evidence of a sleepless night and the trials that followed, marred his handsome features.

Now he slouched against a boulder that protruded from the sheer wall of the ridge, fatigue clearly revealed in the lines of his body. A grimace of pain furrowed his brow as he shifted his position, unaware that she watched. His ministrations at the stream had been gentle, yet he seemed to have detached himself emotionally. He needed rest and nourishment, she thought, acknowledging the gnawing hunger in the pit of her own stomach. Since she couldn't make him sleep, she'd insist on looking at his injuries after they ate.

Tallia struggled to her feet, her legs numb from the duration of her sitting position. The sole of her foot, though still tender, was no longer blistered and raw. Careful not to put unnecessary weight on it, she limped to the fire. As she knelt to fumble through her packs for supplies, her mind returned to Luma. Where could the gari be? She'd never failed to reappear after her night's hunt before.

"Thrul!"

Tallia leapt to her feet at the masculine yowl of outrage. She winced as the sudden action sent a bolt of pain through her foot and up the calf of her leg. As she willed the pain away, she caught a glimpse of creamy fur disappearing over the edge of the outcropping. Her questing eyes sought Tynan. He dangled a tawny gari cub before him in disbelief. Tallia, too, stared at the creature in stunned surprise until comprehension dawned. Something in the disgusted look on Tynan's face cracked the tight strain of the morning's events. Uncontrollably, she began to laugh. It felt so good to be able to laugh. The sound rang true and clear, rebounding from the base of the cliff.

"What's so funny?"

The growled demand only heightened her hysterical elation. "You," she uttered breathlessly between giggles. "That look."

For an instant, she thought that Tynan's lips might have twitched in response before the scowl returned. "Very amusing. What were you thinking of, riding a gari due to whelp into the wasteland?"

Tallia sobered slightly, although the irrepressible smile still hovered. "I had no idea she was pregnant. She must have had a very small litter."

"Well, for that you can be thankful—if you're right." Tynan's green eyes scanned the ridge for a sign of Luma with more cubs before they returned to pin Tallia accusingly. "We have no way to carry a large litter." He paused, looking again at the cub still gripped in his hand, although he'd lowered it to rest on his lap. "Why did she drop the thing on me?"

"Gari females always leave their cubs in the protection of the strongest male. And it's not necessarily their mate. Luma's only choices were you and Chaz. I guess she appointed you protector."

"That's all I need," he grumbled, although Tallia thought he looked a tiny bit pleased.

No longer worried about Luma, Tallia proceeded with her meal preparations. Her thoughts centered on Tynan. The sudden realization that she was no longer uncomfortable with his gruff moodiness came as a shock to her. That he was at ease with violence as part of his life should frighten her. Yet, how could she fear a person who'd suffered injury on her behalf? How could she judge in another that which she'd discovered in herself—the capability for violent retaliation? Her brow creased as she wondered about the ebullient surge of destructive energy she'd experienced. Where had it come from? Was it something within herself, or a force contained within her Zarma stone? She desperately needed to confer with Eyrsa.

Absently dishing up the stew which she still found disagreeable due to its high meat content, Tallia hobbled toward Tynan. Were it not for the lean brown fingers gently stroking the ball of bronzed fur in his lap, she might have believed he was asleep. His face was completely obscured by the huge hat pulled low over his forehead. "Tynan," she called softly, "eat. It will help you heal."

Slowly, he raised the hat, lifting his head to gaze at her. Tallia almost wilted beneath that potent emerald stare. She felt lightheaded at such odd moments, most frequently when subjected to one of Tynan's soul-searching scrutinies. *It's just the sun*, she assured herself, forcing herself to return his stare. But her eyes fell to the full lips above that whiskered jaw. Warmth curled in her abdomen, ruthlessly stealing her sense of equilibrium as she remembered the texture of his mouth on hers.

"Here," she said, shoving the plate into his grasp, mortified by the sudden huskiness in her tone. Quickly, she limped off a few steps before seating herself, feigning concentration on the food before her.

Tynan continued to study her for a moment. Some very male part of him, ego no doubt, felt enormously pleased by the flush that had crept into her cheeks. He had enough experience with women to know that she found him attractive. Yet, knowing that also made it hard for him to control his own fascination. The image of welcoming outstretched arms and bared ivory flesh flashed through his mind and the rush of heat in his loins caused him to shift uncomfortably. "Ow!" he yelped as his sudden movement prompted the forgotten cub to sink its sharp baby claws into his thigh. "Cursed beast." Between the cub and pain stabbing his side every time he took a deep breath, he was extremely uncomfortable.

He looked up to find Tallia observing him quizzically. Now it was his turn to feel the warmth of embarrassment slowly creeping up his neck. Hoping that his dark complexion hid any signs of his discomfort, he turned his attention to the meal with a gusto quite beyond that befitting such simple fare.

His hunger appeased, Tynan set aside his plate and moved the cub to a spot beside him. He allowed his thoughts to retrace the path they'd been following before Tallia had interrupted him to eat. Who had sent Bodan? Tynan suspected in all probability it was the same man who was also the leader of the band who had killed his family. Bodan was not the type to offer his loyalty to many men and there would be few fearsome enough to hold it. "Do you know why anyone would want to harm you?" he queried abruptly.

The timing of Tynan's question startled her. Frowning slightly, she stared into the distance as she struggled to control the painful memory of her torment at the hands of Bodan and his men. Had the incident been the one foretold in her dream? Still, she knew of no one who would wish her harm. "No," she finally replied, shaking her head.

Tynan hated to remind her of the horror she had suffered, but he desperately needed answers to the questions racing through his mind. "Tallia, I know this is difficult." He paused momentarily, his eyes holding hers. "Do you have any idea what those men were after?"

To his relief, her answer revealed no hesitation or emotional torment. "No. They kept asking who my real parents were. It had to be simply a case of mistaken identity."

Tynan wasn't convinced her analysis was accurate, but he said nothing, continuing to examine her thoughtfully. Abruptly, he realized that her face was almost entirely healed. The swollen, distorting contusion had all but disappeared, only a slight discoloration remained. He'd been so preoccupied with his thoughts and his need for solitude when he'd returned to camp that he hadn't noticed. Awareness struck him like a blow. The woman truly was a healer!

He didn't know why he should feel so surprised, but some part of him had refused to acknowledge Tallia as a Zarmist. The acknowledgement of her healing power reminded him of that other power. Hesitantly, he voiced the question that burned to be asked. "Tallia, what power did you use to k—," he stopped, searching for a less graphic word, "overcome Bodan."

Tallia's eyes clouded with misery. She had taken a life, and the knowledge twisted knifelike within her. She stared at the empty plate in her lap. "I don't know," she mumbled, barely audibly, then continued more forcibly, "I am a healer, Tynan." The note of pleading in her tone told him she sought reassurance.

"I know. You're almost completely recovered."

Tallia nodded, her eyes distant, her thoughts following other patterns. "Eyrsa told me that the Zarma stone amplifies the natural powers of a healer. That's why they wear them—to augment their empathetic abilities." Her hands twisted with agitation in her lap.

She remained silent so long, that finally Tynan prompted her. "And?"

Taking a deep breath, she met his eyes. "If the Zarma stone merely amplifies one's natural abilities, then the potential for murder comes from within me, and has been inside me all the time."

Tynan shook his head. "You obviously weren't in control of the power you wielded, or you wouldn't be so distressed at the realization that you . . . killed."

Tallia acknowledged his deductions with a brief nod.

The unusual power Tallia was capable of wielding left him curious, and a little apprehensive. Zarmists were often reclusive people. Still, the ones he had encountered in the past had not been capable of employing lethal abilities. At least, he was *almost* certain they couldn't. True Zarmists felt compelled by destiny to heal, and Tallia had said that the Zarma stone merely augmented their natural abilities.

Hating his own apprehensions, Tynan forced the next question. "Can you learn to control the power? Or, is there a possibility that, angered, you might harm someone who is not a serious threat?"

Tallia gazed at him in stunned surprise. The thought hadn't occurred to her. Could it happen? Of course. Anything was possible. Unless—unless she learned to master the force within her. Until she reached Twin Suns, and could seek Eyrsa's help, she'd have to deal with it alone. Despising the doubtful expression in Tynan's eyes, she responded with more assurance than she felt. "Now that I know it exists and what it feels like, I can control it."

"You're sure?"

"Yes, I'm sure."

"Good." His concern abated for the present, he leaned back, resuming his reclining position against the boulder.

"Tynan, will you allow me to attend to your wounds now?" She made a sweeping gesture encompassing his chafed wrists, his wounded arm, and bound torso.

"Yes," he muttered, hating the necessity.

"Good." She retrieved her herbal pouch before crouching down at his side. Forcing her mind to ignore the abrasive texture of the fine black hair on his arm, she bathed the laceration with a solution of aloe sap diluted with water. Despite her tenderness, she felt his arm tense beneath her grasp. Inwardly, she winced. She hated to cause him pain, but it was unavoidable.

The cleansing finally completed, she rested her hands on his arms, opening her mind to his pain. She twitched at the blast of torment that invaded her senses. Tallia focused on the injury. Drawing on the ethereal essence of her healing force, she probed the wound, directing her curative energy to the damaged flesh.

Tynan, watching her actions, found himself mesmerized by the sudden luminous glow of her pearly complexion. Her breathing slowed; her eyes closed. Almost imperceptibly, her hands moved, tightening on his wrists. A peculiar tingling, almost like a vibration, passed between them. As the sensation increased, the pain receded. Then Tallia removed her hands, startling him with the hastiness of the treatment. He looked down, fully expecting to find that she'd been unable to do more than ease the pain, and gaped in surprise. All that remained as proof of the injuries to his arm and to his wrists was a faint redness almost invisible against his bronzed flesh.

He was still staring in disbelief, when Tallia's timid fingers took the end of the wrapping around his midsection. Gently she unravelled it to expose his bruised rib cage. Unfortunately, the removal of the bandage also bared more of his solid muscle-corded abdomen.

Tallia gave herself a mental shake to keep her eyes from roving appreciatively over that broad expanse of hair-roughened chest. The fiery warmth of his flesh as her hand brushed against him sent waves of awareness dancing along her nerve endings, disrupting her concentration. She took a deep breath to steady herself, unaware that Tynan, observing her closely, was aware of her confusion and suffered from a similar sense of heightened perceptions.

Tallia lay her hands as lightly as possible over the discolored area on his side. Closing her eyes and senses to her attraction to him, she compelled her mind once more into its healing trance. Journeying slowly past the ruptured blood vessels in the area, she sought the source of the breaks. Weariness was taking its toll. *Once more*, she pleaded silently, forcing her mind to roam further, to the source of Tynan's pain. Directing all her energy to the point, she envisioned the fusing of the bone. Finally came the subtle communication. It was done. She sagged with a combination of relief and fatigue.

"Tallia, are you all right?" Tynan's voice jerked her upright almost instantly.

"Of course, I'm just a little tired," she respond-ed, opening her eyes. A broad expanse of bronzed chest layered with thick, curling black hair met her eyes. Unfamiliar sensations, heightened by her lassitude, invaded her body. She could not raise her eyes. She was captivated by the beauty of his vigorous body.

"Tallia." The word was a shuddering whisper. Tynan lifted her jaw with a gentle finger to look into her pale smokey eyes. The unbridled adoration he saw there elicited a faint groan from his lips. Gently he pulled her toward him.

Oblivious to all but the anticipation of feeling those strong arms cradling her body, and those firm full lips caressing hers, Tallia leaned into him. His lips closed over hers; his tongue probed deeply into her mouth. Her senses swirled. A kaleido-scope of color burst behind her eyelids as tremendous heat rushed to her limbs. She was melting. Goddess above! Her heart pounded so erratically in her chest she could barely breathe. She was dying! Yet, not even for life would she break this spell. Her fingers curled into the thick hair at his nape, holding his mouth to hers.

Tynan felt her willing body pressing against his. His blood boiled with desire for the beautiful young woman in his arms. Then, reason intruded. Tallia belonged to a noble house. She was a Zarmist. Her destiny didn't lie with a man who roamed the wasteland and who rarely returned to civilization. She deserved better. He would never forgive himself if he took what she in her naivete was offering. Slowly, he withdrew from the embrace.

"Tallia," he whispered, his voice so choked he barely recognized it as his own. "We have to stop now. In another moment, it will be too late."

Her confused eyes lifted to his. "I don't understand."

He sighed. "I know you don't. Someday, you will. When you marry."

The sudden hurt in her eyes was almost more than he could bear, feeling as he did. He was spared further torment by Luma's arrival with another cub. She immediately set it down in the shade of a boulder near Tynan, retrieved the one beside him, then lay down to nurse her offspring. Tallia slipped from his embrace. Refusing to look at him, she moved to lavish attention on Luma. Breathing a heartfelt sigh, Tynan attempted to calm the feverish pace of his heart.

They passed the remainder of the day resting, recuperating. Despite Tallia's sudden silence,

Tynan found the opportunity to relax for a time enjoyable.

The next morning they rose early. The feeble rays of the rising sun failed to provide even a small measure of heat. Rather, as they journeyed on, the day seemed to grow progressively cooler beneath the dismal gray of a heavily overcast sky.

"It's snowing!" Tallia exclaimed, watching the first silent flakes falling starlike and settling daintily on the soft fur of her cape. Awed by their sparkling perfect pattern, she allowed a faint smile to touch her lips.

Was there any use in warning her of the danger? Tynan wondered. Snowstorms in the wasteland were brutal, unrelenting in their severity and suddenness, often fatal to those unprepared.

Captured by the childlike wonder in her expression, Tynan halted his words of caution. At times it was difficult to distinguish the woman in her from the child. There was a purity in the way she viewed the changing prisms of nature. The snow, Tynan thought, was pure like Tallia and yet possessed a subtle, uncompromising ability that could kill. He frowned as the memory of Tallia's face, distorted with anger and pain, flashed into his mind. Perhaps the snow's deathly abilities were more like Tallia than its purity.

"It's such a quiet beauty, isn't it?" Her serene voice interrupted the direction of his musings.

He nodded absently as his eyes began to search for shelter.

Noting the deepening chill in the air, Tynan pressed his legs tighter against Chaz, silently urging the beast to quicken his pace. The muscles quivered along the stallion's back and Chaz turned his dark head to look at his rider. Tynan patted his neck in reply. The faralk's instincts had never been wrong and his actions confirmed Tynan's growing suspicions. This storm would be a furious one.

"Come on, keep up," he barked at Tallia as she allowed Luma to prowl unhurriedly from one side of the path to the other. Ignoring her hurt look, he pressed Chaz into a trot, forcing Tallia's cat into a quicker pace to keep up.

Despite the earliness of the afternoon, the darkening sky generated the impression of impending night. Ahead stretched the barren, hostile wasteland. The stunted trees, few as they were, would be unable to protect them from the wrath of a storm. Making a quick decision, Tynan turned Chaz from the path, eastward.

"Where are you going?" Tallia shouted after him, halting the tawny cat where Tynan had exited the trail.

"To make camp," he replied sharply without slowing Chaz. If his memory served him right, there was a slight bluff a few miles ahead. He hoped they would reach it before the storm struck. Glancing back to make sure Tallia was following, he set Chaz a quicker pace, glad to see that Tallia was pushing Luma to lessen the distance between them.

Tallia checked the security of the cubs in the saddlebags as they hastened toward the promise of shelter. The storm, like a hidden enemy suddenly sensing its prey's escape, leapt angrily from the sky, transforming the soft, drifting flakes of snow into hard-driven, biting chips of ice. The world abruptly became a swirling, dancing sea of white.

Tallia manuevered Luma until she could almost reach out and touch the faralk's side. Here there was a little respite from the harsh wind that jerked at her cloak and the brittle bits of snow that stung her cheeks.

"Take hold . . ." The wind whipped away the last of Tynan's shouted words as Tallia grabbed at the end of the rope he tossed toward her. Her fingers numb with cold, she struggled to secure it through Luma's harness. Finally successful, she crouched lower on the animal's back, burying her face in the warmth of the gari's thick fur.

Time, too, became their enemy, relentlessly moving forward as the blizzard held them in its greedy clutches, making every movement an effort of will. The boundaries of the snowy world in which they seemed the only inhabitants continued to close in on them. Tynan pressed on, the image of the bluff rising in his mind like a beacon.

Tallia pulled her stare from the hypnotizing, shifting wall of white, concentrating instead on the sure-footed steps of the faralk. One foot, then the other, disappeared into nothingness. Endlessly, the dark hooves reached into the calcimine whirlpool. The blizzard roared in her ears. The biting wind chilled her until she could no longer ward off the shivers that shook her body. Tallia clapped her hands over her ears, desperately trying to will away the shrill pernicious scream of the storm's fury as it enveloped her, threatening to choke the breath from her.

Tynan peered ahead, striving to discern the shape of the escarpment through the blinding force of wind and driven snow. It was all he could do to make out the shape of Tallia's mount beside him. Surely, they should have reached shelter by now. Perhaps he had misjudged the location. He closed his eyes momentarily and prayed that was not the case. He saw Tallia waver in her saddle. How much more could she take? Bending from Chaz's back, he ordered her to grasp his arm as he hoisted her onto the faralk's massive hind quarters. She would be a little more protected from the wind's fury behind him.

Guilt stabbed at Tynan as Chaz stumbled. He was asking the animal for more than he should. He knew the beast's loyalty would not allow him to quit until he had given all he had. New warmth surged into his chilled limbs as he turned savage anger against the storm.

"No!" The wind whipped the rebellious word away into the ravenous void of hungry white. *Damn you*, he cursed silently, *you won't beat me*. He bent close to Chaz's ear. "Just a little more, my friend, just a little more."

The wind abated a degree as the protective rise appeared before them. But only Tynan saw the abutment, with its rocky overhang and shallow cavelike shelter. Tallia, exhausted from Bodan's attack and beaten by the elements, slipped quietly into a world of oblivion, unaware of Tynan's strong arms as he lifted her from the faralk's back and carried her to the haven of the abutment.

Tallia drifted aimlessly through the passages of her mind. She saw her life, laid out before her like a valley stretching in the light of the rising sun. Around her neck the Zarma stone glowed with mystic power and all she touched grew and was healed. But somewhere within herself existed an empty cavern, a space leaving her less than whole. A vision flashed through her mind. She saw Tynan, tall and proud on the crest of a rise. He stood, his broadsword raised high, and she appeared by his side. A strange misty blue aura enwrapped them, binding each to the other. What did it mean?

Another foretelling? Was Tynan the element that corresponded to the void? With sudden startling clarity she knew he was. Somewhere in her cloudy future, she would have need of Tynan's strength, and he of hers. Drawing upon the bond that would be forged between them, they would stand together, united. He *was* part of her destiny!

Painful, tingling warmth slowly returned to Tallia's body as Tynan carefully rubbed her limbs. He gathered her trembling form onto his lap, continuing to stroke her icy arms as she surfaced from the haze of semiconsciousness. Shuddering convulsively in reaction to the cold, she studied him with new awareness.

Lifting her head she stared into the emerald depths of his eyes searchingly. Her body quaked once more with an uncontrollable shudder; this one induced, not by cold but by fear. What did her future hold? Why would there be a need in her life for a man of violence?

As their gazes locked, a peculiar tension developed between them. Tynan's hands stilled. Immobilized by the intensity of the contact, Tallia moistened her lips nervously.

Tynan's breath caught in his throat at the unconsciously seductive gesture. She was beautiful. Even with her skin flushed and blotched with cold, she was exquisite. Once again he found himself trapped by the strange magnetic quality of her silver-eyed gaze. Unaware of his action, he placed a hand on either side of her face and slowly lowered his lips to hers in a caress as gentle as a sigh.

Startled by the potency of the subtle touch, Tynan jerked his head back. What was he doing? Yet something in her eyes drew him. Once again, he battled his instincts, reminding himself that she was vulnerable, innocent. Then his heart skipped a beat as she reached one small trembling hand up to caress his stubbled chin. Surely she didn't realize the effect her touch had on his body which, even now, pulsed with the heat of his need. A need that was more than sexual. He needed to feel life and warmth, erase the icy remnant of death's clutch from his mind.

"One day we will have need of each other, you know."

Her husky murmur struck a cord deep within him. What did she mean? Suddenly, it no longer mattered. The last of his resolve shattered. Driven by his own desires, the remnants of his self-control having traitorously deserted him, he bent to taste the fullness of her trembling lips once more.

Gently he lowered her onto his cape and stretched out beside her, pulling the fur around his shoulders. She lay trembling and passive in his arms as he hugged her to him with a possessiveness that unnerved him. An inner voice warned against his actions but the undeniable pressure of Tallia's body quivering against his own drove it from his mind. He needed her. His lips traced a path from her mouth to the beckoning hollow at the base of her throat. An involuntary moan escaped her, fueling his passion. Then, tentatively, she began to caress him in return.

Tynan's embrace felt warm and solid. Above the ridge, the wind howled and the snow swirled in a blind fury. The sound of the white death faded into the recesses of Tallia's consciousness as something within her urgently demanded a reaffirmation of life. From the depths of her being, a hunger surfaced, expanding, throbbing.

The fur cape slipped from Tynan's shoulders as she ran her hands beneath his shirt, her fingers flitting across the warmth of his bare skin as if by touching him she could know his very soul, blend with his thoughts, merge into one being.

The fervid rush of her blood heated her skin which, only moments before, had been chilled by the storm. She closed her eyes and reveled in the sensation of his touch. His roughened hands explored the curves of her body lingeringly as he slowly peeled away her clothing, leaving only the thick fur of the cape to cocoon the warmth of their fevered flesh.

Suddenly she felt the unfamiliar hardness of him against her thigh. She tensed, afraid once more. This was wrong! And yet, as his hands continued to massage her, easing the tension from her limbs, it felt right. Oh, so right!

Ripples of insatiable desire ran the length of her body as he gently teased the taut rose-hued crests of her breasts with the tip of his tongue. His gentle, stroking hands eased between her thighs stoking to life a fiery urgency. The uncontrollable blaze consumed her untutored body in liquid warmth. She clung to him; he was an anchor within this vortex of alien sensation. The thick hair on his chest, a soft abrasion against her skin, stimulated her. Sensual hunger ravaged her perceptions.

He clasped her tightly to him. She cried out as he slid slowly into her. A flash of pain. She tensed. He gripped her more tightly, pausing until the spasm passed, replaced once more by the urgency of newly awakened hunger. He moved in the ageless rhythm of procreation. Together they rose on a cloud of passion, soaring. Entwined, merging, the fever in their blood built to a fiery crescendo before the cooling waves of release doused the carnal flames.

Buoyed by exquisite sensation, Tallia felt herself drifting, settling back to the ground like a feather wafting weightless in the breeze. The comforting warmth of Tynan's body enveloped her. She smiled slightly as he pulled her close, safe, protected. Then, exhaustion claimed her and she drifted into a dreamless slumber.

As the first rays of sunlight spilled over the far horizon, clouds of mist rose from the snow-shrouded terrain beyond their shelter. Tallia slipped from the warmth of their makeshift bed to retrieve her clothes. Tynan, resting on one elbow, stretched out on the fur. Never had he felt such desire. Like a smoldering fire which had suddenly burst into flame, the spark of interest he'd had when he'd first seen Tallia had built into a raging passion. The intoxicating sensations, so temporarily appeased, were already building into a voracious hunger for more. And yet, his thoughts plagued him. It could not last. He could not allow his yearning to persist.

Tallia smiled at him a little shyly as she dressed. Affection and trust emanated from her, glowing in the radiance of her eyes. If he moved closer, he was sure he would feel it, comforting, warming, like the heat from a campfire. Already he felt the pain and guilt of his half-formed decision. His actions would destroy her trust, and in that moment he despised himself.

Stopping in mid-action, she cocked her head to one side, listening intently. All Tynan heard was the gentle lowing of the wind, eased now since the storm had passed. He watched as Tallia struggled into her clothing then crept out from under their shelter and across the snow toward the end of the bluff.

The stifled whimpering had been as clear to Tallia as the frosty vapor of her breath. Somewhere in this frozen wasteland a creature mourned and the sorrowful sound tore at her heart. Irresistibly drawn, she followed the sound around the point of the escarpment and up toward the peak.

Diligently, she picked her way up the slope through the icy tumble of rock. She paused, peering down over the edge. Below, Chaz grazed in the sparse grass in the ridge's shelter and Luma curled beneath a stunted bush, near the sheltering overhang, nursing her cubs. Again, she listened for the sound. When it came, the closeness startled her. Circling a large boulder, she found the source of the cries.

The wolflike female lopii had sought shelter in the boulder's shadow but it had provided little protection from the storm's fury. The frost of the lopii's last breaths whitened the slender muzzle; her graceful length, gaunt with hunger and the demands of nursing, lay stiff now in the arms of death. Beneath the female, drawing life from the diminishing heat of her body, a pup whimpered, confused by his mother's sudden stillness. He nuzzled his tiny shape against her, seeking reassurance and comfort.

Tallia squatted near the pup's mother and ran her hand through the animal's blood-encrusted fur. Her injuries had prevented her from reaching shelter. The pup looked up at Tallia, his eyes dark against his gray, silver-tipped fuzzy coat. Planting small paws defiantly in the snow, he attempted a defensive growl.

"So brave." Tallia kept her voice low, gentle and soothing. "I'll not hurt you." When she made no move, the pup relaxed. His sad mournful look passed to his mother and then back to Tallia. "Come, silver lopii. You must be hungry. Poor thing." Discreetly, she held out her hand resting it on the mother's flank.

The pup regarded the gesture warily before inching forward to sniff her fingers. The scent of his mother's fur lingered on her hand. Reassured, he rested his head gratefully against the warmth. As Tallia drew her hand back, he followed, needing the comfort and protection she offered. Unsteadily, he clambered into her lap, the whole back half of his body wiggling as he attempted to wag his stubby tail while licking her fingers. Secure now, he allowed her to bundle him in her arms and carry him back to camp.

Tynan was adding dung chips to the blaze when Tallia seated herself within the circle of the fire's heat and let the pup tumble to the ground.

"Great god!" Tynan jumped back as if the tottering animal would attack him.

At the harsh tone of voice, the pup yelped and ran back into the circle of Tallia's legs. Crouching down, he stared at Tynan from behind one of her boots.

"Put him back before she comes looking for him," Tynan demanded angrily as his eyes made a quick, thorough search of the immediate area. "You can't just pick up a lopii pup." The ferocious nature of the animals, especially a mother protecting her young, was well-known in the wasteland. Few crossed a lopii and escaped without something to show for it.

"I'm afraid she can't help him anymore. Her last act was to give her own warmth to save him."

"Well, you don't think you're going to keep him, do you?" The disbelief echoed in Tynan's question.

"He has no one else," Tallia answered, her own determination rising. "He's too young to fend for himself. I can't just leave him." She ran her fingers in a caress through the fur.

As Tynan moved to stand over her, the pup leapt from behind Tallia's leg with a shrill bark to pounce on his foot. Tallia couldn't stifle the giggle that bubbled from her lips and the action even coaxed a reluctant smile from Tynan though he shook his head in disapproval.

And so the lopii pup, dubbed Silva, joined Luma's cubs—after considerable persuasion on Tallia's part. Eventually, seeing that the pup posed no threat to her offspring, Luma simply ignored him.

The sun, when it fully emerged, was as brilliant and warm in its intensity as the night had been dark and cold only hours before. A fog of steam rose from the quickly thawing ground in thick wraith-like tendrils. As the morning progressed, the moisture in the air around them disappeared quickly; small streams of running water raced over the frozen ground on the beginning of its journey to the sea. The little that was absorbed by the shallow, parched soil was greedily sucked up by the thirsting plantlife. As they breakfasted silently, Tallia noted with amazement small wildflowers in a bountiful array of colors opening their fragile petals to capture the sunlight.

Tynan saddled Chaz in silence, pondering the turmoil within himself. He'd given in to his male weakness. He'd lost control of himself, something he had vowed would never happen. Tallia compelled him more than any woman he had ever known and yet, he knew he could never call her his own. There was no room for love in his world of solitude. The icy grip of vengeance would not release his heart. Could he ever look at her and not see Tynara, not see death, not feel the anguish?

Tallia was not the type of woman who indulged in casual relationships. He'd discovered the proof of that himself. Neither was she likely to have associated with women who did. After his irresponsible conduct, she no doubt expected marriage and that was, quite simply, an impossibility. The hopelessness of any future together was painfully obvious. He didn't belong in her world, an environment of love and solace and she could never adapt to his often violent, nomadic, revenge-filled life. Shame for his previous actions and regret for what he was about to do threatened to choke him. But she'd get over him. He wondered if he could say the same about himself.

Forcing aside his dreams and desires, he watched as she approached. She reached to wrap her arms around him. A wrenching ache filled his chest as, wordlessly, he thrust her roughly aside to finish securing his pack. Peripherally he observed the play of confused emotions across her face. Tears shimmered briefly in her narrowed eyes as she straightened proudly and silently walked away.

Tynan felt his insides coil into a tight knot. Turning sharply on his heel, he refused to allow himself to follow her, to take her into his arms as his senses demanded he do. The sooner they both accepted the reality of their situation, the better. He mounted Chaz and urged the faralk northwest.

Tallia heard him ride out. Dazed, she deposited the cubs in her saddlebags, picked up the lopii pup, and followed. Why had Tynan coldly rejected her? Had the glory of their lovemaking not affected him? Did men not feel the same way women did? She felt despair and anger seething within her chest. Recalling the previous result of her rage, she hastily suppressed the emotions. She'd asked nothing of him. She'd not smothered him with protestations of love, something Dayna had said made men uncomfortable. So why had he spurned her friendship?

Love? Did she love him? No, she didn't think so

but she liked him very much. If men treated women in this manner, why had Dayna found them so appealing?

Hurt, confused, and disillusioned, Tallia unseeingly allowed Luma to follow Tynan, and the seventh day of the journey passed in agonizing slowness. The world seemed dull, gray and unattractive. Tallia slouched wearily in her saddle by the time Tynan halted to make camp. Seeking the comforting presence of the animals that evening, she brushed first Luma's coat and then Chaz's. Although she fought it, her mind roamed and she glanced frequently over her shoulder at a silent, brooding Tynan where he squatted before the fire, clutching a cup in his hand, taking his turn at cooking. That he was troubled, she knew. However, the fact that he'd refused to converse with her in any way hardened her heart toward his suffering. After the way he'd treated her today, he deserved to agonize. He'd receive no pity from her.

Turning back to the faralk, Tallia froze in terror as a strange face materialized amid the rocks beyond Chaz's shoulder. The image of ridged amber features, long, thin black hair, and perfectly round black eyes, mirroring a surprise as deep as her own, appearing out of nowhere in the gathering gloom of the wasteland's dusk was too much.

She screamed ear-splittingly and her scream was echoed almost immediately by the intruder whose face contorted with shock and fear at her piercing shriek. It was more than Tallia's shattered nerves could stand. Scrambling backward as swiftly as possible, without taking her eyes off the apparition,

she summoned Tynan in a distinctly unfeminine squawk. That her summons had been unnecessary with Tynan seated only a few yards away, she did not consider for she'd not taken her eyes off the face long enough to note that Tynan now stood beside her. The sudden uproarious laughter that erupted *did* draw her attention. She whirled in shock at the sound of Tynan's uncharacteristic rumbling laugh. Her eyes widened with dismay. Had he gone mad?

"Letai," Tynan called, still chuckling, "it's good to see you."

The visage over the boulder smiled hesitantly before a lithe form rose, revealing that the face was definitely attached to a body. Her heart's erratic beating slowed, as Tallia studied the man curiously when he dropped down from the stone before them. He was clad in a fur tunic that covered his torso, hanging to just above his knees. His flesh was no darker than Tynan's tanned, weathered skin but was strangely yellowish. Over one shoulder a bow was casually draped, a slender quiver of arrows, their feathered ends displaying a variety of different plumage, protruded over the other.

As Tallia observed him, he began waving his arms and moving around in a manner that suggested to Tallia that he was either highly agitated about something or a very high-strung person. Watching him wide-eyed as he jabbered incomprehensibly, literally jumping off the ground a number of times, she revised her opinion. He was both agitated and high-strung.

To Tallia, the stranger's extreme excitement was underscored by the fact that he was barely four feet tall. Tynan later told her that this was characteristic of Letai's race, but at the moment she could only wait for the commotion to subside.

"Tallia, I'd like you to meet Letai," Tynan said, stepping back to allow them to greet each other. The man touched his forehead briefly with two fingers before extending his upturned palm toward her. Tallia hesitated. At her obvious reticence, Tynan burst into a fresh bout of laughter which earned him a censorious expression from both his companions. "Letai has been my friend for a long time. You can return his greeting in the same manner he just displayed."

Tallia mimicked the gestures and added, "I'm pleased to know you."

Letai grinned in return, bobbing his head enthusiasticly.

To Tallia's disgust, Tynan immediately reneged on his cooking duties. As she took over the preparation of the meal, Tallia surreptitiously regarded the two men, amazed at the transformation in Tynan. She'd never seen him so relaxed, so open. She didn't bother attempting to follow the conversation which was conducted in a strange combination of her own language and the Hytola dialect.

Handing the men each a plate, she sat a short distance away to enjoy the vast panorama of the night sky, just beginning to be studded with stars. The first of the moons had risen, bathing the barren landscape in soft silver light. Tallia found that her mood had lightened.

The muted sounds of conversation lulled her pensive spirit. She relaxed, permitting her mind to drift aimlessly, admiring the shadowy landscape, recalling pleasant memories of home. She realized that the urgent calling of Eyrsa's message no longer haunted her as it had in Maurasia. The anxiety had eased. She felt certain that she would have sensed Eyrsa's concern if whatever dilemma had prompted the message still bothered her mentor.

Tallia turned and watched the men. They sat within the glowing circle of the firelight, Tynan bent forward with apparent interest in the conversation. Letai leaned back, relaxed except for his hands which moved in quick furtive gestures with almost every word. Once or twice Tallia thought he motioned toward her, but he looked away quickly as if to conceal his expression.

The two friends exchanged news of all that had happened since their last meeting, and Letai provided much useful information about the immediate vicinity. Tynan was particularly pleased to learn of a small herd of herti in a nearby valley. Finally Letai approached the subject that interested him most.

"She's very pretty," Letai remarked to Tynan. "Very innocent, I would guess." He waited for some remark, some expression to indicate Tynan's thoughts. He smiled at his friend. As usual, no trace of emotion showed on the tanned face or in those startling green eyes.

Tynan shook his head and allowed a smile to play across his features. He leaned forward. "Get to the point." Inseparable as boys, their friendship had developed into a life-long one and Tynan felt comfortable challenging Letai's observations.

Letai smiled back. "I'm curious about the girl." He bobbed his head slightly in her direction.

"I've agreed to escort her across the wasteland. That's all." Tynan ignored the way Letai raised his brows dubiously. "She needed an escort and I was traveling in this direction." He barely succeeded in keeping the explanation from sounding like an excuse. Why was he so defensive? Was there more to it than that? He wasn't sure anymore.

Studiously regarding the toe of one leather-bound foot, Letai nodded.

"How is your father?" Tynan maneuvered the conversation toward a less disturbing subject.

"He asks after you. He's curious concerning your path in life."

Tynan remembered again old wise Moural's revelation to the eighteen-year-old boy who awaited the seer's words so eagerly. "Seek a destiny that is greater than your own," he had muttered. "That is the way to truth and freedom." Tynan's mind returned to Letai's query.

"My path remains unchanged," he responded.

Letai nodded again.

The hours passed unnoticed, and when Tallia slipped back into camp, she pulled her bedding near the fire. The easy camaraderie between the two men dispelled the tense atmosphere that had enveloped her relationship with Tynan. She drifted to sleep, lulled by the muffled sound of their voices.

In the morning, Letai bid his good-byes and bent to pat the lopii pup.

Tallia tugged on Tynan's sleeve. "Do you think Letai would like Silva? We'll soon reach Twin Suns, and the pup is too young to fend for itself."

Tynan nodded wordlessly. Walking toward Letai, he scooped the puppy into his arms and offered it to

Letai as he muttered an explanation in the native's language.

Letai bobbed his head happily, jabbering a reply, as he took the animal from Tynan's grasp. Waving, he quickly left, disappearing beyond the ridge.

Tallia felt a twinge of regret. His presence had prompted a change in Tynan, one of which she approved.

CHAPTER SIX

FIVE DAYS HAD PASSED SINCE LETAI'S VISIT AND Tynan's amiable mood had not even lasted the first morning of Letai's departure. The past few days had been days of silence with only the most cursory conversation between them, and Tallia was heartily sick of it. Soon the sun would slip beneath the distant mountains and once more they would make camp. Each would carefully avoid encountering the other's gaze, turning away quickly if an accidental contact should occur. She knew it would happen for that was how it had been ever since the day after the snowstorm. It was disconcerting and ridiculous for two adults to behave in this manner. Yet Tallia did not know how to alter the situation since Tynan had made his feelings abundantly clear.

Once more the pain of his rejection overwhelmed

her, and she had to swallow against the lump in her throat. *Enough*! she told herself sternly. Though she turned her gaze with determination on her surroundings, she was unable to divert the direction of her thoughts. Perhaps it was her fault. Had she done something to make him feel threatened in some way?

Once more the foretelling scene flashed through her memory—she and Tynan together. Despite his reticence, they would remain bonded. How and why, only Destiny would reveal. Meanwhile, she resigned herself to the coolness of his moods, content to bide her time.

A bitter breeze chilled the air, and clouds of steam issued from her mouth with each breath. Now that winter was upon them, small patches of dry snow swirled along the cracked, frozen ground, amassing against a small stone or beneath a clump of brittle brown grass before being picked up once more and hurled onward by the relentless wind. She shivered despite the warmth of her enveloping fur. Her feet were numb with cold, and yet her hands had darkened three shades due to constant exposure to the sun. It was a strange place, this wasteland.

Ahead of her, Tynan halted, then disappeared into a small aperture in the base of the cliff they had been traveling along. Tallia waited for him to reappear. She hoped he would deem the sheltered area suitable for camping. Absently, she rubbed her hands in the warmth of Luma's neck ruff. "Come on," she muttered impatiently, her eyes fastened unwaveringly on the fissure. Sitting still in this weather, even for a few minutes, was worse than riding the entire day. The icy cold penetrated to the bone as soon as one stopped moving.

Tynan emerged and beckoned with a brief wave before disappearing once more into the opening. Sighing in relief, Tallia coaxed Luma forward.

After the incessant droning of the wind, the calm inside the cleft seemed absolute. The area between the walls wasn't large, a path barely three feet wide, but at its end it widened into a roughly circular region perhaps ten or twelve feet in diameter. To her, bone-tired as she was, it was sanctuary. She dismounted and began removing her supplies.

"We need meat."

Tynan's voice drew her attention. Turning, she met his gaze, and her eyes fixed on the hypnotic movement of his full mouth, the motion of his firm jaw. Why must the man be so handsome?

With a start she realized she'd failed to hear anything he'd said. A guilty flush stained her cheeks. "Pardon me?"

"I said, I'm going to try to find bigger game. This weather will drive all the smaller animals to shelter. We won't be able to rely on hunting nightly."

Tallia nodded. "All right. I'll have the fire going when you get back."

He gazed at her with an expression of total exasperation. "You certainly didn't hear much of what I said. Did you?"

Embarrassment deepened the rosy hue of her face as Tallia opened her mouth to apologize.

Without giving her the opportunity to utter a word, he continued, "I just finished telling you, don't start the fire. The chips are almost gone."

Turning away, he retrieved his bola. "I'll probably be awhile," he muttered over his shoulder as he once more mounted Chaz, "depends on how far I have to go." Then he left.

Tallia returned to the task of relieving Luma of the supplies. Envisioning the backside of one arrogant, domineering, and all-too-handsome male, she vented her anger on the unsuspecting pack as she landed a well-placed kick with extreme satisfaction. "Sarcastic, overbearing . . . wastelander!" she muttered under her breath. Feeling marginally better, she took a deep breath and set about establishing camp while Luma settled in to nurse her cubs.

A short time later, Tallia sat down on a boulder to survey the fruits of her labors. Yes, everything was ready. Now, she just had to wait for Tynan to return. She had grown more accustomed to their predominately meat diet. Still, she missed the foods she'd been raised on. Her mouth watered as she pictured Eyrsa's special casserole, a culinary delight comprised of herbs and vegetables cooked in their own juices within a golden crust. Oh, it would be nice to get home.

Home. The single word induced visions of Twin Suns and all she loved. Wistfully, she turned her gaze to the northern sky. Could they view the same clouds? *Probably not*, she concluded. Then her brow furrowed a moment in puzzlement. Something was wrong.

The clouds, normally forced along at tremendous speeds by the strength of the ever-present wind, hung lifelessly in the sky. Had the wind died? But that was unheard of. Winter in the wasteland meant wind. Only in the summer months did it occasionally cease to blow. Curiosity compelled her to walk through the short passage to the entrance. As she stepped from the shadows into the light, she halted, staring in amazement.

Before her stood a woman. No, not stood . . . floated. Tallia swallowed nervously. Was it a revenant? The ghost of an ancestor? Somehow, she'd always imagined spirits as insubstantial wisps, ethereal. Yet, this woman seemed corporeal—almost. There was something about the magnitude of her beauty that made Tallia think she could not possibly be an ordinary being. The woman's eyes, a brilliant blue that would rival the cerulean tint of the sky on a clear summer day, gazed at her with gentleness and compassion. Her features, so perfect that they could have been carved by a master craftsman from flawless ivory, were framed by abundant gleaming masses of ebony hair. Her figure, both revealed and concealed by the unusual clothing she wore, was as flawless as her face.

Suddenly, Tallia was released from her spellbound reverence by the realization that the woman beckoned her. She took a step forward at the gesture only to be stopped by an upraised hand. Confused, Tallia finally found her voice. "I don't understand. What do you want of me?"

The lady indicated the cleft in the wall before motioning once more that Tallia should follow her.

"You want me to bring my things?" Tallia hazarded a guess.

The reply was a nod and a beautiful smile.

Still, Tallia hesitated. "But what of Tynan's equipment? My mount can't carry it all, and I don't like the idea of leaving his things unguarded."

For an instant, the woman frowned. Then, apparently arriving at a solution, she smiled once more. Indicating that Tallia should move aside, she moved slightly forward, stopped, and closed her eyes.

Tallia waited, more curious than frightened by the unexpected encounter. Without taking her eyes off the woman, she realized that the wind truly had died. The wasteland was totally silent. There was not the slightest rustle of grass or whisper of snow. She shivered with apprehension. It felt wrong. The woman, her arms outspread, drifted back from the entrance to the cleft. Tallia looked at the fissure, and her eyes widened in disbelief. Tynan's large pack of supplies floated through the air, past where she stood to a point some forty feet from the wall of the cliff. As the equipment settled to the ground, Tallia was unable to control a gasp of astonishment. The pack now appeared to be nothing more than an average-sized boulder quite like any of the hundreds of others dotting the landscape.

Swallowing, Tallia returned her stunned gaze to the lady. She was once more gesturing in the direction of the aperture. Unable to think clearly, Tallia did as she was bidden. Re-entering their campsite, she began gathering her supplies. Absently noting that the cubs had finished nursing, she placed them in the large pocket of her saddle. Then, she turned to Luma.

The gari had backed into a corner and now

observed Tallia with wide nervous eyes. "Come
Luma," Tallia said softly, coaxingly. To her sur
prise, Luma hissed quietly at her. "It's all right, girl
I know packs are not supposed to float through th
air. It shocked me too." As she talked in mute
tones to the disconcerted animal, she began loadin
the supplies. "The lady means us no harm." Sh
stopped suddenly as she spoke the words, wonder
ing why she was so positive. Somehow, she was
She'd felt only gentleness emanating from th
woman.

Her packing complete, she mounted Luma an
emerged from the fissure. The lady waited, appear
ing slightly agitated now as her eyes constantl
moved, studying the surroundings.

"Who are you?" Tallia queried as she ap
proached the woman.

Her lips moved in response to Tallia's query, bu
no sound issued. She appeared frustrated. Then, a
if inspired, she nodded with a slight smile as sh
waved her slender hands. Immediately, Tallia fel
the whispery caress of a gentle breeze against he
cheek. As the mystical current of air swirled aroun
her, momentarily stealing her breath, she heard
sound.

"Gal . . . aa . . . cia," the wind sighed.

Then, as if the passage of time disquieted her, th
lady once more gestured to the west. Too stunned t
do otherwise, Tallia set Luma into motion. Th
gari, now calm and exhibiting no fear of the unusu
al presence, followed the woman without guidance
as Tallia retreated into stupefied thought.

It wasn't possible. Tallia did not possess th

exemplary characteristics she had always assumed necessary for one to be worthy of divine intervention. Galacia was a goddess. Goddesses simply did not concern themselves with the lives of ordinary people. Perhaps it was a dream. A wonderful, confusing dream. If she dared speak of it, nobody would believe her anyway. Even Eyrsa would probably think her mad. No, it was better if she acknowledged it only as a dream.

Suddenly, the ground trembled. Uttering a feline hiss of fright, Luma stumbled as a second, more violent vibration rocked the terrain. The very atmosphere quivered. Tallia clutched at Luma's ruff as she felt the sudden rush of wind against her face. Around her, the landscape began flashing by at an astonishing pace. Looking down with total disbelief, she saw that Luma no longer trod the land. They were airborne, suspended in the air behind the goddess, propelled along at a speed no gari was capable of. Tallia closed her eyes against the dizzying scene. This wasn't happening. It was only a dream.

Within minutes, she felt their forward motion stop. Cautiously, she opened her eyes. Luma stood within the shifting mists of a cloud. A few feet away, the goddess floated, gazing down at the land below with an expression of concern. *We are standing on a cloud? I have gone mad!* Once more she shut her eyes tightly. "When I open my eyes the dream will be over," she muttered.

Tynan had ridden Chaz in a northwesterly direction in search of the herd of herti when the wind died, suddenly and totally. He halted. The slight uneasiness he'd felt all day intensified as Chaz snorted nervously. Something was wrong. Even the great stallion sensed it. But what? What warning was to be found in this unnatural stillness?

He turned to study the mountains in the east. Their summits constantly shrouded in clouds, the enormous monoliths had never been successfully climbed and a passage through them had yet to be discovered. No one knew what lay beyond them. But, somehow, Tynan knew they were responsible for the constant chilling winds that swept the wasteland. What could have happened to change that? There was no physical indication.

His nerves strung taut, he nudged Chaz forward. Whatever happened, they needed to eat. Still distraught by the unusual silence, Tynan finally reached the area he knew was usually frequented by small herds of the deer-like herti. For a moment, he thought his trip had been fruitless. Then, at the far end of the grassy gorge he discerned movement. Carefully, he advanced.

The sight of the herd increased his anxiety. They huddled together, almost motionless, not grazing, not walking. Like small statues, they remained immobile, not even running as he approached, perplexed. Normally the herd would have scattered, racing in all directions. Then he would have chosen his kill and run the animal to ground, entangling it with his bola and then ending its struggle with one quick slash of his hunting knife.

Dismounting, he walked slowly toward the herd. They shuffled nervously at his approach, but remained firmly grouped. Within three feet of the nearest herti, he stopped to study the animals. Small nervous movements rippled their hides constantly. He looked into their eyes and swallowed at what he saw there. Stark terror. The animals were frozen with terror.

Once more Tynan turned his gaze to the mountains. What was wrong? His own nerves began to quiver. Whatever it was he needed to get back to Tallia as soon as possible. Detesting having to kill an animal that simply waited to die, Tynan quickly closed the distance between himself and the nearest herti. A quick slash of his knife and the animal was down. The remainder of the herd, almost unanimously, uttered a panicked bleating sound and skipped away a few feet. There, they regrouped and continued to eye him, the terror in their eyes undiminished.

More than a little unnerved by the situation, Tynan quickly draped the herti across Chaz's broad withers. The faralk, too, was unusually skittish, his eyes wide and frightened. "I know, boy. I know," Tynan muttered as he mounted. "Let's get out of here."

Traveling as quickly as possible with the cumbersome herti dangling against Chaz's hindquarters, they'd only gone a couple of miles when the first faint vibration rippled through the land beneath their feet. Chaz slowed. Tynan studied the terrain, worry creasing his brow. The next shudder, a scant minute later, was not so gentle. Its turbulence threw Chaz completely off stride and the beast screamed in terror. Tynan attempted to urge him on.

Thoughts of Tallia, and how she'd fare, clamored in his brain. For the first time ever, the faralk fought Tynan's guidance.

Without pausing to think, Tynan jumped to the ground and quickly relieved Chaz of his burdens, dumping the saddle and limp herti unceremoniously to the ground. Chaz reared. Snorting with fear, he spun and raced off in the opposite direction.

Again Tynan felt the ground tremble. The soil beneath his feet began to buck and heave. He gasped for breath in the now dust-thickened air, struggling to keep his balance. All around, the earth seemed to lift, groaning as it writhed in the agony of its transformation. A quake! He'd heard of them occurring far to the south. Never had he imagined himself in the midst of one. He didn't know what to do, and the feeling of helplessness terrified him almost as much as the sight of the upheaval around him.

Tallia! Why had he camped in the foothills! Even without the disrupting violence of a quake, the eroding rock walls were sometimes subject to slides. A vision of her trapped, helplessly crushed beneath tons of stone, invaded his mind. He began to run, weaving and stumbling over the convulsing terrain. *Tallia! Tallia*! Her name resounded in his brain, a rhythmic litany to which he ran.

When Tallia opened her eyes, nothing had changed. Galacia hovered nearby, and Tallia leaned forward to see what held the goddess's interest below.

Her eyes widened in shock and dismay. The

landscape, bathed in the final rays of the setting sun, shuddered and buckled. Enormous gaping cracks opened, belching clouds of dry sandy soil before indiscriminately swallowing everything in their splintering path. "Tynan!" Frantic, she searched the scene below with panicked eyes. Turning urgently to the goddess, she forgot all thought of reverence and madness. "Goddess, what of Tynan? Can you help him?"

The shifting terrain seemed to become more volatile the farther east Tynan traveled. Enormous boulders were swallowed whole into gaping crevices that appeared suddenly in ground that a second before was solid. He lost count of how many times he fell. Doggedly, he rose to continue. He could see little before him but a huge cloud of dust as the powdery soil was lifted and flung in all directions. His lungs burned, and his palms and knees stung where the pitted soil had scoured his skin. Ignoring it all, he prayed, *Let her live.*

Suddenly, a wide fissure fractured the ground behind him, the pulverizing sound grating in his ears. The earth beneath him bucked upward with one mighty thrust, and like a doll, he was lifted and flung to the ground. Dazed, the breath knocked out of him, he could only lay there as a hail of rock from a nearby outcropping descended all around him. He felt a tremendous blow to his head and fought against a wave of dizziness. It was no use. Blackness descended.

The goddess shook her head, regret and pity in her gaze.

"He could be hurt!" Tallia exclaimed in desperation.

Once again the goddess shook her head, spreading her hands in a gesture of helplessness.

For an instant, Tallia stared at her uncomprehendingly. She was a goddess, wasn't she? Why couldn't she help Tynan? Was it too late? She forced herself to ask the question, dreading the response. "Will Tynan live?"

The goddess smiled gently and nodded.

Staring down through the murky air, Tallia sought to locate Tynan in the midst of the upheaval. The clouds of silt rose and hung over the landscape, obscuring it from her searching eyes. She looked again at the goddess. He had to be all right. His hunt had probably led him away from the quake site.

She waited as the dust-cloaked sun sank inevitably into the horizon, blanketing the land in night. Still Galacia gave no indication that it was time to return to the shudder-wracked land below. Although the worst was over, intermittent aftershocks continued to ravage the terrain. The sound of rock being pulverized within gaping fissures continued to reach her ears as minutes stretched into hours.

Tynan groaned. His head hurt and something tugged at him. Painfully, he opened his eyes and turned his head, wincing at the tormenting ache induced by the movement. With agonizing slowness, he sat up. Extending his hand in the direction of the tug, he encountered a horn. Chaz! He expelled his breath in relief. At least he wasn't about to be devoured by some denizen of the wasteland.

Abruptly, memory returned. The quake! Tallia! He had to find her. "Come here, boy," he spoke softly to the faralk. Using the animal's foreleg as a crutch, Tynan slowly pulled himself erect. Blinking away the wave of dizziness, he stood.

The wasteland was cloaked in one of the blackest nights he'd ever witnessed. There were no moons or stars. Straining, he could discern Chaz as a slightly blacker shadow against the darkness. He would have to rely totally on the faralk to return him to camp.

As he attempted to mount, devoid of stirrup or saddle, he realized the ground still trembled with occasional aftershocks. The shudders were minor compared to the earlier ones. Still, in his unsteady state, the next reverberation was enough to knock him to his knees. Cursing with little restraint, he struggled once more from his ignominious position, awkwardly pulling himself onto the patient faralk. Clinging to Chaz's mane, he managed to right himself despite the lightheaded feeling that refused to leave him.

Tynan judged that it couldn't be more than two or three miles to camp. The herti valley hadn't been more than five miles away. He and Chaz had traveled a couple of miles on the return journey before the quake, and he was certain that he must have run at least another mile.

Thoughts of Tallia invaded his brain once more. Was he too late? Had it all been in vain? Relentless images of what he might find flitted through his mind. No! She had to be alive! He refused to contemplate life without her.

I love her! The conscious realization struck him like a blow. He'd tried so hard to hold himself distant, to keep himself from feeling. But somehow she'd breached the wall he'd constructed around his heart. He swallowed against the tide of emotion that twisted savagely in his chest. The thought that he might never hold her again was almost unbearable.

And as Tynan, lost in the clutches of these new and raw emotions, sat immobile upon the wide sturdy back of the faralk, Chaz picked his way slowly and carefully over the now unfamiliar terrain. When Tynan absently began taking note of his surroundings once more, the blackness of the night had begun fading to gray. Another hour and it would be dawn. They couldn't have much farther to go. Could they? He peered ahead.

The sun's rays filtered through the dust-filled air, bathing the altered landscape in hazy golden light as Tynan and Chaz finally came into view of the cliff wall. Tynan caught his breath. It was no longer a wall. Closing his eyes, he sent a prayer to Toleme, son of Yaewel, before attempting to urge the faralk to a faster pace. Chaz would not be hurried. The stallion continued to pick his way sure-footedly over the rubble-strewn ground.

As Chaz neared the spot where Tynan had left Tallia in the cliff's crevice, Tynan's eyes widened in astonishment. Luma lay nursing her offspring with apparent nonchalance. Nearby, sitting in the shadow of the pile of rubble, calmly munching hard tack from his opened pack, was Tallia.

His entire being trembled with the force of a wild, uncontrollable emotion. Awash in a strange sea of feeling, too potent for expression, he took refuge in anger. "How can you just sit there so calmly?"

Startled, Tallia's head jerked up. Smiling joyously, she jumped to her feet and moved to meet him.

"I thought you were dead!" His dark brows pulled together in a scowl as he stared at her accusingly.

"I'm fine," she replied, her smile of welcome faltering as his angry frown halted her steps.

"Well, *I* might have been dead," he shot back.

"I knew you weren't." Her reply was placid.

Tynan caught a slight movement to his right. He jerked Chaz to a halt, his hand instinctively moving to the hilt of his dagger. Amidst the rocky debris only a few feet away, a man sat motionless. Tynan dismounted, moving slowly forward, frowning as each jarring step induced an answering jolt of pain within his battered skull.

Suddenly Tynan recognized the man. "What are you doing here?" There was no reply, not even the flicker of an eyelid.

"What is Jenk doing here?" he demanded of Tallia, though his eyes never left the man.

"I have no idea. When I got back a few minutes ago, he was standing here, alone, without a mount."

"Got back!" He moved so he could see them both, eyeing Tallia with surprise. "Where did you go?"

Tallia chewed her bottom lip indecisively. "It's a long story. I'll tell you later. All right?" She responded, putting him off in the hope that he'd forget about the incident.

Meeting her anxious gaze, Tynan found all the emotions he'd experienced when he thought he might never see her again rising once more to the fore. Unable to trust his voice, he nodded and walked over to the still motionless Jenk. "Jenk, I want to know what you're doing here. Were you following us?"

Silence. The man didn't even seem to be aware of his presence. Reaching out, Tynan grasped his shoulder. "Jenk," he called again, shaking him.

Finally, there was a response. Jenk slowly lifted his face toward Tynan. The expression in the man's eyes was one of paralyzed shock.

The quake had really affected him. "Jenk, snap out of it. The quake's over." Tynan paused, waiting to see if his words penetrated the man's dazed condition. There was no change in Jenk's stunned expression.

Once more Tynan shook him, more forcibly. "Great god, man! Snap out of it. I want to know what you're doing out here. Where is your gari?"

Mechanically, emotionlessly, Jenk replied, "Threw me. Ran away when the quake struck."

"Where are your companions?" Jenk was not the type to travel the wasteland alone.

"Ran too," again he replied almost entirely in a monotone, his eyes still glassy, mirroring intense shock.

Tynan heaved an exasperated sigh. What was he going to do with him? He didn't even like the man. "Were you following us, Jenk?"

Jenk shook his head slowly. "Intercepting."

"You knew we'd pass near here?" Tynan queried incredulously. "How?"

Jenk shrugged. "Most do."

"You were after Tallia," Tynan stated baldly. "Why is she so important to you?"

At his words, Jenk turned to look at her. With surprise, Tynan noted the man's eyes widen with something akin to fear as he shook his head. "Not normal," he muttered.

Tynan shifted his gaze to the lady in question. She was standing a few feet away, eyeing them with obvious uncertainty. Tynan frowned in consternation. What had happened? Jenk had evidently suffered a rapid reversal of opinion concerning Tallia's worth. "What makes you say that, Jenk?"

For the first time his voice held some expression. "'Tisn't right. Ordinary people don't come riding out of the sky. She's a sorceress or something."

Riding out of the sky? Now Tynan was really confused. "You must be mistaken, Jenk," Tynan spoke softly, for the first time feeling the stirring of compassion for the man.

"I'm not!" Jenk shrieked. "I knew nobody'd believe me!" He rose and began backing away from Tynan, yet all the while his fearful gaze rested on Tallia. "Sorceress!" he screamed, his face frozen in rigid lines of panic. Then, as though fearing retaliation, he ran, stumbling, occasionally glancing back over his shoulder, until he was out of sight.

Frowning, Tynan turned to Tallia. "Want to tell me what that was all about?"

"No," Tallia replied quite honestly. Damn Jenk!

She hadn't wanted to try to explain what had occurred. How could she? Her story was unbelievable.

"Fine," Tynan replied. "We'll leave it at that. For now." He moved to gather up their supplies. "We better move on. There may still be aftershocks from the quake and this spot isn't safe. We'll retrieve my saddle, if possible, then make camp elsewhere."

Tallia smiled in relief. Hurrying, she began packing her things and saddling Luma before he changed his mind.

After finding Tynan's battered, but serviceable, saddle, minus the slain herti, they traveled less than five miles before he sighted a sheltered area that he deemed suitable. He'd managed to stun a slightly befuddled toiphat as they moved, so as soon as they halted Tallia set about preparing a well-banked fire while he skinned and skewered the animal. For the first time, Tallia's mouth actually watered at the thought of eating meat. She was ravenous.

Waiting impatiently for the fire to die down enough to cook the meat, she observed Tynan. He'd moved off to sit against a large stone, but his posture concerned her. He'd drawn his knees up and rested his arms across them in order to cradle his head. It was the pose of a man in pain. Tallia ached for him. Would he accept her help? His churlish behavior upon finding her this morning had made her fully aware that his attitude of the last few days remained unchanged, and she was apprehensive of his reaction.

Hesitantly, she rose and closed the distance between them. Longing and compassion swelled within her breast and she reached out to touch him. Only at the last instant did she remember that he might not take her touch kindly. Her hand faltered, hovering above his shoulder. "Tynan, are you hurt?"

"Yes," he replied without looking up. "Something struck my head."

"Will you let me tend it?"

"Yes," he agreed.

Relief flooded her. Kneeling at his side, she slowly, gently, ran her fingers through his thick ebony hair, searching his skull. She felt him wince with discomfort as her fingers brushed the swollen lump on the left side of his head. Careful not to apply unnecessary pressure, she took a deep breath and opened her senses to his pain. Dizziness assailed her. How could he withstand such misery? Her mind probed the region. His skull was not cracked, but there were a number of ruptured blood vessels. With infinite patience, she directed the healing energy of her mind, mending as much of the damage as possible. As always, some of the healing would be left to time. Slowly, the swelling lessened and the pain diminished. She had done all that she could.

Opening her eyes, she found herself drowning in the warm depths of Tynan's emerald gaze. Hope and anticipation paralyzed her. She remained imprisoned by his heated gaze as he turned to her.

"The pain's almost gone," he murmured huskily. "Thank you."

Tallia was incapable of response. Her heart raced. Desire, heady heart-stopping desire, shone in his eyes. Then, slowly, hypnotically he leaned closer. An involuntary sigh of resignation escaped her as his lips closed over hers. Her eyes drifted shut as her senses, attuned to his nearness, soared, and all coherent thought fled.

There was only Tynan, strong, demanding, his powerful arms enfolding her, drawing her with him to the ground. Soft moans of mutual surrender punctuated their ardor as they rediscovered their passion. She gasped as his calloused hand closed over her bared breast, his thumb gently stimulating the erect nipple. Feverishly, she broke away to divest herself of her confining leather attire.

Tynan rose, his passion-darkened eyes never leaving her as he emulated her actions. Trembling with the depth of her desire, Tallia let her eyes rove over his body. He was magnificent. Euphoria swelled within her, along with the stirring of passion, and she smiled.

"Come here."

His gruff masculine voice sent shivers up her spine. His eyes glistened with a carnal hunger older than time, and Tallia could not have refused if she'd wanted to. The charged atmosphere of desire and need eddied and swirled between them. They were a man and a woman—nothing more. The warmth of his muscle-corded arms closed around her, cradling her against his heart. She closed her eyes, reveling in his sensitive, caring caress until his lips closed over hers once more.

Slowly, with infinite care, Tynan lowered her upon their discarded clothing. She was so beautiful, so giving. There were no pretensions within the depths of those crystalline eyes. He exulted in the desire he read there. Pure, unadulterated sensuality. He loved her. Gods above! He did but the words lodged in his throat.

She was so young, so impulsive. What if what she felt for him was mere infatuation? Could he stand it if, after admitting his love, she gently, but firmly, flung it back in his face? He couldn't! Then, too, what kind of life could he offer her? As a Royal Executioner he'd be away much of the time in the service of his king. She was vibrant and alive, needing love, needing a man's affection. Could he stand it if she took a lover? No! Although he loved her, he could do naught but let her go. He would cherish the time they had together. And as they soared to the heights of sensual delight, heart-wrenching pain at the realization of the limit of their time together misted his vision.

Tallia, curled contentedly at his side in the aftermath of their lovemaking, looked into his face and saw the sadness there. "Tynan? What is it?" She stroked the soft hair on his chest in an unconsciously possessive gesture.

"I was just remembering how worried I was after the quake. I thought I'd lost you." With that small truth, he effectively avoided revealing the actual cause of his disquiet.

"Well, you didn't lose me and I didn't lose you. We're together. And I'm about to fade away from starvation."

Banishing all thought of the future to the recesses of his mind, Tynan grinned. "I thought I'd appeased your appetite."

Giving him a reproving glance, negated by the answering grin on her own lips, Tallia rose to dress. "You did quite well," she responded primly. "However, the toiphat is what I need to appease my rumbling stomach."

CHAPTER SEVEN

KROGAN SURVEYED THE CRAMPED CABIN WITH distaste. He'd been waiting three days for word of his wastelander hirelings and, although the cabin was kept meticulously clean by two quiet, unobtrusive servants, the rudimentary quarters were less than acceptable compared to his luxurious apartments in the castle at Maurasia. Regardless of his disgust for his unacceptable surroundings, he could not tarry much longer. An extended absence this far from Maurasia could rouse speculation, which was what he had tried to avoid by keeping his association with the less desireable elements of society unknown.

Thus far, the private meetings in this remote wooded area bordering the northwestern edge of the wasteland had remained secret, mostly because Flagan had handled them. But Flagan had been assigned to the more important task of monitoring every move made by Krogan's beloved uncle, King Quillan.

But Krogan was tempting fate by remaining too long. The nearby town of Lamos was relatively prosperous for a border town, and there was much traffic in the area. He didn't want to chance someone recognizing him. He would order Flagan to find another rendezvous place after this engagement.

A hesitant knocking on the door roused Krogan from his morose reflections. "Enter," he commanded, welcoming the diversion.

A short, unkempt, rather portly fellow entered the cabin. Krogan, ever the fastidious lord, was careful to maintain his distance, unobtrusively brushing his nose with a perfumed handkerchief to counter the offensive odor of the man. "What is it, Dack?"

"One of your men contacted me in Lamos and asked me to bring him to meet with you."

Bodan at last? "Send him in immediately."

"Yes, my lord," the man responded with noticeable relief as he backed out of the room.

Krogan smiled humorlessly, his men's obvious fear of him satisfying.

Within seconds, the door opened once more. The condition of the second man was enough to make the first appear almost clean. He was tall, although he slouched noticeably, and thin, with a bobbing larynx.

"What's your name?" Krogan demanded irritably. Another new man! He would have to be careful that he did not begin to lose control of them. Where was Bodan? Flagan had assured Krogan that he'd ordered Bodan to remain an observer in the proceedings.

"Rizo, my lord."

"Where is Bodan?"

"Dead, my lord."

"Drop the 'my lord,' for a time, and give me a full report on the proceedings with the girl," Krogan ordered impatiently.

"Yes, my lord. I mean—" He eyed Krogan nervously.

Krogan clenched his fists, stifling the inclination to invade the man's mind for the details he wanted. He had to use his power with discretion, for to let the extent of his abilities become widely known too soon could jeopardize all his plans. In the past he'd let his anger and impatience overpower him and only by using the fear of those who'd witnessed those incidents had he managed to preserve his scheme, and to control his men. He took a deep breath. "Continue, Rizo."

"Well, we caught them unawares just before dawn as ordered. That Tynan fellow put up quite a fight, but we handled him. Then, we proceeded with the girl as ordered." Rizo paused uncertainly. "You won't believe the rest," he stated with conviction.

"I assure you, Rizo, I will. What happened with the girl?"

Hesitantly, and then with more confidence as he noted that Lord Krogan listened attentively, Rizo launched into an animated and descriptive account of their encounter in the wasteland. Bodan was the only one who'd actually been killed by the sorcer-

159

ess, he assured Krogan. Nevertheless, Rizo was
certain that she was a sorceress. Who else could kill
in such a manner?

"Who indeed?" Krogan mused, a speculative
gleam lighting his eyes. "Anything else?"

Rizo concluded by detailing his own narrow
brush with death in the form of a monstrous
demon-beast, and his heroic attempt to save the life
of his poor comrade before the man was impaled
upon the beast's rapier-sharp horn.

Fully aware of the wastelanders' characters,
Krogan was certain no such attempt had been made,
but it mattered little. He had the information he
required. Bodan had disobeyed his orders only to
observe and paid with his life. Appropriate.

"That's about all, my lord."

Krogan nodded abstractedly, his mind already
straying in other directions. "Dismissed." He barely heard the closing of the door as Rizo backed out
of the room.

So, there *was* another contender to the throne to
rid himself of. The fact that Quillan had never
officially proclaimed his nephew Krogan as his heir
had raised suspicions in Krogan's mind. Krogan
had undertaken a search through his network of
informants for children who displayed unusual
abilities, abilities connected only with the royal
bloodline. That search had lead to Tallia of the
House of Darnaz in the Fiefdom of the Twin Suns.
To verify his suspicions, Krogan had devised a
brutal test, utilizing the wasteland animal, Bodan.
He had instructed Flagan to give Bodan a set of
false names, names which Krogan had invented,

and to tell Bodan that Flagan needed to confirm that these were Tallia's real parents. Of course, Tallia could not possibly give Bodan the names Krogan sought. The test had been designed merely to provoke an instinctive response from one of royal blood. The result had confirmed Krogan's suspicion. She was Quillan's daughter, a contender for the throne. .

Taking a seat, Krogan pondered the ramifications of his discovery. He'd been a young boy when the goddess, Coran, had first appeared to him in a dream and had revealed to him the full extent of the power he possessed. Grandiose pictures of godlike reverence bestowed upon him by his people had been painted by her in his boyish mind. "Learn to wield your powers," she had said, "and all of Karaundo will one day be ours."

According to Coran, to gain the monarchy of Karaundo, he had to defeat a contender for the throne in psychic combat. This rival would be a direct descendant of the royal bloodline's House of Tuhan. When that had been accomplished, he would become Coran's right hand.

She'd stated that she had disobeyed the rules of the game when she'd revealed the nature of his abilities, allowing him to practice using them and becoming proficient in wielding them. His opponent had no such knowledge.

For a while, Krogan had been blinded to her ambition by her beauty and the forbidden knowledge she continued to impart through his dreams. But as he grew older, he no longer liked the idea of sharing the rule of Karaundo with the goddess of

161

sorcery. Oh, certainly he had Coran's intervention to thank for his powers. But why should he share with Coran that which was his by right? As long as he never fought a "psychic" battle with an heir possessing powers equal to his own, the terms of Coran's prophetic encounter could never be fulfilled. And so, he'd attempted to insure that none of Quillan's heirs had survived infancy. Obviously, he'd failed. Still, the monarchy would come to him anyway once his cousin, Tallia of the House of Darnaz, was dead. Who, other than his beloved nephew, would King Quillan name?

Tallia Darnaz of the Fiefdom of the Twin Suns would have to die without ever knowing the reason why. Her abilities decreed that she would have to be killed from a distance. The deed would involve careful planning. He refused to risk fulfilling the prophecy by facing her himself.

Tallia basked in contentment as the last two days had been almost idyllic. Tynan had been as attentive and caring as a man of his solitary nature could be, and she was now certain that lovemaking was a very addictive habit. Not wanting to destroy her happiness, she firmly pushed aside all thought of the ever-nearing end of the journey.

As though echoing her thoughts, Tynan's rich baritone broke the silence. "We'll be in Lamos tonight."

For an instant, she stared at him blankly. So soon? She'd hoped to enjoy the wasteland solitude longer, away from the intrusion of others. "Lamos?" she echoed.

"Mmhmm," he responded, turning to scrutinize their trail.

"That's only about a day from Twin Suns. Isn't it?"

Sensing her anxiety, and feeling the same turbulent emotions himself, he met her gaze compassionately. "One day," he murmured. "You'll be home tomorrow evening."

"Oh," she whispered. It was too soon. She needed more time. She was certain that, somehow, in some way, Tynan's life path coincided with hers but she hadn't determined how to convince him of that. All she knew was that he was important to her future, and that she needed him.

Total silence spread between them for the next few miles as each became immersed in melancholy thoughts of parting. Finally, Tynan spoke, "I'd really like to know what you did to scare Jenk so badly."

Tallia frowned and chewed her bottom lip. She thought he'd forgotten about that. Reflectively, she gazed off into the distance. How could she disclose the nature of what had happened in a way that would be plausible?

"Why don't you want to tell me?"

She sighed. "You won't believe me," she stated matter-of-factly. "You'll think I'm insane."

"I'd never think you insane, Tallia. I promise to reserve judgment, all right?"

Uncertain as to the wisdom of her telling him, Tallia began to relate the happenings on the day of the quake. She stopped occasionally, looking at Tynan quizzically, but his expression remained impassive. "Well, anyway," she began the conclusion of her fantastic tale, "Galacia seemed confident that you would survive, so I stayed with her until the quake ended. Actually, even longer than that. She seemed to want to make sure that all the aftershocks were over before she took me back to the cliff area."

"Why do you constantly say *she seemed*?" Tynan interrupted.

"I couldn't hear her when she spoke."

"Why?"

"I have no idea," Tallia frowned in consternation. "I could see her lips move, but I heard nothing."

Tynan nodded. "What happened then?"

"Well, Luma and I just followed Galacia, traveling back toward the east. Finally, I could see the cliff beneath us. You know what that looked like. I didn't see Jenk there, so when Galacia signaled that it was safe to leave, we did."

"Descending from the sky, as it were," Tynan stated. That's how Jenk had described it.

"Well, yes, but Galacia controlled the descent. If she hadn't, we would have fallen."

"I see." She had been right. He did think she'd lost her mind. But if she'd suffered derangement, then Jenk suffered the same affliction. Was collective insanity in the aftermath of a quake possible? If Tallia and Jenk were sane, then . . . then what? Maybe the whole damned world was insane. He shook his head. It was totally beyond him to arrive at a logical conclusion.

"So what happened when Jenk saw you?" he

asked. He might as well get the complete story, although he was beginning to wish he hadn't pressed her.

"Not much," Tallia replied. "I didn't even notice him standing there in the rubble until he screamed. By then I was more than halfway down. When Luma and I . . . landed, he was sitting there, staring blankly at me. Just as he was when you arrived."

Tynan didn't really know what to think. He certainly did not believe that a goddess had intervened to save Tallia's life. But he was beginning to be aware that strange powers did exist for which he had no explanation. Tallia's encounter with Bodan had been proof of that. Perhaps some supernatural force had interceded on her behalf using the guise of the goddess, Galacia. Thrul! He didn't believe he was actually thinking these things.

"Well," Tallia prompted, "what do you think? Do you believe me?"

Tynan looked at her with a pained expression. "I don't know what to think or believe. So," he continued with determination, "I'm not going to think anything." With that decision made, he encouraged Chaz to increase his pace.

"I told you!" Tallia shouted at his back.

"Remind me of that the next time I press you for details!" he yelled over his shoulder.

Tallia grinned. At least he hadn't told her she was mad, she thought as she urged Luma to close the distance between them.

Within an hour they sighted Lamos's outskirts. Tynan halted and began removing his supplies from Chaz's back. Curiously, Tallia watched him. What was he doing? Opening his pack, he removed a few items, securing them on his body. Then, he carefully hid the remaining supplies within a small pile of boulders before walking back to Chaz. She observed him as he hugged the animal and spoke softly. Seconds later, Chaz left them, racing back into the wasteland.

Now Tynan turned to her. "Mind riding double?" he asked with an engaging grin. "Saves me walking the last mile."

"Why did you send Chaz back?" she asked incredulously.

"I didn't, he went. I plan on spending the night in town. There's no stable for faralks."

"Oh." She hadn't thought of that. "It must be very inconvenient for you at times."

"At times," he acknowledged, "but the advantages far outweigh the disadvantages."

Tallia nodded. "Still, how will you find him tomorrow when you need him again?"

Tynan shrugged. "He'll be here shortly after dawn." He grasped Luma's mane with one hand. "May I?"

"Oh, of course." Her curiosity regarding Tynan's unusual association with the faralk had made her forget his initial request to share her mount. She moved back on the gari's long back to accommodate him.

She was just beginning to enjoy the new experience of riding double, and the opportunity it afforded to hug his magnificent torso, when they entered the small border town's outskirts. In appearance, Lamos was much like Promise—perhaps a little larger, offering more services for travelers. She had been there a couple of times with her father to obtain supplies which the fiefdom did not produce.

They halted before the town's inn. A relatively large structure in comparison to most of the buildings, it appeared clean and well-kept. Tynan left her outside while he inquired as to lodging and stabling. Minutes later he emerged.

"I rented two rooms for the night. Yours is across the hall from mine."

"Two!" exclaimed Tallia. "Why two?" Almost immediately she bit her lip in consternation. Dayna's influence had not been *all* good. She was becoming much too forward.

"You're very near home, Tallia. I thought it best. It's possible you may meet someone you know."

"Oh." So, he was worried about her reputation, was he? That should have been her concern. Should have been, but wasn't. She didn't care a pentar for her reputation right now. She would worry about it later. What she wanted was one last night in his magnificent bronzed arms.

"Here's the key," he said. "Take your supplies and go on. I ordered baths for both of us. I'll take Luma and the cubs around back."

A bath! A real bath! The mere thought transported her into blissful anticipation. "All right. Will you come get me for the evening meal?"

"Yes," he responded.

Two hours later, clean and replete after sharing a delicious meal that included vegetables, Tallia settled back in her chair to enjoy Tynan's company.

Rising, he walked to the window and looked down on the street below. "I'm afraid I'll have to send you back to your room for a while Tallia. I have some things to take care of."

"What things?"

"Business," he replied curtly.

"Oh."

The haunted expression that she'd seen less and less frequently of late, except at sunset—it was always there at sunset when he retreated into solitude—was back in his eyes. Still, whatever bothered him, he didn't want compassion. That part of him remained locked away and she was at a loss as to how to breach the wall he'd constructed to contain his suffering.

"Certainly," she responded softly as she rose. "I'll see you later then."

"Later." She'd reached the door when he abruptly spoke again. "Tallia?" His voice sounded slightly strangled.

"Yes?"

"I . . ." he paused, clearing his throat. "To reach Twin Suns from here, ride due east until you reach a shallow gully. Then, follow the ravine north."

Her eyes widened in alarm. "Why are you telling me this?"

He shrugged fatalistically. "You probably won't need to know. Forget it."

She eyed him uneasily for a moment, but he remained silent, his gaze once more riveted on the street below. Forget it! She couldn't forget it. What kind of business did he have to take care of anyway? Slowly, thoughtfully, she opened the door and crossed the hall to her own chamber.

Standing with her ear pressed to the door, she listened for the sound of Tynan's departure. Whatever his business was, if it meant he might not return, she intended to know about it. A few minutes later she heard his measured tread on the floor boards outside. Carefully, she opened her door a crack to observe him as he moved down the hall. As soon as he'd turned the corner to descend the stairs, she followed.

Tallia stood in the shadows between the tavern and a bathhouse. Tynan's business had taken him into the tavern. Every once in a while, when the street was clear of pedestrians, she moved around front to peer cautiously through the window. What kind of business involved entering a tavern, finding a table in the rear of the room, and sitting drinking alone? He'd been in there almost an hour and the last time she'd looked nothing had changed. The firm tread of booted feet on the boardwalk made her duck back quickly. Oh well, she could wait. As long as Tynan's business remained so uneventful, she didn't have to worry.

Tynan sipped from his second mug of rastan. The people in this town seemed to be more accustomed to the presence of wastelanders. No one had yet made any comment about his appearance, though a pair of ladies *had* crossed the street to avoid meeting him. Oh well, it was part of the job which reminded him that he would have to go to Maurasia for a meeting with King Quillan upon leaving Tallia. Damn! The thought of parting was painful.

169

With determination, he once more turned his attention to the tavern clientele. He'd studied the hands of every man present. All of them possessed the normal number of fingers. What would he do if Four-Finger didn't show up? He had to assume that Dack would be a regular client, since his contact with wastelanders could not be scheduled. Tynan hadn't wanted to consider that Dack might not show today, but it was now beginning to look like he should have considered that possibility. Bored, he began digging the dirt out of the gouges in the table with the point of his dagger. He'd wait another hour. No more.

The banging of the door signaled a new arrival, a short, slightly overweight, filthy man. Moving to the bar, rather than to a table, he ordered a bottle. He did not wear a wastelander's garb but something in his swagger prompted Tynan's scrutiny. His patience was rewarded. The hand that grasped the bottle had only four fingers. So, this was Dack.

Another man entered and took a seat at one of the tables near the door. Tynan gave him only a cursory glance before picking up his mug and moving to the bar. Taking up a casual position near Dack, he cleared his throat. "You're Four-Finger Dack, aren't you?" he asked conversationally.

"Who's asking?" the man growled.

"Keane."

"We met before, Keane?"

"No. A fellow told me about you."

"Yes. What fellow might that be?"

"Sal."

At this, Dack turned to look at him for the first

time. "Where was this?"

"The wasteland."

Dack was obviously curious now, his lips curling in an attempt at a smile, but his eyes remaining cold. In fact, they were a pair of the iciest eyes Tynan had ever seen. The only word capable of describing them was "soulless." This man, he suspected, had no conscience.

"What did Sal have to say?" Dack queried with a measure of wariness, before tilting the bottle the bartender placed before him and draining a fair portion of its contents.

"Said you were looking for a woman," Tynan responded casually.

Dack snorted. "So, I like women. What of it?"

Tynan ignored his comment. "If I had in my possession the particular woman Sal told me about," he paused to let the words sink in. "Who would I deliver her to for payment?"

"Don't know what you're talking about," the man growled, lifting the bottle to his lips again.

"I think you do."

"Even if I did, couldn't tell you."

"Why?"

Dack shrugged. The half bottle of liquor he'd drunk during their conversation seemed to be affecting him. Yet, not even inebriation could mask the trace of fear Tynan saw momentarily in the man's expression.

"You're afraid of him!" Tynan remarked with forced incredulity, baiting him. Most men of Dack's caliber did not admit fear easily.

Four-Finger's eyes narrowed menacingly, but he

said nothing, refusing to rise to the bait.

"You won't tell me his name."

"Uh–uh," Dack shook his head emphatically. "Say," he remarked, an expression of drunken cunning on his face, "if you got this girl, how do you know she isn't runnin' away right now?"

"I tied her up at the inn," Tynan lied absently. He felt instinctively that Dack's leader was the same one who had controlled Bodan's group two years ago. If this leader inspired such fear in all his men, it would explain why Tynan had had so much difficulty learning his identity. Once again he seemed to be getting nowhere. Firmly, he tamped down his impatience. "Can you tell me where to find him?"

"Who?" Four-Finger frowned in puzzlement, having lost the thread of the conversation.

"Your boss."

Dack shook his head. "Not until you're cleared."

"What do you mean, cleared?"

"I tell him what you look like, who you are, where you been. He decides."

"I see." Well, infiltrating the group, even if he found a pretext other than Tallia, was out of the question. If the man had been the same one who'd ordered his family killed, he'd recognize Tynan before long. The family members of the House of Keane were unmistakable in their resemblance to each another. Somehow, he *had* to get Dack to reveal the man's name.

"Say, you look kinda familiar," Dack remarked as he stared at Tynan with alcohol-fogged concentration. "You sure we never met before?"

Tynan grinned mirthlessly. So, Dack remembered the faces of those he killed. It was more than he could say for most of the men who'd participated in slaying Tynan's family two years ago. He'd had to inform a good many of them as to the reason for their death sentence.

"Positive," Tynan responded with finality. He'd have to divert the man quickly back to the conversation. If they talked long enough, perhaps Four-Finger Dack would become drunk enough to forget his fear of his leader. "If I can't take the girl to him, what do I do with her? There're lots of greedy fellows in the world who might try to steal her for the payment."

"Ah, I don't think you need to worry about that," Dack responded with careful enunciation, trying valiantly to appear sober. "Nobody knows he wants her but a few of us."

"And I don't have to worry about you?" Tynan asked with just a trace of disbelief.

"Sure you do. Why d'you think I'm standin' here talkin' to you," Dack replied, abandoning enunciation, as he leaned forward conspiratorially, almost knocking Tynan over with his breath. "I'm pumpin' you for information," he admitted.

"I see." This conversation was going absolutely nowhere. "And have I given you any?"

"Sure ya"—he belched loudly—"'ave. I'm good at it you know. Even better when"—another belch—"I 'aven't been drinkin'."

Tynan nodded. He had to extract the information he needed from Dack before he executed him. But how? He retreated into thought. It was a mistake, for once more Dack took to studying him.

Suddenly, Dack banged down his bottle. "I know you," he growled. "And you're no wastelander."

Tynan tensed, the wariness that had become so inherent to his survival coming to the fore. "Oh?" he responded casually, in an attempt to preserve the conversation. He didn't want to execute a drunken man. It wouldn't be right, somehow. "What makes you say that?"

"You said your name was Keane. But it's Tynan. I heard about you trackin' us . . ." He paused and craftiness entered his expression. "You goin' to fight me, Tynan? I live here you know. People know me. They don't know you."

Tynan shook his head. Dack's time would come, but not here, not now. He'd been patient for two years, a little more time meant nothing to him. He wanted this man in the wasteland where he would become the animal he was. He'd hoped to lure him to a midnight rendezvous on some pretext or other, but discovering the identity of the man who'd engineered the deaths of his family had become almost an obsession. Obviously, his persistence in that direction had been a grave error. Now what?

"Your mum was good," Dack whispered hoarsely.

Tynan looked up sharply, his cold emerald gaze pinning the man.

"Ha, got your attention now, do I?" He paused, waiting for a reaction. There was none. "Told you I liked women. Ye're mum was the first *lady* I ever had. Soft." He shook his head in disgust. "They die too fast."

Tynan grit his teeth, the pain and anguish assailing him like a volley of arrows. "We'll meet again," he said tightly, rising to leave. His back turned, Tynan heard the scrape of steel.

CHAPTER EIGHT

TYNAN PIVOTED AND MET FOUR-FINGER DACK'S eyes. He saw the anticipation, the lust for blood, the joy of inflicting pain all mirrored within those shallow depths. Was that the last sight his mother had seen before she died? In that instant, he pronounced Dack's sentence. Death! Almost absently, he noticed the steadiness of Dack's hand holding the broadsword. Four-Finger obviously was not as inebriated as he'd acted.

Baiting the man, Tynan turned. Every sense alert, his muscles taut, he took another step away. He wanted it to be obvious to all present who had instigated the fight. His retreat worked.

"Wastelander!" Dack shouted as he lunged.

Tynan side-stepped, turning to face the man, his own sword in hand. The room plunged into a deathly silence, and no one noticed the unobtrusive entry of a young woman, nor her movement to one side of the door from where she could freely observe the fight.

Tynan and Dack crouched slightly, circling, their weapons to the fore. Those at the tables nearest quietly and speedily vacated the area. Dack made his move, charging bullishly, relying on his burly strength to give him the advantage as he whipped his massive sword viciously back and forth. Tynan leapt aside at the instant that Dack was within reach, sending his foot flying at the wastelander's ribs. It connected, hard, but elicited only a slight grunt as the wastelander plunged past, his sword biting deeply into a table. Regardless of his weight, Dack was solid, and within seconds had regained his equilibrium.

He spun to face Tynan, rage contorting his features. Once more they circled. Again, Dack charged, hacking wildly. Tynan leapt aside, but not quickly enough. He felt the tip of the sharp blade graze his belly even as his foot connected with Dack's chin. Backing off, Dack shook his head to clear his vision, and Tynan waited, studying his opponent.

The next time Dack began his rush, Tynan sprang to meet him. The clash of metal meeting metal reverberated through the room. Hack. Block. Slash. Parry. The sound of steel on steel rang again and again through the room as muscled arms brandished the heavy weapons with apparent ease. Once more Tynan slashed and his weapon managed to break through Dack's guard. His blade cut, but not deeply enough. Dack slashed, Tynan blocked. Their weapons locked. They grappled. Muscles bulged;

tendons strained. Neither weakened.

Once more Tynan used the kick-fighting ability he'd learned from Letai. Kicking with both feet at Dack's knees, he curled his spine using his weight to pull Dack down. As he felt the floor beneath him he used the momentum to throw the man over his head. Dack's weapon flew out of his hand as he connected with the floor. Immediately, Tynan was on his feet.

"You busted my knees!" the wastelander shrieked at Tynan, rage and disbelief warring in his voice.

Slowly, Tynan moved to stand over the man, as the tavern customers, certain the fight was over, began to stir.

"You don't fight right," Four-Finger accused between moans of pain.

Tynan shrugged. For a moment, he gazed at the man at his feet. This man had debased and defiled his mother and sister. This man deserved to die. Almost casually, he removed his dagger from his waistband. Then, as though discarding the blade in his hand, he released it—with deadly accuracy.

When Tallia entered the tavern, she swore that she would not interfere unless it was to preserve Tynan's life. She'd remained tensely observant during the fight, but the two men appeared to be evenly matched. Besides, she didn't think Tynan would appreciate any help. Not that she knew what to do anyway. Yet, she knew that if Tynan's life depended on her, she'd do something. The fight appeared to be over now, and people were beginning to move around. Perhaps she should simply slip back to the inn. That way he need never know that she'd followed him. She began sidling toward the door.

Suddenly she saw one of the men in the room move but something in the man's stance halted her. Like the other patrons present, he appeared to be moving to view the man on the floor, but something was odd. He was positioning himself in a manner that would allow him to approach Tynan from behind. His right fist was tightly closed, his arm rigid.

Instinctively, Tallia slipped through the crowd, keeping him in sight. A few more feet, and she would be at Tynan's side. If only these men would move out of the way. She gasped. Behind Tynan, the man raised his arm. In his hand was a dagger. "No!" Her intended scream of warning emerged as a whisper as horror choked her voice. Her heart pounded with dread as she leapt automatically to close the distance, placing her back at Tynan's. The dagger was descending. Time stopped.

Once more she felt the heat of her Zarma stone penetrating her chest, radiating through her limbs. *I will not kill*, the thought reverberated in her brain. The power coursing through her swelled, less potent, different. With determination, she concentrated on the descending blade rather than the man wielding the weapon, attempting to channel the energy battling for release within her. She felt the effluence of a burst of puissant energy. The dagger shattered. The force of the charge radiated outward, striking the man. Helpless in the face of the psychic release, he flew back hitting the wall with enough force to rattle the windows in their panes. Sliding down the wall, he crumpled to the floor, his eyes staring blankly.

Tallia stared at him in horror. "No, not again," she moaned. "Not again."

Tynan had turned in time to witness the incident. At the sight of the man's upraised weapon, he knew instantly what was happening. Yet, before he could react, the blade disintegrated and the man, as though lifted by unseen hands, was flung forcibly away. Having witnessed Tallia's power before, he was not quite as stunned as the crowd, many of whom were simply looking around curiously, wondering what had happened. Only those closest stared speculatively at the shaken young woman standing at his side.

Grasping Tallia's hand, ignoring her almost incomprehensible muttering, he moved quickly to examine the man. He was alive. There was a pulse.

Rising, he grasped Tallia by the shoulders, shaking her slightly, forcing her to focus on him. "It's all right. He's alive," he whispered hoarsely.

Confused, she looked from him to the man on the floor and back again. "H–he is?" Hope warred with disbelief in her trembling voice.

"He is," he assured her. "Come on. Let's get back to the inn." Grasping her hand once more, he pulled her through the milling crowd to the door.

By the time they reached the inn, Tallia had calmed.

"What were you doing there?" Tynan demanded as he halted before the building.

"I was worried about you. You made it sound as if you might not return. I just wanted to make certain you did. I didn't interfere until it was absolutely necessary, Tynan."

He gazed at her thoughtfully for a moment, then nodding, he opened the door to the inn and guided her inside.

Tallia automatically followed Tynan to his chamber, was only vaguely aware of his movement about the room as she withdrew her Zarma stone from its place of concealment beneath her tunic. Absently, she studied the smooth lavender stone; her fingers caressed the surface, warm from the heat of her body. Why had she never suspected its power? Why had Eyrsa not prepared her for the eventuality? She sighed, perplexed. The cord from which the stone dangled was becoming frayed. It would have to be replaced soon or she'd lose it. Thoughtfully, she removed the cord from about her neck and placed the stone gently on the night stand.

She turned to observe Tynan who sat with an air of deep despondency upon the edge of the bed. Hesitantly, she moved to join him. She couldn't begin to understand what had happened tonight, and having witnessed Tynan's killing a man bothered her. Yet, she knew within her that Tynan was good.

The bed moved slightly beneath her weight but he didn't even seem aware of her. Compassion brimmed in her eyes as the sight of the exhaustion and despair in his expression tore at her heart. With gentle fingers, she reached to massage his tense shoulders. He appeared oblivious to her ministrations but patiently, she waited. Perhaps tonight he would talk to her, let her share his burden— whatever it might be.

Tynan clenched his fists. He was so tired of it. Tired of it all, the endless traveling, the gutwrenching need for revenge, the death and killing. Would it never end? Goddess above! How he missed his home! And yet, his brief visits there brought nothing but pain. He had only to stroll through the vast hall of Ravencrest to hear the voices of his mother and father raised in loving banter. Could he ever go home? Or would he forever hear Tynara's vibrant laughter echoing within those sturdy stone walls?

Gradually he became aware of the delicate touch of kneading fingers easing the tension from his muscles. Tallia. How he loved her! Could he declare his love? Ask her to wait for the time when he could make her his wife? No, it would be unfair to her.

Slowly, he turned to meet her unusual crystalline gaze. There was compassion there, a deeper empathy than he'd ever seen in another's eyes. Confusion and inquiry were mirrored there as well. But was there love? He didn't know. He reached to stroke her soft cheek.

"Beautiful Tallia," he murmured, and suddenly he realized he wanted to share his secret. And if there be condemnation or pity in her gaze, so be it. Tomorrow would be their last day together anyway.

Rising, he avoided her gaze and touch as he strode to the window. Looking sightlessly at the street below, he wondered how to begin. It was difficult. In two years he'd rarely spoken their names. Hesitantly, he began to speak. "My father was Torden. Torden of the House of Keane in the Fiefdom of Ravencrest, senior advisor to King Quillan." He paused, remembering.

The silence stretched, and Tallia was afraid to utter a sound lest he not resume.

"He was ailing," Tynan murmured. "Had been for quite some time. The king had tried to help him, but there is little call for the healing abilities of a king, so Quillan was no longer as accomplished as he once was. And the palace Zarmists were useless. Finally the king, distressed at my father's illness, for they were friends, ordered him to seek out an accomplished healer—a Zarmist in a fiefdom across the wasteland. He believed this woman was extremely accomplished." Tynan turned to look at her. Seated quietly on the bed, she listened attentively. "I believe this woman was your governess. But we never reached the fiefdom."

Tallia's eyes widened with surprise at his pronouncement, but she refused to interrupt his tale with distracting questions. Watching the play of emotions crossing his handsome features, she waited. His expression became bleak, and from his lips issued a tale more horrific than anything Tallia could have imagined. His terse description painted vivid scenes of dreadful carnage on the canvas of her mind.

Tynan spared himself nothing. The most minute details of that sight had been engraved in his memory. And though his throat grew tight, he spoke on, relentlessly.

Silent tears rolled down Tallia's cheeks as she listened. It was if the wall, once breached, had crumbled into dust and now, the story must be told in its entirety.

"I watched the sun set in the horizon as I held my dying sister in my arms. That sunset was the only beauty left in that ravaged landscape. Only when darkness fell could I let her go. Her body was stiff and cold. Tynara was no longer there." He choked, unashamedly brushing the tears from his face as he continued to stare blindly through the window.

"She always loved the sunset. I shared that last one with her, and almost every one since. She'd been defiled and beaten and yet, her final thought was of me. 'Live, Tynan . . . live for us both,' she said."

He turned to Tallia, suddenly realizing that her understanding did matter. "But how could I?" he asked. "The knowledge that the animals who'd murdered my family lived was like a cancer in my gut. The need to avenge the honor of the House of Keane became an obsession." He fell silent. There was little change in Tallia's expression. She continued to gaze at him compassionately. Did she understand what drove him? Could she ever comprehend? "The man you saw me kill in the tavern tonight was one of those who raped and murdered my mother. Bodan was also one of the men. Two others remain. One of those is the leader, the man who ordered my family butchered. I *will* find him."

He leaned against the wall, staring across the room in silence for a very long time. Tallia thought perhaps he would say no more. She was at a loss. What could she say or do that would have meaning? "Sorry" was such an inadequate word. It conveyed nothing of how she felt. Shocked and horrified, yes. But, too, she felt that she understood at least a small measure of his grief. Vengeance? Well, perhaps she did not understand that. But would she, if it had been her family? Probably.

"I'd been trained as a royal guard when I was

younger," Tynan resumed quietly. "King Quillan, perhaps sensing that Ravencrest was no longer the place for me, offered me a permanent position. I declined, for by then I knew what had to be done. And, when he asked my reason for refusal, I told him truthfully. It was then that he made me an offer I couldn't refuse.

"It seemed that the lack of lawful influence in the wasteland and border towns had long been worrying him. He'd begun assembling men of honorable character to whom he granted absolute authority to dispense justice in those lawless areas. I became a member of this elite guild, a Royal Executioner." He stopped briefly, half expecting to see a look of horror on her face, but her expression hadn't altered.

"Few are even aware of our presence but we exist, and our numbers grow." His voice became impassioned. "One day, the land will be unified under our laws. It will not fall to the lords of the fiefdoms to fortify themselves against marauding bands. The border towns will be peaceful, not subject to the raids of those who take pleasure in fear. And the wasteland will be a place of serenity. Wild, forever changing. But the only danger will be from nature."

Tallia rose and walked toward him. "It is a noble vision," she said softly as she wrapped her arms about his lean waist, burying her face against his chest. There was nothing else she could say. The horrors he had described continued to replay in her mind. What could she possibly say to help ease his pain? Tynan enveloped her soft form in his arms.

"You're still bleeding," she said, touching the long slash on his belly.

He nodded silently, seating himself.

Tallia gently bathed the wound, then once more performed the healing ritual that Tynan was becoming accustomed to. It was only later, when she returned the basin of water to the stand that she realized she had performed the service without the directing influence of the Zarma stone. The small mauve talisman rested undisturbed on the stand where she had left it earlier. Had her abilities so surpassed those of other Zarmists then? How was it possible? Yet, the question seemed somehow insignificant at this point. She filed it away at the bottom of a growing list to ask Eyrsa when she reached home.

Tynan observed her as she moved gracefully about the room. When she returned to his side to be cuddled once more, he opened his arms willingly. She said nothing more about all that he had revealed. Did she understand? Had she judged him and found him lacking? Was her very silence condemnation of the path he trod in service to his king? He didn't know, and he could not bring himself to ask, but she offered compassion, and that he could not refuse. Tonight, for the last time, he would bury himself within her soft, scented body, and for a time he would forget.

That night, sated with Tynan's lovemaking, Tallia slept deeply and dreamed. It was a replay of a brief time when she'd ventured out from the college without permission in order to witness a royal procession.

The city hummed with a life and a pulse all its own. Tallia found herself fascinated by the vibrancy of the people she observed. From her vantage point on the hill that housed the palace, she viewed the entire city of Maurasia as it sprawled in the valley below and flanked the shore of Lake Randalia.

The first carriage of the royal procession conveyed the pages. Resplendent in bronze-toned apparel, each page held a corner of an enlarged replica of the Scroll of Peace. Conceived and inducted by Toleme, the first king of Karaundo, the scroll contained the major laws of the land which incorporated the beliefs of equality, liberty, and harmony, and advocated that all rulers, from the king down to the lords of the fiefdoms, should govern by the means of clement guidance.

The next coach carried squires garbed in deep forest green trimmed with gold. Each ceremonially held a feathered quill to a facsimile of the Royal Chronicles which recorded the births, deaths, and major accomplishments of the citizens of Karaundo. Also initiated by King Toleme, the practice spanned hundreds of years. The actual volumes of the royal chronicles would occupy many shelves in the palace library.

Her eyes moved beyond the squires to the third conveyance. The buglers had now reached the gates, and the procession halted. Guards dismounted with a regal flare and swept wide the orifice. Royal flag bearers, eyes forward, sat erect upon copper-furred gari. Even the enormous felines seemed composed, resting quietly beneath their riders as the flags flapped languidly over their heads. The lone occupant of the third carriage rose and bowed.

Tallia was not disappointed when the carriage

conveyed not the king, but his nephew. Lord Krogan was expected to be the next to occupy the throne and he was commonly heralded as the heir.

As she watched his gracious bows and ready smile, Tallia felt a shiver of precognition. She sensed a peculiarity beneath the veneer of magnanimity. For a fleeting instant, Tallia sensed malevolence, and that Krogan was not what he seemed to be.

Abruptly, Tallia woke. Perspiration soaked her limbs and uneasiness fogged her mind. The dream had been much more vivid than the reality, yet the two became intertwined, inseparable. The dream prompted and intensified her distrust of Lord Krogan's character. But what significance did it have?

The next morning at dawn, after a restless night's sleep, they left the inn and Lamos. Chaz waited near the concealed supplies. Wordlessly, Tynan saddled Chaz and mounted, once more taking the lead. They spoke little throughout the day. Neither knew what to say. It was late afternoon when they left the wasteland, emerging into the meadowed terrain that bordered the fiefdom.

Twin Suns sprawled lazily at the foot of Mount Coran. Overhead, scattered clouds cast elongated shadows across the neat swaths that patterned the golden fields of late autumn. Lee of the mountain stood Darnaz castle, its stone walls the color of molten lead draped in flame as the sun burnished the masses of clinging ivy crimson. Huge stone cairns bordered the main entry to the fiefdom and before them stood a woman.

"Eyrsa!" Tallia shouted joyously. Her eyes shining, and forgetting all but the moment, she turned to Tynan smiling happily. "Look Tynan, it's her."

He smiled indulgently. "How can you tell from this distance?"

"It's her. I know it is." She urged Luma to a faster pace.

He let her go, watching as she raced across the prairie and dismounted, enthusiastically embracing her beloved governess. When he reached the gate, they were conversing in low tones. So, this was Eyrsa. He studied the old woman who was stooped and frail in appearance. Yet, when she met his gaze he felt her vigor and strength.

She came forward. "Tallia tells me your name is Tynan."

"That's right, my lady," he replied respectfully.

"Eyrsa," she said briskly. "Just Eyrsa." She surprised him somewhat by fearlessly taking hold of Chaz's horn to hold the beast's head. "I'm informed we owe you two hundred gold pentars for your services as escort."

Tynan shifted his gaze to Tallia. She stood apart, looking fragile and uncertain. Their parting was taking its toll on her as well. The thought that she cared for him gladdened his heart. Perhaps it wasn't love, but she *did* care.

He turned his attention back to Eyrsa. "There's no charge, my lady."

"Eyrsa!" she snapped, meeting his gaze, holding it. Time passed with interminable slowness as he looked into those ancient eyes. He had the uncomfortable feeling that she could perceive the very essence of his being. Abruptly, she nodded sharply. "I thank you for delivering Tallia safely," her voice had softened noticeably. "Will you at least accept our hospitality as payment?"

"Thank you, but I must be going."

"Farewell then, Tynan, until you return."

"I will not be returning," he responded hesitantly, wondering if something Tallia had said had created such a misconception.

Once more, Eyrsa looked deeply into his eyes. "Yes, Tynan," she murmured, "you will."

Her certainty left him slightly unsettled. "Farewell." Once more he met Tallia's gaze, pausing expectantly. Would she reveal some indication of her feeling for him? His throat grew tight. Lifting one hand in a brief wave, he pivoted Chaz and headed toward the wasteland.

Sadly, Tallia watched his departure, unaware that Eyrsa observed and interpreted the play of emotions on her face.

A deep sense of loneliness penetrated her soul; a part of her felt suddenly empty. He had come to mean a great deal to her, and yet there had been no way to ask him to stay; nothing could have deterred him from his duty. A part of her understood that. She was home now. His task was done. He could ride away and forget. She blinked back the tears that dampened her long lashes. Agonizingly she watched as he commanded the faralk to a gallop. The dark wastelander on a midnight-black beast faded from her life just as he faded from sight beyond Twin Suns' rolling hills.

Tallia drew herself up proudly and lifted her head. Forcing a tight smile for Eyrsa's benefit, she took the dear old lady's arm and, leaving Luma to follow complacently, they turned toward the castle. "Did you tell Father that I was coming home?"

Eyrsa shook her head. "He'll know soon enough," she responded, lifting her eyes to the imposing building before them. "He'll know soon enough."

CHAPTER NINE

SENSING TALLIA'S NEED TO BE ALONE, EYRSA HESI-
tated at the door. "Look to the animal, then
come to my room. We will talk before we
distract your parents from their work. Once they've
overcome the shock of your homecoming, I'm
certain they'll monopolize you for the remainder of
the evening."

Tallia nodded, a slight smile curving her lips as
she envisioned the evening ahead of demanded
explanations followed by a boisterous reunion.
Luma growled impatiently, and she patted the
gari's neck. "Yes, Luma. We're home." She turned,
absently letting the lines go slack as the cat headed
for the stable.

Inside, she removed the saddle and draped it
across the tack rail. Luma's cubs, freed from the
saddle pouches, tottered unsteadily underfoot.

Scooping them up, she led Luma to her enclosure. Contented now, the cat dropped down onto the thick bed of straw and stretched out to nurse the cubs Tallia placed beside her.

"I wish I was as glad the journey is over as you seem to be," Tallia whispered as she knelt to stroke the soft fur of a cub. Luma replied with a loud throaty purr.

Tynan's presence filled her mind. His face, his voice, his movements, characteristic of only him, were painfully vivid.

Tallia rose. Wearily, she retrieved her pack and left the building, gazing around as she crossed the graveled path to the main house. Nothing had changed, yet she found herself viewing her surroundings with different eyes. The thick grass, fawn-colored in the waning autumn, the garden's trellis arch visible through the bared vines of the climbing roses, the paths strewn with golden leaves were part of the Twin Suns she loved. Yet, as she looked beyond the safety and security that it represented, it suddenly seemed listlessly hollow. Was she allowing her mood to influence her perceptions? Her eyes wandered again to the crest of the hill where Tynan had faded from sight.

Forget him, she commanded silently, trying to force the memory of his face from her thoughts. "Forget as he surely will," she muttered bleakly.

She mounted the steps and entered the keep. Sounds of meal preparations issued from the direction of the kitchen, but the wide main hall was deserted. The door to her father's study was closed, as it almost always was at this time of day. Her mother would be overseeing the kitchen staff before retiring to her chamber for a short rest before the evening meal. Silently, Tallia crossed to the corridor that lead to Eyrsa's chamber.

Although she had missed her family dreadfully, she was quite willing to postpone her reunion with them for a short while. Her father would not be pleased by her unexpected return and she had her list of questions she wanted to ask Eyrsa. Besides, as Eyrsa had said, they would deal with her father soon enough. Lamplight spilled from beneath Eyrsa's door, for dusk approached quickly in these autumn days. Tallia quietly opened the thick oaken portal and entered the room, dropping her supplies.

Eyrsa sat patiently before her writing desk, her eyes closed and Tallia noted the dark circles beneath them. Was her frailty more pronounced? Perhaps having not seen Eyrsa for so long had just made the changes more noticeable.

"You're ill, aren't you?" she murmured, concern creasing her smooth brow.

Eyrsa's eyes fluttered open at her words. "I'm fine. Just tired." A faint apologetic smile accompanied her words.

"I came as quickly as I could." Tallia explained, crossing the room to kneel at Eyrsa's feet.

Eyrsa nodded as she reached to stroke Tallia's sable hair. Her blue-gray eyes glazed slightly and she stared past Tallia thoughtfully. Finally, as if gaining strength from the girl's presence, she stood. "Sit." The Zarmist indicated the edge of the bed.

Tallia did as she was bidden. Patiently, she waited for Eyrsa to put her thoughts into words.

"Before we confront your parents, I wished to

speak to you alone. I didn't summon you because of my health," the elderly woman began hesitantly. "A foretelling . . ." She paused.

"What did you see?" Tallia prompted in a hushed whisper. The consternation that lined Eyrsa's face betrayed her anxiety.

"I saw your life threatened in a vision." Eyrsa shook her head as though eradicating the worry. "What I saw does not have to come to pass. Only if things remain unaltered will the outcome of the vision be unchanged. It is important that you know that. We can change the future. Dreams are only symbolic. There is time. You must make use of that time."

Tallia listened solemnly. Had the wastelanders' attack been a part of Eyrsa's vision? The swaying apparition of Bodan's shocked, contorted face shifted into her thoughts. Guilt and remorse racked Tallia's mind. "I killed him," she whispered almost inaudibly.

Eyrsa's head snapped up. "What?"

Having no need to shield her emotions from Eyrsa, Tallia lifted her face, repeating her admission. "I said I killed him. The man in the wasteland. The one who attacked me." Shock and confusion laced her tone, but there were no tears, only a heavy knot of guilt in the pit of her stomach. "He kept asking who my parents were. I felt a power coursing through me. It escaped me. I . . . I raised my hand and I killed . . ." Her voice faltered.

Eyrsa's jaw tightened; her eyes narrowed. So there was more than had been revealed to her. Did someone suspect Tallia's identity? The need to complete Tallia's training in the "key" became more urgent. But how had Tallia killed?

She moved to sit beside Tallia, enfolding her within the comfort of her embrace. "What do you mean, you raised your hand?" she questioned carefully.

"I didn't touch him. I just raised my hand." Tallia turned to Eyrsa, her pale gray eyes pleading for comfort and understanding. "I could feel his heart in the palm of my hand, as though it rested there. I hated him. I hated what he was doing to me, what he did to Tynan." She choked out the words. "I envisioned his heart there. I felt it. I closed my hand and I crushed the life from it with my mind." As though confirming her explanation, Tallia nodded conclusively. "I killed him."

Eyrsa sat silent, shocked. Never had she heard of the power being so strong. Never strong enough to kill. Rising, she began to pace the room with renewed energy. "Take your things." She gestured to Tallia's packs resting, forgotten, near the door. "You've had a long journey. You need rest and nourishment. There's a tray of food in your room. Eat it and sleep for a time. In a short while, we'll speak with your parents. Then, we'll see if we can make any sense of this." She guided Tallia firmly to the door.

Eyrsa needed time to think. The girl was distraught, reasonably so, but she must be encouraged to recall the events exactly. Eyrsa would wait until she'd rested. Meanwhile, she would contemplate the ramifications of Tallia's story.

Tallia nibbled halfheartedly at the food left for her before exhaustion claimed her. Fully clothed, and ignoring the chill of her room, she crawled onto her bed and curled into a ball beneath the thick overspread.

As Tallia slept, Eyrsa rummaged through Arilan's library, pulling down volume after volume, thumbing through yellowed pages but finding no answers to the myriad of questions that swirled through her mind. There was no reference, no mention of such a lethal ability. Yet she knew Tallia and believed what she had said. The method would be similar to the healing process—the envisioning of the infected area, the reconstruction with thought, only in reverse.

Eyrsa glanced around for something to experiment with. Outside, across the courtyard, a gaggle of kohens clucked and pecked insistently at the pebbled ground. Eyrsa concentrated her energy on one particularly plump, rust-colored bird. Envisioning the heart, she sought to reenact Tallia's feat. The fowl, impervious to Eyrsa's attempts, continued to scratch at the ground. Eyrsa frowned. Perhaps, the distance was too great. She turned from the window and pulled the bell cord to summon the caretaker, Garth.

When he appeared several moments later, she instructed him to bring her one of the kohens. Though he raised his brows quizzically, he did as she asked. Returning with a squawking kohen clutched firmly under one arm, he deposited the bird at her feet. It strutted defensively around the room, black beady eyes searching for a means of escape.

Garth remained, obviously intent on seeing for what purpose Eyrsa wanted the creature. She ig-

nored him and again focused her thoughts. She saw
the kohen's heart, and wrapped her mind around it.
Minutes passed. She felt the drain of energy. The
force she expended was enough to cure almost any
ailment, set bones, reduce fevers. Yet nothing. The
bird stretched its feathered neck to peer at her.

"Take it away." She ignored Garth's quizzical
expression as he removed the bird.

A trace of a smile tugged at her lips. *He probably
thinks I've gone senile.* Frowning, she proceeded to
contemplate the outcome of her experiment. She'd
had years of training, yet her expertise combined
with the memories of her Zarmistic ancestors and
the enduring power of her own mind had not been
enough. She'd been unable to duplicate Tallia's
deed.

Eyrsa returned to her room. Quillan's libraries
were much larger than these. Perhaps her half
brother could find what she had not. It was imperative that she inform him of Tallia's actions and of
the very real possibility that someone suspected the
girl's true identity. She allowed her mind to drift, as
it was so often wont to do these days. Almost
eighteen years ago she had brought a tiny baby girl
to Rashana and her new husband and asked them
to raise the "orphaned" child as their own. Until
now, nothing had happened to lead Eyrsa to believe
that anyone suspected her secret. Seating herself,
she forced her mind to focus and drifted effortlessly
into a telepathic trance.

For days, Quillan had mulled over the concern
which Eyrsa had transmitted telepathically to
him. Nightly forays into the library had, thus far,

proved fruitless and he was growing desperate. He wanted to spend all his time in pursuit of an explanation for the variance in Tallia's abilities but instinct prompted caution. He must not be observed. Once again he quelled his impatience. He could not afford to rouse suspicions, not with Tallia so near the age of maturity. Determined to conceal his preoccupation, he turned his attention to the duties awaiting him. In just a few more hours, he'd continue his quest.

The halls were silent, shadowed in darkness as Quillan moved stealthily down the winding back stairs toward the library near the rear of the castle. Apprehension gripped him as he entered the yawning expanse of the silent room. His lantern flickered, an insignificant pinpoint of light in the tenebrous void of the cavernous chamber. The archives housed the works of many generations, and the dusty volumes lined the walls and partitions. Overhead, cobwebs hung, mute evidence of the lack of intrusion.

His worries plagued him. Was the answer to why Tallia possessed the killing ability to be found in this place after all? His eyes narrowed. The futility of this exercise struck him once again as he gazed down the rows of books disappearing into several small recesses positioned around the room. Thousands remained yet to be scanned. Where did he begin tonight?

Since he could not remember any ruler of Karaundo who had possessed the power to kill with psychic mastery, and he had already looked through some of the latest rulers' works, he reasoned that he should find the oldest records. Slowly, cautiously, like an intruder afraid of waking the ghosts of centuries past, he meticulously worked his way toward the far recesses of the vast room, trailing his fingers over bindings encasing long forgotten words of wisdom.

Musk. The aroma of age. His fingers slowly roamed the leather-bound volumes embossed with elaborate letters of gold. So many. The icy flagstones numbed his bare feet. He'd forgotten his slippers; now he would have to go back to his room to get them. As he turned toward the door a small beacon of radiance lit the room. He started, almost dropping his lantern. Between himself and the exit hovered a diaphanous indistinct form.

Frozen with fear and indecision, he stared. The features solidified, becoming discernible. It was a woman, slender, beautiful. Her long blond hair writhed around her as if buffeted by invisible currents and her translucent body began to acquire substance. Gradually, Quillan came to the startling realization that she beckoned him. The icy temperature of his feet forgotten, he followed, mesmerized. Was this a dream? The ghost a figment of his imagination?

She led him to the left, to a dusty densely shadowed corner. There, she halted, silently pointing at the shelf before her. Quillan approached, wary, frightened, but too curious to do otherwise. He glanced at the shelf she indicated. Unable to discern the titles, he brushed the thick coating of dust from the bindings. A single book drew his eye: *The Private Journal of Toleme, First King of Karaundo*. Was this what the apparition had wanted him to find? Drawing the volume gently from its resting place, he turned to face her. Yet, even as he pivoted, she was fading, a gentle smile upon her incorporeal features.

Lifting his lantern higher, Quillan stared in bewilderment at the place were she had been. Was his tired mind playing tricks on him? Or had he truly seen someone? He squinted at the volume illuminated by the pale flickering light. His hand trembled slightly as his fingertips caressed the gold-leaf lettering on the book's binding. The pages within this tome had been penned by the immortal hand of the god-king Toleme himself! Once more, his hand quivered as it felt the edges of the ancient manuscript. Would he find the information he sought on these yellowed pages? Lifting his head, he peered into the shadowed recesses of the room once more, seeking confirmation from the ethereal presence who had guided him to the volume. None was forthcoming.

Thoughtfully, he retraced his steps, returning to his chambers. Climbing into his bed to warm his chilled feet, he propped the text on his upraised knees and simply stared at it. These pages would hold insight into the life of a god. Was he, Quillan, ready to receive it? He took a deep breath and opened the cover.

The journal described Toleme's home, according a view into a place and a society very different from Quillan's. The Raunarian race maintained a civilization where all beings were equal, and every citizen of the realm had a voice. Most decisions were handled by an elected tribunal of twelve of the Raunarians. But certain decisions were of such paramount importance that the entire race's agreement was necessary before implementing those decisions. So advanced were many of the philosophies and aptitudes described that they lay beyond the scope of Quillan's understanding and of his planet.

When Toleme was initiated into maturity, he took the oath taken by all of his race, to preserve and to protect the balance of the universe. So sensitive were the minds and intellects of these people that they could sense the distress of a distant planet or star. They knew things that it was impossible for a human mind to fathom.

Disease and aging had apparently been virtually eradicated from Toleme's home dimension. It was only when citizens traveled into other dimensions that, in rare instances, a malady occurred. Death was a rare occurrence and the Raunarians aged so slowly that they lived thousands of years, making them almost immortal. Death, when it did occur, was such a traumatic event for the people that the entire populace linked minds, becoming one being, sharing their grief.

Slowly, as his mind began to grasp the meaning behind the words he read, Quillan perceived the fallacy that even now prevailed among his own people and in their religious beliefs. Toleme had not been a god, but rather a being from another dimension, another realm of existence. Coran and Galacia, his sisters, were powerful, psychic entities, not goddesses. Yaewel was merely a member of the elected tribunal, and the father of Toleme and his two sisters. Neither they nor any of the others who lived in their realm were divine. They were not infallible beings.

Quillan paused in shock. A centuries-old belief, and the basis for the very lifestyle of the people of Karaundo, had been eradicated in a matter of moments. The very history of his people was being rewritten, and it was almost more than he could comprehend.

The responsibilities of ruling his own small world of Karaundo had left Quillan with little spare time to wonder about what lay beyond its boundaries. But as he read not only did Toleme speak of a civilization beyond the mountains of Karaundo, but he spoke of other dimensions and of many worlds among the stars, some of which were populated. Quillan struggled to understand. How could a man or woman who lived hundreds of human lifetimes and who traveled among the stars not be a god?

According to Toleme's journal, Karaundo's first inhabitants had imperiled the existence of their home planet with their greed and ambition and were on the verge of extinction. Centuries ago, those who survived fled their planet only to face death among the stars. The tribunal of twelve had decided that the only compassionate thing to do was to aid the remnants of the dying civilization. Yet, such interference had to be undertaken carefully, taking into consideration the history of the race. Thus, the people were guided to an isolated area of the young planet now known as Karaundo. For mutual protection, they were isolated from the more aggressive inhabitants who lived beyond the mountains.

The people from the stars began with nothing but

the diverse knowledge from their past. On Karaundo, they were granted the opportunity to begin anew. The tribunal hoped that the people had learned from their past mistakes and would be able to revitalize and rebuild their civilization in harmony with the nature of their new world. It was not to be.

The people began to regress. The land given into their hands began to suffer. Plants and animals were killed without thought for reproduction. Within a few short lifetimes, the territory was imperiled.

Finally, the tribunal could stand by no longer. Despite the ideology against interfering perceptibly in the lives of primitive species, they feared for the continuance of the environment they were bound to protect. It was at that time that Coran and Galacia were sent to guide the new people of Karaundo, to educate them concerning the delicate balance of their new home.

However, the other-dimensional sisters had abilities beyond the imagination of mere mortals, and the people exalted them as goddesses. It was due to this adoration that the plan failed. Coran, drunk with the power she wielded, encouraged the promulgation of greed among the primitive people, enjoying the control she held over them.

Galacia, lacking Coran's intoxication with domination, could not control her sister's ambition. Once again, Yaewel and the tribunal were forced to intervene. As punishment for their actions, the two sisters were ordered back from the planet and forbidden to interfere ever again in the lives of the people of Karaundo. In addition, Coran was exiled from her own race's peaceful dimension, denied forever the companionship of her own kind. Only in matters which involved the accord of the entire Raunarian race would she be notified by the tribunal.

Next, the tribunal of twelve directed Toleme to succeed where his sisters had failed. He, too, was revered as a god by the people although he tried many times to discourage the belief. His mental abilities were held in awe and fear. His physical form, though humanistic except for the ageless quality of the flesh, was considered the quintessential form of male beauty.

As Toleme worked with the people of Karaundo, he began to love them despite their many faults, for they were eager to learn. He instructed them in living in harmony with the land that supported them. Yet, even in this instance, it was proven that edicts are not made without reason. The price of interference in the lives of primitive people soon became evident. Toleme fell in love.

He requested permission before the tribunal and his father, Yaewel, to marry the Lady Shalaun. The council, unprepared for such an extreme request, did not deny his petition outright. He was ordered to continue his work on Karaundo while they considered the ramifications of granting his request.

Days later, Toleme was summoned before the tribunal for their response. He was told that, in this instance, it was necessary for Toleme to achieve the agreement of the entire Raunarian race. Should

Toleme acquire the accord of his fellow citizens, the tribunal would attach some stringent conditions of its own.

First, Toleme would be denied access to his own dimension throughout the course of a human lifetime. It was not known definitely what effect this would have on him, but it was suspected that it would shorten his life span considerably. Second, he was to relinquish all mental abilities except those which would aid him in being a good and benevolent ruler. Thus, he would retain the talent for telepathic communication, the proficiency for healing, and the ability to discern truth in another's words. The aptitude for telekinetic battle would be relinquished, as would all capabilities that could be misused in his position of authority.

These conditions were attached with good reason. Although the tribunal was reasonably certain of Toleme's inherent good will, his committment to benevolent guidance might not be inherited by his future offspring. But his abilities *would* be, and the understanding of them would be conveyed upon his death. Thus, due to the possible peril represented by Toleme's progeny, the curtailing of his psychic power was deemed necessary.

In the following Karaundo year, Toleme gained the approval of everyone in his society for his petition except from his sister, Coran. Although exiled, she retained her vote and she directed her embittered reply directly to Toleme. If he desired union with Shalaun, then he would have to attain agreement from the tribunal that Coran was, in the future, to be granted a second chance at guiding the people of Karaundo.

The hour grew late, but Quillan was unable to lay the journal down. It was engrossing, riveting, this view of Karaundo's first king. He read on through the entries.

Shalaun! Quillan reread Toleme's exacting details concerning the woman he would wed. The description fit too well to be coincidence. It had been she who had guided his steps in the library.

King Quillan looked up from the book, staring across the room and through the window at the first hues of dawn lighting the sky. Once more he bowed his head to peruse the yellowed pages. He still had a third of the book to read. He would not sleep until he was finished.

Before Shalaun could wed Toleme, she had to acquire powers equal to his. Toleme was charged with the construction of a "key," a pyramidal structure constructed on a high point in the land which channeled the cosmic energy of the universe. When entered, this energy focused on the human mind, amplifying, or bestowing when necessary, certain abilities. Because of the tremendous power of the "key," the construction included a fail-safe security mechanism. No one whose character leaned to the darker side of human nature could penetrate those amorphous walls. This security served to preserve the compassionate nature of Toleme's descendants' consorts as well as to prevent the misuse of power by unscrupulous people.

Quillan paused. His own wife and queen, Jhysine, had survived the "key." The only humans who had successfully entered and emerged from the "key," other than those who wed the past rulers of Karaundo, were Zarmists. The "key" appeared to attract healers who valued the strange stones found within for the enhancement of their abilities. Healers who utilized the Zarma stones became known as Zarmists, a special breed of healer.

The journal had revealed a lifetime of happiness for the two lovers. Then Shalaun had preceded Toleme in death. Toleme's following pain-filled entry, an apparently unrelated paragraph that nonetheless revealed untold depths of anguish, remained in Quillan's mind.

"How can you possibly triumph, my grandchild? Especially when the rules the tribunal has set forth forbid me to warn you of what the future holds. I have revealed as much as I dare of the tale leading to the establishment of the Prophecy. Forgive me if you can for being unable to provide you with answers to the dilemma you will face."

Quillan's heart pounded erratically. Prophecy! His mind skipped back over the years to the dream. He always thought of it that way, for it was the only time he'd felt the touch of what he'd assumed to be divine guidance. Galacia had intervened to spare his child's life. She had warned him that his daughter's life was in danger and had hinted at a prophecy. In the trying times following, he'd thought of the incident often, but until now had been unable to understand the significance of the event.

Quillan flipped the page. Blank paper glared up at him. Desperately, he thumbed through the rest of the book. There was no more. Toleme had neglected to relate the Prophecy. The reason for Tallia's enhanced talent still eluded him.

He frowned in concentration. In that long-ago dream, Galacia had foretold of amplified abilities. She had connected maintaining the secret of Tallia's heritage with a prophecy! The same prophecy? It had to be. He had to discover its contents, find the reason behind Tallia's uniqueness. Once more he flipped through the pages of Toleme's journal. Nothing! Carefully, he checked the binding. No, there was no indication of anything concealed within.

Dejected, Quillan slumped back against the head board. How could Toleme have poured his heart and soul into these pages and then not have penned that which he knew his descendants would need to know? True, he'd written that he had revealed as much as he dared.

Quillan chewed thoughtfully on his lowered lip. Still, if he had been Toleme he would have found a way to reveal the Prophecy. Tapping his fingers on the cover of the journal, he nodded slowly. He felt he knew the man in the journal, and he was certain Toleme had secreted the details somewhere. Now all he had to do was discover where the first king had hidden it.

Toleme would not have been willing to chance the discovery and destruction of the journal and the Prophecy before they could be of use. He had carefully omitted it from the one place where one would expect to find it, the journal, and yet hinted at it enough to propel some future descendant to search for it. Tomorrow night, Quillan would make a thorough search of the library. Drawing the covers up, he carefully tucked the journal beneath his pillow. He'd better get some sleep.

Later that day, Quillan rose and dressed, slipping the journal inside his robe. He was not about to leave it laying around for prying eyes. At the moment it was best not to trust anyone. The book would remain his secret, at least until he found the prophecy—which he was determined to do. Then he would share his discovery with Eyrsa.

Time seemed to pass with agonizing slowness. Quillan forced himself to keep his mind on his work as he sat through several appointments, signed various permits and documents, and, with a few privileged members of his court, mulled over the invitation list for the dinner party to be held in honor of his sixty-third birthday next month.

When at last the afternoon's duties were accomplished, he ate a hearty supper and excused himself with muttered comments about hours of paperwork. The tension within him had increased to the point of bursting and, fearing that he would be unable to hide it much longer, he retired to the privacy of his room.

Once there, Quillan waited impatiently for the sounds of activity to fade as the castle's occupants sought their beds. Intent on being prepared for a long evening, he donned his slippers and resumed pacing. Finally, he pulled the journal from its hiding place and reread several sections, grateful to find something capable of occupying his thoughts for the next few hours.

Finally all was quiet, and he stealthily left his

room. But hearing a whisper of sound behind him, he turned a corner, heading away from the rear staircase, and quickly ducked into the shadowed recess of an alcove. Silence. No, there it was again; the slight sound of a footfall. He hugged the wall, peering from the shadows into the dimly lit corridor beyond. Who dared follow him?

The lean silhouette of a darkly garbed figure stepped into view, then paused uncertainly; the man's features were obscured by the darkness. Then the figure took a step forward. Pale light cast from one of the wall lanterns fell across his face. Flagan! Krogan's man! Why? Quillan, frowning in perplexity, retreated silently into the densest shadow, waiting. Finally, Flagan moved on. Peering furtively from the alcove, Quillan ensured he had not been seen before swiftly retracing his steps to the stairs and making his way cautiously to the library. As he slipped inside and closed the oaken door, he let out a sigh of relief, listening. The library was silent, the only light the faint glow from his own lantern.

Retracing his steps of the night before, he gently replaced Toleme's journal. It would be safer where it had been, unread, these many years. He blew lightly on the dusty shelf and watched with satisfaction as the particles settled, masking the evidence of his intrusion.

Careful not to disturb anything else, he let his eyes roam over the volumes that bordered Toleme's journal. *Zarmistic Craftsmanship*, *Maps of Karaundo*, *Poetry for Children*. None seemed an appropriate selection for the forbidden secret that

Toleme would have hidden. *Think like Toleme*, Quillan mouthed silently. *Think like Toleme*.

Hopefully, he gazed around for the apparition. "Help me, please," he whispered into the silence. No reply. All right then, he'd have to do it himself. He stared at the rows of books, refusing to consider the possibility that he was wrong about Toleme recording the Prophecy. If he were Toleme, he would have hidden it there somewhere. The room was seldom used and potential niches for concealing a small document were endless.

Quillan leaned against the bookshelf and began to logically reconstruct what Toleme's thoughts might have been. Hiding the Prophecy in another book was unlikely, as it would be too difficult to locate, and would have not endured. Something that would withstand the passage of time, perhaps something associated with the royal line. The throne! No, it was portable and constructed of wood. There simply weren't that many things that remained unchanged over hundreds of years, almost nothing within the castle. But the castle would endure for centuries!

His slippered feet swished over the irregular flagstones. Slowly, he circumnavigated the room, noting each nook and cranny, letting his mind go blank, his eyes wander randomly.

He muttered as a heavy slab of stone shifted slightly underfoot and the toe of his slipper snagged on the loose mortar. He moved on, then stopped, turning slowly to stare at the offending piece of rock. His heart thumped slowly in his chest, its rhythmic beating intensifying in his ears. He clenched his fist to still the sense of excitement that surged through him. Was it possible? He walked back slowly, his gaze riveted on the pale gray slab as if looking away might allow it to disappear. Setting his lantern on the floor, he squatted next to it. Only one corner jutted up and even that would have been undiscernible unless you were looking for it.

"Perhaps you have helped me after all," he whispered to the absent lady. Impatiently he removed the loose piece of mortar. The resulting gap left just sufficient room for his fingers. He slid them under the lip of the flat rock and pulled. The stone grated eerily against the neighboring slabs as Quillan hoisted it enough to slip his other hand beneath.

He felt along the solid dirt floor compressed by centuries beneath the weight of the rocks. His fingers inched forward, groping blindly. There! He had brushed something. The crackle of aged parchment reached his ears. He held his breath, carefully withdrawing the soiled paper. *Please let it be what I seek*, he beseeched. Replacing the stone and the mortar, he moved to hold the message nearer to the lantern.

"Forgive me." It began in Toleme's now familiar penmanship. Quillan rose, tucked the parchment inside his robe, flattening it against his chest. He would wait to read it within the privacy of his chamber. "Thank you," he whispered to the empty room. Surely his steps had been guided this night.

King Quillan barred his door and set the lantern on the worn writing desk. With trembling hands he extracted the age-old warning from beneath his cloak and placed it on the desk. For several breathless moments he only stared, afraid to read the forbidden words, fearing the contents of the terrible prediction. Finally, he sat and bent over the paper.

"Forgive me. I understood not the full consequence of the contract and now I have endangered those of my blood, those of Shalaun's womb. I knew Coran and Galacia had forged the fatal Prophecy. I gaze upon their perennial youth and curse my aging form and my part in this charade. But what they could not predict were the tortures of my final hours, my final desperation.

"I could not rest without knowing what penance I had bequeathed. Compelled, I gained entrance through the Gate and slipped into the tribunal's private archives. On these next pages, I have copied the letter of the Prophecy so that you may be forewarned. I cannot leave without imparting this knowledge. Threats and promises once made mean nothing to me now. The Prophecy is Coran's reparation, her payment for the permission I once sought. I had hoped then that Galacia, in her compassionate wisdom, would be able to temper Coran's demands with some measure of justice. The results are yours to judge, the final move yours to ponder. My prayers are with you."

Quillan took a deep breath and folded the page back. What was the "Gate" that Toleme referred to? Quillan shrugged and looked down at the paper. The words, faded by time though still legible, had obviously been recorded by a trembling hand. He began to read the Prophecy as his own hand shook.

"We, the sisters of Toleme, accord our agreement to his request with the following stipulations. I, Coran, decree, that at such time in the future as chosen by myself, Toleme's descendants shall battle for the right to the throne. Both combatants shall be granted full Raunarian abilities. Should my chosen challenger triumph, I shall be pardoned and permitted to share the staff of power, reigning again, unsupervised, on Karaundo. The battle shall be fought to the death without Raunarian interference and the results shall be decreed final.

"I, Galacia, stipulate that neither contestant may challenge the other until they have reached maturity. Beyond that, I add only that invisible bonds shall not tether the hands of my defender, only the heart, and thus be allowed. Past indiscretions shall not hinder but strengthen. A unity of love will enhance psychic power."

Puzzled, Quillan reread the Prophecy. Coran's dictates were straightforward, to the point, even heartless. Galacia's words were cryptic, adding a meager stipulation, enlarging only on the demand of no interference.

"Both combatants shall be granted full Raunarian abilities," the words leapt from the page. Tallia was one of the combatants then! It explained the abilities she possessed, the proficiency that no other in history had—except the one who would be her adversary. Instinctively, he guessed that Tallia was Galacia's combatant. But who, from among the many direct descendants of Toleme, had Coran chosen? Krogan? He didn't want to believe it of the nephew he'd raised as a son. Yet, who possessed a stronger position and motive?

His mind returned to Tallia and the Prophecy. He felt a shiver of fear; icy fingers of premonition pinched at his nerves.

Tallia hesitated in the hallway outside her father's study. Eyrsa's implacable voice carried clearly to her ears. "I summoned Tallia home because I have need of her."

For a moment there was silence. Tallia could picture her father seated behind his desk, his brows drawn together in a scowl. "I will not tolerate this undermining of my authority," Arilan's voice was hard with anger. "Tallia is to complete a year at the college before beginning her own practice."

"I have already taught her more than she will learn in two years at the conservatory." Eyrsa's tone was low, uncompromising.

"Nevertheless, her practice will have more credibility if she has completed the time there. She *will* return."

"So it is for appearances' sake that the child is to waste her time? Tallia's skills will inspire credibility."

"I will be the judge as to what is a waste of time. The discussion is closed. She will be allowed a brief time with us, but ultimately I will make arrangements for her return. When do you expect her to arrive?"

Tallia bit her lip indecisively, then stepped firmly into the room. "Hello, Father."

Arilan rocked back in his chair, staring at her, his

mouth open, momentarily speechless. "How . . . When . . ." He turned to Eyrsa.

Before he could begin another lecture, Tallia crossed the room and gave him a quick hug. Arilan straightened, frowning. "How exactly did you get home?"

"I had a very reliable guide. As you can see, I have arrived safely."

Arilan shook his head, annoyance mirrored in his expression. Tallia drank in the sight of his familiar features. She hadn't realized how much she missed her parents until this moment. His face was dear to her no matter what expression it held. "I missed you, Father."

Arilan sighed, a resigned smile tugging at his lips. "I missed you too. Who else could possibly cause all the trouble you do?" He turned once more to Eyrsa. "Still, I would have appreciated being informed of your intentions. Please keep that in mind."

"As you wish," Eyrsa conceded, knowing that she would have done nothing differently. With Arilan, it was always better to present the accomplished deed.

Rashana was called and, as usual, welcomed Tallia with open arms, pleased to have her daughter once more ensconced beneath the safety of her own protective wing. Explanations, such as they were, were repeated and the family spent the next hour imparting their various pieces of news.

In the days that followed, Eyrsa questioned Tallia occasionally, but there seemed little else she could reveal of the method used to kill Bodan. And, because thinking about it seemed to distress the girl immensely, Eyrsa soon left the subject alone.

Then in a telepathic communication she received the distressing warning from Quillan. She sensed the alarm and apprehension that gripped him, leaving a discernible quiver in his thought pattern. How was she to prepare Tallia to utilize abilities she, Eyrsa, did not possess? Resolutely, she turned her attention to giving to Tallia all that she was capable of, though she feared it might not be enough to prepare Tallia for the fulfillment of the Prophecy.

Now Tallia sat across the table from Eyrsa. The Zarmist's pale gray eyes met Tallia's. "The power within you is strong, stronger than any I have encountered before." She paused, forming the words in her mind before continuing. "Perhaps the experience in the wasteland has already honed it."

She made no mention of Quillan's warning. Although she sensed the time of the Prophecy was near, now was not yet the time for enlightening Tallia. She needed to understand the magnitude of Tallia's ability. "I have a request to make." Her eyes locked with Tallia's. "I would like to attempt a link with your mind."

Tallia nodded. There was nothing in her thoughts that she wanted to hide from Eyrsa; in fact, Eyrsa would see all the questions Tallia had stored in her mind during her journey across the wastelands, questions which seemed so insignificant now. Tallia suspected that any attempt to hide even those from Eyrsa would be ineffectual. Eyrsa had a sixth sense and, although she would be courteous and not probe into forbidden areas, sooner or later she would know the truth of Tallia's involvement with Tynan.

Tallia felt the link, a light touch like a butterfly flitting across the petals of a flower. Relaxing, the probing strengthened into fingers of mist that enfolded her thoughts, delving deeper and deeper into her consciousness and then even beyond. Abruptly, it was gone. Tallia opened her eyes, and Eyrsa's startled expression frightened her.

"What is it?" she whispered. What was in her mind that had so shocked her governess? Surely the memories of her time with Tynan had not. Eyrsa had never been one to condemn the actions of another for the sake of propriety. "What do you see?"

"You are strong, even stronger than I imagined," Eyrsa muttered hoarsely. "But you will need to be. There is so little time. I must give you my wisdom. Coupled with your instinct, it may be enough."

"Why?" Tallia pleaded for answers. "What is in the future that requires so much of me?"

"That will be answered in time, child. In time." She squeezed Tallia's hand reassuringly before releasing it.

"Does Tynan have a part in my future?"

"I think your association was meant to occur. The true implications of your actions have yet to unfold."

A thought occurred to Tallia. "These strong abilities I possess, are they the reason I was able to heal Tynan without the aid of the Zarma stone?"

Eyrsa nodded. "Your abilities are far beyond the mere augmentation of the Zarma stone. It can do naught but aid you. You will discover that much you do will not require the stone. If you'll think back, you'll remember the first time you healed. It was without the aid of the stone. Do you recall the llamahare?"

Tallia nodded with dawning comprehension. "I had forgotten."

"I knew your talents far surpassed the normal when you were very young. In order to protect you, I attempted to conceal it."

"Protect me from what?"

"Even I do not know that yet. The time for revelations has not arrived," Eyrsa responded gently.

"Can you teach me to control the power, to understand myself?" Tallia pleaded.

Eyrsa smiled compassionately before continuing with her characteristic astuteness. "It is not Tynan you need fear, nor the emotions you feel. I sense another and he is very powerful. I cannot instruct you in the control of abilities I do not possess. The only thing I can do is bequeath my own experience. The 'key' represents the only source of knowledge to you now."

"The key?" Bewilderment accentuated Tallia's question.

"A place in the mountains. It was conjured centuries ago, a triangular pyramid of strange mist. It enhances and enlightens—if one is fortunate enough to pass within its walls, for it is protected by a peculiar force that prohibits anyone possessing nefarious qualities from gaining admittance. It is the source of the Zarma stones."

Tallia felt for the stone suspended on the leather

thong around her neck. "You've been there then?"

Eyrsa nodded. "But I received only an augmentation of my healing powers. For you, I predict more, much more. There is little you can do to prepare for this trial. But the sooner you attempt to enter that guarded realm, the better."

CHAPTER TEN

CONCEALED WITHIN THE NIGHT'S DARK MANTLE, Tynan traversed the western edge of the wasteland. Relying on Chaz's nocturnal vision, he enfolded himself deep within his cape, concentrating on the sounds around him: the mournful howl of a lone lopii; the subdued hum of insects made sluggish by the winter chill; the slither of a reptile in the dry grasses followed by the piercing scream of the toiphat which became its victim. But the noises of the wild served only to accentuate his loneliness. Before, solitude had been a treasured companion. Now, memories plagued him: Tallia's feminine form outlined by the firelight; her soft voice asking yet another question; her wrinkling of her nose as she dutifully collected dung for the fire. Tallia. Always Tallia. Like the sorceress Jenk thought her to be, she'd invaded his mind and his heart.

Nothing exorcised the images that played and replayed within his mind. He'd ridden hard and fast since he had last seen her, stopping only when weariness overcame him. Even in his dreams he found no escape, no refuge.

He sighed. It was time to make camp. Chaz, though possessing endurance far beyond that of a gari, needed rest. Within two days he should reach Ravencrest. There he would exchange mounts, releasing the faralk to return to his own kind for a time. Then he would continue on to Maurasia to report to his king.

To his left, he caught a faint flicker of light. Fire? He passed an imperceptible communication to Chaz and the faralk halted. Silently, Tynan dismounted and felt the weight of his broadsword bump against his shoulder. His senses already probing ahead, he absently adjusted the placement of his baldric.

Furtively he advanced, crouching, creeping silently forward through the thick grasses until he saw the campfire. Close enough to distinguish the silhouettes of two men, he warily lowered himself to his belly and proceeded more cautiously. With serpentine stealth, he maneuvered through the dry grasses until he could look into the shallow basin. He studied the men's features. Carefully, he searched his mind for the descriptions of men sought by the Royal Guild but no details corresponding to these men came to mind.

He began to back away when the blond young man shifted. His cape opened and Tynan stared. He couldn't be so lucky! He scrutinized the figure again. Yes, there it was, a sliver of pink. Could this possibly be the eleventh man, the one from whom he would learn the leader's identity?

This man, if it was he, had been the hardest to locate. He'd left Bodan's band shortly after that terrible day two years ago and had seldom been seen since. The description Tynan had obtained from other wasteland band members had been vague: young, blond, average height, average appearance, the only distinguishing mark a minuscule scar near his right eye. But, he'd been told, the young man appeared to have a fixation for a woman's pink scarf which he rarely removed from around his neck.

Using every bit of cover the barren wasteland offered, Tynan wormed his way toward their encampment. He could see them clearly now, hear their conversation.

"Kal, couldn't you find a way to come home? A short visit, that's all I'm asking," the younger man was saying.

"If I was discovered, my presence could jeopardize all your lives. I can't return until I can prove that I didn't kill Thirza."

Tynan had waited long enough. Tall, menacing, darkly clad, he stepped out of the night. The younger man shrieked a warning, and Kal sprang up, turning simultaneously, his sword drawn. But his grip was unsteady and the weapon was knocked from his grasp by the forceful blow of the massive broadsword wielded by Tynan's steel-sinewed arm.

The point of Tynan's sword hovered a hairbreadth from Kal's throat. He glanced at Kal's companion, hardly more than a boy. "Leave," he commanded.

"What are you going to do?" the boy asked despite his fear as he backed away.

Tynan remained silent. His cold emerald eyes glowed in the light of the fire, intensifying the warning.

Kal sighed. "Go, Denak. Go home." There was resignation in his tone as his eyes met Tynan's. Tynan saw no fear there, only acceptance. Neither man moved as they listened to the sound of Denak's frightened scrambling as he saddled his gari and rode away. Then, there was only silence—the savage silence of a wasteland night.

"Do you know who I am?" Tynan queried, his voice unemotional, only his eyes mirroring the cold determination that had burned within him like a wintry flame for two years.

Kal studied him. "One of the king's men?"

Tynan felt a certain surprise. So the existence of the Royal Guild of Executioners was becoming known, which he knew was inevitable.

"Look," Kal spoke, then abruptly halted, nervously eyeing the weapon at his throat. Lifting his gaze once more to Tynan, he continued, "If you'll just put that aside for a moment, I can explain."

"Explain!" Now Tynan really was surprised. How did the man propose to explain his involvement in mass murder? "What in the name of Coran are you talking about?" Tynan demanded impatiently.

Kal appeared startled. "You're not a Royal Guard from Maurasia?" he asked hesitantly.

Tynan grit his teeth. "Sit down," he ordered, lowering his sword but maintaining his firm grasp upon the thick handle. "Why, may I ask, would you expect a Royal Guard to be in the wasteland?"

Kal eyed him uncertainly. "I just thought . . ." Kal halted, swallowing. "I mean I escaped and . . ." Again he stopped. Suddenly, wariness entered his expression. "If you're not a Royal Guard, then why are you here?"

Sustaining his vigilance, Tynan turned to inspect the ground for a comfortable spot to sit. "How did you come to be with Bodan?" he demanded, still facing away.

There was no response.

Seated, he looked once more at the young man. He had thought there might be some merit in listening to him. This sudden reticence in Kal's attitude brought a flash of anger to Tynan's emerald eyes. "I asked you a question?"

"I'm sorry. I . . ." Kal hesitated, shifting to avoid Tynan's piercing gaze. "I didn't hear you. I'm deaf," he finally blurted. "Have been for years now."

Tynan's eyes widened in surprise. "How did you understand what I said before?" he queried suspiciously. He'd only encountered one other deaf person, and that man had been unable to communicate except on the most basic levels.

Obviously uncomfortable discussing his handicap, Kal's response was both defiant and defensive. "I watch your mouth. I can tell what you say by the way it moves."

Tynan studied him briefly then finally nodded. He thought he understood now and, despite the nature of his exchange with Kal, he couldn't help feeling a twinge of admiration for the young man's ability to adapt. "I asked you how you came to be with Bodan." He noted the way Kal watched the movement of his lips.

Kal swallowed. "When my fianceé, Thirza, was murdered, I was falsely accused of the crime. I fled here, to the wasteland. Bodan and his men were the first people I ran into."

"That your fianceé's?" Tynan asked, indicating the pink scarf.

The young man nodded, fingering the material sadly.

Tynan sensed that Kal was not a hardened animal like the other members of Bodan's band.

"Who are you?" Kal asked.

"My name is Tynan, Tynan of the House of Keane," he said quietly, watching Kal's reaction closely.

"House of Keane." An expression analogous to horror entered his eyes. "It was on the side of the caravan wagon, House of Keane, Fiefdom of Ravencrest." Kal shuddered.

For the first time, Tynan saw not fear of reprisal, but genuine remorse in the face of one of Bodan's accomplices. "I need to know the identity of the man who hired Bodan."

Searchingly, Kal met his gaze. For endless seconds, he said nothing. The fire crackled; a lopii howled; Tynan waited.

"I heard you were tracking us," Kal murmured. "What are you going to do with me?"

Now it was Tynan's turn to hesitate. He'd vowed to execute every wastelander responsible for the death of his family. But faced with this sensitive, tortured young man, his resolution wavered. "Depends on what you had to do with what happened," he finally said.

"Nothing!" Kal yelled. "Nothing," he repeated in a near whisper. "I tried to stop them. Bodan told me to sit back, to watch and learn, or die." His shoulders slumped. His gaze fell to the ground at his feet. His posture reflected guilt and remorse, not the fear Tynan had expected. "I sat there and watched because I was afraid. I was afraid to die." He raised his head and met Tynan's stare, his eyes pleading for understanding if not forgiveness. "So I did nothing. I still see their faces in my dreams. My mind creates the sounds of the screams I could not hear."

Tynan swallowed. To his surprise, there was compassion in his heart for this young man. He had felt only fathomless apathy for so long. Was he growing soft? Or was the need for revenge lessening in the face of time? "Live, Tynan. Live for us both." Tynara's words echoed in his mind. He made a decision. "If you can tell me the name of the man who hired Bodan, I will spare your life."

"Had I not been able to read lips I never would have learned it. It is not a name they spoke freely and for good reason. But I speak truthfully."

Tynan nodded. Praise Galacia, perhaps there was some justice in this wasteland. He had come so close to failing that he practically trembled with anticipation. And but for this young man's disability, he might forever have been denied the successful conclusion of his quest for himself and the king. He concentrated on Kal's words.

"After the deed was done that day, a man named Flagan came to speak with Bodan and to deliver payment. But he was not the leader. He merely relayed instructions. I watched them speak from a distance. The name I read upon his lips was Krogan, Lord Krogan." Kal hesitated. "I swear 'tis true," he assured Tynan. "A man named Torden was the object of the assassination. I don't know why they killed the others." Again he shrugged. "That is the kind of men they were."

Lord Krogan! Why would the heir to the throne want Tynan's father dead? Had Torden inadvertently posed a threat to King Quillan's nephew? He had no answers and his gut wrenched with hatred. He knew not how, but someday the opportunity for retribution would come. If Lord Krogan was guilty, then he would die by Tynan's hand.

Rising, he sheathed his broadsword in its scabbard. He whistled shrilly, and the sound was immediately answered by the soft thud of approaching hooves. "Go in peace, Kal," he said softly.

Kal watched incredulously as the large man with the blazing emerald eyes and somber clothing mounted a gigantic red-eyed demon-beast, the animal as black as the night itself. Almost convinced in that brief moment that his visitation from Tynan of the House of Keane had been supernatural, he sent a silent prayer of thanks to Galacia.

"Go home, Kal. I will speak to the king and your name will be removed from the roster of the Royal Guard." With that, Tynan pivoted Chaz and rode into the night. As soon as he'd put some distance between himself and this spot, he'd make camp. He needed to be alone. He needed to think, to plan.

Tallia paced within her chamber. Today the large room with its brilliant tapestries offered none of the

comfort she remembered. "Visit the 'key,'" Eyrsa
had advised, and trepidation swelled in her heart at
the thought of it. She sensed the visitation would
alter her in ways she could not imagine. And yet,
the thought of forever being plagued with this
swirling uncertainty was even more untenable.

She strode to the window. Wistfully, she let her
mind register each detail, committing to memory
the view of Twin Suns and the surrounding acres of
prosperous land. Would she see them with altered
perception after this day? With that thought she
realized she'd made her decision. Eyrsa believed
the "key" was the answer so Tallia would go
tomorrow at dawn.

Almost unwillingly, her eyes were drawn to the
mountain. It was diminutive as mountains went,
yet still imposing. It would take her much of the day
to reach its summit. And, although nearly snowless
despite the season, it would be cold. Having often
gone far afield seeking rare herbs, she was no
stranger to day-long excursions so the journey itself
did not frighten her. But she knew she must prepare
properly. Tomorrow was her eighteenth birthday,
an appropriate day to begin the voyage of discovery
into her future.

Composed now, she turned to survey her room.
The massive four-poster bed occupied the center of
the north wall, its sunny yellow overlay cheering the
chamber. Her wardrobe, hand-carved by the
fiefdom's finest carpenter, inhabited a large area on
the opposite wall. Beside it, neatly arranged in a
compartmentalized cabinet, was her herb collection. She moved to it, slowly running her fingers

over the labels as she inhaled deeply of the myriad scents.

Turning once more, she caught sight of her reflection in the mirror. A new maturity strengthened her features. Her eyes no longer reflected the outlook of a young girl. How would Tynan perceive her now if he saw her?

Why did he keep intruding on her thoughts without warning? She had known that their journey would end so why had his leaving haunted her? Had a link been forged between them? Was she mistaken in her assumption that destiny compelled them to walk the same path? *Forget him!* she instructed herself. But the image of the solemn man in black would not be purged.

Tallia refused to acknowledge the pain in her heart. The unbidden tears that came to her eyes at the oddest moments, she attributed to anxiety. Erotic dreams and alien yearnings she ascribed to Dayna's affliction of "addiction to sensual pleasure." Although she'd not really taken her friend seriously at the time, circumstances had prompted her to alter her perception. Immersing herself in the task of self-discovery had helped in combating her unfulfilled desire. She sighed, her eyes once more going to the window. Mount Coran drew her gaze again and with determination, she squared her shoulders and left the room. Preparations for tomorrow would keep her from dwelling on her troubling emotions.

The next morning at dawn, having dutifully informed her family of her excursion to the Zarmist's "key," Tallia departed. Leaning heavily on her cane, Eyrsa walked with her to the gate. Her gnarled hands trembling from strain, she squeezed Tallia's arm in a silent gesture of reassurance. For the first time Tallia viewed Eyrsa as an old woman, and realized that the healer's strength was perhaps not as enduring as it seemed.

They reached the gate, and still Eyrsa had not spoken. Tallia turned, impulsively, hugging her. "I love you."

"I know that, child," Eyrsa replied quietly as she returned the embrace. Stepping back, she stared at Tallia, her gaze enigmatic.

"What is it?"

The old healer shrugged. "A feeling. Nothing more." She turned to view the mountain, then slowly closed her eyes, concentrating. "There is someone or something who will seek to keep you from the 'key,'" she murmured. "Keep your mind clear and your heart pure."

Despite her resolve, Tallia shivered and for the first time in her life, felt very insecure.

"Go, Tallia. It must be done," Eyrsa directed, her voice brisk now. Without further comment, she turned to make her way back to the fortress.

For a moment, Tallia stared wistfully after Eyrsa, longing for the return of bygone days when she'd been a child trailing after her governess. Then, shaking her head to dispel the fruitless yearning, she mounted Luma and turned toward Mount Coran.

The sun shone brightly, bathing the meadow in its pure golden light. The birds warbled, and the sound of water trickling in a nearby brook soothed her nerves. And she allowed herself to forget, for a time, the purpose of her journey as she basked in the simple pleasure of her surroundings.

By midday, she'd traversed most of the foothills. Stopping to eat in a sun-dappled forest glade, she noticed that the temperature had dropped. It would continue to decrease the higher she climbed. She donned her cape as she studied the slope above. Farther up, the slant of the mountain became steeper and much rockier and her tension increased.

Firmly tamping down her fears, she mounted the gari and continued. Within moments, she'd left the last of the forested area behind and before her rose Mount Coran, barren and imposing. The climb became more difficult, the landscape more alien. Mists swirled above her, alternately cloaking and exposing the view of her route. Narrow ledges, like livid scars on the face of the landscape, snaked their way up the mountain. She dismounted, having to abandon Luma to continue on foot. The large cat simply could not maneuver on the narrow stone paths.

A cold swirling mist wrapped its clinging tendrils around Tallia's ankles as she made her way carefully along the worn rock path that cut across the face of the mountainside. Clouds hugged the cliff, obscuring her view of the valley below, and the enormous granite mesa loomed before her. Carved by nature's hand into a dramatic triangular plateau, it was the home of the "key." Apprehension sent a shiver through her. Eyrsa had been able to tell her so little about the mysterious powers that radiated from the amorphous walls of the "key." Was she truly ready for this? Tallia breathed deeply, attempting to calm the tremors of uneasiness that haunted her mind.

Reaching a wider ledge, she found a flat boulder and sat down to rest. The steep climb had sapped her strength and she needed this time to think, to clear her mind of doubt, as much as to regain her faltering determination.

She wouldn't give up. The answers to the questions that plagued her were in the "key." As she closed her eyes and took several deep breaths, willing her body and mind to relax, she felt the tension slipping away. She sensed that only by being at peace in her body, soul, and mind, could she successfully enter the doorway to the unknown and return victorious.

Feeling the restoration of her inner balance, Tallia finally rose and made her way across the rocky retreat. The path, steeper now, cut between two sharp pinnacles of stone and twisted upward to the summit, to the mesa once more mantled in mist. Obscured, the path seemed to reach into the clouds and beyond. A sense of the ethereal drew an uneasy sigh from Tallia. Did she perceive a presence near? Or was it her imagination? The sense of the illusory intensified as even the faint breeze faded, leaving Tallia alone in the stillness and the thickening shrouds of mist. Inhaling deeply, she drew on the well of serenity within her, and calm descended over her once more. This was her destiny.

Abruptly, she cocked her head and listened. From the distance the pounding of hooves grew louder, the sound amplified by the echoing granite cliffs. She peered through the heavy veil of white that surrounded her. It was impossible! No animal could race at such a speed in this terrain.

Suddenly, the beast was before her. It reared, its dark hooves flashing dangerously close. The ruby glow of the demon-beast's eyes cut through the mist, pinning her against the rock at her back. The breath expelled from its flaring nostrils felt hot against her skin and its angry snort resounded in her ears. It was like Chaz, and yet it wasn't.

The mist-dampened rocks cut into her back as she pressed tightly against them, flattening her palms on the cold hard surface. Mesmerized by the ebony apparition before her, she could do nothing but stare in disbelief. The thick hooves flashed again and she shrank from the fury as the animal's almost human scream pierced the air.

Suddenly rational thought penetrated the numbing fear in her brain. It was impossible for the beast to be there; it was an illusion. The instant she reached that conclusion, the animal wheeled and raced away, straight off the side of the mountain, emitting one final shriek of rage that echoed from the rocky cliffs.

Tallia clenched her fists and fought to restrain the leaping of her pulse as she watched the beast fade into the distance, its hooves thundering on the clouds. As the vision was swallowed by the mists, Tallia felt reality return—the heavy pounding of her heart, her quick gasping breath.

Did the demon-beast's appearance have some significance? Eyrsa had said someone or something would seek to stop her. Was the apparition meant as a threat? A warning perhaps? Tallia glanced again at the path beyond. Squaring her shoulders and allowing herself a moment to strengthen her resolve, she turned toward it.

She stepped forward, cautiously finding a secure foothold on the damp rocks. With painstaking care, she completed her climb to the gigantic triangular mesa. As she stepped onto its wind-worn surface, her heart quickened with trepidation then slowed with relief. Then her eyes found what she was seeking—the "key." Not even Eyrsa's description had prepared her for the absolute magnificence of the mystical creation towering over her. Its nebulous periphery shimmered in the muted rays of the sunlight penetrating the clouds overhead—a pyramid of prismatic light.

Spellbound, her fear forgotten, Tallia studied the shifting, hypnotic patterns generated by the walls of the mutable enclosure. The enchantment of the scintillating effulgence lured Tallia and she walked toward it.

Suddenly, an inhuman shriek pierced the air, releasing her from her trance. She screamed as human skulls, their eye sockets glowing with fiendish light, rushed at her from beyond the "key." Their mouths opened and deafening wails of hopelessness bombarded her ears. Fear pounded in her breast urging her to turn, to run.

Clasping her hands over her ears to shut out the sound that attempted to rob her of her will, she summoned all of her inner strength and resolve. She could not go back. Behind her was death, for an incautious descent would surely result in a fatal fall. Before her was her future, her destiny. Anger, stubborness, and determination burst within her and her eyes radiated her innate fortitude as her spine stiffened with outrage. Who sought to deny her the knowledge of her destiny?

She looked at the skulls once more, knowing they were illusions, the seeds of fear. "Leave me!" she commanded, her voice ringing with an authority she'd not known herself capable of. But then, there was much she'd discovered lately. A final mournful wail drifted on the air as the skulls disappeared as though they'd never been.

Once more, Tallia advanced toward the lucent, amorphous "key." Her determination tempered the hypnotic quality it induced within her, but she was still awed and revered the cabalistic obelisk of mist. Standing before it, she felt that she should have been able to see inside the edifice but the walls were opaque.

Hesitantly, she reached out. As her hand came into contact with the shimmering cloud, coruscating sparks of energy radiated down her arm, flashing into the air around her. The effect was not painful, but calming, revitalizing. Her brief hesitation gone, she stepped forward. For a moment, she saw only the effulgence of sparkling energy glittering around her. Then she was within.

No light penetrated the structure, and yet its walls radiated a brilliance that illuminated the area. The impression was of an enormous cavern. Its stone floor was smooth, polished, littered with small pebbles. The Zarma stones, Tallia realized. Slowly, she advanced. Except for the almost imperceptible sound of her soft tread, the silence was absolute. *What now*? she wondered.

Abruptly, she came upon a diaphanous, insubstantial curtain like a spider's web. She could see intricate threads woven into complicated designs that were beyond the capabilities of human hands. Hesitantly, she reached out, touching it. For a brief moment, she fancied that the material clung to her fingers and then it was gone, dispersed by the force of a hot desert wind that flailed violently all around her, leaving her unscathed but for a fleeting moment of breathlessness.

The hot dying wind left in its wake an air of expectancy. She sensed a presence near, but the influence was not frightening. Turning, she saw a gossamer spectral image near the rear of the chamber. Hesitantly, she walked toward it, studying it, but her concentration was pointless, for the apparition remained hazy, genderless.

Unexpectedly, it disappeared. Tallia halted, disappointed, then realized that another filmy curtain hung before her, spanning the entire area from ceiling to floor. Had it been there all along? She wasn't certain. Before she attempted to bypass it, an eerie lilting music, unlike any she'd ever heard, filled the chamber. Startled, she pivoted to locate its source but she couldn't as it appeared to emanate from all around her.

Gradually she became aware of shifting patterns on the veil. She turned to face it once more and was awe-struck. She cautiously retreated as the figures in the three-dimensional moving picture before her appeared to step out of the confines of the curtain. Warily, she observed them. Slowly, she realized that if she concentrated she could see through them. They were only representations. Reassured now, she studied the fascinating phenomenon.

She saw people, dressed unlike any she'd ever seen, standing before a mass of twisted silver metal. They appeared distressed. The scene shifted and the music became more violent. People, garbed now in shapeless animal skins, warred. Others, enslaved, toiled beneath enormous loads while the enslavers cracked whips upon their already-scarred backs. Tallia cringed. How could such things happen? Then she remembered Bodan. Yes, someone like him could perpetrate such cruelties.

The colors shifted, merging, re-forming, the spectacle one of sweeping vistas rich with natural bounty. Tallia could almost smell the richness of the world around her as the music enhanced the serenity of the vision. Then, once more the music became discordant as people so feral that they seemed almost bestial returned to the scene. Thoughtlessly, they raped the fertile land, leaving nothing but waste in their wake. Tallia felt sickened. Why must she view this?

Once more the colors bled as though running down an artist's canvas before coalescing and reorganizing. Two women appeared on the scene. Both dark-haired and beautiful, they exhibited tremendous powers as they attempted to guide the people away from their doom. They were the goddesses, Coran and Galacia, Tallia realized, although, puzzlingly, in the scene before her they appeared to discourage the people's worshipful attitude. At least, Galacia did. Coran, after an initial attempt to discourage the conduct, actually seemed to foster it by performing incredible feats to further awe the people. Before long, the demeanor of those who followed the goddess Galacia appeared to anger the goddess Coran. Again, wars ravaged the land.

And so the shifting scenes continued, some of which she understood, while others were incomprehensible to her. And always, the alien music flowed. She saw the arrival of the first king, Toleme, son of the god, Yaewel. Scenes of love and despair, of death and birth, of royal consorts entering the walls of this very "key," all played on. She saw King Quillan and his queen, Jhysine, weeping at the funerals of three children. Then she saw them hurrying secretively along darkened corridors, a babe in Jhysine's arms. She screamed as she witnessed the horrifying spectacle of the queen falling from a castle parapet to her death.

Then abruptly, as the colors converged and solidified once more, she realized she looked at herself. She stood in a glass-domed enclosure upon a gleaming marble-tiled floor. Opposite her stood Lord Krogan. His eyes gleamed with hatred as he lifted his hands and Tallia saw herself flung back by the force of his power. Behind Krogan, the goddess Coran materialized smiling triumphantly. "No," Tallia moaned, denying the truth of the vision.

Immediately the scene reversed and was replayed. This time though, it was Krogan who died, thrown back by the ebullient release of Tallia's energy. The goddess Galacia appeared behind the image of Tallia, compassion shining from her eyes. "No," she whispered, once more denying the outcome of the vision. She remembered the release of that force in the wasteland and the terrible burden she felt for having committed the act. As a healer, she treasured life. She could not kill again. "Why?" she shouted hoarsely to the altering patterns on the veil as tears brimmed in her eyes.

As if in answer to her question, another scene came into focus. Now Tallia saw herself staring wistfully out an unfamiliar window, her hand resting lightly on her swollen stomach as she searched the horizon. A tall dark-haired figure in black entered the room, and the image of herself turned joyously to meet him. But, when she reached out to embrace him, he faded, becoming insubstantial. Tallia's likeness was left grasping only air, and once more she turned to gaze despondently through the window.

"Tynan," Tallia whispered yearningly. Instinctively, her hand went to her flat midriff. Did his child even now grow within her? Her head seemed to nod of its own accord. Yes, she was pregnant with Tynan's offspring. The revelation did not shock her for she knew. Somehow the awareness of it had been buried deep within her, hidden from her conscious mind.

Gradually, Tallia became aware that the shifting colors of the veil were behaving differently now, shimmering incandescently as sparks of energy flew around her. The cavernous chamber darkened. A jagged-edged bolt of coruscation flashed from the ceiling, splitting the diaphanous curtain of shifting light patterns. Tallia felt it fall upon her, enveloping her. Scintillating sparks of energy danced upon her flesh, stimulating her nerve endings. Power coursed within her, surging, amplifying.

She felt the psychic energy of her mind expanding, becoming all-encompassing. She had the ability to do things she never dreamed possible, and yet, even as she gained this knowledge, her mind sought further, seeking understanding of the proficiency required to direct and to control her power. But only partial knowledge was forthcoming.

Slowly, the wind rose in the chamber once more, this time chilling. Its mournful wail echoed and re-echoed as its icy touch raised goose flesh on Tallia's arms. The wind increased as the scintillating coruscation of energy decreased. Then abruptly there was nothing. Absolute silence reigned as once more only the walls radiated soft light, illuminating the enormous room. All was as it had been when she'd entered.

It was done then, and yet she was left with only more questions. What did it all mean? She walked through the shimmering wall of the "key" into a world still bright with daylight. Surprised, she looked at the position of the sun. She had thought it would be near sunset, but obviously time was suspended within the mystical confines of the "key."

Cautiously, she began her descent from Mount Coran along the steep mountain paths. There were so many unanswered questions. Could Eyrsa help her understand?

Dazed and only partially conscious of her actions, Tallia traversed the path down the mountain. The revelations spun wildly within her mind, one instant startlingly vivid, the next obscured, overlapped with other visions. The enormous weight of her confusing destiny pressed despairingly in on her as she rode Luma across the meadow behind the Darnaz castle. Dismounting, she sent the intelligent animal ahead. The walk would do her good. She needed time to think, to absorb the serenity of her surroundings.

CHAPTER ELEVEN

I N THE GARDEN EYRSA GATHERED HERBS. METICU-
lously, she plucked the last resinous, oval
pennyroyal leaves, placing them in her apron
alongside the fluffy, yellow camomile flowers for
brewing carminative teas. Pausing, she took mental
inventory. She required more black bryony root. It
was invaluable in the prevention of water retention
and she didn't want to be without a sufficient
supply.

Wearily, she tucked a strand of white hair into its
netting before massaging the back of her neck. Only
a few years ago she'd been able to work unrelenting-
ly but now even the slightest exertion was a strain.
She hobbled slowly to the garden's gazebo. She'd
rest there for a moment to still the heavy thudding
of her heart.

At the door of the belvedere, she halted abruptly
as a searing pain stabbed her breast. Instinctively,

she raised her numbing fingers, clutching convulsively at the agonizing constriction. Reeling, she stumbled to a wooden bench before collapsing, huddling against the consuming torture of the immense weight on her chest. The herbs spilled unnoticed from her apron, scattering across the plank flooring. *I will live*, the familiar litany swelled in her mind, expanding, crowding out the pain.

Gradually, the spasm relinquished its hold, loosening the tight bands that strangled her heart and lungs. As her rasping, laborious breathing slowly returned to normal, Eyrsa released her grip on the bench's splintered frame. Cautiously lowering herself to her knees to retrieve the herbs, she sighed deeply. There was no medicine to cure the dull ache in her chest. Time, in its merciless pursuit, was catching up with her. Soon it would wrap its greedy fingers around her, but not yet. She remained too stubborn to let it win. Tallia needed her and Eyrsa would not forsake destiny by passing from this earth before accomplishing what was required of her. She had to see Tallia once more.

The lines around her cool gray eyes deepened as a frown creased her forehead. Intently, she stared through the gazebo's latticed walls, across the russet branches of the laurel hedges. As if straining to hear Tallia's soft footfall above the whisper of the cool breeze, she tilted her white-haired head slightly. The garden's peacefulness, broken only by the occasional twittering of the elusive blue-breasted sparlark, endured.

Wrapping her heavy shawl tightly around her hunched shoulders, she rose. With her gnarled, aging hands, trembling now, she bound her curative stalks and roots within the sweep of her apron. Again she surveyed the horizon, searching the azure sky for some unknown sign. Shivering as a portentous chill undulated up her spine, she left the shelter of the circular summer retreat. Slowly, she made her way through the topiary, beneath the trellis arch draped in the dry foliage of climbing roses, and across the thick lawn to the keep.

She paused briefly at the base of the thick stone steps to regain her breath before ascending. The massive oaken doors of the keep opened with a protesting creak. Inside, she allowed herself to rest briefly against the ancient wooden portals, leaning her head against their enduring hardness as she gazed across the fortress's massive central hall. The door to Arilan's study was open, and she could see him bent studiously over his ledgers. Taking a deep breath, she shoved away the lethargic tiredness that had become her constant companion.

In her room, Eyrsa emptied her apron onto a low writing desk beside the bed. Today's collection would not join the packets stored throughout the room, for she didn't have the strength to sort them. Tiny bundles bound with twisted strands of dyed hemp permeated the atmosphere with their scents. The array before her represented the knowledge of many generations. As a Zarmist, she guarded the secrets of her trade as parsimoniously as a miser would his gold. Her healing powers were instinctive, inherited, an inner knowledge bestowed upon few.

Eyrsa removed her cherished indigo prayer crystal from its bed of aromatic herbs and set it on her desk. She'd always been particularly proud of her crystal. It differed slightly from others like it in that it seemed to hold dancing stars in its depths. Mined from the mountains of Karaundo and blessed in the temple in Maurasia, the indigo crystals were said to provide a link with the gods.

Now, she focused her gaze on those distant stars and directed a silent prayer on wings of faith to the father-god, Yaewel. *Guard the life of your child, Tallia. Protect her from harm. As always, I bow to your will.* Her prayer complete, Eyrsa reverently raised the crystal to her lips before replacing it on its bed of purifying herbs.

A sense of uneasiness invaded Tallia's mind. Lifting her troubled eyes to the threatening cumulus overhead, she shuddered. A corresponding cloud hovered on the horizons of her mind. The foretelling remained indistinct, shrouded in mist on the edge of her consciousness.

Her first premonition that something was wrong struck with jolting intensity. The fortress sat silently in the late-afternoon sun; nothing stirred. Yet, it was more than that. Tallia sensed something altered within the vined walls. There was no sign of Eyrsa who she had been certain would hurry to meet her upon her return. Concentration on the obscure visions of the "key" vanished as dread grew, rooting itself in her heart. She began to run.

Her breath came in ragged gasps as brambles clutched at her, tearing her clothing. Through the thin soles of her leather slippers, sharp rocks cut into the bottoms of her tender feet. Tallia ignored the physical pain that was not as great as the growing terror that captured her heart and drove knifelike into her soul.

She stumbled through the castle gate and across the yard as the premonition grew. Throwing open the double doors, she raced to Eyrsa's room.

Her eyes closed, Eyrsa lay unmoving in her bed, her lined face pale against the ecru coverlets, her shallow breathing barely discernible beneath the blankets that covered her.

Breathless, Tallia ran to her side, dropping to her knees beside the bed. At the slight sound, Eyrsa's eyes fluttered open, her gaze riveted on Tallia as she weakly lifted a shaking hand.

Taking the extended hand in both of her own, Tallia pressed it gently against her cheek. "I'll make you well," she promised, unable to keep the trembling from her voice. "I need you."

Slowly, Eyrsa shook her head. Her voice rasped when she finally spoke. "You don't need me." She withdrew a tattered journal from beneath her spread. Caressing the faded navy cover, she ran her fingers over the fraying edges. "In these pages lies my past, bits and pieces of emotion, stores of memories, some good, some bad, but all there nonetheless." She coughed feebly. "I can help you more this way. There are things . . . Only through death can you utilize the true extent of my knowledge."

"No," Tallia pleaded. "Don't leave me. Not now. I've seen what is required of me. I'm not strong enough to defeat him without you."

Eyrsa's gaze sharpened. "A defeatist attitude will forfeit the battle before it has begun. Strength comes in ways often not expected." Her voice, though weak, was uncompromising.

Eyrsa's expression softened. "What I do now, I do for you. Someday, you will understand that. I am with you always, even though I am gone." She gripped Tallia's hand tightly. "Remember that," she wheezed.

Helplessly, Tallia watched as pain constricted her governess's features. Closing her eyes, she forced herself to concentrate on Eyrsa's ailment. She would heal her. She had to. She loved her, needed her, now more than ever. Her Zarmistic mind focused. She saw Eyrsa's heart palpitating irregularly, weakened by disease. She revolted at the fading will to live she discerned in Eyrsa's consciousness, the compliance with death. She focused her power, feeling it surge within her. Her Zarma stone glowed luminously, its heat radiating around her. For an instant she saw the response in Eyrsa's talisman. Then the color faded, the old Zarmist's stone reverting to a lifeless gray. Tallia felt the warmth drain from Eyrsa's mind and body. Slowly, Eyrsa opened her eyes and studied Tallia quietly.

Tallia bent closer to hear the faintly uttered words. "Hold my hand now, girl. Form the link. What I will give you, I do so freely. I have always loved you as my own daughter. These things I bequeath can belong to no other."

Gripping the aged, arthritic hand firmly, Tallia extended her mind to Eyrsa's. Eyrsa's Zarma stone once more glowed with energy. Perhaps this was the way. Could she save her with the mind link? Stiffening at the jolt of energy that leapt from

Eyrsa's body and mind into her own, Tallia clung desperately to Eyrsa's hand.

She realized, even as she felt them becoming her own, that the visions flashing through her mind were Eyrsa's memories. She saw a young girl with sable hair, much like her own, learning the art of healing—Eyrsa. She saw Eyrsa marry, and felt the tremendous love Eyrsa shared with a man Tallia had never known, for he'd died; and Eyrsa's grief became hers.

She saw Eyrsa, middle-aged, her hair only faintly tinged with gray, lifting a baby from a lace-embroidered bassinet. The exquisite blanket was removed, and the child was then wrapped in a homespun, woolen scarf. With the infant pressed tightly against her chest, Eyrsa slipped down darkened corridors and into the night, stealing silently away.

The image shifted to Eyrsa, as a young woman, huddled in the shade of an arched stone bridge. A stream trickled by at her feet and sent glimmers of reflecting lights across her youthful face. Smiling, she rose to meet a boy. Tallia's mind hesitated, seeking recognition. Somehow, it eluded her and the nexus compelled her mind back to the memory. He strode firmly, confidently toward Eyrsa. But as he reached her, his commanding attitude changed. He reached out and hugged her to him.

"My sister," he whispered. "I hear your loneliness in my mind."

The scenes kept coming, increasing in speed as Tallia relaxed within the psychic bond. Another vision obscured the last. Tallia frowned. It was happening too fast. Each scene flickered into her mind taking root in her unconscious before she could analyze it or comprehend its haunting significance.

She saw a young couple embracing. They were strangers to her, though some aspect of their features struck a note of familiarity.

"Go," the woman said, and as she pulled away Tallia saw that she was with child. "You are pledged to another."

The anguish was evident on the man's face. "I will always love you."

"No. Love her," the woman pleaded. "For there is more at stake here than mere love."

The man could not deny her words. "Never again will marriages be prearranged. Never again will those destined to love have to turn their backs on their true emotions."

"That would please me," the woman whispered. "But still, it is too late for us. Please go before it is more than I can bear. You have granted me the child. She will be my strength. Through her I will always have you."

"She will be a great Zarmist," the man predicted.

The woman nodded. "I will call her Eyrsa."

Tallia started as she realized she had passed beyond Eyrsa's memories. Like the "key," this strange mind link, aided by the glowing Zarma stones, revealed flashes of the past.

The sensation of the bond had altered. Memories and scenes from minds she had never known flashed into her consciousness. She sensed that these were people who had gone before Eyrsa, her ancestors. Their knowledge, too, imprinted itself in

251

Tallia's mind; their experiences became hers. She felt her power growing, fortified by their unselfish giving. Their lives played out before her mind's eye. Images darted past, constantly changing, and a kaleidoscope of memories, continually shifting, swept her back through the early days of Karaundo and even beyond, into the swirling mists of another realm.

Abruptly, the transfer ceased. Tallia slumped against the bed, exhausted. After taking several deep breaths to clear her mind, she raised her head expecting to encounter Eyrsa's all-knowing gaze, the expression of wisdom that Tallia had grown accustomed to over her years of training.

Tallia's heart froze. Eyrsa was still, staring sightlessly past Tallia, her body lifeless. With disbelief, she shook Eyrsa's inert form. The stunning realization slowly crept through her and a burning lump rose in Tallia's throat, threatening to choke her. She swallowed against it and stubbornly repressed her tears. Eyrsa would not have wanted tears. Gently, she closed the healer's eyes, confused by the peaceful expression on Eyrsa's face. Eyrsa had willed this, willed her own death so that she might pass on her strength, her memories to Tallia, sacrificing herself for something beyond her comprehension because she felt it necessary. Tallia's expression hardened with determination; she *would* be worthy of Eyrsa's gift.

Across the wasteland in the capital of Maurasia, King Quillan trembled and dropped to his knees. Several aides rushed to his side but he brushed them aside with hastily muttered assurances and escaped to his room. He felt the cold surge of emotion that forewarned of Eyrsa's departure, the fluttering of breath, the transference of power. Eyrsa's death left an aching void in his heart, a cold abyss and he wept at the loss of his half sister.

As the agony of shock and grief subsided, he rose and crossed his room to the window. Over the walls of Maurasia, beyond the distant wasteland and into the purplish mountains, he sent his pleading call across the miles. He had to be sure but there came no reply. She was truly gone.

Finally, he sat before the polished desk and withdrew a sheet of crested parchment, placing it in front of him. Dipping the quill in the inkwell, he jotted several instructions and then quietly, purposefully, he folded the parchment and sealed it with wax. The time had come. He summoned an aide and instructed him to find Tynan of the House of Keane immediately. Tynan was the man most suited to the task, for not only did he know the wasteland, but he had earned Quillan's trust as had his father before him. The letter must be delivered personally into Tynan's hands and from them to Tallia of the House of Darnaz.

Quillan began to pace the parquet floor, letting his thoughts roam sadly over the memories of his half sister, knowing she could never be replaced in his heart.

Tallia stood in the doorway to her father's study. She felt numb, her motions involuntary, uncontrollable. "Eyrsa's dead." The emotionless sound of her voice brought Arilan to his feet. As he reached her side, she collapsed into his arms, the bolstering strength of her determination fading.

"She's gone." Her voice quavered with the force of the grief that robbed her of coherent thought, leaving nothing but the piercing pain in her heart. "Eyrsa's gone."

The funeral passed in a blur of anguish. Paralysis gripped Tallia's emotions; she could not cry. The bleak gray sky corresponded to the numbing dark cloud that blanketed her mind as she stood dry-eyed and silent during the eulogy. She stared blankly past the villagers as they filed by, deaf to their words of condolence, blind to the evidence of their grief.

When it was over, Tallia followed meekly, holding on to Arilan's arm as he led her back to the castle. Her family, though distraught with their own pain, tried to comfort her. Rashana administered a strong brew, forcing Tallia to drink it. The potion induced a deep dreamless sleep but even that did not diminish Tallia's loss.

One week later, Tallia stared across the sheltered garden, past the frost-blackened roses that still clung tenaciously to the framework of the latticed arch. She felt only emptiness within the walled confines, within herself. Eyrsa was gone, and with her a part of Tallia had died. She clenched her slender fingers around the Zarma stone to stop their trembling and walked toward the gazebo, unaware of the tears that trickled down her cheeks.

Languidly, she ran her fingers across the interwoven pattern of the structure's walls as she halted in the doorway and gazed longingly at the vacant seat before her. The first sob struck her like a blow, racking her slim form, forcing her to grip the doorway to remain on her feet. The emotion she had held in check for so long would no longer be denied; she was forced to surrender to the agony that consumed her. Slowly her grip on the doorframe slackened as she slipped down its length. Falling to her knees, she wrapped her arms around herself as though the action might ease the ache. Her head bowed and her shoulders shook with the force of her sorrow as she finally allowed her grief to surface.

"Why?" she demanded angrily through her tears. "I need you." She raised her face to the sky then covered it with her hands as a fresh burst of tears wet her cheeks. "Eyrsa!" But only silence answered her mournful plea.

When Tallia finally emerged from the garden, she brushed away the last of the tears. Though her reddened eyes gave evidence of her mourning, a new resolve showed in the set of her chin. She squared her shoulders and delved deeply into her soul. Her destiny was clear. There was much to do, much to learn. No one could ever fill the spot Eyrsa held in her heart, but she knew now that the Zarmist would always be with her, perhaps not physically but in spirit. She recalled Eyrsa's quiet presence and welcomed the memories with an eager heart, relieved that they brought some small measure of peace.

Crossing the yard, she re-entered the manor.

Unerringly, she sought Eyrsa's room. Closing the door quietly, she moved to the aged writing desk and pulled up the chair. The time had come to lay the past to rest. Slowly, she emptied the contents of each of the drawers and nooks. Examining each item, she placed them in a lined basket—the yellowed pages of a now unbound notebook; a piece of ribbon; thick packets of dried herbs; and stalks of flowers, their petals crisp with age. They were all a part of Eyrsa, no matter how small, how trivial, and each was afforded a treasured place in the woven basket.

From the chair by the window, Tallia retrieved the lace shawl that had always adorned Eyrsa's shoulders and folded it on top of the other items. From the mantel over the fireplace, she took down the oval frame that held a miniature hand-painted portrait of Eyrsa. Lovingly, she ran her hands over the face that smiled at her from within the gold-embossed frame. These things were her inheritance, a part of her as surely as they had been a part of Eyrsa. With a sad sigh, she carried them from the room, closing the door with finality behind her.

Quietly, she made her way up the stairs to her own chamber. Inside, she opened the lid of the heavy chest at the foot of her bed and placed the basket inside. Removing the notebook, she touched the basket again in a silent homage before closing the chest and turning to her desk.

For several minutes she stared at Eyrsa's journal, then, with a sigh, picked it up and folded back the cover. A sealed enveloped slipped from between the pages.

Tallia picked it up and broke the seal. Carefully, she unfolded the yellowing paper. A frown creased her brow as she scanned the contents of the letter and noted the signature scrawled across the bottom of the page. An icy chill crept into her fingers and the message fluttered to the floor.

CHAPTER TWELVE

TALLIA STARED BLANKLY AT THE PAPER AT HER feet. For an instant her mind rejected its implications. King Quillan's daughter! It wasn't possible. Or was it? She resembled neither Arilan nor Rashana, a fact that Tallia had never given much consideration to. But now it tolled like an alarm inside her head.

Why was she here, hidden away in the Twin Suns Fiefdom? Momentarily she felt a sense of betrayal. Who else knew of this? Her parents? Others? She frowned. *No,* she thought. Surely she would have felt the difference in her family's and servants' attitudes. This was Eyrsa's secret, carefully guarded for the past eighteen years. The confusing images she'd witnessed in the "key" began to fit into place.

Bending, she retrieved the document. The statement of birth certainly appeared official, giving

Tallia's name, place, date, and time of birth. The thick wax seal near the bottom belonged to the royal House of Tuhan and King Quillan's eloquent scrawl filled the line reserved for the father's signature. The mother's signature, smeared by moisture, was illegible. Queen Jhysine, Tallia recalled, had died the year after her birth. That fact, learned in a lesson years earlier and then forgotten by Tallia, came back now with startling clarity. Was she then the legitimate child of the royal family?

Why had Tallia never seen this man, this king, who was her father? Why this deception? Why the secrecy? The unanswered questions marched intractably through her thoughts.

Reopening the chest, Tallia withdrew the basket. Meticulously, she searched it for some other sign, some further confirmation of the document's contents. She found nothing. Sitting in the middle of her bed, the contents of the basket spread before her, she sat in silence for a long time, allowing the reality of the situation to imbed itself in her mind. She had no doubt that the circumstances of her birth, so long hidden, were true. But that truth didn't impart understanding. She needed answers. She needed to speak to Eyrsa. Repacking the basket slowly, she considered the situation. Then, reaching a decision, she left the room.

Across the garden, at the far end, shaded by trailing branches of an ancient anwista tree, Tallia halted before the barred metal gates to the graveyard. At its center, rising imposingly above the simple markers surrounding it, was the crypt. Tallia walked softly toward it. The silence there always seemed more intense, as though all nature quieted in honor of the dead. She halted, studying the stone structure before descending into the depths of the tomb. Eyrsa's chamber, being the newest, was the nearest, but still at least twenty feet back.

Beyond Eyrsa's shrine were those of Arilan's mother and father, though they were several years older. The stone casing that enclosed Eyrsa's coffin rested on a dais several feet above the damp floor. As Tallia reached it, she dropped to her knees, heedless of the moisture. Laying her arms across the cold stone, she rested her head in her hands and stared vacantly into the cavernous darkness beyond, her mind whirling with questions. Absently, she traced her fingers over the brief inscription engraved on a small metal plaque embedded in the rock. She'd seen it earlier. It read, simply, "Eyrsa, Zarmist."

"What do I do now? What will become of me and the child within me?" Tallia let the words flow, hoping that by speaking aloud she could discern her own answers, formulate her own plans. But, in her mind, they tumbled together confusingly. "Do I stay here? Do I wait? Do I tell the others? Should I speak to him? King Quillan, I mean. Oh, Eyrsa, you have bequeathed me your knowledge, yet I am unsure now of my path. My destiny always seemed so clear before. But where does it lead to now?" Her plaintive cries went unanswered.

The tears that trickled down Tallia's cheeks now were not from grief, but were curative, a deep healing process that she let run its course. It was almost an hour before she finally struggled to her feet and massaged the numbness from her limbs. In silent acceptance of Eyrsa's death, she walked slowly to the entrance, re-entered the world beyond and returned to the castle.

In her room, Tallia paced. What was she to do? The foretelling of the battle, revealed in the "key," clearly marked her as one of the opponents. Was it a result of her newly discovered blood tie to the throne? It had to be. Yet, she still did not understand fully why the confrontation was to occur. What events had lead to the provocation of this battle? How could she possibly hope to survive without Eyrsa's advice and guidance? Would King Quillan help her?

Dropping into the chair, she rested her elbows on the desk, her chin in her hands. Could she talk to her parents? What would they say? Would their expressions confirm or deny her belief that they knew nothing of her true identity? She sighed. There was no one else and they were still her parents. Perhaps they could help her sort through the tumult in her mind.

She found Rashana and Arilan together in her father's study. They weren't working, though Arilan's thick ledgers sat open on his desk. They sat quietly on a sofa, watching the flames in the fireplace, content with the silence and each other. Tallia almost hated to interrupt the peaceful moment. She hoped that someday she would find such easy companionship.

"Tallia." Rashana smiled at her and patted the worn leather beside her. "Come sit awhile." Arilan shifted so all three of them could sit comfortably.

Tallia noted that they both studied her with concern. They knew her deep attachment to Eyrsa and were still cautious in their references to the

Zarmist. Rashana had comforted Tallia on Eyrsa's death but time had been what Tallia needed more than comforting words.

"I found a document in Eyrsa's things," Tallia began hesitantly. "I thought it best if you saw it too." She extended the parchment to Arilan. Tallia waited as he read, her heart pounding loudly against her ribs as she held her breath. His lined brow creased in thought as he passed the paper to Rashana and stared incredulously at Tallia.

"Could it be?" Rashana whispered, looking first at Arilan and then at Tallia. "Why would Eyrsa not have told us?"

Arilan shrugged. "The same reason she never told Tallia I suspect."

"You didn't know then?" Tallia knew without hearing the answer. Their expressions were answer enough. The contents of the certificate had startled and surprised them as much as it had her.

"No," Arilan replied.

Rashana shook her head. "Eyrsa brought you to us when you were only a few weeks old. Of course, she didn't have to ask twice if we would raise you. I've always thought of you as my daughter. I just assumed you were orphaned," Rashana explained.

"We should have told you," Arilan added. "I'm sorry, Tallia."

She pressed her hand over his. "You did what you thought best. I've never wanted for anything and you'll always be my parents. You raised me, loved me, taught me right from wrong. There is no reason to be sorry."

Rashana reached over and gave her a quick hug.

Tallia continued, a frown of confusion marring

her face. "But why did Eyrsa never tell me, even when she knew how little time she had left? And why did the king give me to Eyrsa and why has he never so much as inquired as to my well-being?"

"I'm sure there must be a good explanation for all this," Arilan stated, "which I wouldn't mind hearing myself."

"Do you think then that I should seek an audience with King Quillan?"

Arilan stared thoughtfully into the fire. Finally he nodded. "Come spring, we'll all go. I think we're all owed an explanation."

Tallia made no reply.

"We must be discreet," Arilan continued. "There may be a good reason why he's never claimed you, and why he gave you to Eyrsa. We must be careful not to form hasty conclusions which could result in false accusations and inadvertent harm to the king's reputation. I suggest that this remain our secret for a while longer."

Tallia nodded. She couldn't agree more. There was something threatening about losing your identity so suddenly.

"Goddess above!" Tallia exclaimed, as the reality of the situation struck her. "I'm his only child, his true heir."

"Mmmm." Arilan nodded. "I wonder if this charade was for your protection? I suspect someone of King Quillan's forthright nature must surely have had justification for removing you from the castle."

"I just can't imagine how he could bear to part with you," Rashana interjected. "His wife passed away shortly after your birth. It must have been a terrible blow to him, losing both her and you."

Tallia nodded. She needed time alone. "I think I'll go to my room for a while if you don't mind."

They smiled understandingly, and Tallia felt a twinge of pain compounded by the secret she held. They would always be her parents, always be special, no matter what the birth certificate said. Soon they would be grandparents. For now, though, she would continue to keep that knowledge to herself. Her emotions were in too much turmoil, her decisions not yet made. Impulsively, she wrapped her arms around her mother and then her father, bestowing upon them grateful hugs, then hurried from the room as the tears brimmed her eyes and the ever-present nausea overpowered her.

During the following two weeks, she mourned Eyrsa's passing in silence, recapturing their moments together in her memory. She spent the long hours poring through the tattered pages of Eyrsa's journal, surprised to realize that many of the entries were now her own memories, instilled by the fusing process Eyrsa had instigated at the moment of her death. Reading the words brought the visions sharply into perspective and she found she could relive many of the incidents. Even Eyrsa's cures and potions were now permanently fixed within Tallia's consciousness.

So this was what Eyrsa had meant her to inherit, not only her knowledge, but her memories and those of generations before her. The clarity and realism of those remembrances brought Eyrsa back and the aged Zarmist began once again to fill the void in Tallia's existence.

Tallia alternated between the journal and Arilan's library. She suddenly found herself hungry for knowledge concerning the royal house, any knowledge. Often she sat long into the night, studying some particularly interesting article. She discovered the repetitive mention of the special royal powers and placed her hand gently on her stomach and wondered if her child would have those abilities.

Tynan halted on a rise just south of Darnaz castle. In these, the winter months, he had been forced to skirt much of the barren wasteland now perilously wrapped in the grip of ice and frigid cold. Even pushing himself and Chaz to the extent of their endurance, it had taken more than a month to reach this spot.

King Quillan's instructions had been clear. He was to return Tallia of the House of Darnaz to Maurasia immediately. The king had not expounded on the reasons behind that request and Tynan had not had the opportunity to question the imperative. Now his mind resounded with questions. Who *was* Tallia of Twin Suns that Quillan would request her presence? Why was her arrival in Maurasia so important that Quillan had postponed Tynan's duties in the wasteland?

He was unsure what Tallia's reaction to this summons would be. After his departure almost two months earlier, he wasn't certain what his reception would be. He touched the king's letter, tucked inside his shirt, to reassure himself of its presence. He would need it to convince Tallia to come with him, he was certain.

The fact that she appeared to have accepted his departure so easily galled him. He'd half hoped she would have pleaded with him to stay. In fact, he'd even had a speech ready to deliver in that event, explaining all the reasons why he felt they could not share a life together. But, in the moments spent preparing the speech, he'd forgotten that it was he who loved, and that his love was not reciprocated.

For a moment, he allowed his thoughts to roam, recalling the haunting visions of her which he had yet to escape—Tallia's oval face framed with the length of dark hair, and her innocent, trusting eyes with just a trace of something imperceptible flickering in their depths. The nearer he drew to his destination, the more vivid the recollections became. His nerves tightened, until he thought surely they would snap.

He forced his mind back to the king's request. He would simply be the king's messenger. There was no room in his life for the emotion he felt tossing uncontrollably beneath the surface of his carefully maintained facade.

In the library, Tallia looked up suddenly from the open book before her. Something had disturbed her concentration but she was at a loss to explain exactly what it was. Absently, she closed the book and leaned back in the chair. Pensively, she waited for a repeat of the almost indecipherable touch.

Distantly, a solid rapping at the main door

echoed within the stone confines of the walls. She listened intently to the muted sound of Garth's footsteps. Unconsciously holding her breath, she waited, straining to hear. A brief conversation of muffled unintelligible words drifted into the room.

Probably someone from the village, she thought, refusing to acknowledge the exhilaration that sent tremors quivering to the tips of her fingers. She rose and met Garth in the hallway.

"A messenger from the king." Garth's tone indicated his curiosity. "He requests a meeting with you."

"Is the fire lighted in the sitting room?" Tallia had the most peculiar urge to run, to hide.

Garth nodded.

"Are my parents back yet?"

The caretaker shook his head.

She swallowed nervously, furtively glancing around, ensuring that everything was clean and in its proper place. She shook her head slightly, surprised by her state of uncertainty.

"Show him in. I'll be right there."

Instead of following the servant, she went to the kitchen and prepared a tray of snacks and a pot of hot tea. The methodic actions gave her time to still the trembling of her hands. More confident and relaxed now, she carried the tray toward the sitting room. *Is this it*? she wondered, thinking that perhaps the king had learned of Eyrsa's death. Was she about to get the answers to the questions that still tormented her?

Tynan stood before the fire, letting the warmth penetrate his numb hands, trying to concentrate on wording his request. His anxiety astounded him. What would be her reaction to his presence?

When Tallia entered the room, she saw only the back of a tall man with wavy, ebony hair, his wide shoulders still cloaked in black cohabear fur. It was enough. The tray dropped the last few inches onto the table, cups and spoons clattering noisily against each other. Her initial reaction after the shock of recognition was disbelief, then elation, then disappointment. They rebounded within her, one following the other in rapid succession.

Tynan turned slowly to face her. He looked more handsome than he had when he'd left only seven weeks ago. Neither moved. Finally, his face expressionless, he took a seat near the fire.

"You needn't have used the king's name to gain admission here," Tallia rebuked softly. Her emotions roiled within her and she struggled to control them. He must not see her confusion. She would not be affected by his cool aloofness.

Tynan didn't reply as he reached inside his shirt, and produced a crumpled piece of paper, offering it to her in silence. He didn't trust himself to speak. A flood of desire, induced by the sight of her, rose perilously close to the surface. He needed time to regain control before he trusted his voice.

Tallia regarded the letter cautiously. Finally she reached out, stretching a little, maintaining her distance. She knew it was irrational after what they'd shared only a few short weeks ago, but she felt awkward, unnerved by his presence. She thought she'd mastered the rampant craving for his touch, but his mere presence rekindled the consuming emotion. Why? What was there about this man that drew her to him? Hesitantly, she accepted the letter without touching him. She was afraid the lightest brush against his skin would sear her like a red-hot fire. She backed away before opening the message.

Quickly, she read the note. *No explanation then*, she thought. King's Quillan's missive was brief. He requested her immediate presence in Maurasia. All would be explained on her arrival. Tynan, his trusted envoy, was to escort her. Tallia refolded the parchment.

Tynan tossed uncomfortably in the bed. Sleep eluded him. Whether due to the unaccustomed comfort of a soft mattress, or the thoughts and visions of Tallia that refused to leave his mind at peace, he was uncertain. She'd made no comment upon reading the message; in fact, she had not seemed surprised, but expectant.

Curiosity burned within him. What connection linked her to the king and what was the reason for sending him across the wasteland to retrieve her? Tallia had remained silent as she refolded the message, and he suspected she would not confide in him. Her response had been cool. Yet, for an instant when she'd first seen him, he thought he'd seen a brief flash of happiness in the depths of her expressive eyes. Had he imagined it?

With detached efficiency she had directed a servant to prepare a room for him, and then to oversee the packing of the items she would require for travel. He should have been relieved by her coolness. Hadn't he once encouraged just that reaction? It was safer. Why then would his heart not listen to reason?

Eventually, sheer exhaustion pushed the tortuous musing from his thoughts as weeks of hard travel and inadequate sleep took their toll.

Through the thick cloud of sleep he dreamed of illusive specters. Eyrsa was there and, beyond her, faceless shapes that beckoned as they wavered back and forth, the transparent folds of their robes billowing hypnotically in the mist curling at their feet. Within the grip of his dream, he tried to move, attempted to shift his leaden legs over the edge of the bed.

The visions faded as a more brilliant glow filled his thoughts. The new, glimmering apparition was his mother, then Eyrsa, Tynara, then Tallia and suddenly a strange combination of all four that left his mind groping for recognition as it tried desperately to determine who the face most resembled. She smiled and he felt the confusion slip away. Comforting darkness blanketed his thoughts, plunging him back once again into the depths of dreamless slumber.

Tynan shivered. The room seemed suddenly cold, the bed unexpectedly hard. His eyes snapped open, searching the unfamiliar confines of the stone chamber, and he shook his head to clear the cobwebs that deadened his thoughts. He was no longer in the keep. How had he come to be there, in an alien stone chamber? He rose stiffly to his feet.

The pyramidal stone walls peaked overhead, three of them appearing to be of solid stone. The fourth side was cloaked with a shimmering semitransparent gauze that allowed a view of the moon-lit valley below. Somehow he had been transported up the mountain. Had Tallia or someone else drugged the meal he had consumed before retiring? How else could they have brought him there without waking him?

He'd soon find out. He strode toward the exit and reached out to brush the diaphanous cloth aside. As his fingers touched the smooth surface, he jerked his hand back in surprise. Icy cold to the touch, the gauze was smooth and solid, as impenetrable as the three rock walls. He retreated in awe as the material began to shimmer with pale lavender light, gradually becoming a kaleidoscope of shifting colors that converged into altering patterns depicting changing scenes.

First there was the smiling multifaced woman. Her image was quickly replaced by one of Tallia and himself, naked, wrapped in each other's arms, making love beneath star-studded wasteland skies. He saw Tallia staring at him with the same haunted, melancholy expression that she had tried so hard to hide as they had spoken their good-byes a few weeks before.

The scene shifted again. It was Tallia, rocking slowly before the fireplace in the king's palace. He frowned, unable to understand the connection. As he moved toward her, the scene became enlarged. She lifted her head and smiled lovingly at him. As he reached her, he saw the child held in her arms. The baby opened his eyes. Tynan gasped audibly. They were a piercing emerald green—his eyes, his child!

He heard the rising howl of the wind. Still his

gaze remained fixed on the vision before him. Like
a sheet of ice, the gauze wall shattered, cascading in
a shower of crystal shards to litter the stone floor. In
a luminous flash they became drifting, spinning
eddies of mist. Like the cold breath of death, the
wind whistled through the rocky cavern, sweeping
the lavender fog, twisting it up and around him.
The vortex grew, entrapping him within the circle
of its clinging grasp. Dizziness clouded his mind and
he sank to his knees. The stone floor disappeared
and he felt himself falling, spiraling through a black
void of howling wind, plummeting through space
and time.

"Galacia." The whisper echoed within the walls
of his mind. "Galacia." He heard the name again as
a flash of flame surged around him, encircling him,
imprisoned by the windy barrier around him. The
murmur was harsh, a voice that quivered with age.
Then a thousand voices merged within his head, all
speaking simultaneously, insinuating that he had
no right to enter the "key," all questioning his
intentions, his background, his lineage. Tynan
clamped his hands over his ears to block the
deafening sound but found the source was within
him, and the sound was only intensified.

Instinctively, he straightened and shouted out at
the unseen interrogators. "I am Tynan of the House
of Keane."Remembering his heritage, he mentally
dared anyone to deny his rights. A surge of energy
invaded his body and his mind, and with it came the
knowledge that the "key" was the source of psychic
power. Yet, even as his brain fought to grasp the
myriad fragments of knowledge amassing there, it

was gone from his conscious mind.

Tynan felt a jolt as his knees struck the floor. The wind and the voices were gone. In the fleeting heartbeat between the time he felt himself dropping to his knees and the time he felt the ground, the sensations had come and gone. His vision cleared. He was in the room in Darnaz castle. For an instant he thought he saw the face of the woman again, shimmering opaquely across the room. His eyelids felt heavy, so heavy. He fought to keep them from closing but failed. Descending like a thick cloak, the darkness engulfed him and he slumped to the floor.

Tynan tossed uncomfortably on the too-soft mattress and as he turned, a bar of sunlight crossed his face. He opened his eyes and raised his hand to massage his temples to alleviate the pounding in his head. Sitting up abruptly, he recalled the dream. It was as vivid now as it had been the night before. Every detail remained firmly implanted in his memory.

Had he been cursed with one of Tallia's foretelling dreams or had his own desires, incited by her nearness, conjured the scenes to haunt him even further? Had it been a message? Was there some possibility of a life together for them?

No, he'd had nothing to offer her when his desire had consumed him in the wasteland, and he had nothing now. How could he commit to her when vengeance ruled his life? Even now his soul hungered for it, demanded that he restore honor to the House of Keane. There was no other means to appease the cold knot of rage that lay constantly coiled in his gut like a viper. It had commanded his steps since the day his family had perished and he had entered into the king's service, this hatred that refused to leave him in peace, refused to allow his mind to stray far from those horrendous memories. He could not give of himself until he had banished that gnawing pain.

But how? How could he prove Krogan's guilt? Would the king believe him? The man was too powerful, too ensconced in the hearts of the people of Karaundo. Oh, yes, Krogan had disguised his hypocrisies well.

Tynan frowned. Why did the hands of fate forever guide him to Tallia of the House of Darnaz? Was it the Zarma stone? he wondered as he recalled wise old Maural's prediction. Was he destined to follow her for the rest of his days, always afraid to draw too near, lest he become ensnared by his own desire or her innocent passion? Where did this journey lead? Where did it end?

And the child? Did it grow within her now? Or was that merely a foretelling, a vision of things to come? He wondered if a confession of his love would be a relief to Tallia or merely a more unwelcome tie to bind her to a destiny she did not desire.

Tynan watched Tallia carefully as they prepared for their journey. A silent communication passed between her and her parents, something he did not understand for he thought their expressions revealed more than sadness at a temporary parting. Was it resignation, acceptance he read there? Why? He noted the anguish in her parents' eyes as they bid her good journey, and once more memories of his own loss hardened the planes of his face.

The first morning on the trail confirmed Tynan's suspicions as Tallia doubled over behind a clump of trees, racked by waves of nausea she could no longer hold at bay. Was she unaware of the child? Or did she think him so ignorant that he would not guess, even with this evidence?

"Are you all right?" he queried solicitously in the hope that she'd confide in him.

"Fine," Tallia responded.

Tynan felt the anger well up in him. Obviously she intended to conceal his child from him.

The journey was pure torture, an endless series of frosty mornings and frigid evenings broken only by the monotony of endless riding. Neither Tallia nor Tynan would bend enough to break the silence they both held onto.

Tallia prayed for the trip to end as the reins of self-control on her emotions were so tight that she felt surely she would break. She pulled her fur closer to her, a gesture of protectiveness that was not due entirely to the chill.

Tynan of the House of Keane had come back into her life, but the association would once more be brief. She knew by the haunted expression in his eyes that he'd not yet completed his chosen course. There had been naught between them but wanton passion, and she carried its fruit within her womb. But she'd matured in the last few months. Her destiny, though she still did not understand it fully, was more compelling than even she had imagined.

She could no longer allow her emotions and her desires to control her actions.

She had Eyrsa's strength and determination. She wouldn't let herself need him, child or no. Yet, she couldn't help but remember her past certainty that a bond had been forged between them. *No*, Tallia thought, denying the memory. Although she cared for him deeply, she didn't need him. Her determination to reject her emotions fueled her temper and tore at her insides with a voracious hunger that grew with the long days of travel.

Tynan slowed his pace to allow for her condition, thankful that if she noticed she made no comment. During the many days of silent travel, he made a decision. When she told him about the child, he would ask her to marry him. She wouldn't be encumbered with his presence, for his duty to the king would keep him away much of the time. She need never know of his love, something she obviously didn't want. But perhaps she'd admit that she needed his help to raise the child.

As they neared Maurasia, Tynan eyed the horizon. Another day at the most and they'd be there. He frowned. Four weeks of travel and still she had not told him of the baby. Should he approach her, inform her that he knew, demand to know her intentions and the reason for her secrecy? No, that was not the way. His lips tightened grimly. He would wait.

Relieved to be almost at the end of the tortuous trip, Tallia let Luma plod unhurriedly behind Chaz. She missed the security of the fiefdom, and her growing anticipation and trepidation at meeting King Quillan left her edgy, nervous.

Tynan turned to tell her to hurry. He'd had as much of this tense, silent companionship as he felt obligated to endure. A spark of sunlight reflected from the rocky cliff above, drawing his attention. An arrow hissed through the air, imbedding itself in the soil at Chaz's feet. Another swiftly followed.

CHAPTER THIRTEEN

TYNAN BELLOWED A WARNING EVEN AS HE BENT, scooping Tallia into his arms from her seat on the gari. He goaded Chaz, racing for a mound of boulders at the foot of the cliff on their right. More arrows rained from above. Jumping from Chaz's back, he deposited Tallia within the confining space between two large rocks. "Stay here," he commanded briskly.

Numb with surprise, Tallia observed him as he moved off through the jumble of stone. Her heart stopped every time his body became exposed to the cliff above. The sharp points of the arrows clicked against the rocks around him, and she held her breath every time she lost sight of him. Who were the men above? Why had they attacked? How many were there? The questions whirled through her mind like a maelstrom.

Then she remembered the abilities she possessed, still so foreign to her. Perhaps she could discover the answers. She closed her eyes, sending her mind soaring, drifting like a feather propelled by a gentle updraft. Up, up to the cliff above, seeking. There, she'd touched an unfamiliar mind. One. She moved on. Another, two. And the process continued until she'd touched the essence of ten unknown minds. Great goddess! Ten! And only Tynan against them. She had to do something. But what?

Tynan! her mind cried out in fear and frustration.

Yes. What is it? The reply was hesitant, confused, but clear.

Tallia's eyes dilated in surprise. How had Tynan heard her call? Quickly gathering her wits, she communicated what she'd learned. *There are ten of them.*

A brief pause followed in which Tallia perceived only uncertainty. Then his reply came. *I'll get behind them. Lure them one at a time.*

Tallia stared across the rugged bluff. She could no longer see Tynan as he moved up the face of the steep boulder-cluttered hillside far to her right. She feared for him. Was there more she could do to help? Once more she sent her mind spiraling. She would do more than briefly touch their minds this time. Now she sought their thoughts, their reasons.

Slowly, as she made contact with one of the men, she moved past the ineffectual barriers of his insipid mind. This one thought only of the drink and women to be bought when the job was done. She moved on to the next man, repeating the process. She recoiled. Never had she felt a mind so corrupt, so slovenly. Touching it made her feel contaminated, but she forced herself to continue. Bloodlust was strong in this one; he enjoyed killing. He was here to kill. . . . *No!* She withdrew in horror.

What is it, Tallia?

Tynan had sensed her distress! She forced composure. *Nothing. I'm just frightened.*

She stared at her hands in dismay. These men were after her, were being paid to kill her. Her association with Tynan had endangered his life. "Oh, Galacia, what can I do?" she murmured.

A searing pain stabbed her chest. She felt the hurt as though it were her own, yet instantly realized it wasn't. *Tynan!* her panic-stricken mind screamed. There was no response. Seconds later, a black-garbed form tumbled from the rocks above to land with a sickening thud. "Tynan!" she shrieked. All thought of personal safety gone, she clambered from the concealing rocks.

"There she is."

Tallia turned as the hoarse shout penetrated her frenzied mind. An arrow released from the rocks above sailed toward her. Her limbs refused to operate. Time seemed suspended, slowed. She could only stare, mechanically watching the agonizingly slow descent of the razor-tipped shaft.

In a burst of fire, Coran clothed in a garment of shimmering flame appeared before her. Her long black hair billowed behind her on the eddies of a nonexistent wind. She raised her hand and the arrow halted. Her scornful laughter echoed, rebounding from the cliff above. Thick mist formed around her, swirling, expanding. Shapes became visible. Flying beasts with fangs of lightning sprang from the ground, spreading spectral wings, expanding, multiplying until their shadowy forms blocked the sunlight. Jagged bolts of energy flashed within their eye sockets as they opened their mouths. Wind rose, roaring, hurling debris before it.

Tallia heard the terrified screams of the men above and she heard Coran's throaty triumphant laughter. Like ragged tusks of energy, lightning flashed once more from the mouths of the beasts. And then, silence. The attackers, the wind, and beasts were all gone. Only the strange mist and the woman remained. She turned now to face Tallia, smiling a secretive, evil smile. "It is not yet your time to die," she said, and then she was gone. Only the ghostly echo of her spiteful laughter lingered.

Tynan! Tallia's mind, incapable of dealing with the bizarre occurrence, returned to her original purpose. She peered into a thick mist that only seconds before hadn't been there. Where was he? Like a moth drawn to a flame, she followed her instincts.

Suddenly, through the strange wisps, she saw a shadow. Riveting her gaze on the vague form of the faralk, Tallia unconsciously sought contact with Chaz's mind, following his mental trail as easily as a well-defined path. Desperately, she peered into the mist surrounding the beast.

"Tynan," she called as she broke into a run. Wildly, she raced across the broken, rocky ground. "Tynan!" she screamed again, willing away the dark cloud of foreboding that pressed down upon her, choking her, piercing into her heart like a dagger.

An anguished cry of despair escaped her lips as she recognized his shape, twisted beside a tumbled pile of rocks. In an instant, she reached the spot where he lay. Falling to her knees beside him, she gently lifted his head and placed it in her lap. He stared up at her with glazed eyes as she ran her fingers through his dark hair and wiped away the trickle of blood from his brow.

Tallia struggled against the surge of rage that threatened to release her carefully controlled psychic energy. She forced her mind from thoughts of revenge against those who had harmed him. Instead, she concentrated on her deep desire to heal his pain. The glow of the Zarma stone deepened to a brilliant violet beneath her light tunic and she clutched the powerful talisman, feeling its warmth in her palm.

Slowly, she placed her other hand on Tynan's forehead, opening her mind to his pain. Tears of compassion and shared torment clouded her vision. Impatiently, she shook them away. At each of his labored breaths, red froth bubbled from his chest, staining the shaft of the arrow protruding from his flesh. Hesitantly, she grasped the instrument of his torture. Closing her eyes, she summoned her strength then quickly jerked the wooden barb free. Tynan's body jerked beneath her hand as the pain penetrated his unconscious state.

Now her mind probed the damage. So much hurt! Broken bones, a crushed vertebrae, punctured lung, fractured skull, death. Even now it crept upon him. Did she have the strength to heal so much? To rob Death of his prize? *Live, Tynan*, she prayed. Tears clouded her vision as she looked down upon his handsome features.

"My life," she whispered, knowing he did not hear her. Her voice trembled with the strength of her emotions. "I would give my life for you,

Tynan." The searing energy built inside her, flowing from the tingling tips of her fingers. Her surroundings faded from her consciousness until only the sight and thought of Tynan occupied her entire being. Tallia felt the force as it pulsed from her hands into his still form. She summoned every last ounce of energy she had to give, and still more was required. *Please*, she pleaded silently. But the light of the Zarma stone began to flicker, its power drained. She had no more to give. She'd failed! Her shoulders sagged in defeat. Debilitated by her efforts, she welcomed the black veil of oblivion as it hovered, then descended. She collapsed, sprawling across Tynan's motionless body.

Tynan's eyes fluttered open. Warmth bathed his face as the afternoon sun cast slanted rays from atop the slope. A few yards away, Chaz and Luma waited patiently. The warmth from Tallia's body penetrated his sore limbs and he wrapped his arms around her possessively.

He'd been shot! He remembered the arrow, the strength leaving his limbs, the fall. There'd been pain as his body tumbled, striking sharp stone. Then when he'd landed amid a pile of boulders he remembered the excruciating agony as his bones splintered. He'd felt the coldness of death in his limbs and yet, he was alive! A vague memory of Tallia leaning over him surfaced.

"Tallia." He shook her gently. Instantly concerned by her lack of response, he frowned. "Tallia." Her body remained limp and flexible in his grasp as he shook her again.

Instinctively, he guessed that she had healed him,

giving too much of herself. Frantically, he searched for a pulse on her slender white throat, now frighteningly cold. It was there, faint, but unmistakable. She needed warmth, rest, and nourishment. He rose, staggering beneath the onslaught of dizziness and weakness that assailed him. Stumbling, he retrieved the thick cohabear cape, spreading it on the ground near her. Then, with more effort than he would have thought he'd need to lift her slender form, he moved her onto it, cocooning her within its warmth.

He held her, rocking her gently back and forth as if the strength of his love alone would revive her. As the realization of the ineffectiveness of this action finally penetrated his fogged thoughts, he set about making camp. At least it provided a slight diversion, displacing some of the desperation that filled him.

A short time later, having made a nourishing, if somewhat tasteless, broth of dried meat and water, he returned to her side. Her flesh had warmed somewhat, and he took that as a good sign. "Tallia," he murmured, shaking her gently. There was no response. For the first time in years, Tynan felt truly frightened. He had no idea what to do, how to help her. "Oh, goddess Galacia," he moaned, "don't do this to me."

Then, abruptly he remembered the strange mind contact Tallia had initiated earlier. When had he been granted psychic ability? The night of the dream? No sooner had the question been asked and it was answered. All that had been implanted in his mind surfaced. He could contact Tallia again! Could he stir her from her cataleptic trance? Cautiously, uncertain of his ability, Tynan closed his eyes, focusing, probing her unconscious.

He perceived vague shadows, fear for him, fear for his child and he felt the pain of that knowledge anew. *Tallia, why didn't you tell me?* But there was no response to his query. He delved more deeply. Hopelessness. Defeat. She'd failed. She blamed herself for his death. *I am alive! Tallia, do you understand me? It's Tynan.* Again there was nothing, not even the flicker of an eyelid. She lay as still as though death had already claimed her.

Not knowing what else to do, he tried again. *Tallia, it's Tynan. Live! Do you understand? You will live. For your child. Our child. Live.* He thought of telling her of his love, but instantly stifled the inclination. He was too unsure. Why had she not admitted to him that she carried his child? Instead, he continued, repeatedly bombarding her unconscious mind with the simple command to live, as he chafed her hands, restoring warmth to her slender fingers. Finally, there was a reaction to his ministrations, a faint moan.

Relief washed through him and his temples pounded with the rush of blood returning to his white face. "Tallia," he called. Her eyelids flickered, slowly opening. She stared at him, confusion mirrored within the crystalline depths of her eyes. "Everything's all right," he assured her. "Here." Lifting her, supporting her slender shoulders, he held the cup of broth to her pale lips. Hesitantly, then gradually more eagerly, she sipped the revitalizing liquid.

Slowly, her strength began to return. She rested, restoring her energy. As the sun sank on the horizon, she watched Tynan, waiting for him to move off, to yield to the call of his private torment. He stayed instead by her side, ignoring the reddening sky. A quiet calm settled over her heart. Had he beaten it? Had this brush with death driven the torment from him or was this only a brief respite?

Feeling much more herself, except for a slight trembling of her limbs which betrayed a measure of strength not yet regained, she moved to assist in the preparation of the evening meal. She waved off the protest that was evident in his expression and he finally accepted her aid though he observed her closely.

As she told Tynan of Coran's appearance and intervention, Tallia found herself wondering what possible motive the goddess could have had to save her life. Neither could Tynan suggest a plausible explanation as to Coran's purpose.

The close companionship of their first journey together was reestablished, and Tallia found herself wishing they could simply remain there. But tomorrow they would continue their journey—to Maurasia and the king, a father she'd never known. What then? What reaction would that revelation draw from Tynan? Even to herself, the knowledge seemed dreamlike, unreal. She forced it from her thoughts, intent on relishing these last few hours with Tynan.

The next morning, Tynan said farewell to Chaz, knowing that the animal would return to the secluded wasteland valley where they'd first met. When Tynan returned to his wasteland duties, he would find Chaz there.

Midafternoon the next day, Tallia and Tynan

rode through Maurasia's central square. Tynan rode the pack gari that Tallia had taken to carry her belongings. The embossed metal gates to the castle grounds stood before them. Tynan had insisted she wear the Twin Suns circlet upon her forehead. "Respect is more often achieved through position than deed," he had said. Not wanting to plague him with unanswerable questions, she complied with his suggestion.

Now for the second time in her life she viewed the magnificent sight before her. Manicured lawns swept up the gradual slope and lombar trees stretched skyward, their leafless branches casting skeletal shadows on a white cobbled lane that twisted up to the summit of the hill. There, in regal majesty stood the king's castle, its turrets reaching for the heavens, sun-bleached white against a cerulean sky.

They halted before the embossed metal gates. "Tynan of the House of Keane seeks admittance," he informed the guard.

"State your business," the guard demanded belligerently.

"The king's business," Tynan responded sharply.

The guard hesitated. Tallia received the distinct impression that he enjoyed exploiting his position. He studied both Tynan and Tallia carefully "I've seen you here before," he admitted grudgingly to Tynan, "but what's the lady's business here?"

Tynan's emerald eyes flashed warningly and Tallia saw his jaw clench with irritation. "The lady's business is her own," he responded coldly. "Open the gate."

The guard was obviously startled by the ring of

287

command in Tynan's tone and his eyes narrowed with dislike. Yet, he didn't quite dare defy the order. With deliberate slowness, he swung the gates open.

They passed through, winding their way up the hill. Tallia's uncertainty increased in proportion to their nearness to the castle. What was her father like? Would he be disappointed in her? How should she act? The questions resounded in her mind, increasing her nervousness.

Absently, she followed Tynan's lead. They halted before a massive stone staircase. Two young men left their positions before a carved pillar, and took the bridles of the garies. "Stable them please," Tynan requested.

"Yes, lord," they replied simultaneously.

Then Tallia and Tynan climbed the endless flight of marble stairs. The enormous doors were opened by uniformed doormen and they entered an antechamber so vast that the fans suspended from the ceiling looked to be no more than the size of coins. Tynan halted before the desk of a clerk. "Tynan of the House of Keane in the Fiefdom of Ravencrest seeks audience with the king on the king's business," he stated formally.

The man nodded and waved an imperious finger at a guardsman who immediately hurried off to relay the message to the king.

"Be seated," the clerk directed, indicating a row of rather uncomfortable-looking, but attractively carved, wooden chairs.

Tallia's hands twisted nervously in her lap. She wanted nothing more than to run from this ostenatious world of the nobility, back to Twin Suns. She did not belong there, and yet she knew she no longer belonged at Twin Suns either. Her life had been irrevocably altered. She glanced at Tynan. He lounged in his chair with apparent ease. For all the time he spent in the wasteland, he was more conversant with this world than she.

"Tynan of the House of Keane," the clerk's voice rang out. "King Quillan will see you now. Please follow the guard." Tynan rose, drawing Tallia with him.

Tallia's heart leapt into her throat. She was absolutely terrified and she clutched Tynan's arm with painful intensity. His eyes flicked briefly to hers, mirroring puzzlement at the depth of her anxiety. Then he smiled reassuringly. Whatever the king's business with Tallia, Tynan knew of Quillan's gentleness. Soon her apprehension would be eased.

The guard led them down a maze of hallways before stopping in front of a pair of thick wooden doors. Opening one, he ushered them inside and closed the door quietly behind them.

Tallia's eyes scanned the length of the throne room. Portraits of past kings and queens adorned the thirty-foot walls. From the center of the lofty, domed ceiling an enormous chandelier hung suspended by chains of gold and lit the immaculate marble flooring. Intricately designed cushioned chairs lined the walls on either side, and at the opposite end of the spacious chamber, a man sat upon the throne. Except for the three of them, the room was unoccupied.

"May I present Tallia of the House of Darnaz in the Fiefdom of the Twin Suns, your majesty?" Tynan's loud announcement coupled with her own intense nervousness made her jump.

"You may," the king's voice rang out. "Come forward."

Tynan urged her ahead, taking up a position two paces behind her and to her left. They reached the center of the room, and she now saw clearly the man who sat before them. From Eyrsa's memories came recognition. Garbed in munificent robes, and with a small gilded, but otherwise unadorned, crown upon his head, Quillan was a figure who commanded respect despite his obvious advancement in years. Instinctively, she halted, granting obeisance to the "king", for this intimidating man represented nothing of the "father."

"Stop," his commanding voice rang out. "A daughter does not bow before her sire. Come here, child."

Tallia swallowed and continued.

Stunned, Tynan remained rooted in place, watching the tableau taking place before him. Daughter? Tallia? It didn't make sense. How was it possible? Now his eyes traveled between them, father and daughter. Yes, there was a resemblance. The eyes, Tallia's unusual eyes, were the same as those of his king. He remembered when he had first met her and had wondered about the familiarity of her eyes. Why hadn't he made the connection then?

His shocked brain refused to function any longer. Only the paralyzing emotion of hopelessness remained. How could he hope to win her love now?

In his mind, despite his status of Lord of the Fiefdom of Ravencrest, he was no longer her equal. At least at one point, he had allowed himself to hope that once his duty to the king had been fulfilled he could return to her side and try to capture her heart. But now he saw that hope dashed away.

Quillan observed the young woman walking slowly toward him. She was the image of her mother and his eyes misted as his arms ached to embrace her. But he could not, not yet. To her, he was still a stranger. Leaving his throne, he walked to meet her. Grasping her small fragile hand in his, he looked deeply into her wide nervous eyes. "Come with me," he directed gently. "We will go someplace less formal to get to know each other."

Tallia hesitated. She wasn't sure she should ask, but she needed someone familiar with her. "May Tynan join us, your majesty?" For an instant, King Quillan looked startled and Tallia feared she'd committed a breach of conduct.

Actually, Quillan had completely forgotten the presence of the young man. That wasn't like him, not at all. Normally, he would have requested that Tynan remain a guest for a time and then would have suggested a later informal conclave in which they'd discuss the details of the journey. Now he sensed a bond between this daughter he'd never known and the son of the finest man he'd ever befriended, Counsellor Torden. His eyes narrowed thoughtfully. "Of course he may join us if that is your wish."

He smiled at Tallia's obvious sigh of relief. "I am

not that fearsome, child," he murmured for her ears alone. His smile broadened at her flush of embarrassment. Then he turned to Tynan. "Will you come with us?"

"Certainly, your majesty," Tynan replied, having regained a certain amount of his aplomb. If what was to follow would help explain the myriad questions once more dancing in his brain, he didn't want to miss it.

"Your journey was uneventful?" Quillan asked him as they walked.

"Not quite, my lord. But by the grace of Galacia we are here."

"Hmm," Quillan nodded. "Remind me to discuss it with you later."

"Yes, Majesty. I will," Tynan responded.

They were seated in the king's sitting room within his private suite; a comforting fire danced within the hearth, and mugs of mulled wine had been placed before them. The silence stretched on as King Quillan stared with thoughtful concentration into the flames, apparently oblivious to Tynan and Tallia. Tallia sipped from her mug, waiting quietly. Finally, he turned to regard her.

"There is much you don't yet know or understand, Tallia," he remarked solemnly, holding her gaze. "It has fallen to me to attempt to explain it to you. I know you are brimming with questions, but I believe they will all be answered in due course."

Tallia nodded and murmured, "Yes, your majesty."

"Please dispense with my title. If you cannot call me Father, then Quillan will do." He waited for

Tallia's assenting nod before turning to Tynan. "Much of what you are about to hear has never before been told. I would ask your word of honor that nothing you hear will be repeated."

"You have my word, Majesty."

Quillan searched Tynan's features briefly, then abruptly nodded and turned once more to stare into the leaping flames. "The exact beginning is hard to determine," he muttered. Then sighing, he began to speak. "Years ago, I married your mother, Jhysine. We were happy, but childless for a long while. My younger brother, Rhys, and his wife were killed in a fire, leaving Krogan an orphan at the age of nine. We took him in and raised him as our own. Then, one gloriously happy day, ten years after our marriage, Jhysine announced her pregnancy. We were blissfully happy in anticipation of our parenthood. The child was born, a beautiful boy.

"But he died in infancy." His brow furrowed in remembered pain. "Twice more she conceived and twice miscarried before my sons could be born. You might have had three brothers, Tallia," he said, turning to look at her with sorrowful eyes. "Our grief was boundless. We, who loved children, were being denied the opportunity to give our love. The Zarmists were baffled, for there was no apparent reason for Jhysine not to carry a child to term."

His eyes misted with sorrow, and Tallia felt compassion for Quillan. She could not share his sorrow for she'd never known the people for whom he mourned. But she understood it, remembering her own anguish at Eyrsa's death. This man who was both her king and her father was human. The sense of intimidation she'd felt earlier dissipated.

"Jhysine was afraid to have another child, and it was that fear which made her secretive when she discovered she once again carried a child. She told only me, and insisted I divulge the news to no one. Using her poor health as an explanation, we ensconced her at our summer retreat." He paused, starting thoughtfully at Tallia. "You look much like your mother. Your eyes and hair are mine, but your features are hers."

For a long while, Quillan was silent. Tallia glanced at Tynan. He sat patiently, his thoughts undisclosed by the expression on his face. Noting her perusal of him, he met her gaze. A strange and poignant emotion she couldn't decipher resided within those emerald depths. Was he angry with her?

Disturbed without quite understanding why, she turned her attention back to Quillan. His hair was graying with age, yet almost as dark as her own. Lines of time etched his features. He was striking, definitely not handsome, though he might have been years ago, with a strong well-muscled physique that could have belonged to a much younger man. She had never met him, and yet he seemed familiar. He radiated the same sense of vitality that Tallia had always felt in Eyrsa's presence.

Finally, he began to speak once more. "Before you were born, the goddess Galacia came to me in a dream. She revealed many strange things, much of which I did not fully understand at the time. She made reference to the Prophecy that would never reach fulfillment if you did not attain maturity.

And I have since found a journal and the writings of the Prophecy."

He paused, pursing his lips pensively. "I'm straying. It is so hard to keep events in sequence. The dream," he said as though focusing his thoughts. "The goddess indicated to me the incredible psychic power you would acquire, more potent than any member of the royal line since the founding of the sovereignty. At the time, I automatically assumed your abilities would be analogous to Eyrsa's and my own but possessing greater range, more strength. I now know that assumption was erroneous, for it is true only in part.

"But most important, Galacia revealed that your life was imperiled; evil threatened your existence and the peace of our land. She stressed that your birth and heritage must be concealed, even from you, for there was one who would seek your death. Your mother and I could never establish contact with you, never see you. Not until you were grown. To do so would have jeopardized your life and inadvertently all of Karaundo." Quillan's voice faltered and he cleared his throat.

"I have suspected since then that the one who would threaten your existence was also responsible for the deaths of your brothers. But I have no evidence to lead me to him."

Again he stopped, looking at Tallia with an expression of such love and longing that she felt for the first time she gazed upon not a king, but her father. "After losing three children to what, I suspect, was some type of poison, I knew I would do anything to preserve your life. I even placed guards outside the conservatory for Zarmistic healers when Eyrsa informed me she sensed danger for you here. They were ordered to watch over you, protect you as long as you remained in Maurasia." He shook his head. "Again I have strayed. Back to Galacia's warning. I had to devise a means to protect you but I had to plan. So, I did not confide my dream to Jhysine immediately, not until I felt certain I could guarantee your safety.

"My half sister Eyrsa became an integral part of my plan. Born of love but not of a queen, she and I were as close as any brother and sister could ever have been. According to the law at the time Eyrsa was born, she should not have been allowed to live, for the royal decree is such that no illegitimate lines must be allowed to propagate. The law was a safeguard, preventing contention for the throne. But my father cared deeply for Eyrsa's mother, and he could not deny her the child, the only thing he could give her. However, in an effort to maintain the laws of Karaundo, Eyrsa was allowed to live only on the condition that she would be rendered sterile at birth. I explain this only so that you will understand why she had no children of her own and why you became the child of her heart.

"It was to Eyrsa that I entrusted the safety of you and your mother until your birth. I told Eyrsa of the dream and she informed me that she had been haunted by a similar occurrence. After your birth, we agreed that she would take you. No one was to learn of your existence lest we jeopardize your safety. It was imperative for you to reach adulthood.

"Eyrsa took on the responsibility of raising you, preparing you for your place at my side." He paused, shaking his head. "Neither of us knew or suspected the nature of the Prophecy that was to unfold, but we both recognized the urgent warning Galacia issued. Perhaps if we had known of the Prophecy sooner we might have instructed you differently."

He halted, staring toward the window for a time. "Jhysine was never quite the same after you were sent away, often spending long hours on the parapet just staring north. She wanted so much to lavish her love on you and yet, it was not meant to be.

"Eventually, she became pregnant again and for a while was happy. She was determined to keep this child with her. Her pregnancy had barely begun to show when—" Quillan choked; his throat worked with remembered love and grief. "She fell from one of the parapets," he concluded quickly, his voice hoarse with emotion.

His hands trembled with emotion. "I'm sorry," he said gently to Tallia. "I had thought after all this time, the memory would not affect me so." He took a large swallow of his wine.

"I wish I could have been a true father to you but fate has tricks which often lead us down paths we'd rather not travel. I hope you can understand the reasons for what must seem a heartless act. What we did all those years ago, we did because we loved you enough to sacrifice our own wants for your safety.

"I hope you can forgive me, Tallia. Perhaps now we can recapture some of those lost years."

Tallia could only nod. Her shock at learning that Eyrsa was her aunt and the reason for her own exile overwhelmed her. But as she thought of all Quillan had said, her anxiety dissipated and her doubts vanished. The depth of her father's emotions were evident in his words, his expression, the anguish in his eyes.

"You must be tired from your journey. I will allow you some time to think about what I have said for I am sure it has unsettled you. I'll summon a servant to show you to your rooms." He rose and moved to pull a large bell cord. "We'll talk more later."

"All right," Tallia replied. ". . . Father," she added in a hesitant whisper. The reference brought tears to Quillan's eyes. The designation still felt strange to her, but she'd get used to it. She had no doubt that what she'd heard was the truth, for many of her questions had been answered. Many more questions remained, but there was time. Eyrsa had taught her patience.

A knock sounded, prompting Tynan and Tallia to rise and silently leave the room. Tallia studied Tynan's somber figure thoughtfully as they followed the attendant down the hall. He remained silent, his face devoid of expression. But that was Tynan.

Quillan stared from his window, watching with unseeing eyes the sunlight dancing on the surface of the waves on Lake Randalia. Time had not passed quickly since Jhysine's death. Each day had been a trial of loneliness. And now, Galacia had at last seen fit to grant him the company of his child. Her mere presence was both a balm and a torment.

An urgent knock resounded upon his door. He sighed. The time for private memories was past; the duties of a king claimed him. "Enter," he bid.

A tall, well-built man, wearing the uniform of the king's private bodyguard, approached Quillan. "Your majesty," he said, kneeling to kiss the seal of office that rarely left Quillan's forefinger.

"Rise, Thanal," he directed, thinking the guard seemed unusually fervent in his obeisance. "What news have you?"

"I fear to tell you." Thanal's eyes avoided those of his king.

"You need have no fear of me unless you have committed some grave offence, Thanal," Quillan said with gentle firmness, grasping the young man's arm, urging eye contact. "Now, come, unburden yourself."

"Majesty, I have a friend among Lord Krogan's personal guard . . . " He stopped, shuffling his feet nervously. "I'm sorry, my lord, but I participated in a gambling tourney."

Quillan pretended an expression of severity at the discovery that one of his guards had disregarded the gambling restrictions. Although he enjoyed a good game of chance himself now and then, he always strove to set an example. However, he knew instantly his expression had failed to intimidate Thanal for he sighed briefly with relief before continuing.

"I was to meet my friend in a secluded alcove here in the castle where I would pay him his winnings when I overheard a conversation. It was not intentional, Majesty, and normally I would not repeat a conversation overheard. But, this . . . this is different." He faltered, meeting the eyes of his king. "And even if you do not believe me, I feel it is my duty to tell you."

Quillan looked deeply into the eyes of the man before him, lightly probing his mind. He read only loyalty, sincerity, and fear; there was no deceit. "I will believe you, Thanal. Please continue."

"I was leaning against the wall, when I heard voices as plainly as though they stood next to me. Yet, there was no one near. At first, I didn't listen to their words. Curiosity made me look for the origin of the sound. One of the stone carvings on the wall appeared to be out of place. When I touched it, I found that it moved easily, and behind it was a hole that looked directly into the chamber beyond."

Quillan knew of the existence of several similar peepholes throughout the castle, granting access to many "private" chambers. Nodding his understanding, he moved off to pour himself a drink. He would have liked to invite the loyal guard to join him, but protocol prevented it. Instead, he signaled the man to continue.

"Well," Thanal resumed, "after my curiosity was satisfied, I leaned back to wait for my friend. But the voices continued, and after a time I couldn't help listening. Lord Krogan was speaking to Counsellor Flagan. He sounded angry." Thanal halted, frowning.

"And what did he say?" Quillan prompted, his interest aroused.

"I'm trying to remember his exact words, my lord." His brow remained furrowed as he concentrated on recollecting. "He said that the men failed once again, that they were frightened away by beasts conjured from mist. He called them superstitious idiots." Thanal paused. "At that point Counsellor Flagan said that the girl had powerful protection and that the men could not be blamed for failing."

Quillan's breath froze in his chest. "Continue, Thanal," he ordered more briskly than he'd intended.

The guard nodded. "Then Lord Krogan said that he'd recently discovered that Tallia of the House of Darnaz was your daughter. He said that she must die before you, your majesty, leave this world and her escort with her as he was going to become a problem soon. He asked if Flagan understood.

"Counsellor Flagan said something I didn't hear and then left. That's all, your majesty. I left the alcove after that without meeting my friend. Then I thought about what I'd heard and knew I had to tell you."

Quillan cleared his throat; his heart pounded oddly in his chest. Now he had the proof he needed. His suspicions were confirmed. Yet, he'd almost hoped such verification would never surface. "You will be rewarded for your loyalty, Thanal. Thank you, you may go."

The man bowed and backed from the room.

Quillan continued to stare into nothingness for a long time. Was he not partly to blame for his nephew's actions? Had Quillan not raised Krogan as his own son, even going so far as to prepare him for the throne? And yet, not once had he named

Krogan as his heir—not even in private. Krogan must be very bitter. Torn between his compassion for Krogan and his outrage at his deeds, Quillan made his decision, and left his chambers. Within moments, he stood before the door to his nephew's suite. Summoning all of his strength for the confrontation to come, he raised his fist and knocked.

CHAPTER FOURTEEN

THE DOOR SWUNG OPEN.

The king stared at his nephew, this polite, smiling young man, whom Quillan didn't want to believe plotted the demise of his daughter and himself. Even harder to comprehend was the probability that if Krogan planned Tallia's death, then he, too, had calculated Jhysine's and his male heirs' deaths. Having raised Krogan as a son, he would never have suspected him capable of such cold-blooded ambition. Yet, if Thanal's words were true, and he had no reason to doubt them, then Krogan had masked his true self all these years.

"Uncle, come in."

Quillan attempted to pierce Krogan's facade, but he could not, and stepped across the threshold. Krogan indicated a chair near the fireplace and Quillan sat.

"And to what do I owe the honor of this visit?" Krogan queried, as he leaned casually against the stone mantel.

Krogan reveled in the connotation of superiority his position afforded as he looked down at the older man. He was the more powerful of the two. He knew it instinctively. How long must he continue this charade? Gently, imperceptibly, he sent a probing tendril to seek his uncle's thoughts.

Quillan hesitated. Where did he start? How did he begin questions that if answered truthfully could label his nephew a murderer, a cold, calculating killer? The evidence intimated Krogan's guilt but he had no proof other than the conversation Thanal had overheard.

"Ah." The trace of a sardonic smile flickered across Krogan's face. "It is hard to put into words, isn't it?"

Quillan's head jerked up, meeting Krogan's eyes which gleamed with sadistic hatred. He stiffened at the unexpected expression.

Krogan casually advanced to stand before Quillan's chair. Leaning forward, he braced his arms on either side of the king, and leaned forward until his face was inches from his uncle's. "I killed them all," he hissed. His steely eyes narrowed and the muscles in his jaw pulsed as he clenched his teeth, drawing his thin lips together in a rigid line.

This is the real Krogan, Quillan thought. Evil radiated from him, filling the room, tainting the air, and sending shivers of apprehension crawling along Quillan's spine. He sank into the chair, shrinking against the leather at his back, his eyes wide with disbelief.

Krogan smiled, a wicked, sordid grin. "All of them, my parents, all your heirs, even your wife. And many since then. All who stood in my way." The masquerade was over and he gloried in the sense of horror growing within his dear uncle's mind.

Quillan felt his insides churn.

"Fear not, King Quillan," Krogan emphasized the word "King" with distaste. "It is not in my best interest to dispose of you. Not yet. Your secret was well protected. I admit I am surprised you were able to keep the girl's existence concealed from me."

Quillan's thoughts whirled. To fulfill the Prophecy, Krogan must battle Tallia for the throne. Victorious, he would share his reign with Coran. But if he rid himself of the rightful heir before he harmed the king, the Prophecy could not be enacted. The contest could not be held if only one contender remained. Enlightenment came in a flash. By eliminating his opposition, Krogan was trying to avoid the Prophecy, to cut Coran out of the picture. Krogan would seize the throne by default. What madness! Clever, evil madness!

Thrusting Krogan aside, he stood. "I have misjudged you." His voice was cold, emotionless. How well Krogan had played the part of the devoted nephew. He'd all the while been hiding as a serpent within his walls! And soon the serpent would strike.

But he was still king, and duty demanded action, demanded control. Inner strength and courage swelled within him. Tallia deserved better from her father. Though the Prophecy had revealed a glimmer of the tremendous power to be possessed by the combatants, he would not grovel in fear at Krogan's feet. If he was to die, he would die like a man for the preservation of his daughter's life.

"There are many kinds of power. Strength of mind is but one. I shall see you exposed as the imposter you are. All will know of your evil."

Krogan arched his brows in mock surprise and slowly shook his head as if reprimanding a child. "You forget, Uncle, that I can bend people with my mind. My will becomes theirs and they do not even know it."

Quillan tensed at the harsh bite in Krogan's voice but refused to be intimidated. What Krogan said was true. Quillan could surround himself with guards, warn the people, tell the world of Krogan's sins but it would do no good. If he battled Krogan now and failed, his nephew would receive the knowledge that Quillan intended for Tallia. Only upon his death could he impart it. There was naught he could do to rectify Krogan's past acts of villainy, but he could try to alter the future.

He would bar Krogan from Tallia if it meant spending every minute with the girl himself. And that was what would be required, he suspected, for Krogan made no attempt to conceal his determination. He knew Tallia was strong.

Krogan clenched his fists, squelching his desire to crush the man before him. The king's death now would defeat his purpose to rule alone, answerable to no one. He had no intention of sharing his power with Coran. No, he would not kill the king, not yet.

A horrendous shriek filled the air. Wind rushed and swirled, gathering strength within Krogan's chambers. Papers scattered, strewn before the increasing force of the blast. Quillan felt himself tossed against the wall. Furniture spun wildly and the blazing fire in the hearth roared up the chimney and out into the room. Its engorging flames lapped at the ceiling. Krogan clung desperately to a door-frame. The winds of Thrul stole his breath, plaster-ing his clothing against him as he struggled to remain upright.

She stepped from the midst of the flames, her crimson gown billowing around her, her waist-length ebony hair billowing outward from her face as though possessed of a mind of its own. Her eyes wide with anger, her features contorted with rage, she extended her arm and pointed an accusing finger at Krogan. "You dare defy my will!" Coran shrieked. "You are but a pawn in this game. I shall crush you beneath my thumb like the worm you are. I, who have given you all, shall take it from you, toss it in your face, and let the winds of my anger scatter it across this land like a plague none has ever seen. Deceive not thy maker, Krogan, lest ye be destroyed."

Krogan clutched at his throat, desperately fight-ing to remove the invisible constricting grasp that cut off his breath. His face reddened and his eyes bulged, as his lungs demanded oxygen that was not there.

Her shrill voice drilled into Krogan's mind. "The Prophecy shall be fulfilled, Krogan. You shall battle Tallia. Your victory will instate me upon the throne though I shall act through you. Remember you are but a puppet. I hold the strings of your life in my hand." Coran's wicked laugh resounded within the room. Krogan slumped to the floor, gasping for breath as the invisible band fell from his throat.

Coran spun, pointing her slender finger of death at Quillan and her dark eyes narrowed maliciously. "The decision is mine. Be gone, King, that my rightful position shall not be denied by this spawn of your brother's loins."

Quillan felt his chest constrict, his heart beat with erratic jolts. He dropped to his knees, using the insufficient powers of his mind to battle her onslaught. She was powerful beyond any being he'd encountered. She was Coran, Toleme's evil sister. Pain spread, twisting in thin ribbons across his chest and around his rib cage. His legs and arms numbed, his mind grew hazy.

Vaguely he was aware of the splintering sound as the door burst open. Through blurred vision, he saw Tynan and Tallia rush into the room. He looked back to the fireplace. Coran was gone! Darkness, welcome darkness, descended.

Tallia adjusted the blanket across Quillan's chest. His breathing had regained some measure of regularity. It had taken all her expertise to calm the erratic pounding of his heart as Tynan had carried the king's motionless form from Krogan's room.

She still puzzled over the look Tynan had bestowed upon Krogan. Krogan, apparently shaken by the king's heart attack, had not seen the hatred in Tynan's expression but she had. Why would Tynan harbor such intense dislike for the king's nephew? The "key" had revealed what part Krogan played in her destiny, but Tynan could not know that. She'd wanted to question Tynan but he'd slipped away shortly after helping her get her father into bed.

Krogan paced back and forth. He had smoothed his disheveled hair and summoned servants to straighten the contents of the room. He cursed himself for having let Coran read his thoughts, discover his carefully enacted plot. Now he would be forced to do as she bid but he still held some power over her.

Without him, her hands would be tied. She needed him. He realized her threat had been just that, a threat. An empty threat, in fact. He was her only pawn in this game, and without him, she would lose. He'd play it her way for now. Once the king was dead, he'd battle Tallia. He had no doubts as to who the victor of that exchange would be. He would absorb her power, adding it to his own. He paced impatiently, wondering if such an increase in strength would benefit him, would balance the odds between himself and Coran. Time would tell.

Tallia's head nodded and with effort, she straightened. Outside the evening sparlarks trilled their plaintive cry. Thick clouds blanketed the moon, cloaking the landscape in impenetrable darkness. Sighing, she rose and lit the lantern on the mantel and the flame flickered to life. She adjusted the wick until the light was muted to a soft glow, only enough to see by. Quillan's moan brought her rushing back to his side.

"We have to talk." He spoke with effort, his voice weak.

Tallia smoothed his silver hair from his forehead.

"Tomorrow. We'll talk tomorrow. You've had an attack. You're too weak right now."

"It's important."

"It'll wait. Rest now."

Quillan finally nodded. Surely after Coran's warning, Krogan would not be a threat for a time. Quillan was weak, tired. So tired. His worries abated for the present, he drifted back to sleep.

Tallia brushed away her tears. She had just found him and he was to be taken from her. First Eyrsa and now Quillan. How much more pain was she to endure? How much more could she stand to lose? She buried her face in her hands to silence her sobs.

Early the next morning, Tynan helped her lift Quillan into a sitting position. She fluffed the pillows behind his head. He looked pale and wan, his skin bluish against the white linen. Only his eyes were alert, for all sensation had gone from his limbs and he could not move, not even to lift his arms. She sat down and picked up his hand, holding it gently, allowing herself this one small comfort.

Tynan moved toward the door. This should be a moment spent alone, shared by father and daughter. He sensed Tallia's pain and Quillan's quickly deteriorating health. He would not impose upon their privacy any more than he already had. He did not belong there.

"Tynan, I would like you to stay." Quillan's voice stopped him.

Tynan looked to Tallia who nodded and he returned to the bedside, taking a seat opposite her.

"What I have to say includes both of you." Quillan's voice shook. He hoped he had enough time left to say what had to be said. Tallia pressed his hand reassuringly. He saw the movement but could not feel the pressure.

He stared wistfully at her for a very long time. Then, taking a deep breath, he spoke quietly, revealing his melancholy thoughts. "The night you were born, I held you in my arms for the first and last time, for these arms can no longer feel to embrace you."

Tallia bowed her head. His agony over the sacrifice he'd been forced to make shone in the depths of his gray eyes. His love was apparent in every glance and she clutched his hand more tightly.

Quillan blinked rapidly, struggling to organize his thoughts. The memories were as clear as though the events had occurred only yesterday, potent and painful in the recollection.

"Eyrsa took you away the night of your birth. It had to be. She kept me advised of your progress and I loved you through her."

He closed his eyes for a moment. Tallia envisioned Eyrsa, seeing clearly her part in the sequence of events, always slightly apart, yet always connected by the thin thread of illegitimacy and love. Eyrsa had possessed the royal talent, an attribute that she was forced to hide from all but Tallia. That explained the secrecy in which she had shrouded Tallia's tutelage, constantly insisting that it be maintained. But that had not been the greatest secret she had been entrusted with, pledged to keep from even Tallia until the time for revelation was upon them.

Quillan continued. "I began to train Krogan, originally to divert suspicion. No one was to suspect a true heir existed, and perhaps it was this deception which lead to the situation we are faced with now." His voice faltered. "Yet how could I have been so blind? For even as a child he betrayed me. He admitted to me last night of killing them all. He was only nine when he murdered his parents, ten when he murdered my first child." There! He had said it! He saw the horror, the revulsion in Tallia's eyes, the loathing and anger glittering dangerously in Tynan's, but not surprise. So Tynan had suspected Krogan's true nature then. Quillan should have known Tynan would, for like his father, Torden, he'd always been an accurate judge of character.

"I will kill him." Tynan's expressionless statement jerked both Tallia and Quillan from their thoughts. His voice reverberated with sharp-edged hatred.

"No!" Quillan's adamant command startled Tallia.

Tynan leapt to his feet, the cold knot in his gut twisting mercilessly. "Why do you protect him?" he demanded. "He is responsible for countless deaths. It was he who ordered my family butchered."

Quillan blanched. He hadn't known that. Tynan's hatred was understandable but it would do no good. "Sit." His command brooked no refusal. Tynan reluctantly took his seat, though his disagreement with the king's decision was plain.

"Patience, Tynan," Quillan's voice soothed. "There are nuances here that you do not see. This battle has been decreed by powers greater than even mine. Tallia"—he turned his eyes to hers, holding them, conveying his sense of urgency—"you must read the journal of the man who by the depths of his

312

love inadvertently bequeathed this cursed Prophecy on his heirs. Understand the man," he ordered fervently, "understand his sisters."

Patiently, he proceeded to describe the journal's position in the archives. "When you have read it, replace it. Then seek the corner of a flagstone which is loosened. Have Tynan help you lift it. Beneath it, on a piece of parchment, you will find the words of the Prophecy recorded. Study it carefully, for the Prophecy must be fulfilled. You must battle Krogan."

"Tallia?" Tynan could not conceal his disbelief. "She doesn't have the strength or the means to dispose of him. She is a Zarmist, killing distresses her. She cannot appease the need for vengeance as I can."

"Stop talking as though I'm not in the room!" Tallia's angry retort cut into Tynan's tirade. "Neither do you have the strength to defeat Krogan. He will not battle with a broadsword, Tynan."

"Can you do it? Can you kill him?" Tynan fired the question heartlessly and her hesitation answered his question. "See! He will defeat you! A split second of indecision like that and he will win." He kept his voice harsh. He could not afford to let his love show, especially now. His only hope of saving her, of completing his path of retribution, lay in convincing her to let him take her place. He knew now for certain that somehow, in some way, he had gained psychic ability. His abilities were new and untried, but he was motivated by revenge. "It is not in your nature, Tallia. It *is* in mine. I am an executioner."

Her voice was purposefully calm. "It is my duty,

Tynan. My destiny. Not yours."

"It's suicide. That's what it is."

"Stop!" Quillan's voice halted the angry exchange.

Both Tallia and Tynan fell silent.

The king's gaze moved to Tallia's waist and Tynan's eyes followed.

Quillan asked quietly, "Does he know?"

Tallia blushed guiltily. She should have expected her father to detect the child within her.

"No," she whispered.

"Yes." Tynan's answer brought her head up sharply. "I know about the baby."

"How?" Tallia couldn't repress the word that slipped from her parted lips. The king, too, turned to stare at Tynan, awaiting his reply.

Tynan shrugged. "A dream. Eyrsa showed me in a dream. In some stone pyramid I saw the pictures flashing in the air."

"A stone pyramid?" Quillan's pulse leapt at the words. Had Tynan been in the "key"? Had Eyrsa, bless her foresight, taken him through the spousal initiation? What had his sister known that he did not? What would she tell him now if she could? Certainly, she linked Tallia and Tynan. Was the baby the reason she had judged it necessary or was there something else? Had Eyrsa sensed some invisible bond? His thoughts riveted on the words. "Invisible bond!" They coursed back to the Prophesy. "And invisible bonds shall not tether the hands of my defender, only the heart, and thus be allowed."

Quillan stared fixedly at Tynan. Love binds! He saw it now, obscured behind the hard mask of emerald eyes. Tynan loved Tallia, though she could not yet see it. So clear had Toleme's journal been, he could almost picture Coran snickering at Galacia's cryptic phrases and predictions of the "unity of love." Coran had been completely unaware of the stipulation's true purpose. Praise Galacia! In her wisdom she had found a way. She knew Coran knew nothing of the tight lariat of that emotion as love was alien to Coran, something she had never felt. Galacia had given Tallia an edge, an assistant, a powerful one. He must be careful not to negate that small advantage. He wasn't sure how, but he knew Tynan was vital, Tynan and his love.

His mind worked quickly. He knew he was dying. If he could pass his powers to both Tynan and Tallia perhaps there was a chance. If they were married! Of course! Eyrsa knew! Sensing there was very little time, she had subjected Tynan to the "key." He could only marry Tallia if he had passed that test. He obviously had or he wouldn't be with them now. And who better to rule by her side if Tallia succeeded? Quillan trusted Tynan as he had his father, Torden.

Quillan phrased his words carefully. "There is a way, at least a chance, to defeat Krogan."

Two faces spun toward him, the accusations forgotten for the moment.

"How?" Tynan demanded quickly. He would deal with Tallia's predicament later.

Tallia welcomed the interruption. She had nothing to tell Tynan, no reasons, no explanations. His accusing look had seared her flesh. Once again she sensed that in some way he was part of her destiny. Yet, she fought that realization. She didn't want his life endangered on her account but, neither could she bear the possibility that her unborn child might perish.

Quillan fabricated a small lie. "If you two were married, I could pass my knowledge to both of you. Then Coran might perhaps agree to let Tynan substitute for you in the battle." It was only a small lie. He could pass his power to them both. He knew Coran would never agree to let Tynan do battle for Tallia, but they did not.

"No." Tallia shook her head. "It is my destiny. I refuse to be responsible for the possible death of another."

Quillan interjected, "If married, you might be able to draw on Tynan's strength. It might be enough." He needed to persuade her to form some kind of commitment between them, something that would keep them together until Krogan or Coran instigated the showdown. He sensed it would be soon. He could not hold on to life much longer. Once he was gone, there would be nothing to deter the enactment of the Prophecy.

Silence prevailed as Tallia considered his words. Was this where Tynan fit in? It had to be. He was to be her accomplice, to assist her in this horrendous deed. As daughter of a king, her life was committed to the people of Karaundo. Marriage to Tynan, a man she truly cared for, was not too much to ask.

She looked at first her father and then at Tynan. "All right. It seems the only way."

"A secret wedding. Immediately. Here. Ring for the high priest." Quillan rapped out the ultimatum, ignoring the constricting pain in his chest, the shortness of breath. He would not join Eyrsa until he had seen his wish fulfilled. It was his only hope for Tallia's survival. His psychic aptitude would be his wedding gift to them both.

Tynan did the king's bidding and gave three quick tugs on the bell cord.

"The key is in the top drawer of the desk," Quillan continued. "Once the high priest has been admitted, lock the doors. No one shall enter this room until it is over."

Tynan retrieved the key quickly.

"No one! Do you understand?" Quillan's adamant tone sent a shiver of alarm through Tallia. He was not well and should not be subjected to this kind of excitement. To placate him, she took a seat at his side, muttering calming inanities. In truth, she had no idea what she said, for her mind dwelled on the tall dark figure standing silently at the window as they waited.

A short time later, a knock sounded. Tynan moved to admit the high priest, and the lock clicked shut with finality.

"Marry them." Quillan's explosive order brought a startled look from the thin, aging priest. Tallia forced herself to concentrate on the swishing motion of his long white gown, then at his bald head as he bowed his head in a quick prayer and opened the small book he carried in his hand.

"Do you submit to this union of your own free will?" He began the ceremony and seemed relieved when both Tynan and Tallia answered in the affirmative. The words slipped past Tallia like water cascading over rocks. She caught her name somewhere in the jumble of religious mutterings and croaked out a weak "I will." Tynan's reply came strong and certain as she had known it would. That was Tynan's way. Decide quickly; act immediately; live with that decision.

She knew little of the Prophecy other than what had been revealed to her in the "key." She would battle Krogan for the throne. Would this marriage change her destiny, aid her in some way, or was she merely endangering Tynan with these vows?

"Take my hands." Quillan's voice shook with the effort of speech. The time had come. Tynan recognized his urgent pleading command and grasped the king's hand. He turned to stare at Tallia who remained frozen, motionless.

"No," she cried, stepping back as if burned. She'd seen death before. She knew, that as with Eyrsa, the power exchange would be his last act.

"Now, Tallia," Quillan gasped, blood bubbling to his lips. "Now, before it's too late." His body jerked spasmodically, and Tynan clung to his hand.

"Don't die," Tallia pleaded. "Not you too. Please don't die." Tears coursed down her ashen cheeks but still, she made no move to reach Quillan's side. One despairing sob escaped as the flash of light radiated from Quillan's body. Tynan's free arm snaked out, his fingers biting into the soft flesh of her arm. The power surged through him and leapt into her mind.

The room swirled in a dizzying kaleidoscope of color. The crackle of electricity zigzagged through the link, jolting her to her knees with its intensity. The visions surged into her mind, shifting, changing, becoming a part of her memory. She saw her mother, Eyrsa, her own birth, her father's loneliness, his kingdom, his strengths, his weaknesses and those of the ones who had passed before, all in the span of a heartbeat. Then only silence. Tallia stared blankly at Quillan's lifeless form then fainted into Tynan's trembling, but protective, arms.

The pounding outside the king's chambers aroused Tallia from her grief-stricken stupor. She heard Krogan's angry voice through the thick walls as he ordered the door smashed in. *Too late*, she thought, still dazed by the velocity of the power transfer. Krogan was too late.

"This way," Tynan urged, scooping Tallia into his arms and steering the high priest to one end of the chamber. He led them through the secret panel that separated Quillan's room from the turret stairwell, a method Tynan had used in the past when secretly reporting his covert operations in the wasteland to the king. Holding Tallia in his arms, he reset the wall, followed the high priest down the twisting stairs.

Krogan would have to be faced but not now. Tallia was exhausted and the unexpected force of the power surge had left his own thoughts in disarray. He needed time to rationalize the scenes and revelations that were strangely now a part of his own memory, time to experiment with the overwhelming force he felt surging within him.

"He's gone," Tallia sobbed, her tears staining the smooth material of Tynan's shirt. Desperately, she clung to him, the one solid thing left in her unpredictable life, drawing on his constant inner strength, soothed by the feel of his strong arms encircling her. Was this why she needed him? Had Galacia known the extent of her trials, the depths of her anguish and had given Tynan to her to bolster her resolve?

He thanked the high priest and closed the door to Tallia's private suite. Carrying her to the bed, he gently laid her down, stretching out his hard length beside her. She wrapped her arms around him in an unnecessary attempt to keep him near. He would not have left her side now had the dragon, Coran herself, appeared before him. She was his.

The cost had been monumental but Quillan had bequeathed his knowledge, and with it came the awareness that the king's death had been inevitable. He mourned the loss of his monarch silently as he rocked Tallia's shaking body until her trembling ceased and she slept. Tynan found no such retreat. Her soft whimpers tore at his heart and he vowed no one would hurt her again if he could prevent it. When this was over, if they survived and it was what she wished, she would be free.

Though he knew the toll that separation would extract from his heart, he loved her enough to let her go. Love was not something you could gain by coercion. If she didn't love him, he would accept it. There was naught else he could do.

Krogan's messenger arrived early the next morning. His impatient pounding roused Tallia and she accepted the message. Tynan stood behind the door, hidden from the eyes of Krogan's aide but near enough should Tallia be threatened. The exchange was uneventful. Tallia closed the door as the messenger strode away without requesting a reply. When she opened Krogan's note, she realized none was required.

The missive was brief. "Quillan's entombment will take place two days hence. The heir to the throne will be announced the next day. Conveniently, Coran has decreed that we meet the evening before that announcement." It was signed "Lord Krogan."

So, the battle was to take place on the eve of her father's entombment. She had only two days to glean whatever knowledge she could from the journal and the Prophecy.

CHAPTER FIFTEEN

TALLIA BREATHED DEEPLY OF THE CRISP MORNING air as she leaned from her turret window and gazed down the hill into the square. Already, even as the sun drew its full circumference over the horizon, the mourners were gathering, their haunting murmurings drifting to her ears. She caressed the comforting smoothness of her Zarma stone. She'd read and reread Toleme's journal.

So much had been explained that her mind felt full to bursting with new knowledge, and yet she remained confused. Galacia, Coran, Toleme, and even Yaewel were not deities, and today, on the day of her father's entombment, she felt the need to pray but there was no one to pray to!

She wondered at everyone's unquestioning acceptance of the indecently short period of state mourning accorded King Quillan. But so good was

Krogan's deception, that none dared to suggest his actions were improper. Tallia wondered if she and Tynan were the only ones aware of his true ambitions.

Destiny had decreed this combat. She might not win but at least it would never be said that she neglected her destiny. And if she could, she'd keep the undeserving Krogan from the throne.

Silently, she cursed the doubts that surfaced vaguely in the pool of her thoughts. Eyrsa would have chastised her for harboring such uncertainties. Hadn't she always taught her that anything was possible if you believed in it and yourself?

A sharp rap at the door startled her. So, it was time. She took a deep breath to still her tumultuous thoughts and the quickened pace of her heartbeat.

She followed the servant to the great hall where sweet needled boughs perfumed the air. Sprays of winter snowbells draped the coffin and were arranged in elaborate wreaths about the wide room. Dried roses and waxed lilies added their perfume to the incense-thickened air. The flowers had come from all over Karaundo. Quillan's popularity and his people's bereavement were in evidence everywhere.

Inside the gold-embossed coffin, King Quillan's body had been wrapped with the robe of his office. The thick gold ring of the House of Tuhan still adorned his index finger. He appeared so peaceful, so at rest.

Tallia moved back as several servants entered and began rigging the coffin for the long procession through the winding streets of Maurasia. Across the room she spotted Krogan, his head bowed in feigned prayer, the false aura of sorrow wrapped like a cloak around his shoulders. She knew that in his eyes she would see the greed, the pleasure in the significance of this day.

Tynan stepped from the alcove and stood beside Tallia. Letting his gaze follow hers, he noted the disgust glowing in her eyes. He was no longer the only one to know the truth of Krogan's character. But then, perhaps he had never been alone in his knowledge, for Tallia's first foretelling dream those many weeks ago in the wasteland had hinted at another side to the man. Tynan's gaze held steady as Krogan raised his head and stared across at them.

"How can I possibly win?" Tallia muttered to herself.

"We all do what we must."

She started, gasping in alarm at the unexpected voice from behind. She spun around and looked directly into the emerald stare of her husband.

"What are you doing here?" she whispered, striving to conceal her worry.

He raised his brows in mock surprise. "I was a close friend and in Quillan's employ. As such, I have been assigned to escort the procession. I am also his daughter's husband, in case you have forgotten."

Tallia spun away from him. That had not been the meaning behind her query, and he knew it. Why, oh why, had she ever agreed to Quillan's request? She'd been lulled into believing Tynan could bolster her abilities without danger to himself because she wanted to believe her father's inventions so badly. She knew now after reading the

Prophecy that no one would be allowed to enter the arena but the combatants. This was a battle she would have to fight alone. And yet, she felt certain that Tynan, in his quest for vengeance, would try to interfere. Had she endangered his life once again by becoming his wife?

Krogan approached from across the room. Maliciousness glimmered in the depths of his metallic gray eyes. "Cousin," he began with a sinister smile, "I hope you are prepared."

Tallia met his gaze squarely. Her mind might quail at the thought of what was required of her, her heart might shudder with trepidation, but she would never allow him to sense her apprehension. "I am ready," she replied calmly.

He nodded, peering into her eyes in an attempt to pierce her facade, to discern her true emotions. Tallia purposefully blanked her mind. This was merely the beginning. If Krogan sought to begin this psychological battle here, so be it. She would not crumple beneath his gaze. Finally, his scan unsuccessful, he turned with a sweeping bow and walked away.

The funeral procession wound through the crowd-lined streets. Six silver garies pulled the heavy platform on which King Quillan's coffin rested amid the sprigs of ivy and sprays of flowers tossed by the people of Maurasia. Tallia and Tynan walked on one side, Krogan on the other. Behind the royal entourage, Quillan's pages and soldiers formed a double line, slowing their usually brisk steps to a funereal march. Banners flapped in the stiff breeze chilling the mourners. Tallia closed her mind, willing herself to be impervious to the cold.

Clouds billowed threateningly on the horizon, obscuring the sun's rays and turning the day gray and overcast.

Tallia held her tears in check and ignored the curious stares of the bystanders. Only a select few in the castle had as yet been informed of her true identity and the crowd whispered when she walked in her appointed place beside Quillan's coffin. Tallia straightened proudly. This was one right she refused to have denounced, one privilege that could not be denied her.

The procession seemed interminable as it followed the cobbled streets, winding and twisting along the main avenues. At some point, Tynan had slipped his arm around her shoulders but she wasn't sure when. Only now, as the castle loomed beyond the central square, did she become aware of that comforting warmth.

Today, the crowd would be allowed onto the grounds, following the procession to the royal vault in the secluded garden behind the castle to witness the final resting place of their king. Slowly, they trudged up the long lane, beneath the soughing bows of the lombars, across the crisp, winter-frosted lawn until finally the cavalcade halted before the doors of the secluded tomb.

The massive stone structure was set in a clump of weeping anwistas. Though bare of leaves, the thick trailing branches provided peaceful solitude. Thick vines of ivy, the leaves blackened by cold, clung tenaciously to the structure's sides. Only the front of highly polished slabs of granite was free of the plant's roaming tentacles. Atop the vault, a narrow steeple pierced the sky and proclaimed the avenue of departure for the souls within.

The flag bearers stepped forward as six soldiers lifted the coffin from the platform. King Quillan's banners were rolled and laid in the indentations around the coffin's lid. The crowd hushed respectfully as the doors were swept open.

The high priest stepped onto a raised dais to one side of the doors and carefully unrolled his scroll. His voice droned unheard in Tallia's ears. She sought her memories and those of her ancestors, finding again the visions of Eyrsa and Quillan to sooth the empty ache of loss that threatened to press her to the ground with its heavy weight.

Involuntarily she reached out and gripped Tynan's hand, desperate for his warmth, his solidity. Purposefully, she turned away from Krogan, disgusted by the false show of mourning he enacted for the benefit of those citizens near enough to see it.

The epitaph was read, the coffin transported inside, and the doors laboriously closed. Tallia felt detached, as though she watched a play from a distant balcony seat. Numbed by the cold, she stared at the closed doors, unable to move, rooted to the spot until Tynan tugged gently on her arm to lead her away.

The mourners would stay today and all through the night. Tomorrow, Quillan's heir would be announced and the crowd would finally disperse.

Krogan moved to Tallia's side as Tynan propelled her through the castle doors. "An hour," he hissed. "In the solarium. Be there or forfeit."

Both Tynan and Tallia stared at him incredulously.

"An hour!"

Tynan detected the tremble in her voice and reacted. "Have you no respect? Quillan is just entombed." He challenged Krogan's words in the hope of extracting some emotion, some compassion, from the man.

Tynan's fists clenched at the delighted gleam in Krogan's eyes. He should have known. Krogan obviously planned to use Tallia's emotional distress to his advantage. Tynan stepped forward menacingly, his fingers itching to choke the life from this man who had caused so much pain, but Krogan stood his ground.

"The choice is Coran's, and thus mine. An hour." Krogan turned and walked away, his macabre laughter resounding in the passage.

Trancelike, Tallia followed Tynan to her room. The deep shock had chilled her heart, and Tynan began slowly to massage her limbs, bringing warmth back to her body. His touch soothed her frayed nerves and she submitted to his tender contact until it lulled her into a hazy sleep.

Tynan watched her face, the play of expressions flashing across her features, her dainty brows drawn together in a concerned frown, her mouth trembling with the strength of those emotions even in sleep. He continued to rub his hands over her back and arms, soothing away the tension. She needed rest. The moment of truth was near at hand and he feared for her. She had been devastated by killing Bodan and somehow, Tynan felt sure that the memory of Bodan's distorted face and agonizing death would be her downfall. She lacked the desire to kill. He could only pray that the instinct which had preserved her before would resurface and provide her with the ability to defeat Krogan.

The solarium was silent. Their footsteps echoed eerily on the cold marble tiles as Tynan and Tallia crossed the wide room. Candles flickered in wall sconces, banishing some of the grayness cast by the darkening, stormy sky visible through the glass dome overhead. Tallia shivered and Tynan quickly slipped his arm around her.

From a curtained alcove at the far end of the room, Krogan stepped boldly into sight. He made no move to approach them but rather stared expectantly toward the center of the great hall.

Tallia held her breath. The air was still, but an electrical charge almost visible seemed to crackle between herself and Krogan. The contact was none of her doing and yet she did not feel threatened by it, though it did seem strangely judgmental.

In the peak of the room's central dome, a blue mist materialized, twisting, swirling, obscuring the sky beyond. From the midst of this maelstrom, a voice boomed, "The opponents have been verified and approved."

A streak of lightning lit the firmament. Thunder rumbled menacingly beyond the castle walls as great drops of rain began to pelt down, drumming on the glass, echoing within the confines of the solarium.

The fireplace at the end of the room roared to life, the flames leaping into fiery red-and-yellow tongues. Coran stepped from the heated depths. Her crimson robe glowed with ruby and topaz and seemed to have a fiery will of its own. Her cloak billowed out from her body like a dragon unfolding blood-red wings. Her ebony hair swirled about her and from it, sparks of flame crackled into the surrounding air, tinting it with an angry orange glow. She moved to Krogan's side, seeming to engulf him within her fiery aura.

The cold hand of fear clutched at Tallia's throat as she drew a gasping breath. Even Tynan seemed awed by the theatrical entrance. Coran's evil laugh swirled across the room, momentarily paralyzing her intended victim. Like a snake hypnotizing its prey, her apparition swayed back and forth, the jewel-encrusted robe flickering and crackling like consuming flames.

Tallia stiffened. Could she protect herself and her child from the malevolent force that emanated from Krogan and Coran? Could she possibly emerge victorious? Tentatively, her mind reached out and touched Coran's crimson aura. Instantly, she withdrew, her eyes widening in surprise. Tallia had felt that presence before. It only took that one small contact to recognize the source of the power surge that had bolstered her energy when she'd killed Bodan in the wasteland.

"It was her," she whispered to Tynan. "I felt her presence in the wasteland."

Tynan stared at her then slowly nodded. "She could not allow you to be killed by anyone other than Krogan lest she lose her right to the throne." He frowned thoughtfully, seeking some way to use this knowledge.

Tallia's mind, too, sought the path to elucidation, but drew a blank. How could she defeat Krogan? Coran would not resurface within her today, not that she would want that no matter what the stakes. Her mind was repelled by the evil emanating from the fiery apparition.

Then she felt it, a soothing calm that settled the air around her. She glanced upward and found herself entranced by serenity. A shaft of silvery light pierced the cloud cover and glowed softly as the ray came to rest at Tallia's feet. From the diamond-sparkled mists, Galacia stepped forward. Her robe shimmered in swirling patterns of icy blue, lavender, and sea-mist green. The silver threads that wound through her robe reflected tiny lights in the ebony cloud of curls that cascaded to her waist and fanned out in a wispy halo. Pale blue eyes came to rest on Tallia, and a sweet smile transposed her features. Tallia felt her heart swell with affection for the woman who had carried her to safety from the ravages of an earthquake. Galacia's sparkling azure aura surrounded Tallia and she felt safe and at peace.

"Fear not." Galacia's voice was like the gentle breeze that rippled the placid surface of a lake. "I will protect the child to the limit of my means. Follow your heart, for love is with us always." Tallia watched awed as Galacia's gaze swept to Tynan and then back.

They turned together toward the center of the room as the blue mists descended from the apex of the dome and formed a thick circular fog.

The commanding voice boomed again, "The rules will be stated."

Coran stepped forward. "I, as prophesied, have chosen this time. Both combatants have been granted Raunarian power. The battle shall be to the death without our interference. I have signed my pledge to the Prophecy and yield to all its terms."

"I too yield to the terms," Galacia spoke. "I remind my sister only that the Prophecy also states that the invisible bonds that hold captive the heart shall allow, in this arena, a unity built of love."

"Ha!" Coran snorted contemptuously across the room. "Love will not save her." She pointed a slender finger at Tallia. "Sister, you are a fool. Through that naïveté you have ensured my victory."

Galacia only smiled sweetly. "We will see," she replied in a calm voice.

"Call forth the contestants." Tallia jumped as a masculine voice issued from the midst of the impenetrable blue mists. "Let the combat begin."

Tallia and Krogan moved forward until their forms were engulfed by the thick mist. Abruptly, it lifted, forming a semitransparent, perpendicular dome over them. The battle ground was set. Tallia swallowed against a flood of fear. Her chest felt tight, her breath trapped in her throat, her Zarma stone heavy around her neck. She faced Krogan with determination, steeling herself for the onslaught she knew he would hurl at her.

It struck with numbing force, like a dagger driven into her mind, a red-hot brand that seared her nerve endings in a single instant. She quailed beneath the pain and stumbled back, breaking the electrical surge that twisted in the air between them.

Power surged within her and she forced it through the air in a blinding blue arch. As it struck Krogan, he faltered briefly, bracing himself against the energy surge. It splintered, arching away from him in a thousand harmless scintillae and Krogan smiled.

Tallia could sense another energy within her, more powerful, lying dormant. It was what she needed to win. Yet even as the realization surfaced, her heart rebelled. Winning meant killing. Murder. She who had been reared to save lives must take a life. Tynan was right; she couldn't do it. Her breath came in quick urgent gasps. She had to do it quickly, for Krogan was preparing for another assault. Taking a deep breath, she drew on that other power, so ancient, so lethal.

She hurled a poisonous blue radiance which flared and undulated swiftly across the arena, gaining speed as though eager for the kill. It halted abruptly before reaching her opponent. She couldn't harm him with the light of her psychic assault. Bodan's pain-contorted image flashed in her thoughts and the light wavered.

Across the marble tiles, Krogan analyzed her attack. She had not the will, the greed for power that possessed him and strengthened his resolve. He'd seen the glow flicker and knew she struggled with her own hidden demons. But no matter, he didn't need to depend on Tallia's pangs of conscience to defeat her. She presented only a scant resistance. He would squash her and be done with it.

Tallia froze as the brilliant beam of crimson light spun from Krogan's mind. The air crackled and hissed, streaked with sparks, as red met blue, slowly forcing its way across the arena.

Beyond the barrier, Tynan clenched and unclenched his fists. Tallia was no match for Krogan's hatred for she did not know how to hate. It was a struggle for her just to protect herself, and how long could she maintain that position? He started as the air snapped again with fierce intensity as Krogan sent another blood-red surge pulsating along the charged cord of electricity that seemed to bind the two combatants. He felt Tallia's pain as she raised her hands to her head and fell to her knees.

Tallia trembled. Heat filled her mind and consumed her very body. Her pulse pounded at her throat, and her chest constricted, trapping her breath within her lungs. She opened her mouth to inhale but there was no air. Her vision blurred as she struggled to regain her footing.

Krogan unleashed another blast. She saw it arching toward her and tensed. Was it to be over so quickly then?

A shimmering wall of blue ice moved around her, enveloping her in soothing coolness. She felt the pressure of a gentle hand on her shoulder. Her eyes flitted sideways in disbelief. On either side of her, Eyrsa and Quillan stood straight and strong. Krogan's barrage struck the barrier, sending splintering fissures across its surface but the blue aura held.

Coran's shriek of outrage filled the air and she shouted at Galacia, "Get them out! The rules—"

Galacia interrupted her sister's ranting, "State that those bound to Tallia by love shall be permitted in the arena. They are not Raunarians."

Coran's anger burst into an illusory flaming cloak that leapt from the ground and surged around her. "I will still win! Even together they are no match for Krogan." She hurled her commands to Krogan. "Kill her! Now!"

Another red bolt jarred the ground and heated the air around the protective circle. Tallia's voice shook as she stumbled to her feet, half expecting the Zarmist to vanish at any moment. "You've come back. Can you help me?" Tallia pleaded.

At Eyrsa's apologetic expression, Tallia turned to her father but he shook his head. "We can but lend our love as support. You and Krogan are the first descendants of Toleme to possess aggressive abilities. We are unable to take a life."

"Then I am doomed." Tallia stared blankly past Eyrsa and Quillan as their images faded. "For, even in my own defense, the taking of a life is abhorrent to me. I am a healer."

Tynan stared at Tallia. She had conjured some sort of ice wall against Krogan's onslaught. Within its circle, she mouthed silent words that did not reach him. Mesmerized, he heard Coran's accusations and Galacia's reply. Had they gone insane? There was no one in the arena but Krogan and Tallia and yet Coran's outrage burned around her in a crimson mantle of flame. What could he not see? Was there someone there to whom Tallia spoke? Galacia's words stuck in his mind. "Those bound by love shall be allowed to enter."

Tynan watched stunned as a streak of red light shattered the icy wall around Tallia. It melted away in a hiss of vapor, and Tallia's defense vanished. Krogan seemed to gather his strength, converging all his energy for one stupendous bolt of death. As though in slow motion, Tynan saw it arch into the air, gathering momentum and growing while Tallia stood helpless in its path.

"No!" The word felt torn from his very soul. He threw himself at the wall of the arena. He could not stand by and watch her killed. Krogan had taken too much from him; he would take no more.

Tynan burst through the barrier unscathed. He felt the power granted within the "key" surge to his mind. He gathered it, converged it into a solid shaft of force, and hurled it at Krogan as he ran. Blinding, the luminous prismatic ray found its mark and sent Krogan crashing back. Beyond the wall, Coran's face contorted with rage. A puissant ball of flamelike energy flashed from her fingertips, striking the barrier only to scatter and dissipate harmlessly. A misty blue tentacle whipped from the wall and wrapped around her arms, immobilizing her, preventing her further interference.

Tynan halted between Tallia and Krogan. The wall had offered no resistance to his entrance. Galacia's carefully worded appendage to the Prophecy had provided the means. Tallia could not defeat Krogan, but he could. He felt it deep within him, the avenging spirit snapping its angry tail, spurring his anger. He wanted Krogan dead, had wanted it since his family had been massacred, though then he had not known the identity of the man he hated.

Krogan struggled to his feet, rage and confusion etched on his face. Never before had he felt the power so strong in another and Tynan had reason to battle, even beyond his love for the girl. Still, Krogan had been taught by a master. He would never admit defeat. His eyes narrowed into thin slits as he conjured a swirling maelstrom of searing force. It built around him, twisting and roaring, shooting flame-hued rays of energy from its apex. He breathed deeply and beckoned every ounce of strength, directing the wildly spinning vortex at Tynan.

Tynan felt the heat upon his face. Visions of his parents, his brother, and Tynara flashed through his thoughts. He felt his heart grow cold, empty. He clenched his fists at his side and let the anger surface, erupting, spewing forth. Like a burgeoning tidal wave, the green light rolled across the span of the solarium, dwarfing the fiery tornado and crushing it beneath the weight of his vengeance. It surged over Krogan, engulfing him in its midst. Like a giant eddy, it spun, faster and faster, sucking Krogan into its wake, tossing him like a leaf upon the crest of an oceanic whirlpool.

Tallia's touch broke Tynan's concentration. The emerald light dimmed then faded, leaving only empty silence. Krogan lay lifeless, his glassy eyes staring sightlessly skyward. Coran's scream cut through the stillness.

The heavy masculine voice boomed again, "The Prophecy is fulfilled." The blue mist curled upward, drawing Galacia and the livid Coran in its wake, coiling about the sisters and fading into nothingness.

Tynan remained with his back to Tallia for several seconds. When he finally turned, the haunted expression had left the depths of his eyes, but there was no sign of triumph. "It is over."

"I . . ." Tallia struggled for words. "Thank you."

Tynan felt the ache in his heart. He wanted desperately to embrace her, to hold her to him. If

337

only she felt the same things for him as he felt for her. If only she could love him. But she had made it clear that he had no place in her life. Only Quillan's request had allowed him to tarry this long. Tynan stared into Tallia's eyes. He would let her go. He had to. Enslaving her with a promise made to a now dead king would not bring him her love.

"You are free now, free to be queen. I will sign the annulment tomorrow." Tynan kept his expression impassive. She could never love him, not she who revered life and detested killing. When she gazed upon him, she would never see any more than the death he had scattered in his path. Quillan's wish had been fulfilled, but now he must go. He was a wastelander, a nomad.

Tallia observed his cold expression. He had performed his duty, kept his pledge to the king. Now that it was over, he wanted no part of her. She felt a inexplicable burning in her chest.

"You will stay for the coronation." She struggled to find an excuse to keep him near if only for another day.

He bowed politely. "As you wish."

As he turned and walked from the room, her mind screamed out for her to act, to halt him. But she knew not what to say, so she said nothing.

Tallia stared at the gold-trimmed robe that had been carefully draped over the chair by her wardrobe. The sounds of activity from below set her pulse racing. For several hours now the people had been arriving, filling the temple and the hall beyond, all eager to claim the best view of their new ruler. She took a deep breath. They expected to see

Lord Krogan walk down that flower-strewn aisle, bow, and be crowned the new king of Karaundo. What would be their reaction to her, a stranger, an unknown face, the secret daughter whom King Quillan had acknowledged in his will?

She tapped her foot impatiently on the flagstone floor as the matron twisted the last strands of her rebellious hair into the elaborate coiffure that crowned her head. A few disobedient curls even now fought free and wisped across her forehead.

"That's fine." Tallia raised her hand to dismiss the woman.

Relieved, the servant relented and, bowing, left. Alone, Tallia rose and moved to stand before the floor-length mirror beside the wardrobe. Her gown was simple, white satin folding gently to the tips of her slippers, tied with a braided gold rope, the ends of which almost reached the floor. She reached up and touched the single chain of diamonds around her neck that had been presented by Quillan's chief aide only this morning. Custom, he had advised, and handed her the velvet case before leaving to arrange the details of the coronation. She had removed her Zarma stone and replaced it with the precious gems.

Tallia gave a sigh of resignation. She had not suspected the price of this position. Loneliness already wrapped itself around her. Gone were the carefree days roaming the fields of Twin Suns. Gone was the easy rapport she had with all she knew. Now it was, "Yes, my lady. No, my lady." Already she was highly sick of it. And Tynan, he too was beyond her reach. Goddess above, how she missed Dayna. Dayna who cared not a fig for propriety, whose honesty and sense of humor knew no class distinctions.

Dayna! When all of this was over, she would invite her to visit, perhaps offer her the position of Royal Zarmist. She smiled slightly in remembrance of Dayna's irreverence. It would definitely be refreshing to have somebody around who actually spoke her mind.

Retrieving the thick scarlet robe, she hoisted its heavy weight onto her shoulders. Sliding her arms through the slits in the sides, she fastened the emerald clasp at her throat.

There was, she reflected, one good thing about her newly acquired status. She returned to her seat to wait for the enactment of that benefit. Tynan should have received her summons by now and was probably on his way. She wondered what reaction he would have to her request for his presence at her side during her coronation. After all, he was the one who had reminded her that he was her husband, a close friend of King Quillan's and, fortunately, in the employ of the head of the House of Tuhan.

She jumped to her feet at the pounding on her door. Taking a deep breath to regain her composure, she answered, "Enter."

As the door swung open, Tallia's breath caught in her throat. Deep emerald eyes met her own gaze with direct scrutiny and thick black brows raised slightly in silent approval of her appearance. She felt the heat of her blush as it crept up her throat and over her cheeks. Inwardly she berated herself for her schoolgirl reaction but she could not tear her eyes from the sight of him. His dark hair gleamed in the lamplight; his muscular form was accentuated by the tight-fitting black trousers and partially opened ebony silk shirt that revealed a glimpse of the soft black hair that covered his broad chest. No adornments, no jewels, nothing to mar the simplicity of him. This was Tynan. In her life, he was the one rock, the one predictable, unchangeable certainty.

He crooked his arm and offered it to her. Wordlessly, she accepted it and allowed him to lead her down the curving stairs to the curtained alcove below. They would not enter until the announcement had been made. Tallia heard the pounding of her heart in her ears, felt the warmth of his closeness in the shadowed niche. The familiar longing to be wrapped in his powerful arms surged unexpectedly through her.

The chancellor's voice rang out, "Lord Krogan, is dead!"

The volume in the room rose to a roar.

The chancellor waited several minutes before he could continue. When he did, his accusation rang out clearly. "Krogan is responsible for the death of your king. He does not deserve your sympathy."

"I give you the new ruler of Karaundo." The chancellor let his voice roll out over the crowd so it might penetrate the recesses of that secluded alcove. "As named by your king in his will, I present his successor. I give you your queen, Tallia, daughter of King Quillan and Queen Jhysine."

Tallia stepped from the alcove at Tynan's prompting. They paused on the dais. The crowd was silent as all eyes turned to stare.

Tynan stepped from the dais and extended his hand to aid Tallia in her descent. They walked slowly down the aisle as Tallia held her head high to silence the thudding of her heart. She smiled as Tynan squeezed her hand in a quiet measure of reassurance.

As they progressed toward the platform and altar, the crowd hushed. Those nearest her saw the resemblance to the king. Frozen expressions converted to hesitant smiles of acceptance and the chant began, gradually increasing in volume as more and more people joined in until the hall rocked with the force of their voices.

"Long live the queen! Hail, Queen Tallia!"

Tallia returned the smiles, her apprehension diminishing.

"Long live the queen," Tynan whispered in her ear as he drew her to a halt before the temple's two-tiered platform. As he stepped back, she felt a tremendous sense of loss, and turned to him. There had to be some way to convince him to stay, some compromise that they could work out between them. As soon as this ceremony was over, she would speak with him.

Gracefully, she lifted the edges of her gown and stepped onto the first level. Bowing her head to the chancellor, she knelt.

"You have fixed your pledge upon the documents of leadership," he began. "You have vowed to rule with benevolence and kindness and the strength bestowed upon you by those beyond. The crown of responsibility is heavy, and we, the members of the court, will seek to lighten your burden. Be fair in your judgement, Tallia of the House of Tuhan, be righteous in your purpose, and generous with your love." He turned and lifted the vee-shaped band from its resting place on the ivory pillow.

Holding the circlet high for all to see, he pronounced, "I crown thee Tallia, Queen of Karaundo."

Engrossed, Tallia watched the gleaming gold band descend toward her brow.

"No!" The outraged shriek swept from the back of the room. A gust of desert-hot wind grazed Tallia's face and sent the crown spinning through the air. The chancellor stumbled back, propelled by the force of Coran's angry release.

Spinning, Tallia leapt to her feet. Surely, the tribunal would not allow Coran to interfere here.

"We will meet again, Tallia of the House of Tuhan," Coran hurled the words like blazing sparks before her.

A crimson flash of light filled the room as Coran lifted her arms and released her power. Tallia felt her own energy surge. She would have reparation. She turned to Tynan, seeking to draw on his bolstering power. To her dismay, he cast her an agonized look and crumpled lifeless to the ground.

Tallia heard her own scream of anguish penetrate the room but it was too late. Coran vanished in a scintillating blast of illusory flame.

CHAPTER SIXTEEN

TALLIA CROUCHED OVER TYNAN'S COLLAPSED form, and urgently called his name. There was no response. His body felt inordinately cold. Holding panic at bay, she looked up. "You and you," she said, gesturing to two of the closest men. "Help me get him to his chamber."

Inclining their heads with dignity, the two lords she had indicated stepped forward. "As your majesty commands," one replied, moving to aid the other in lifting Tynan's inert form. Distantly, the indulgent tone of his voice penetrated her worry. Damn protocol! She should have summoned guards, she realized. Later, she would send a note of apology to the lords, thanking them for their willing aid. Her eyes once more turned to Tynan as she followed the men from the room, the coronation and the crowd forgotten.

Tynan lay on the bed in his chamber as still and silent as though death had claimed him. Finally alone, Tallia reached out with her mind, searching, attempting to contact his unconscious. She reeled in shock. There was nothing there! Her exploration found only vacuous blackness. How was it possible? His body lived, barely, yet his mind was gone.

She looked down upon the strong masculine features that she loved, and tears brimmed in her eyes. Love? Yes, she loved him. Why had it taken her so long to realize that, to attach the word "love" to the feelings she held? Would her love be enough to help him now? His association with her had endangered his life more than once, and this, this was something she didn't know how to fight. Brushing the thick ebony locks from his forehead, tears ran unheeded down her ashen face. What could she do? What had Coran done to him?

She has stolen his soul, a familiar presence whispered in her thoughts.

"Eyrsa?" Tallia searched the room with eager red-rimmed eyes. There, in a shadowed corner materialized Eyrsa's faint shimmering revenant. "What can I do?" she beseeched.

Follow your heart. If there is a way, you will find it. There is a thread that links his body to his soul. He must be returned before it fades or is severed, or he dies.

"Help me!" Tallia cried in anguish. "Tell me what to do!"

I don't know, child. The ghostly shimmer wavered and was gone.

Tallia paced the room in agitation. How much time did she have? What could she do? She paused, concentrating on the still form on the bed. Yes, there it was. A luminescent filament extending outward, disappearing into the wall. But where did it lead? How could she trace it?

Her eyes narrowed thoughtfully. Coran would not win! She would think of something. Once more she paced the chamber. A multitude of emotions clamored within her, warring for supremacy—love and hope, hatred and rage, urgency and determination. Suddenly she halted.

A Raunarian had perpetrated the crime, so Tallia would appeal to that society for aid. Seating herself, she closed her eyes sending the call from her mind over and over again, *Galacia*. There was no reply, but she refused to allow herself to be discouraged. Her mind ranged farther than ever before, reaching, extending in all directions.

Something changed. She sensed an alteration in the room. Her concentration broken, she opened her eyes. Before her, within an arch of glittering opalescent light, like a rift between worlds, stood Galacia; an alien landscape of shifting colors and patterns stretched into infinity behind her. The woman extended her hand in invitation. Tallia hesitated, but only fractionally, before rising and taking the smooth ageless hand of the woman before her. She glanced back at Tynan's still form. She had no choice.

There was an instant of pain, of vertigo, as she plunged into a whirling vortex of mutating light patterns. She perceived strange presences around her; alien emotions bombarded her senses, passing so quickly she had no opportunity to decipher them. And then, there was only light—bright, blinding light.

They emerged into a hallway or rather the illusion of one. Dimensions were indeterminate; walls did not exist, but rather boundless star-studded space. The floor on which they walked was a narrow path of light, its edges fading into nothingness. Before them, it spiraled into infinity.

Tallia looked at Galacia. Garbed in ivory, the woman's face reflected only serenity. "Where are we going?" Tallia asked in a hushed tone.

"To the tribunal," the woman replied in a voice that was high and pure and as ageless as she, reminding Tallia of the sweet notes of a flute.

"I can hear you now!" Tallia remarked with amazement.

"Coran disregarded the rules of the Prophecy. I am no longer bound by my punishment."

"Punishment?" Tallia queried but Galacia did not respond.

Suddenly, two massive gilded doors appeared before them. At least that's how Tallia perceived the phenomenon, for there was no sensation of having approached them from a distance. Silently, as though propelled by unseen hands, they swung inward.

Tallia and Galacia entered. In a semicircle around the enormous chamber, twelve white columns extended high into the air. Upon the summit of each rested a golden chair occupied by a distinguished person of indeterminate years. Tallia received the impression of extreme age, for although their countenances appeared ageless, wisdom shone from their eyes and snowy hair crowned their heads.

The room remained totally silent, and yet there was animation in the expressions of the people she viewed. Galacia waved an arm in Tallia's direction as though in dramatic introduction, yet no words passed her lips. Of course! These people had no need of verbal speech.

Tallia opened her mind and immediately wished she hadn't. A silent cacophony of disjointed thoughts and incomplete sentences barraged her human mind, none of which could she decipher.

Finally, a man spoke, "So, child, why are you here?" Pristine hair crowned his head. Piercing blue eyes scrutinized her from a face almost totally obscured by a long beard that blended into the white of his robes.

Tallia hesitated. What was the proper form of address to a tribunal member? There had been no mention of that in Toleme's journal. She must be careful not to offend, for her need was great. "My lord, I seek aid in recovering the soul of the man I love."

There was a brief flurry of mental communication before he replied. "I'm sorry, child. Since the dawn of time, we have been forbidden to interfere in the lives of primitive peoples except in situations where the survival of the race is at stake. This is obviously not the case. Again, I am sorry," he said with finality, apparently dismissing her.

Tallia grew desperate, and more than a little determined. "My lord, it is only because a member of your society has broken the very law you speak of that I am here. Does your society not punish lawbreakers? Must the life of the man I love be forfeit because you cannot restrain Coran's wicked ambition?"

For an instant, she felt that in her desperation she had carried her impassioned speech too far. A frown marred the handsome features of the man before her as mental discordance filled the room. She waited anxiously, for there was little else she could do. Galacia, her face an impassive mask, waited with her. Why did she not help her convince the tribunal? What rules were in play that she did not understand?

"Tallia," the man's voice boomed within the vast chamber, "I must reiterate, we are forbidden to interfere in the lives of humans."

"But—" Tallia prepared to argue, to plead if necessary.

He raised a hand to forestall her. "Let me finish, please. My daughter, Coran, will be severely disciplined. She is to be exiled to the Coridian Plane where no laws or rules of science apply. From it, there is no escape without aid from outside.

"However, the process necessary before the punishment can be carried out will not be accomplished in time to save the life of . . ." He paused and Tallia felt a slight tickle in her mind. "Of Tynan. An extremely unfortunate circumstance which should not have occurred. Therefore, we grant you the right to deliver Coran's punishment. This can be done only by you, for as the wronged person, only you have the right to a combat of reprisal."

Having read Toleme's journal, Tallia now realized that it was Yaewel who spoke to her. She frowned in puzzlement. What was he saying? "How do I do this?" Tallia queried.

Yaewel shrugged. "That is up to you. You are a human being, but you have in your possession all the abilities of a member of our society. Anything Coran can do, you can do also."

He paused and there was another brief flurry of communication in which Tallia recognized Galacia's interjection. Then he continued. "You have argued your position well. In view of that, we will allow Galacia, who has been your guardian since birth and whom we allowed to protect your unborn child, to aid you further. However, this aid must be given before the initiation of the combat. Once the combat begins, there will be no further communication."

"I understand," Tallia replied calmly, though her pulse fluttered with trepidation. What did the combat of reprisal entail? "Thank you, my lord." She shifted her gaze to the other members of the tribunal. "Thank you all."

Yaewel inclined his head regally, as did the others, in recognition of her gratitude. Then Galacia grasped her arm to lead her from the room. Once more they tread the strange winding self-illuminating path.

The hall wound on, uphill, downhill, spiraling, all for no reason that was apparent to Tallia. Then, as before, a door once more abruptly appeared a few feet in front of them. It swung open as they reached it.

"Please come in," Galacia invited in her musical voice.

They entered a room which was immediately

recognizable as personal living quarters, yet it was like none Tallia had ever seen before. Tables and chairs had no legs, but rather were suspended by some hidden means. There were no books, ornaments, pictures or decorations of any kind. Although spotlessly clean, the apartment was austere in the extreme.

"Come with me," Galacia directed.

Tallia followed her to one side of the chamber. Galacia waved her right hand, and immediately a three-dimensional picture such as those she'd seen in the "key" appeared.

"Listen carefully to what I tell you, Tallia. This knowledge is indispensible for the task you seek to accomplish."

Tallia nodded, studying the changing scene before her.

"There are many planes of existence," Galacia said. "Some are parallel to your life plane, some are very distant. Occasionally one plane exists within another, occupying the same time, sharing many things, yet governed by a completely different set of laws. You do not need to fully understand this, just know that it is so."

"All right," Tallia responded hesitantly. "The concept is very confusing."

"Yes," Galacia agreed. "Now, the picture you see before us is the Coridian Plane. Study it carefully. Notice how none of the laws of nature function within it."

"It is very strange," Tallia noted. "Some of the trees grow upside down. The stars and sun occupy the sky at the same time. And see there"—she pointed—"a pond that floats through the air. You can see the fish swimming in it."

"It is strange," agreed Galacia. "But those are not the things I wanted you to notice, for many of those occurrences are duplicated in other planes. Look at the horizon. What do you see?"

Tallia peered more closely at the picture. "Well," she said thoughtfully, "it seems to waver."

"Exactly," Galacia responded. "The Coridian Plane is in a constant state of imbalance. Everything changes constantly. In other planes, natural gateways open frequently, allowing travel between them. In the Coridian Plane, natural apertures do occur, but there is no possibility of using them as gateways. The time span involved is too short, mere fractions of a second. This is where, if you are to win the contest with Coran, you must trap her."

"What would happen if you tried to use one of the gates?"

"When the aperture ceased to be, you would no longer exist."

"How will I find the Coridian Plane?" Tallia asked, unable to restrain her impatience any longer. These proceedings were taking an inordinate amount of time, and she didn't know how much longer she had.

"Be patient a little longer, please," Galacia responded softly. "I will tell you shortly."

"How long does it take to pass from one plane to another?" Tallia asked.

"It varies with the planes. How long do you think it took us to come here from your own plane?"

Tallia remembered the strange sensation of vertigo. So that's what had happened. "About five minutes?" she hazarded a guess.

Galacia shook her head. "Less than two, but your material life plane does not border this one." She hesitated. "We gated through three other planes on our way here. It's very difficult to explain. Do you understand?"

"I think so."

"Good. Then we will move on." She waved her hand and the three-dimensional image of the Coridian Plane disappeared. "Come with me please."

Across the room, Galacia placed her hand briefly on the wall. A panel slid aside and a small cabinet appeared. Reaching into a compartment, she removed a strange medallion on a thick golden chain. Flat like a coin, the circular center spun slowly on an invisible axis within a circular band of ebony.

"This amulet allows its wearer to traverse freely between the planes without waiting for natural gates to occur."

"How does it work?" Tallia asked curiously, studying the object.

"It must be worn next to your flesh, for the heartbeat is its source of power. It is active only as long as it is being worn. To traverse the planes, you have only to think the name of your destination. The amulet will gate the way for you."

"But I don't know the name of the plane where Coran has taken Tynan," Tallia protested in distress.

"No," Galacia commiserated, "nor do I. You will still be able to use the amulet to trace them, but the route will be much slower. Simply follow Tynan's lifethread. Whenever the fiber seems to trail off into nothingness, think 'gate.' An arch such as the one you entered with me will appear, and you'll be able to continue."

"And when I've found them, I must trick Coran into following me to the Coridian Plane. Once there, if I gate again quickly utilizing the amulet, she will be imprisoned there. Is that right?"

Galacia nodded. "But you must not attempt to gate directly back to the Material Life Plane. The gate would be open too long, allowing her time to realize what has occurred and follow you. Make certain she is quite a distance from you, then once more simply think 'gate.' The amulet will take you to the nearest plane, and the gate will only be open a matter of seconds. Not long enough for her to reach it and pass through."

"I see." Tallia retreated into thought. She was more frightened than she cared to admit, but she could not allow herself to dwell on the emotion. Tynan's life depended on how well she learned what was being taught. "Once I have confined Coran to the Coridian Plane, how will I retrieve Tynan's soul? Will I recognize him? How do I restore him to his body?" The questions emerged in a deluge.

Galacia replied patiently, "You will recognize him, just as you recognized Eyrsa. Once Coran's mental control has been released, you will be able to speak with him telepathically and guide him back to your own plane. As for restoring him to his body, only he can do that." She paused. "How can I make you understand?" she mumbled.

"Think of the spirit as a foot," she continued after a moment. "A foot that has gone a long time without the restriction of a shoe may find even an old shoe uncomfortable. It has to reaccustom itself to the shoe. So it is with the soul or spirit. Tynan will have to work his soul back into the confinement of his body and reacquaint himself with the restriction. The difficulty will increase proportionally to the length of time his soul is away from his body."

"I understand," Tallia replied in a subdued tone. "Then I had best be about the combat as soon as possible."

"Yes," agreed Galacia. "But there is one other thing. In the other planes, you will meet beings, some human, some not. Many will try to communicate with you. You must, absolutely must, ignore them. If they are of malicious intent, and many are, your acknowledgment of their existence will entrap you. Do not ask me how this comes about, for it is a lengthy explanation that you would probably not understand in any case. Just abide by my warning. Do not see them. Do not hear them. Do not speak to them."

"I'll remember," Tallia assured her. "Do you have any suggestions for the combat? How can I entice Coran into the Coridian Plane without her being aware of it?"

"With that I cannot help you," Galacia responded. "My sister is very egotistical, perhaps that may be of some assistance."

"I'd forgotten she was your sister," Tallia murmured. "You are so very different. Were you ever close?" she asked, and then immediately wished she hadn't for Galacia's gentle countenance mirrored hurt. "I'm sorry. I shouldn't have asked."

"It's all right. Yes, we were close once," she replied, smiling wistfully. "But it was many years ago and we were both different then."

Tallia felt uncomfortable. "I should go now."

"I will take you back to your own plane. From there, you can trace Tynan."

Seconds later, Tallia stepped out of the shimmering arch into Tynan's chamber. He lay as she'd left him, and once more she felt tears threatening her but she forced them back. Tears did not help. Turning to face the arch of opalescent light, she lifted her hand in farewell. "Thank you," she murmured.

Galacia smiled gently in reply, and then was gone.

Once more Tallia focused her gaze on the almost invisible filament that trailed from Tynan's body into the wall beyond. *I am not ready*, a part of her mind insisted. *You will never be more ready*, another part argued. She sighed. She had no idea what she would do, only that she would do whatever was necessary to win, for she was fighting for her husband's life.

Hesitantly, she donned the amulet Galacia had given her, concealing it beneath her tunic. Immediately she felt it warm and begin to pulsate with the rhythm of her heart. With determination, she strode to the wall, fixing her gaze on the thread of Tynan's life. "Gate," she said firmly.

An arch appeared, different than the one she'd seen before, yet similar. The light radiating from its periphery was a dark luminous indigo, like the light of a star. And beyond the gate, the glowing fiber that she must trace stretched on.

She stepped through the gate into a landscape of rippling heat and burning red sands. Deep wide racks, spewing clouds of steam, scarred the terrain. Winged beasts, the like of which she'd never seen, flew overhead in an orange sky, but they ignored her. Tallia walked on, thinking only of Tynan as she carefully skirted the dangerous-looking crevices. Her heart pounded and the heated air scorched her throat. She followed the filament. Within moments that seemed like hours in the inhospitable plane, the trail disappeared into an ocher-colored crag.

"Gate," Tallia uttered hoarsely and then, as a lush green panorama appeared, she stepped eagerly through. A whirling vortex of color spun her around and Tallia fell to her knees upon a rich, grassy, sun-bathed meadow. Why were some gates easier to pass through than others? She shook her head, knowing the question would not be answered, and once more sought the near invisible trace of Tynan. There!

The air was cool, glittering with droplets of thin iridescent mist. A man strolled up a grassy knoll toward her. She remembered Galacia's admonishment and immediately turned her gaze from him. Fixing her eyes once more on the thread, she walked quickly on. The man shouted something in an unfamiliar tongue but Tallia refused to hear him. Over a hill, the filament ended abruptly in mid-air.

"Gate," she said once more and stepped through into a land shrouded in night's black cloak. Three moons shone in the sky above, bathing the alien world in unnatural silver light. Colorless trees reached ghostly leafless limbs into the night sky. Chalky grasses rustled softly beneath her feet. A beast roared in the distance and instinct told Tallia to move quickly.

Suddenly, a creature rose from the ground directly in her path. His pallid face was almost featureless except for the glowing amber of his eyes. "You must not see or hear them," the words echoed in her mind. She saw only the memory of Tynan, alive and vibrant. Without revealing any awareness of the being's presence, she skirted it, walking quickly on. The trace disappeared into one of the ghostly trees.

"Gate," Tallia murmured once more. After a brief vertiginous interval she emerged into a frenzied white world of bitter cold. The blizzard swirled around her, blinding her, robbing her of breath. Within seconds, her hair and eyelashes were sheathed in ice. How was she to survive here long enough to follow? "You can do anything Coran can do," the words echoed in her mind.

She closed her eyes and concentrated. The cold became warmth; the snow became rain; and the roaring wind became a gentle breeze. Tallia opened her eyes, looking around in amazement. Had she done this? In a domed cocoon surrounding her the weather had calmed, while outside its periphery, the blizzard continued to rage. Once more she searched for and found the plane-spanning filament. As she traced it, the protective dome moved with her. Once more, the fiber disappeared into thin air.

"Gate." She emerged into a plane of gray monolithic rock formations. Wind raged and lightning flashed. A translucent duplicate of Tynan's form hovered in the air to her right. Feral laughter echoed from the slight rise of a jagged rock forma-ion in front of Tallia. Coran stood there, beautiful, evil, her red cloak and ebony hair flowing behind her on the eddies of the wind.

"As I knew she would, Galacia has aided you in coming to me. This time, child, you face the goddess herself, not an ineffectual champion. And this time, you *will* die!" She shrieked as her eyes glittered with fanatical hatred, like crystalline diamonds, cutting.

The quietly spoken threat sent shivers like piercing shards of ice up Tallia's spine. She met Coran's gaze, and her mind raced. She struggled to duplicate the deviousness of her opponent's mind. "I learned much from you, my dear ancient aunt. This time I will win, *alone*."

As palpable as a physical blow, she could feel the effluence of Coran's rage. "You know nothing of the power you have. Tricks, mere tricks," the ageless woman derided. She waved her hands dramatically and an enormous red dragon appeared breathing flame.

"You can do anything Coran can do," echoed again in her mind. Tallia concentrated, envisioning a dragon of glittering gold with emerald eyes the size of a gari's paw. From its mouth emanated a storm of ice and hail. The red dragon floundered beneath the icy onslaught, falling, dissipating. Tallia's dragon faded, and she looked at Coran. "But aunt," she mourned loudly, "you teach me naught else but tricks and illusions."

The Raunarian woman descended from the precipice to stand less than twenty feet away. "Die!" Her sudden enraged command momentarily startled Tallia. Coran would no longer work with illu-

sions, and a bolt of lightning shot from her hand
aimed at Tallia's chest.

Shield, grandchild! Toleme commanded in her
mind. *Shield!* Instantly Tallia became aware of his
tremendous abilities, an ancient power. It ap
peared, a shimmering coalescence of prismatic
light that absorbed the force of Coran's attack.

*Do not think to conquer her, grandchild. My sister
cannot be crushed, but she can be subdued. Immobi
lize her. Open your mind to my memories. Sense the
power within you and draw on it. You must win
grandchild, for I cannot spend eternity lamenting
the end to which I have brought you.* Toleme's words
reverberated in Tallia's mind.

Tallia drew on memories buried deep within her.
Foreign thought patterns became hers. She was
Toleme. Tight bands of scintillating blue light
flashed outward, wrapping vise-like around Coran.
Surprised by the unexpected maneuver, Coran
shrieked in outrage. She struggled within the snake
like coils of rippling multi-hued energy. Unable to
raise her arms to deliver the blast of power neces
sary to free herself, the red energy wept from
Coran's fingertips, fanning out ineffectually along
the constricting bands.

Coridian Plane, Tallia thought. The gate opened.
Steadfastly, she maintained her concentration,
drawing Coran with her as she moved. She would
have to find a means of returning for Tynan later;
there was no other way. She passed through the
gate. Her disorientation was worse this time, and
the duration longer. She emerged into the constant
ly shifting landscape Galacia had shown her. She
struggled for stability, knowing that she must re

lease Coran and distance herself from her before risking a "gate". The bands of energy dissipated.

Run! her brain ordered but her legs refused to obey. She stumbled and a cascade of sparking energy flew toward her. Unable to flee, Tallia stopped. The wall of coruscating force had almost reached her. Instinctively, she retaliated and two walls of scintillating power met and clashed. She was thrown back by the force of the telekinetic blast.

She looked to Coran who had also been shaken. Quickly, before Coran could once more initiate an attack, Tallia rose and ran, looking over her shoulder.

She raced on as inhuman shrieks of fury erupted behind her. Once more she looked back. Ragged-edged bolts of deadly lightning flashed behind her. "Gate," she yelled.

Without pause, she rushed into the spectral aperture. She tumbled through time until she felt the tide-washed sands of a beach beneath her feet. Turning, she watched the gate behind her. What would she do if the distance had not been great enough? But, within seconds, the otherworldly rift between planes vanished. Coran had not been able to follow her! A smile of triumph curled her lips. Now, to rescue Tynan.

With a shock, she realized that she didn't know the name of the plane where she'd found him. How would she return to him? Would she have to traverse the planes again, following the thin thread of his lifeline? There had to be a better way.

An idea came to her. She didn't know if it would work, but she had to try. Closing her eyes, she visualized every detail she could remember about the plane where he was trapped. Then, softly, hopefully, she murmured, "Gate."

It worked! Before her, still suspended motionlessly, was Tynan's essence. *Tynan*, she mentally said his name anxiously.

For a moment, nothing. And then, hesitantly. *Tallia*?

Yes, it's me. You must follow me. Can you?

The ghostly shimmer moved, straightened. *Yes*.

With Tynan's spirit beside her, and hope swelling within her, Tallia said quietly, "Material Life Plane," as she envisioned once more Tynan's chamber within the castle walls.

With hope and trepidation warring in her breast, she stepped through the gate. *Come*, she sent to Tynan. He floated forward. *You must re-enter your body.*

That is me? the thought came.

Tallia's heart stopped. Did he no longer recognize his own form? *Yes, that is you*, she responded calmly. *Time is important*, she urged. *Hurry*!

Tynan's essence drifted toward the bed and slowly, very slowly, merged with the still form that lay there.

Hesitantly, Tallia walked forward. She searched for a pulse. Yes, there it was, faint but unmistakable. *Tynan*?

Yes? the response was immediate, unhesitating, and Tallia smiled with relief.

"Tynan, wake up," she called firmly.

His eyelids fluttered and opened. Tears of happiness misted Tallia's eyes, but the words of love she longed to speak stuck in her throat. Did he love her? He'd never spoken of it.

"I feel . . . strange," Tynan said weakly.

"Do you remember what happened?"

His brow furrowed in concentration. "Yes, I think so."

"Then," she murmured, smiling gently as she brushed his hair from his forehead, "you know why you feel strange." Her throat constricted with emotion.

Tynan stared up at her. She had endangered herself to save him and yet she spoke no words of love, hesitated to embrace him. Had she merely been concerned with repaying him for his earlier endeavors? "You no longer need to feel committed to me, Tallia." He forced the words. "You have negated any debt you felt you owed me. I thank you for saving my life."

Debt! She clenched her jaw against the torrent of emotion that threatened to burst from her lips. *Debt?* she wanted to shout at him, *I did it because I love you.* No, there would only be pain in that revelation.

She had to get out of there before she embarrassed herself with an unseemly display. "Rest," she ordered hoarsely. "I will return later." She turned quickly toward the door so he would not see the hurt shimmering in her eyes.

It had been two days since the coronation ceremony and Tallia still avoided him. Tynan was certain that she cared for him, but her love and trust were what he wanted, and those things she seemed incapable of giving. His heart ached at the thought of leaving, but he could not exist this way.

Ravencrest would be balm to his tortured soul. He stowed the last of his supplies in his pack, hoisted it over his shoulder, and left his room.

His decision made, he strode firmly down the long hall.

"Tynan," Tallia's voice echoed within the corridor.

He turned and watched her exquisite form, still slender in her fourth month of pregnancy, as she hurried down the corridor toward him. Carefully, he guarded his expression, though his mind wept at the memory of all they had shared and the realization of what would be lost. "Yes?" he queried briskly.

Her eyes widened with uncertainty at the sight of the pack. "Wh–where are you going?" she asked softly.

"Home—to Ravencrest. It is where I belong." The desire to enfold her in his arms was almost more than he could restrain, but he managed.

As though suddenly making a decision, she looked into his eyes. "And the child, Tynan?"

His emerald gaze hardened as he forced words he did not mean between his teeth. "You are better suited to raising the child. Surely, I would be no more than a bad influence. An executioner should not be a father." She did not love him. Though he desperately yearned to be a father to the child he had sired, it was better this way. He turned once more, striding firmly away.

"Tynan," she called again. Racing after him, she grasped his arm, halting him. Warily, he turned to face her. "Can you ever be free, Tynan?" she asked. "Can you walk away and say you will never think of me again? Will you never be haunted by the memories of those cold wasteland nights, as I am?" Her eyes misted and she swallowed against the emotion welling up inside her.

His eyes lit with a hope he was afraid to allow himself to feel. He grasped her shoulders, unconsciously hurting her with the strength of his apprehensive grasp. "What are you trying to tell me? Say it," he demanded.

She had to tell him *now*. How could she let him walk away without at least knowing for sure that there was no chance that he loved her? The pain of unrequited love would be no worse than the agony of his leaving. "I love you, Tynan," she murmured softly, tears glistening in her crystalline eyes. "I have for a long time. I just did not acknowledge the feeling as love. Even when I did, I was afraid to tell you lest you detested me for attempting to hold you from the freedom your life affords you."

Unable to believe he'd finally heard the words he had longed for, he enfolded her in his arms, crushing her with the enthusiasm of his embrace.

"Could you love me, Tynan?" she murmured softly.

"Could I love you?" he repeated. "Tallia, I love you more than life itself."

Their lips met in passionate mutual surrender. Together, united by the invisible bond of love, they would face the future.

EPILOGUE

TALLIA ROCKED SLOWLY BACK AND FORTH IN A cross-legged position before the blazing fireplace in her bed chamber. The lilting rhythm of a lullaby floated in the air. She gazed lovingly down at the infant in her lap. The baby stretched restlessly and his eyelids flickered open. The emerald gaze studied her intently before one tiny fist jerked into the air accompanied by a imperious cry.

"I think Cade takes after you." She turned to Tynan, smiling.

"It's only the eyes," he retorted. "His temperament isn't mine."

Tallia rose and laid the baby in the bassinet. As Cade's whimpering subsided, Tynan wrapped his arm around Tallia's waist. For several moments, they stood silently admiring the proof of their love. Dayna, now the Royal Zarmist, ordered them from the chamber, stating emphatically that she could handle the heir for a few hours.

Tynan led Tallia through the corridors and out the back doors to a secluded garden at the rear of the castle. They strolled along the shaded paths, past flowering shrubs and aromatic herbs. In the garden's center, a miniature fountain splashed gaily. Tynan sat on one of the marble benches encircling it, and pulled Tallia down beside him. Neither spoke. He wrapped his arm protectively around her shoulder and together they watched the sky changing in hue as the sun hovered on the horizon. Crimson and pink, mauve and lavender, blush and lemon, the colors shifted as the golden orb of flame slipped from sight. Tynan sighed.

Tallia thought back to the night long ago when they had laid to rest the reminders of that which had gone before. The thick flagstone had thudded back into place in the cool library floor with finality. Beneath it, Tallia and Tynan had buried the past, Toleme's journal, the fading pages of the Prophecy, the silent spinning amulet, and all knowledge of the revelation eradicating the existence of Karaundo's deities. They had battled and won. Now, they looked only to the future. They had each other and demanded no more.

Tallia smiled secretively as she twisted to face her husband. Wrapping her arms around his midsection, she lifted her face to his and his gaze met hers.

A telltale pulse throbbed along the line of her slender neck. Desire glowed in the translucent pools of her silvery eyes and Tynan felt a stirring in his blood. He lowered his lips to hers.

Time had only strengthened the love between

367

them, tightened the bond that would endure through all adversity. She had been right all those months ago in the wasteland. It was destiny. They belonged together and neither could be complete without the other.

At last, Tallia thought as she reveled in the fiery demand of his kiss, at last, Tynan had found peace and she had found love. At last, they could share the sunset.